# Hugh was st... ...n he'd ever be...

Tall enough and ne... ...ok down at her and she... ...her chin up.

April explored his face. The sharpness of his nose, the thick slash of his eyebrows, the strength of his jaw. This close she could see delicate lines bracketing his lips, a freckle on his cheek, a rogue grey hair amongst the stubble.

He was studying her, too. His gaze took in her eyes, her cheeks, her nose. Her lips.

There it was.

Not subtle now, nor easily dismissed as imagination as it had been down in his basement apartment. Or every other time they'd been in the same room together.

But it *had* been there, she realised. Since the first time they'd met.

That focus. That…intent.

That *heat*.

Between them. Within her.

It made her pulse race and caused her to become lost in his gaze when he finally wrenched his away from her lips.

Since they'd met his eyes had revealed little. Only enough for her to know, deep in her heart, that he wasn't as hard and unfeeling as he so steadfastly attempted to be.

# BEHIND THE BILLIONAIRE'S GUARDED HEART

BY
LEAH ASHTON

First Published in Great Britain 2017
By Mills & Boon, an imprint of HarperCollins*Publishers*
1 London Bridge Street, London, SE1 9GF

© 2017 Leah Ashton

ISBN: 978-0-263-92303-2

23-0617

Our policy is to use papers that are natural, renewable and recyclable products and made from wood grown in sustainable forests. The logging and manufacturing processes conform to the legal environmental regulations of the country of origin.

Printed and bound in Spain
by CPI, Barcelona

RITA® Award–winning author **Leah Ashton** never expected to write books. She grew up reading everything she could lay her hands on—from pony books to the backs of cereal boxes at breakfast. One day she discovered the page-turning, happy-sigh-inducing world of romance novels… and one day, much later, wondered if maybe she could write one, too.

Leah now lives in Perth, Western Australia, and writes happy-ever-afters for heroines who definitely *don't* need saving. She has a gorgeous husband, two amazing daughters, and the best intentions to plan meals and maintain an effortlessly tidy home. When she's not writing, Leah loves all-day breakfast, rambling conversations and laughing until she cries. She really hates cucumber. And scary movies. You can visit Leah at www.leah-ashton.com or Facebook.com/leahashtonauthor.

For Jen—who writes beautiful messages in cards,
talks with her hands and giggles at all my jokes.
Thank you for all your help with this book,
and for your belief in my writing.
You're fabulous, Jen. I miss you.

# PROLOGUE

THE SUNSET WAS PERFECT—all orange and purple on a backdrop of darkening blue. Just the right number of clouds stretched their tendrils artistically along the horizon.

The beach, however, was not so perfect.

It had been a warm Perth day, so April Molyneux hadn't been alone in her plans for a beachside picnic dinner. Around her, people congregated about mounds of battered fish and chips on beds of butcher's paper. Others had picnic baskets, or brown paper takeaway bags, or melting ice cream cones from the pink and white van parked above the sand dunes.

There were beach towels everywhere, body boards bouncing in the waves, children building sandcastles, women power walking along the beach in yoga pants, gossiping at a mile a minute. Then a football team jogged by, shirtless and in matching deep purple shorts.

April wanted to scream. This was *not* what she'd planned.

This was *not* a private, romantic, beachside *tête-à-tête*.

Evan lay sprawled on their picnic blanket, his back turned away from April as he scrolled through his phone.

Today was their wedding anniversary. Three years.

#anniversary #threeyears #love #romance

Right now April felt like dumping the contents of the gourmet picnic box she'd ordered all over his head—sourdough baguettes, cultured butter, artisan cheeses, muscatels and all.

'Do we *have* to do this?' Evan asked, not even looking at her.

'You mean spend time with your wife on your anniversary?' Her words were sharp, but April's throat felt tight.

The sea-breeze whipped her long blonde hair across her eyes, and she tucked it back behind her ears angrily. She sat with her legs curled beneath her, a long pale pink maxi-dress covering her platinum bikini. She stared daggers at Evan's back. His attention was still concentrated on the screen of his phone.

'You know that isn't what I meant.'

She did. But she'd spent weeks leading up to today, posting photos of their wedding to her one point two million followers.

#anniversary #threeyears #love #romance

She'd organised for the Molyneux family jet to take them up north, up past Broome. She'd found the perfect—*perfect*—private beach. She'd had the stupid picnic box couriered up from Margaret River, and she'd had her assistant organise a gorgeous rainbow mohair picnic blanket, complete with a generous donation to the Molyneux Foundation.

And then Evan had called from work as she'd been packing her overnight bag. He'd asked if they could cancel their trip. He didn't really feel like going, and could they stay home instead?

Coming to this beach had been the compromise.

It wasn't even about the beach, really. Just the photo.

All he needed to do was smile for the camera and then they could go home and eat their fancy picnic in front of the TV. Or order pizza. Whatever. It didn't matter. And Evan could eat silently, then retreat to his study and barely talk to her for the rest of the evening.

Just as he did most nights.

Again, April's throat felt tight.

Finally Evan moved. He shifted, sitting up so he could face her. He took off his sunglasses, and for some reason April did too.

For the first time in what suddenly felt like ages he looked directly at her. Really intensely, his hazel eyes steady against her own silvery blue.

'I don't think we can do this any more,' he said. Firmly, and in a way that probably should have surprised her.

April pretended to misunderstand. 'Come on—it's just a stupid photo. We need to do this. I have contractual obligations.'

For product placement: The mohair blanket. The picnic box. Her sunglasses. Her bikini.

Donations to the Molyneux Foundation were contingent on this photograph.

Evan shook his head. 'You know what I'm talking about.'

They'd started marriage counselling only a year after their wedding. They'd stopped trying for a baby shortly afterwards, both agreeing that it was best to wait until they'd sorted things out.

But they hadn't sorted things out.

They'd both obediently attended counselling, made concerted efforts to listen to each other...but nothing had really changed.

They still loved each other, though. They'd both been clear on that.

April *knew* she still loved Evan. She'd loved him since he'd asked her to his Year Twelve ball.

To her, that had been all that mattered. Eventually it would go back to how it had used to be between them. Surely?

'I'll always love you, April,' Evan said, in a terribly careful tone that she knew he must have practised. 'But I don't love you the way I know I should. The way I should love the woman I'm married too. You deserve better, April.'

*Oh, God.*

The words were all mashed together, tangled up in the salty breeze. All April could hear, repeated against her skull, was: *I don't love you...*

His lips quirked upwards. 'I guess I deserve better, too. We both deserve that love you see in the movies, or in those books you read. Don't you think? And it's never been like that for us.'

He paused, as if waiting for her to say something, but she had nothing. Absolutely nothing.

'Look, I would never cheat on you, April, but a while ago I met someone who made me think that maybe there was a bigger love out there for me, you know?' This bit definitely wasn't practised—his words were all rushed and messy. 'I respected you too much to pursue her. I cut her out of my life and I haven't been in contact with her. At all. I promise. But I can't stop thinking about her, and I...'

His gaze had long ago stopped meeting hers, but now it swung back.

He swallowed. 'I want a divorce, April,' he said with finality. 'I'm sorry.'

She could only nod. Nod and nod, over and over.

'April?'

Her throat felt as if it had completely closed over. She fumbled for her sunglasses, desperate to cover the wetness in her eyes.

'Let's just take this stupid picture,' she said, her words strangled.

His eyes widened, but he nodded.

Awkwardly, they posed—only their shoulders touching. April took the photo quickly, without any thought at all... but amazingly the beach in the photo's background was perfectly empty just for that millisecond as she pressed the button on her phone.

To her followers it would seem perfect.

A private beach, a handsome, loving husband, a glorious sunset...

Silently she cropped the image, then added her caption and hashtags.

Three amazing years with this guy! #anniversary #threeyears #love #romance

But she deleted the last hashtag before she posted it:

#over

Hugh Bennell's gaze was drawn to the black door at the top of the grey stone stairs. The paintwork and brass door hardware all looked a bit dull—and not just because the sun was only just now rising on this rather dreary London morning. A handful of leaves had gathered where a doormat should be, and a single hopeful weed reached out from beneath the doorstep.

He'd have to sort that out.

But for now he simply wheeled his bike—lights still flashing from his pre-dawn ride—straight past the steps that led to the three-storey chocolate and cream Victorian end-of-terrace, and instead negotiated a matching set of steps that led downwards to his basement flat.

Inside, the cleats on the base of his cycling shoes clicked on the parquet flooring, and his road bike's wheels squeaked noisily. He hung the bike on its wall hanger, immediately across from the basement front door. Above it hung his mountain bike, and to the right of that was the door to one of his spare bedrooms.

That door was painted white, and the paintwork still gleamed as fresh as the day he'd had the apartment painted. He noted that the brass knob still shone—in fact his whole house shone with meticulous cleanliness, just as he liked it.

Hugh settled in at his desk after a shower, his dark hair still damp. The desk was right at the front of his apartment, pushed up against the window. Above him foot traffic was increasing as London got ready for the workday. From his viewpoint all he could see were ankles and feet—in heels and boots and lace-up shoes. The angle was too acute for anyone passing to see him—he'd checked, of course—so he could leave his blinds open, allowing natural light to filter across his workspace.

He placed his mug of tea on the coaster immediately to the right of his open laptop. Beneath that lay the day's to-do list, carefully formulated and handwritten the previous evening.

He'd always loved lists, even as a young kid. He remembered his mum's bemusement when he'd stuck a list above his bedside table to remind himself what to pack for school each day of the week. He'd found it calming to have it all written out—a much better alternative, he'd thought, to his mother's panicked realisations at the school gate and her frantic delivery of forgotten sports shoes at morning break.

*'A neat freak with lists!'* His mum had laughed. *'How could you possibly be mine?'*

To the bottom of his list for today he added *Paint front door and polish brass.*

He was certain the team at Precise thought his penchant for paper lists eccentric for a man who owned and ran a multi-million-dollar mobile app empire—but then, the team thought him eccentric for many more reasons than that.

A reminder popped up on his screen for a nine a.m. appointment, and he clicked through to sign in for the online meeting. Already four of the five other attendees were logged in, their faces visible via their webcams in a grid to the right of screen.

But in Hugh's box there was only the generic grey silhouette—he never chose the video option, and he kept the camera at the top of his laptop taped over just in case.

Because, for Hugh Bennell, maintaining his privacy was non-negotiable.

*He* was in control of exactly what he revealed to the world.

His laptop dinged as the final attendee arrived.

'Looks like everyone's here,' Hugh said. 'Let's get started.'

# CHAPTER ONE

*Six weeks later—London*

APRIL FELT GOOD.

She was thirty-two, and her first ever job interview was today.

Sure, she'd been interviewed for the couple of internships she'd had back at uni, but they didn't count. Today was her first real-life *I actually really, really want this job* interview.

That was significant.

She smiled.

Around her, the Tube train was packed. Everyone looked completely absorbed in their own world—reading a book, swiping through a phone, gazing out of the window into the blackness of the tunnel.

Nobody noticed her. Nobody realised how momentous this day actually was.

Since her disastrous wedding anniversary there'd been weeks of numbness for April. There'd been shock, then anger, then the awfulness of telling her mum and her sisters, Ivy and Mila. There'd been weeks of meetings with lawyers and endless discussions about property settlement. There'd been tears and wine and long conversations.

Time had seemed to go on and on. Especially at night, when she'd been alone in her ridiculously too big concrete-and-angles home. Mila had stayed a few nights to keep her company—but she had her own life and a partner to worry about. Her mum had stayed every night for a fortnight, determinedly focusing on the practicalities of lawyers and legal details. Ivy had brought her son, Nate, to visit regularly—although she had been mortified when the toddler had accidentally pushed a salad bowl off the table, shattering it into millions of pieces.

'Don't worry about it,' April had reassured her. 'It's one less thing we need to decide who gets to keep.'

At first, sorting out the things that she and Evan had bought together had seemed vitally important. Maybe it was the focus it had given her—or maybe there was more of her ruthless businesswoman mother in her than she'd thought.

But as the weeks had worn on, and she'd spent more time staring at her ceiling, not sleeping, all their *stuff* had begun to feel meaningless.

As it probably should for a woman with a billion-dollar family trust that she held with her sisters.

So Evan could have everything. Of course he could have everything.

*I don't love you...*

April didn't sugar-coat what Evan had said. He'd wrapped it up in superfluous words to blunt the blow, but that didn't hide the reality: Evan didn't love her. He'd never loved her—at least not the way April had loved him.

In those endless nights she'd analysed that relentlessly.

How could she not have known?

*I don't love you.*

*You.*

Who was she, if not married to Evan?

The feminist within her was horrified that she could even ask herself this question. But she did. Again and again:

*Who was she?*

This woman Evan hadn't loved enough. This woman who had been oblivious to the end of her marriage.

*Who was she?*

She was thirty-two, single and had never worked a day in her life.

Her home had been a wedding gift from her mother.

Everything she'd ever bought had been with a credit card linked to the Molyneux Trust. She had been indulged by a family who probably didn't think her capable of being anything but a frivolous socialite. Why would they? She'd applied herself to nothing else. Her days had been filled with shopping and expensive charity luncheons. Her evenings with art gallery openings and luxurious fundraising auctions. She'd spent her spare time taking photos of herself and posting them online, so millions of people could click '*like*' and comment on her fabulous perfect life.

What a sham. What a joke.

She hadn't earned a cent of the fortune she'd flouted to the world.

And her husband hadn't loved her.

She was a fraud.

But no more.

April smoothed the charcoal fabric of her pencil skirt over her thighs. It wasn't designer. In fact it had probably cost about five per cent of the cost of her favourite leather tote bag—which she'd left back home in Perth.

She'd left everything behind.

She'd booked a one-way ticket to London and opened up a new credit card account at her bank—politely declining the option to have the balance cleared monthly by the Molyneux Trust. From now on she was definitely paying her own way.

She'd also located her British passport—a document she had thanks to her mother's dual citizenship of both Australia and the UK.

Only then had she told her family what she was doing.

And then she'd ignored every single one of their concerns and hopped onto her flight the next day.

Now here she was. Three days in London.

She'd found a flat. She'd bought reasonably priced clothes for the first time in her life. She'd researched the heck out of the environmental sustainability consulting firm where she was about to have an interview.

Oh—as she noted her long ponytail cascading over the shoulder of her hound's-tooth coat—she'd also dyed her hair brown.

She felt like a different person. Like a *new* person.

She even had a new name, of sorts.

The name that was on her birth certificate and her passport: April Spencer.

Like her sisters, she'd made the choice to use her mother's surname within a few years of her father leaving them. But she'd never bothered having it formally changed.

Turned out that had now come in handy.

Today she didn't feel like April Molyneux, the billionaire mining heiress whose life had collapsed around her.

Today she was April Spencer, and today she had a job interview.

And for the first time in six weeks she felt good.

As Hugh probably should've expected, it had rained through the remainder of September and then most of October. So it was a cool but clear November morning when he retrieved the tin of black paint from beneath his stairs and headed out from his basement to the front door of the main house.

It was just before sunrise, and even on a workday Islington street was almost deserted. A couple walking a Labrador passed by as he laid out his drop cloth, and as he painted the occasional jogger, walker or cyclist zipped past—along with the gradually thickening traffic.

It didn't take long to paint the door: just a quick sand-down, a few minor imperfections in the woodwork to repair, then a fresh coat of paint.

Now it just needed to dry.

The door had to stay propped open for a few hours before he could safely close it again. He'd known this, so he'd planned ahead and dumped his backpack—which contained his laptop—in the hallway before he'd started work. Now he stepped inside, his work boots loud on the blue, cream and grey geometric tessellated tile entryway.

He yanked off his boots, grabbed his laptop out of his bag and then on thick socks padded over to the grand staircase ahead of him. To his left was the first of two reception rooms on the ground floor—but he wasn't going to work in there.

Instead he settled on a stair third from the bottom, rested his laptop on his jeans and got to work.

Or at least that was the plan.

Instead his emails remained unread, and the soft beep of instant message notifications persisted but were ignored.

Who was he kidding? He was never going to get any work done in here.

It was impossible when his attention remained on insignificant details: the way the weak morning sunlight sauntered through the wedged-open door to mingle with the dust he'd disturbed. The scent of the house: cardboard packing boxes, musty air and windows closed for far too long. The light—or lack of it. With every door but the front door sealed shut, an entryway he remembered as bright with light seemed instead gloomy and...*abandoned*.

Which, of course, it was.

He hadn't stepped foot in here since the day he'd moved into the basement.

Back then—three years ago—it had been too hard. He hadn't been ready to deal with this house.

Hugh stood up, suddenly needing to move. But not out through the front door.

Instead he went to the internal door only a few steps away and with a firm grip twisted the brass knob and yanked the door open.

He hadn't realised he'd been holding his breath—but he let it out now in a defeated sigh. As if he'd expected to see something different.

But he'd known what was in here.

Once, this room had been where his mother and her second husband had hosted their guests with cups of tea and fancy biscuits.

That would be impossible now. If any antique furniture remained, it was hidden. Completely. By boxes. Boxes that filled the room in every direction—stacked neatly like bricks as tall as he was—six foot and higher.

Boxes, boxes, boxes—so many he couldn't even begin to count.

Hugh reached out to touch the nearest box. It sat on a stack four high, its plain cardboard surface slightly misshapen by whatever was crammed within it.

Some of the many boxes that surrounded it—beneath, beside and beyond—were occasionally labelled unhelpfully: *purple treasures…sparkly things.*

Others—the work of the woman Hugh had employed to help his mother—had detailed labels and colour-coded stickers: a relic of Hugh's attempts to organise his mother's hoard into some sort of system.

But his mother had resisted—joyfully creating ridiculous categories and covertly shuffling items between boxes—and in the end her frustrated assistant had correctly informed Hugh that it was an utter waste of time.

Which he'd already known—but then, what option had he had?

Doctors, specialists, consultants…all had achieved nothing.

How could they? When his mother knew exactly what she was doing?

She'd been here before, after all. Before Len. When it had been just Hugh and his mum and her hoard. And her endless quest for love.

With Len she'd finally had the love she'd searched for for so long. A love that had been powerful enough to allow her to let go of all the things she'd collected in the years since Hugh's father had left them. Things she'd surrounded herself with and held on to so tightly when she'd been unable to possess the one thing she'd so badly wanted: love.

Without Len his mother had believed that her hoard was all she'd had left. And, despite still having Hugh, despite his desperate efforts, it hadn't been enough.

He'd been helpless to prevent the hoard that had overshadowed his childhood from returning.

Hugh closed his eyes.

There was so much *stuff* in this room that if he walked another step he would walk into a wall of boxes.

It was exactly the same in almost every room in the house—

every living space, every bedroom. Except the kitchen, halls and bathrooms—and that was only because of the staff Hugh had employed and his mother's reluctant agreement to allow them into the house each day.

So that was all he'd managed: to pay people to keep the few bits of empty floor space in his mother's house clean. And to clear a safe path from her bedroom to the front and back doors in case of a fire.

Really, it was not all that different from how it had been when he'd been ten. Except this time he'd had loads of money to outsource what he'd only barely managed as a kid.

And this place was a hell of a lot bigger than the tiny council flat he'd grown up in.

He opened his eyes, but just couldn't stare at those awful uniform boxes any more.

Back in the entry hall, Hugh grabbed his laptop and backpack, ready to leave…but then he stilled.

The new paint on the door was still wet. He wasn't going anywhere.

But he also wasn't going to be able to work—it would seem that three years had done nothing to ease the tension, the frustration and the hopelessness that those damn boxes elicited within him.

Even waiting another three years—or ten—to deal with them wasn't going to make any difference.

They'd still represent a lot more than they should.

They needed to go. *All* of them.

This house needed to be bright and light once again. It needed to breathe.

So he sat back down on the bottom step of the grand old staircase, knowing exactly what he was going to do.

It was time.

It had started with confusion at the supermarket checkout.

'Do you have another card?' the checkout operator had asked.

'Pardon me?' April had said—because, well, it had never happened to her before.

It had, it seemed, happened several times to the not particularly patient operator—Bridget, according to her name tag. She'd studied April, her gaze flat, as April had tried what she knew to be her correct PIN twice more.

And then, as April had searched hopelessly for an alternative card—she'd cut up every single card linked to the Molyneux Trust back in Perth—Bridget had asked her to move aside so she could serve the next in a long line of customers.

April had dithered momentarily: was she supposed to return the Thai green curry ready-meal, the bunch of bananas and bottle of eye make-up remover to the shelves before she left?

But then the weight of pitying stares—possibly only imagined—had kicked in, and April had exited the shop as fast as she'd been able, her sneakers suddenly unbelievably squeaky on the supermarket's vinyl flooring.

Now she was at home, still in her gym gear, on her buttersoft grey leather couch, her laptop before her.

For only the second time in the four weeks since she'd been in London she logged in to her internet banking—the other time being when she'd set up her account at the bank. Her fully furnished flat didn't come with a printer, so she'd have to scroll through her credit card statement onscreen.

But it was still easy to see the reason for her mortification at the checkout—she'd maxed out her credit card.

How was that even *possible*?

She'd been so careful with her spending—more so as each still jobless week had passed.

She hadn't bought any new clothes for *weeks*. She'd stopped eating at cafés and restaurants, and had instead become quite enamoured with what she considered a very English thing: convenience stores with huge walls of pre-made sandwiches in triangular plastic packaging. And microwaveable ready-meals for dinner.

They must only be costing a few pounds a meal, surely?

She *had* joined the gym, but that had seemed very cheap. And fortunately the flat came with Wi-Fi, so she hadn't had to pay for that.

So where had all her money gone?

Five minutes later she knew.

With pen and paper, she'd documented exactly where her money had been spent.

Her rent—and four weeks' deposit—was the biggest culprit. Only now did it dawn on her that even if she *did* get one of the many, many jobs she'd been applying for, her starting salary would barely cover her rent. With absolutely nothing left over for sandwiches in plastic triangles.

She flopped back onto her couch and looked around her flat.

It was small, but—if she was objective—not *that* small. And it was beautifully furnished. *Expensively* furnished. Her kitchen appliances were the same insanely priced brand she'd had back in Perth. Her small bathroom was tiled in floor-to-ceiling marble.

She even had a balcony.

But she couldn't afford a balcony. She couldn't afford any of this.

Because she didn't have any money. *At all*.

Not for the first time in four weeks, she wondered if she'd made a terrible mistake.

The first time had been after she hadn't got the first job she'd been interviewed for.

Now, several job interviews later—and many more applications that had led to absolutely nothing—her initial optimism astounded her. She literally had a degree, an internship and then almost ten years of nothing.

Well—not *nothing*. But nothing she was about to put on her CV. A million followers and a charitable foundation that she'd established herself could possibly sound impressive to *some* HR departments. But they weren't relevant to the environmental officer roles she was applying for.

And, just as importantly, they would reveal her real name. And she just couldn't do that.

Although it was tempting at times. Like tonight. How easy it would be to still be April Molyneux and organise the reissue of one of the many credit cards linked to her insane fortune? By this time tomorrow she could be eating all the Thai green curry she wanted.

She could even upgrade to a far more impressive flat.

April pushed herself up and off the couch, to search for something to eat in her lovely kitchen.

Her fridge was stocked only with expensive Australian Riesling, sparkling designer water—also expensive—a partially eaten wheel of camembert cheese—expensive—and the organic un-homogenised milk that she'd bought because she'd liked the pretty glass bottle it came in—probably also more expensive than it needed to be.

April felt sick.

Was she really so disconnected from the reality of what things cost?

Her whole life she'd known she was rich. But she'd thought she still had *some* sense of the reality of living in the real world: without a trust fund, without the mansion your mum had bought for you.

She'd liked to think she'd projected some sort of 'everywoman' persona to her Instagram and Facebook followers. That despite the good fortune of her birth that she was really just like everybody else.

She poured herself a bowl of probably overpriced granola and used up the rest of her fancy milk, then sat back in front of her laptop.

Earlier today, before heading to the gym, she'd scheduled the next couple of days' worth of social media posts.

April *Spencer* might be in London, but April Molyneux—to her followers, anyway—was still in Perth, effortlessly adjusting to her new single life.

Before she'd dyed her hair she'd made sure she'd honoured every single product placement agreement she'd signed, and had posed for months' worth of photos. She'd taken even more selfies, with all manner of random backgrounds—she'd come up with something to caption them with as she needed to.

Plus she still took random photos while here in London— the habit was too ingrained for her to give it up completely. She just made sure her hair and anything identifiably London wasn't in any of the photos. So the book she was reading… the shade she'd painted her toenails…that kind of stuff. All was still documented, still shared, interwoven with her blonde April photos and carefully coordinated with her assistant back home—thankfully still paid for by the Molyneux Foundation.

So her social media life carried on. Her followers continued to grow.

And what were they seeing?

She scrolled down the page, taking in her last few years of photos in a colourful blur.

A blur of international holidays, secluded luxury Outback retreats, designer shoes, amazing jewellery, beautiful clothes, a gorgeous husband and attractive—wealthy—friends.

They were seeing an unbelievably privileged woman who had absolutely no idea what it was like to exist in the real world.

April slapped her laptop screen shut, suddenly disgusted with herself.

And ashamed.

The whole point of all this—the move to London, her quest for a job, living alone for the first time in her life—had been about finding herself. Defining who she was if she wasn't Evan's wife. Or one of the Molyneux heiresses.

But so far all she'd achieved was a self-indulgent month during which she'd patted herself on the back for 'living like a normal person' but achieved absolutely nothing other than a new, reasonably priced wardrobe.

She knew her mum, Ivy and Mila all assumed this was just a bit of a game to her. They assumed that once she did eventually get a job she'd supplement her income with Molyneux money. On reflection, no one had pointed out the now damned obvious fact that she couldn't afford this apartment.

And, unlike April, they would know. Mila had never used her Molyneux fortune: she knew exactly how far a dollar or a pound could stretch. And Ivy had dedicated her life to building up the Molyneux fortune—so she knew, too.

She couldn't even be annoyed with them. Up until tonight, and that stupid, sad 'declined' beep at the cash register, they'd been right.

They'd been right to think that their pampered middle sister couldn't cut it in the real world.

And, if she was brutally honest, she hadn't even been trying. She'd *thought* she had, but people in the real world didn't have no income for a month—and no savings—and then casually take their time applying for some mythical perfect job while living in a luxury apartment.

She flipped her laptop open again.

She needed to find a job. Immediately.

# CHAPTER TWO

SHE HAD A nice voice, Hugh thought.

Unquestionably Australian. Warm. Professional.

She didn't sound nervous, although she did laugh every now and again—which was possibly nerves. Or possibly not. Her laugh was natural. Also warm. Pretty.

Hugh's lips quirked. How whimsical of him. How unlike him.

Currently, April…he glanced down at the printed CV before him…April *Spencer* was answering the last of his four interview questions.

Rather well, actually.

He leant back in his chair, listening carefully as her voice filled the room, projected by the speakers hooked up to his laptop.

This was the third interview his recruitment consultant had organised, although the other two applicants had been quite different from April. One an art curator, another an antique specialist.

Both complete overkill for the position. He'd been clear with the consultant, Caro, that his mother's collections were not of any monetary value—although Caro *had* made some valid points that knowledge of antiques and curation skills might still be of use.

But still… He felt as if employing either skill-set would be pretending that all those boxes were something more than they actually were. Which was a hoard. A hoard he wanted out of his life.

'…so I feel my experience working for the Molyneux Foundation demonstrates my understanding of the importance of client privacy,' April said as she continued her answer. 'I regularly dealt with donors who requested their names remain absolutely confidential. At other times donors wished for their donation—whether it be product, service or otherwise—to be announced at a date or time suitable to their company. In both scenarios complete discretion was essential.'

'But your role at the foundation, Ms Spencer, was as social media coordinator,' Hugh prompted, scanning her CV. 'Why would you have access to such sensitive information?'

There was the briefest pause. 'It's quite a small foundation,' April said, her tone confident. 'And I worked closely with the managing director. It was my job to schedule posts and monitor comments—I needed to know what to announce, and also what comments to remove in case anyone gave one of our generous benefactors away.'

From the notes Caro had provided, it seemed April's work with the Molyneux Foundation had been the reason she'd been put forward. Hugh had made it clear that a proven ability to maintain strict confidentiality was essential for this position.

'And you're available immediately?' he asked.

'Yes,' April said.

Hugh nodded at the phone. 'Right—thank you, Ms Spencer,' he said. 'A decision will be made shortly.'

Then he ended the call.

After the interview April left the small meeting room and returned to the recruiter's office.

It had all been rather bizarre. She'd come in this morning expecting to be assigned to an interview for something similar to her two jobs so far—both short-term entry level social media roles to cover unexpected leave—and yet she'd been put forward for a job unpacking boxes, with a phone interview to take place almost immediately.

Across from her, at her large, impressive desk, sat Caroline Zhu, the senior recruiter at the agency April had been working for since her supermarket debacle three weeks earlier.

'I'm sorry,' April said. 'I don't think the interview went particularly well.'

Terribly, actually. She felt she'd answered the questions well enough, but Hugh Bennell had barely said a word. Certainly not a word of encouragement, anyway.

'Possibly,' Caro said, in the no-nonsense voice that matched her jet-black no-nonsense ponytail. 'But unlikely. It's been several years since Mr Bennell has required my services, but I'm certain his interview technique has not changed. He is not one for superfluous conversation.'

April nodded. Yes, she'd got that.

It fitted, she supposed—her frantic internet searching in the short period of time she'd had before her interview had revealed little about Hugh Bennell. She knew of Precise, of course—practically everyone with a smartphone would have at least one app from the company. April, in fact, had about six, all related to scheduling, analytics and online collaboration. But, unlike other international tech companies that were synonymous with their founders, Hugh Bennell was no more than a name on the company website—and the subject of several newspaper articles in which a string of journalists had attempted to discover the man behind such a massive self-made fortune.

But all had failed.

All April had learnt from those quickly skimmed articles was that Hugh had grown up in council housing in London, the only child of a single, hard-working mother. As soon as he'd left university it had been as if he'd wiped all trace of himself from public record—she'd found no photos of him, and his Wikipedia entry was incredibly brief.

It was strikingly unusual in this share-everything world.

Mysterious, even.

Intriguing, actually.

'You'll know soon enough,' Caroline continued. 'In my experience, Mr Bennell makes extremely swift decisions.'

'Are you able to tell me a bit more about the position?'

Caroline raised an impatient eyebrow. 'As I said, the information Mr Bennell provided is limited. He has a room full of a large number of boxes that require sorting and disposal. Not antiques. Nothing dangerous. He requires someone trustworthy and hardworking who can start immediately. That's all I can tell you.'

'And you thought I was suitable because…?'

'Because you're keen to work as much as possible for as much pay as possible. You were quite clear on that when we first met.'

True. After some judicious reimagining of her work experience—she'd repositioned herself as April Spencer, Social Media Manager at the Molyneux Foundation, which was technically true—she'd turned up at the best-reviewed temp agency within walking distance of her overpriced flat at nine a.m. the Monday after her credit card had been declined.

She'd been absolutely—possibly over-zealously—clear in her goals. To work hard and earn as much money as she could. In fact, she'd even found a night job, stacking shelves at a supermarket near her new home.

She needed her credit card debt cleared *pronto*. She needed money *yesterday*.

Fortunately Caroline Zhu had seemed to consider her desperation-tinged enthusiasm a positive.

The phone rang in pretty musical tones.

'Ah, here we go,' Caroline said, raising her eyebrows at April. She picked up the phone, had the briefest of conversations that ended with, 'Excellent news, Mr Bennell. I'll let the successful applicant know.'

She hung up and turned back to April.

'Just as I thought,' Caroline said. 'I'm rarely wrong on such things. Mr Bennell has selected you as his preferred candidate. You start immediately.'

'Unpacking boxes?'

'For a mouthwatering sum an hour.'

'I'm in,' April said with a grin.

Caroline might have let slip the slightest of smiles. 'You already are. Here's the address.'

Hugh Bennell's house was beautiful.

It felt familiar, actually—she'd stayed with her mum and sisters at a similar house for Christmas, many years ago. It was the year she and her sisters had campaigned for a white

Christmas and, like so many things in her childhood and adult life, it had just happened.

She straightened her shoulders, then knocked on the front door.

She'd been told Hugh Bennell would be meeting her—which had surprised her. Surely the boss of a company like Precise had staff to deal with a lowly employee like herself?

But then, she'd supposed he also had staff to *interview* lowly employees like herself—and he'd already done that himself.

If anything, it just added to the general sense of mystery: mysterious boxes for her to unpack, complete with a mysterious billionaire CEO who was mysteriously hands-on with the recruitment of unskilled labour.

It was late morning now. She hadn't had time to change, so she still wore what she now considered her 'interview suit'. Her shoes were freshly polished, and her hair was looped in an elegant low bun that she was rather proud of. Her stylist back in Perth would be impressed.

The liquorice-black door opened.

And revealed a man.

A tall man. With dark hair, dark stubble. Dark eyes.

Dark eyes that met her own directly. *Very* directly.

Momentarily April felt frozen beneath that gaze.

*So this is what a mysterious tech billionaire looks like.*

Jaw-droppingly handsome.

She blinked. 'Good morning,' she said, well practised from years of socialising at every event anyone could imagine. 'I'm April Spencer. Are you Mr Bennell?'

He nodded. 'You got here quickly.'

'I did,' she said. 'The agency emphasised the urgency of this placement.'

Silence. But, despite her usually sparkling conversational skills, April didn't rush to fill it. Instead she simply stood still beneath Hugh Bennell's gaze.

He was still looking at her. Unreadably but intensely. It was a strange and unfamiliar sensation.

But not entirely uncomfortable.

There was something about him—the way he stood, maybe—that created a sense of calm. And of time.

Time to take a handful of moments to study the man before her—to take in the contrast of his black hair and olive skin. To admire the thick slashes of his eyebrows, the sharpness of his cheekbones, the elegance of his mouth.

He was more interesting than gorgeous, she realised, with a slightly crooked nose and an angular chin. His too-long hair and his stubble—forgotten, she was sure, rather than fashionable.

But it was that sum of those imperfect parts that made a darkly, devastatingly attractive whole.

And definitely not what she'd been expecting.

Whatever she'd thought a mysterious billionaire who deliberately shunned the spotlight would look like, *this* was not it.

He was also *nothing* like Evan.

That realisation came from left field, shocking her.

April blinked again. *What was she doing?*

'Please come in,' Hugh Bennell said. As naturally as if only a beat of time had passed.

Maybe it had?

April felt flustered and confused—and seriously annoyed with herself.

She'd just met her new boss. She needed to pull herself together.

She was probably just tired from the long hours she'd been working.

*But did tiredness explain the way her gaze documented the breadth of her new boss's shoulders as she stepped inside?*

Nope.

There was no way she could pretend she didn't know what the fireworks in her belly meant. It had just been a *long* time since they'd been associated with anyone but her husband.

And a pretty long time since she'd associated them with Evan.

She squeezed her eyes shut for a second.

*No.* No. No, no, *no*.

She had not flown halfway around the world to turn into a puddle over a man. Over her *boss*. No matter how mysterious.

That certainly wasn't why she was working two jobs and sharing a room in a truly awful shared house.

She'd come to London to live independently. Without her mother's money for the first time in her life and without Evan for the first time since she was seventeen.

And she needed this job. She certainly needed the very generous hourly rate.

She *didn't* need fireworks, or the heat that had pooled in her belly.

'Miss Spencer?'

April's eyes snapped open. 'Sorry, Mr Bennell.'

'Are you okay?' he asked.

He did have gorgeous eyes. Thoughtful eyes that looked as if a million things were happening within them.

'Of course,' she said with a deliberate smile.

He inclined his chin, somewhat sceptically. 'I was just saying that we'll run through your responsibilities in the kitchen.'

She nodded, then followed him down the narrow hall beside the rather grand if dusty staircase.

As they walked April did her absolute best to shove all thoughts of fireworks or heat firmly out of her mind—and her body. Frustratingly, Hugh's well-worn, perfectly fitted jeans did nothing to help this endeavour.

Neither did the unwanted realisation that—for the first time since Evan had told her he didn't love her and her sparkling life had been dulled—she felt truly alive.

April Spencer was beautiful.

Objectively beautiful. As if she'd stepped off the pages of a catalogue and into his mother's house.

For a while he'd stood and just *looked* at her, because he'd felt helpless to do anything but.

He'd looked at her chocolate-brown hair, at her porcelain skin and her crystal blue eyes. At her lips—pink, and shining with something glossy. At her fitted clothes and the long coat cinched in tight at her waist.

He'd expected a backpacker. Someone younger, really. Someone he could actually imagine lifting and shifting boxes.

This woman was not it.

This woman was poised and utterly together. Everything about her exuded strength and confidence. As if she was used to commanding a room. Or a corporation.

Not rummaging through boxes.

It just didn't fit.

He'd let her in, but then he had turned to face her—to question her.

He needed to know who she was and what she was doing here.

But when he'd turned her eyes had been closed.

He'd watched her for a second as she'd taken deep breaths. In through her nose. Out through her mouth. And it was in that moment—while that knowledgeable gaze had been hidden—that he'd sensed vulnerability. A vulnerability that had been completely disguised by her polish and her smile.

And so, instead of interrogating her, he'd asked her if she was okay.

And instead of calling the agency back, asking for someone more suitable, he'd led her into the kitchen and handed her a confidentiality agreement to sign.

That moment of vulnerability had long gone now, and the woman in his mother's kitchen revealed nothing of whatever he'd seen.

But he *had* seen it. And he of all people knew that people were rarely what they first appeared. He'd spent most his life hiding all but what people absolutely needed to know.

So for now he wasn't going to question April Spencer.

But he *did* acknowledge her incongruity, and he didn't like that this project to clear his mother's house already felt more complicated than he wanted it to.

April laid his pen on top of the signed paperwork. 'All done, Mr Bennell,' she said with a smile.

'Call me Hugh,' he said firmly.

'April,' she said, with eyes that sparkled.

He was again struck by her beauty, but forced himself to disregard it. The attractiveness of his employees was none of his concern.

He nodded briskly, and didn't return her smile. 'You'll be working alone,' he said, getting straight to the point, 'and I've provided guidelines for how I want items sorted. It should be self-explanatory: paperwork containing personal details is to be saved, all other papers to be shredded and recycled. Junk is to be disposed of. Anything of value should be separated for donation. I've provided the details of local charities you can contact to organise collection.'

April nodded, her gaze on the printed notes he'd left for her.

'Is there anything other than papers you want kept?' she asked.

'No,' he said.

Maybe louder than he'd intended, as her head jerked upwards.

'Okay,' she said carefully. 'And how do I contact you if I have any questions?'

'You don't,' he said. 'I'm not to be disturbed.'

Her glossy lips formed a straight line. 'So who *can* I contact?'

He shrugged dismissively. 'You won't need to contact anybody. It's all made very clear in my instructions. Just send me an email at the end of each day with details of your progress.'

'So you *know* what's in the boxes? Caroline implied that you didn't, which is why you need me to sort through them.'

Hugh shook his head. 'It doesn't matter.'

April met his gaze. 'So you trust me to go through a whole room of boxes and make all the decisions myself?'

'Yes,' he said. 'It's all junk. You aren't going to stumble across a hidden fortune, I promise you.'

She looked unconvinced.

'And besides—it's not a room. It's the whole house.'

Her eyes widened. 'Pardon me?'

He ran a hand through his hair. He just wanted this conversation to be over and to be out of this place. This stuffed full, oppressive house which this woman only complicated further.

'Yes,' he said. 'Three floors. Leave any furniture where it is. Don't lift anything too heavy. I've left you a key and the security code. I expect you to work an eight-hour day.' He stopped, mentally running through any further extraneous details he should mention. 'If there's an emergency—*only* an emergency—you can call me. My number is listed in the documentation.'

'That's it?' she said.

'That's it,' he said.

'Great,' she said. 'Where do I start?'

'I'll show you,' he said.

Minutes later they stood before a wall built with pale brown cardboard.

'Wow,' April said. 'I've never seen anything like this before.'

*Hugh had.*

'Did you buy the place like this?' she asked.

'Something like that,' he said, needing to leave. Not wanting to explain.

She'd work it out soon enough.

'I'll get this sorted for you,' April said, catching his gaze.

He already had one foot in the foyer.

She spoke with assurance—*reassurance?*—and with questions in her eyes.

But Hugh didn't want to be reassured, and he certainly didn't want her questions. He hated the way this woman, this stranger—*his employee*—thought he needed to be somehow comforted.

He'd barely said a word since they'd entered this room— what had he revealed?

'That's what you're here for,' he said firmly.

Nothing more.

Now he could finally escape from the boxes, and his breath came steadily again only as he closed the front door behind him.

# CHAPTER THREE

TWO DAYS LATER April sat cross-legged amongst a lot of boxes and a lot of dust.

She was dressed in jeans, sneakers and a floppy T-shirt—her jumper having been quickly removed thanks to the excellent heating and the many boxes she'd already shifted today—and yet another box lay ready for her attention. Her hair was piled up on top of her head, and the local radio station filled the room via her phone and a set of small speakers she'd purchased before she'd realised she had absolutely no money.

But she was glad for her previous financial frivolity. This massive house was creaky and echoey, and she'd hated how empty it had felt on her first day, when she'd been sorting through boxes wearing a pencil skirt, heels and a blouse with a bow—in total silence.

Bizarre how such an overflowing house could feel so empty, but it did.

Music helped. A little.

Now, on day three of her new job, already many boxes lay flattened in the foyer. The shredder had disposed of old takeaway menus and shoe catalogues and local newspapers. And she'd labelled a handful of empty boxes for donations. Several were already full with books and random bits and pieces: a man's silk tie, a mass-produced ceramic vase, eleven tea towels from the Edinburgh Military Tattoo—and so much more. It was nearly impossible to categorise the items, although she'd tried.

But much of the boxes' content was, as Hugh had told her, junk. The packaging for electronic items, without the items themselves. Gossip magazines from ten years ago, with British reality TV stars she didn't recognise on the covers. Sugar and salt packets. Pens that didn't work. Dried-out mascara and nail polish bottles.

It was all so random.

Initially she'd approached each box with enthusiasm. What was she going to learn about the person who'd packed all these boxes from *this* box?

But each box gave little away.

There was no theme, there were no logical groupings or collections, and so far there was absolutely nothing personal. Not even one scribble on a takeaway menu.

Hugh hadn't given anything away, either.

It was hard in this house, with all its mysterious boxes, not to think about the rather interesting and mysterious man who owned them all.

Were they *his* boxes?

April didn't think so. That morning in the kitchen, those clear but sparse directions and neat instructions had not indicated a man who collected such clutter. There was something terribly structured about the man: he exuded organisation and an almost regimented calm.

But that had changed when he'd shown her this room. The instant he'd opened the door he'd become tense. His body, his words. His gaze.

It had been obvious he'd wanted to leave, and he had as soon as humanly possible.

So, no, the boxes weren't his.

But they didn't belong to a stranger, either—because the boxes meant *something* to Hugh Bennell.

Her guess was that they belonged to a woman. The magazines, toiletries… But who?

His wife? Ex-wife? Mother? Sister? Friend?

So—with enthusiasm—April had decided to solve the mystery of the boxes.

But with box after box the mystery steadfastly remained and her enthusiasm rapidly waned.

On the radio, a newsreader read the ten o'clock news in a lovely, clipped British accent.

*Only ten a.m.?*

Her self-determined noon lunchbreak felt a lifetime away.

April sighed and straightened her shoulders, then carefully sliced open the brown packing tape of her next box.

On top lay empty wooden photo frames, one with a crack through the glass. And beneath that lay two phone books—the thick, heavy type that had used to be delivered before everyone had started searching for numbers online.

The unbroken wooden frames would go to the 'donate' box, and the phone books into the recycling. But as she walked out into the foyer, to add the books to the already mountainous recycling pile, a piece of card slipped out from between the pages.

April knelt to pick it up. It was an old and yellowed homemade bookmark, decorated with a child's red thumbprints in the shape of lopsided hearts.

*Happy Mothering Sunday!*
*Love Hugh*

The letters were in neat, thick black marker—the work of a school or kindergarten teacher.

And just like that she'd solved the mystery.

She started a new category: *Hugh*.

She wasn't making a decision on that bookmark, no matter what he said.

She'd let him know in her summarising email that evening.

The email pinged into Hugh's inbox shortly before five p.m. As it had the previous two days at approximately the same time, with the same subject line and the day's date. Exactly as he'd specified—which he appreciated.

She did insist on prefacing her emails with a bit of chatter, but she'd stuck to his guidelines for updating him on her progress.

Which was slower than he'd hoped. Although he didn't think that was April's fault—more his own desire for the house to be magically emptied as rapidly as possible.

That option still existed, of course. He'd researched a business that would come and collect all his mother's boxes and take them away. It would probably only take a day.

But he just couldn't bring himself to do that.

He hated those boxes—hated that stuff. Hated that his mother had been so consumed by it.

Despite it being junk, despite the way the boxes weighed so heavily upon him—both literally and figuratively—it just felt...

As if it would be disrespectful.

Hi Hugh,
I've found a bookmark today—photo attached—and I've put it aside for you. If I find anything similar I'll let you know.

Otherwise all going well. About two thirds through this room...

Hugh didn't read the rest. Instead he clicked open the attachment.

A minute later his boots thumped heavily against the steps up to his mother's front door. It was freezing in the evening darkness—he hadn't bothered to grab a coat for the very short journey—but the foyer was definitely a welcome relief as he let himself in.

April was still in the kitchen, her coat halfway on, obviously about to leave.

'Don't panic—I didn't throw it out,' she said.

'Throw what out?' he asked.

He hadn't seen her since that first morning, and she looked different in jeans and jumper—younger, actually. Her cheek was smudged with dust, her hair not entirely contained in the knot on top of her head.

'The bookmark,' she said. 'I'll just go grab it for you.'

'No,' he said. 'Don't.'

She'd already taken a handful of steps, and now stood only an arm's length before him.

'Okay,' she said. She inclined her chin in a direction over his shoulder. 'It's in a box out there. I've labelled it "Hugh".

I'll just chuck anything in there that I think you should have a look at.'

'No,' he said again. 'Don't.'

Now she seemed to realise what he was saying. Or at least she was no longer wilfully ignoring him. He knew how clear he'd been: with the exception of any paperwork that included personal details, April was to donate or trash *everything*.

'Are you sure?'

Hugh shrugged. 'It's just a badly painted bookmark.'

Up until a few minutes ago he'd had no recollection of that piece of well-intentioned crafting, so his life would definitely be no lesser with it gone.

'I wasn't just talking about the bookmark,' April said. 'I meant anything like that. I'm sure more sentimental bits and pieces are going to turn up. And what about photos? I found some photo frames today, so I expect eventually I'll find—'

'Photos can go in the bin,' he said.

Hugh shoved his hands in his jeans pockets. Again, he just wanted to be out of this place. But he didn't leave.

April was watching him carefully, concern in her clear blue gaze. He was shifting his weight from foot to foot. Fidgeting. He *never* fidgeted.

He wasn't himself in this house. With all this stuff. Now that the boxes had necessarily flowed into the foyer behind him the clutter was *everywhere*.

April had left an empty coffee mug on the kitchen sink.

Now he skirted around her, making his way to the other side of the counter, grabbed the mug and opened the dishwasher. It was empty.

'I've just been hand-washing,' April said. 'I can wash that before I go—don't worry about it.'

Hugh ignored her, stuck the plug in the sink and turned on the hot water. Beneath the sink he found dishwashing liquid, and squirted it into the steaming water.

As the suds multiplied he was somewhat aware of April shrugging off her coat. He had no idea why it was so important for him to clean this mug, but it was.

'You can go,' he said, cleaning out the coffee marks from inside the mug. He realised it wasn't one of his mother's—it was printed with the logo of a Fremantle sporting team he didn't recognise and had a chip in the handle. It was April's.

He rinsed the mug in hot water and placed it on the dish rack.

Immediately it was picked up again—by April.

She was standing right beside him, tea towel in hand, busily drying the mug.

He hadn't noticed her move so close.

She didn't look at him, her concentration focused on her task. Her head was bent, and a long tendril of dark hair curled down to her nape.

This close, he could see the dust decorating her hair, a darker smudge creating a streak across her cheekbone.

She turned, looking directly at him.

She was tall, he realised, even without her heels.

Today her lips weren't glossy, and he realised she probably wasn't wearing make-up. Her eyelashes were no longer the blackest black; her skin wasn't magazine-perfect.

She didn't look better—or worse. Just different. And it was that difference he liked.

That she'd surprised him.

He hadn't been able to imagine her unpacking boxes—but she looked just as comfortable today as she had in her sharp suit. And her gaze was just as strong, just as direct.

He realised he liked that, too.

It should have been an uncomfortable and unwanted realisation. Maybe it was—or it would be later. When his brain wasn't cluttered with boxes and forgotten bookmarks and had room for logic and common sense…and remembering who he was. Who *she* was.

Boss. Employee…

For now, he simply looked at the surprising woman beside him.

'I know this is your mum's house,' she said. 'I get that this must be difficult for you.'

Her words were soft and gentle. They still cut deep.

But they shouldn't—and his instinct was to disagree. *They're just boxes. It's just stuff. It's not difficult in any way at all.*

He said nothing.

'Do you want me to come back tomorrow?'

Had she thought he might fire her over the bookmark?

He nodded sharply, without hesitation. Despite how uncomfortable her kind words had made him. Despite how unlike himself she made him. How aware he was of her presence in this room and in this house. How aware he was of how close she stood to him.

'Okay,' she said. 'I'll leave my mug, then.'

He didn't look at her as she stepped around him and put the coffee mug into an overhead cupboard.

By the time she'd shrugged back into her coat, and arranged her letterbox-red knitted scarf he'd pulled himself together.

'See you tomorrow,' she said, with a smile that was bright.

And then she was gone, leaving Hugh alone with a sink full of disappearing bubbles.

April's roommate was asleep when she got home from stacking shelves at the supermarket, so she went into the communal living room to call her mum.

For once the room was empty—usually the Shoreditch shared house tended to have random people dotted all over the place.

Evidence of the crowd of backpackers who lived here—three from Australia and two from South Africa—was scattered everywhere, though. Empty beer bottles on the cheap glass coffee table, along with a bowl of now stale chips—crisps, they were called here—and a variety of dirty plastic plates and cups. One of the other Aussie girls had had a friend dossing on the couch, and his sheets and blankets still lay tangled and shoved into a corner, waiting for someone magically to wash them and put them away.

Which would happen—eventually. April had learnt that

someone would get sick of the mess, and then do a mad tidy-up—loudly and passive-aggressively.

On a couple of occasions in the two weeks she'd been here it had been her—a lifetime of a weekly house-cleaning service meant she definitely preferred things clean, even though she'd had to look up how to clean a shower on the internet. She'd then realised that her relatively advanced age—she was the oldest of the group by six years—meant that everyone expected her to be the responsible, tidy one who'd clean up after everyone else.

And that wasn't going to happen.

She was too busy working her two jobs and trying to stay on top of her April Molyneux social media world to add unpaid cleaner to the mix. So she'd coordinated the group, they'd all agreed on a roster…and sometimes it was followed.

So April ignored the mess, cleared a spot on the couch and scrolled to her mum's number on her phone.

'Darling!'

It was eight a.m. in Perth, but her mum was always up early. She'd finally retired only recently, with April's eldest sister Ivy taking over the reins at Molyneux Mining. But so far her mother's retirement had seemed to involve several new roles on company boards and a more hands-on role in the investments of the Molyneux Trust.

So basically not a whole lot of retirement was going on for Irene Molyneux. Which did not come as a surprise to anyone.

'Hi, Mum,' April said. 'How's things?'

'Nate is speaking so well!' Irene said. 'Yesterday he said "Can I have a biscuit, please?" Isn't that amazing?'

Irene was also embracing the chance to spend more time with her two-year-old grandson. After five minutes of Nate stories, her mum asked April how she was doing.

'Good,' she said automatically. And then, 'Okay, I guess…'

'What's wrong?'

And so April told her about the bookmark, and her new boss's crystal-clear directive. She didn't mention the details, though—like the sadness she'd seen in Hugh's eyes in the kitchen. His obvious pain.

Her mother was typically no-nonsense. 'If he isn't sentimental, it isn't your role to be.'

But that was the thing—she wasn't convinced he didn't care. Not even close.

'I don't know. It just doesn't feel right.'

'Mmm…' her mother said. 'You can always quit.'

But… 'It pays almost double what I was earning at my last placement.'

'I know,' Irene said.

Her mum didn't say anything further—but April knew what she was thinking. She was torn between supporting April in her goal to pay off her credit card and live independently—a goal she'd supported once she'd been reassured April wasn't going to end up homeless—and solving all her problems. With money.

Which was understandable, really. Her mother had, after all, financially supported April her entire life. And April honestly had never questioned it. She was rich—it was just who she was. Her bottomless credit cards had just come with the territory.

But, really, the only thing she'd ever done that really deserved any payment was her work for the Molyneux Foundation. And besides a few meetings she'd probably spent maybe an hour or two a day working for the foundation—with a big chunk of that time focused on making sure she looked as picture-perfect as possible in photos.

It had been a cringe-worthy, shamefully spoiled existence.

'You understand why I need to do this, right? All of this: living here, living on *my* money, living without the Molyneux name?'

'Yes,' Irene said. 'And you know I admire what you're doing. And I'm a little ashamed of myself for being so worried about you.'

This was cringe-worthy too—how little her family expected of her. Her fault as well, of course.

'But that's my job,' Irene continued. 'I'm your mum. I'm supposed to worry. And I'm supposed to want to fix things. But, if I put that aside, here's my non-mum advice—keep the job. Keep working hard, pay off your debt and move out of that awful shared house. It'll make me feel better once you're living in your own place.'

'Yes, Mum,' April said, smiling. 'I'll do my best.'

And then she remembered something she'd been thinking about earlier.

'Hey, Mum, did *you* keep that type of stuff? Stuff that we all made at school—you know, gifts for Mother's Day? Finger paintings? That sort of stuff?'

Irene laughed. 'No! I'm probably a terrible person, but I remember smuggling all that stuff out to the bin under cover of darkness.'

They talked for a while longer, but later, when April had ended the call and gone to bed, her thoughts wandered back to that faded little bookmark Hugh had once given to his mother.

*Was* she just being sentimental? She wasn't sure how she felt about her mum not keeping any of her childhood art—but then, had it bothered her until now? She hadn't even noticed. Maybe Hugh was right—maybe it *was* just a badly painted bookmark.

But that was the thing—the way Hugh had reacted…the way he'd raced to see her immediately, and the way he'd washed her Dockers mug as if the weight of the world had been on his shoulders…

It felt like so much more.

# CHAPTER FOUR

'Hugh?'

'We must've lost him.'

'Should we reschedule? We can't make a decision without him.'

Belatedly Hugh registered what the conference call voices were saying.

He'd tuned out at some point. In fact, he could barely remember what the meeting was about. He glanced at his laptop screen.

Ah. App bug fixes. And something about the latest iOS upgrade.

Not critically important to his business, but important enough that he should be paying attention.

He *always* paid attention.

The meeting ended with his presumed disappearance, and his flat was silent.

He pushed back his chair and headed for the kitchen, leaning against the counter as his kettle boiled busily.

He'd left his tea mug in the sink, as he always did. He reused it throughout the day, and chucked it in the dishwasher each night.

*Why had he cared about April's mug?*

He was neat. He knew that. Extremely neat. The perfect contrast to his mother and her overwhelming messiness.

Although, to be fair, his mother hadn't always been like that.

At first it had just been clutter. It had only been later that the dishes had begun to pile in the sink and mounds of clothes had remained unwashed. And by then he'd been old enough to help. So he'd taken over—diligently cleaning around all his mum's things: her 'treasures' and her 'we might need it one days', her flotsam and jetsam and her 'there's a useful article/recipe/tip in that' magazines, newspapers and books.

But he wasn't obsessive—at least not to the level of compulsively cleaning an employee's coffee mug.

It had been odd. For him and for April.

He didn't feel good about that.

He didn't know this woman at all.

That had been deliberate. He hadn't wanted to use the Precise HR Department, or reach out to his team for recommendations of casual workers, university students or backpackers—he hadn't wanted anyone he knew or worked with to know about what was he was doing.

But the fact was someone needed to know what he was doing in order to actually do it—and that person was April Spencer.

And so she knew about his mother's hoard and would know it better than anyone ever had. Even him.

That sat uncomfortably. Hugh had spent much of his life hiding his mother's hoard. It didn't feel right to invite somebody in. Literally to lay it all out to be seen—to be judged.

His mum had loved him, had worked so hard, and had provided him with all she could and more on a minimal wage and without any support from his father. She didn't deserve to be judged as anything less than she had been: a great mum. A great woman.

Her hoard had not defined her, but if people had known of it…

The kettle had boiled and Hugh made his tea, leaving the teabag hanging over the edge of his cup.

April had offered to leave yesterday.

But he'd rejected her offer without consideration, and now, even with time, he knew it had been the right decision.

If it wasn't April it would be someone else. At least April wasn't connected to his work or anyone he knew. Anyone who'd known his mother.

She was a temporary worker—travelling, probably. She'd soon be back in Australia, or off to her next working holiday somewhere sunnier than London, and she'd take her knowledge of his mother's secret hoard with her.

His phone buzzed—a text message.

Drinks after work at The Saint?

It was a group message to the cyclists he often rode with a few mornings a week. He liked them. They were dedicated, quick, and they pushed him to get stronger, and faster.

He replied.

Sorry, can't make it.

He always declined the group's social invitations. He liked riding with them, but he didn't do pubs and clubs. Or any place there was likely to be an unpredictable crowd—he never had, and in fact he'd never been able to—not even as a child. He avoided any crowd, but enclosed crowds—exactly as one might find in a pub—made him feel about as comfortable as a room full of his mother's boxes.

He actually wasn't sure which had come first: Had he inherited his crowd-related anxiety from his compulsive hoarder mother, or had his hatred of bustling crowds stemmed from the nightmares he'd once had of being suffocated beneath an avalanche of boxes?

It didn't really matter—the outcome was the same: Hugh Bennell wasn't exactly a party animal.

Fortunately Hugh's repeated refusals to socialise didn't seem to bother his cycling group. He was aware, however, that they all thought he was a bit weird.

But that wasn't an unfamiliar sensation for him—he'd been the weird kid at school too. After all, it hadn't been as if he could ever invite anybody over to his place to play.

*Want to come over and see my mum's hoard?*

Yeah. That had never happened. He'd never allowed it to happen.

His doorbell rang.

Hugh glanced at his watch. It was early afternoon—not even close to the time when packages were usually delivered. And he certainly wasn't expecting anybody.

Tea still in hand, he headed for the door. It could only be a charity collector, or somebody distributing religious pamphlets.

Instead it was April.

She stood in her coat and scarf, carrying a box.

A box labelled '*Hugh*'.

Hugh's eyes narrowed when he saw her.

April knew she wasn't supposed to be down here, but she just hadn't been able to simply send an email.

He wore a T-shirt, black jeans and an unzipped hoodie, and he held a cup of tea in one hand. He was barefoot and his hair, as she'd come to expect, was scruffy—as if he'd woken up and simply run a hand through it. Yesterday he'd been smooth-shaven, but today the stubble was back—and, as she'd also come to expect, she really rather liked it.

Hugh Bennell seemed to be in a permanent state of sexy dishevelment, and she'd put money on it—if she had any—that he had no idea.

But now was not the time to be pondering any of this.

'Ms Spencer?' he prompted.

Ms Spencer—not April. He definitely wasn't impressed.

She swallowed. 'I'm resigning,' she said. 'I didn't just want to put it in an email.'

A gust of wind whipped down from the street and through the doorway. Despite her coat, April shivered.

Hugh noticed.

He stepped back and gestured for her to come inside.

April blinked—she hadn't expected him to do that. She had a suspicion *he* hadn't either, although his gaze remained unreadable.

Somehow as she stepped past Hugh, slightly awkwardly with the large box, she managed to brush against him— just her upper arm, briefly against his chest. It was the most minimal of touches—made minuscule once combined with her heavy wool coat and Hugh's combination of T-shirt and hoodie. And yet she blushed.

April felt her cheeks go hot and her skin—despite all the layers—prickled with awareness.

How ridiculous. Really only their clothing had touched. Nothing more.

She forced her attention to her surroundings, not looking anywhere near Hugh.

His basement flat was compact and immaculate. Two bikes hung neatly on a far wall, but otherwise the walls were completely empty. In fact the whole place felt empty—there wasn't a trinket or a throw cushion in sight. The only evidence of occupation was the desk, pushed right up against the front window, and its few scattered papers, sticky note pads and pens were oddly reassuring in their imperfection.

They were standing near his taupe-coloured couches, but Hugh didn't sit so neither did she.

Her blush had faded, so she could finally look at him again. Even if it was more in the direction of his shoulder rather than at his eyes. His *knowing* eyes?

She refused to consider it.

'Anyway,' April said, deliberately brisk, 'I found some more things today. A couple of photos of you and your mum and a birthday card.'

She shook her head sharply when Hugh went to speak. She didn't want to hear his spiel again.

'And, look…maybe I should've chucked them out, as you've insisted. But then I found one of those old plastic photo negative barrels—you know? And it had a lock of baby's hair in it.'

She met his gaze.

'*A lock of hair*, Hugh. Yours, I think. And then I was done. I'm not throwing *that* out. That's not my responsibility, and it's definitely not my decision.'

She carefully put the box on Hugh's coffee table.

'So there's the box with your things in it. You can throw it straight in the skip if you want, but *I* couldn't.' She turned around as she straightened, meeting Hugh's gaze again. He gave nothing away. 'I've finished that first reception room, and I've organised for the charity donations to be collected tomorrow.'

Still in her coat and scarf, she felt uncomfortably warm—and not entirely because of the central heating.

'I'd better get going.'

'No notice?' Hugh asked.

His tone was calm and measured. *He* definitely wasn't blushing, or paying any attention when April did.

She was being ridiculous.

'No,' April said. 'I didn't see the point. Clearly I'm unsuitable for the position.'

'What if I made the position suitable?' he said, not missing a beat.

'Pardon me?'

'What if I said you didn't have to make all the decisions any more?' He spoke with perfect calm.

'So I can have a "Hugh" box?'

He nodded. 'Yes.'

'And you'll come sort through it each day?'

Now he shook his head. 'No. I'll come and throw it in the skip each day. But at least *you* wouldn't have to.'

No. That still didn't feel right. April wasn't sure she could let that happen…

*Wait.* It wasn't her call. It *so* wasn't her call.

And that was all she'd asked for—not to be the decision-maker.

The job paid well. And it wasn't very difficult—now Hugh had removed the requirement to throw out intensely personal items.

And she still had her credit card debt, still had a manky shared house to move out of.

It was a no-brainer.

And yet she hesitated.

The reason stood in front of her. Making her belly heat and her skin warm simply with his presence.

His *oblivious* presence, it would seem.

In which case…what was she worried about?

She knew she didn't want to walk straight from Evan and into another relationship, and that certainly didn't seem to be on offer here.

Hugh was looking at her with his compelling eyes, waiting not entirely patiently for a response. He did *not* look like a man who enjoyed waiting.

April smiled.

It had been fifteen years since she'd been single. It was probably normal that her hormones were being slightly over the top in the vicinity of a demonstrably handsome man.

It was nothing more.

'Deal,' she said.

She had nothing to worry about.

But then Hugh smiled back—and it was the first time she'd seen him smile both with his divine mouth and with his remarkable eyes.

*Probably nothing.*

On the following day there was nothing to put into the 'Hugh' box.

So April emailed Hugh with her daily update, put on her coat, went home to her still messy shared house and ate soup that had come out of a can while her housemates drank wine that came out of a box. Later, when her housemates headed out to a bar, April walked around the corner to her local supermarket and stacked more cans of soup—and lots of other things—until the early hours of the morning.

The next day, at the Islington end-of-terrace house, April brewed a strong coffee in her Dockers mug, running her thumb across the chip on the handle as she always did. She then placed it on the marble benchtop just where the light hit it, artistically—or as artistically as a coffee mug could be placed—and took a photo.

Really need this today! #workinghard #ilovecaffeine #tooearly

Then she scheduled the post for shortly after Perth would be waking up.

She knew she'd get lots of questions about what she was working so hard on—which was the point. And she'd be vague, and everyone would assume it was something super-exotic—like a fundraising gala event or a photo shoot.

Not unpacking boxes in a grand old dusty house in London.

April smiled.

Part of her wanted to tell her followers *exactly* what she was doing. To tell them that she actually *hadn't* been doing totally fine after Evan had left her, that she'd run away from everyone who loved her and for the first time in her life had realised how privileged she actually was.

But the rest of her knew she had commitments. Knew that the Molyneux Foundation's sponsors hadn't signed up for her to have an early midlife crisis.

And mostly she knew that she wasn't ready to make any big decisions just yet.

She still hadn't really got her head around the fact that she was single.

Of course she'd looked at other men since she'd starting going out with Evan. She'd even had men flirt with her—quite often, really. Possibly because of her sparkling personality—more likely because of all the dollar signs she represented.

But, regardless whether she'd thought some guy was hot, or if some guy had thought *she* was hot—or just rich—it hadn't mattered. She'd been with Evan. So she'd been able to acknowledge a handsome man objectively and then efficiently deflect any flirting that veered beyond harmless.

Because she'd always had Evan.

She'd always loved Evan.

And now that she *didn't* have Evan, meeting another man wasn't on April's radar. It hadn't even been on her radar as something *not* to do—she hadn't even thought about it. It had been too impossible.

Until she'd met Hugh. And then it hadn't. It hadn't felt impossible at all.

But it still *was*, of course.

Totally impossible. As she'd reminded herself in Hugh's flat, she wasn't going to walk from a fifteen-year relationship into another. And—and this scenario felt far more likely—she *definitely* wasn't going to walk from one rejection straight into another one.

There were lots of things she had learnt she could cope with: having no money, working two jobs—two *labour intensive* jobs, no less—living in a shared house at age thirty-two and having her family on the other side of the world.

But she knew utterly and completely that she couldn't cope with another man rejecting her.

*I don't love you.*

How could those words still hurt so much?

She didn't miss Evan. She understood that their relationship had reached its inevitable conclusion. She definitely didn't want to be with him any more.

But… *I don't love you.*

And he never had.

That pain didn't just go away.

Hugh was already boiling the kettle in his mother's kitchen when April arrived the next morning.

Her gaze flicked over him as she walked into the room, her bag slung over her long coat, her scarf in shades of green today.

'Good morning,' she said, in that polished, friendly tone he was becoming familiar with. She was good at sounding comfortable even when she wasn't.

He could see the questions in her gaze and the instant tension in her stride as she walked towards the bar stools tucked beneath the marble counter.

'Morning,' Hugh said as she dumped her bag on a chair and then shrugged out of her coat. 'I thought I'd help move those heavy boxes.'

Her email last night had explained that she'd found some boxes that would need two people to lift them. He'd considered contacting the temp agency to recruit someone, and then had realised that to do so would be preposterous. He was thirty-six, fit and he lived ten metres away. *He* could move the damn boxes. They were, no matter how much he seemed needlessly to over-complicate them, just boxes. He didn't have to deal with any of the stuff inside them.

She nodded. 'Great!' she said, although he couldn't tell if she meant it. 'I thought you'd just organise someone to come and help me.'

'I did,' he said, then pointed towards his chest. 'Me.'

Her smile now was genuine. And lovely. He'd thought that every time he'd seen her smile. It was another reason he'd considered calling the temp office. But similarly—just as the boxes were only boxes—a smile was only a smile. It, and his admiration of it, meant nothing more.

'It shouldn't take long. I could probably do it myself, but I'd hate to drop one of the boxes and break something.'

The kettle clicked as it finished boiling.

'Doesn't matter if you do,' Hugh said. 'But still—ask me to help move anything heavy, regardless. I don't want you to hurt yourself.'

April blinked as if he'd said something unexpected. 'Okay,' she said.

They took their coffee into the second reception room.

As always, the cluttered space made Hugh feel stiff and antsy—as if he could run a marathon on the adrenalin that shot through his veins.

So far April had cleared only a small section of this room. Once it had been his mum and Len's TV room. They'd sat on the large, plush couch, their legs propped on matching otto-mans, dinner balanced on their laps.

The couch was still there—one arm visible amongst the bevy of boxes.

The heavy boxes were near the window. They were much bigger than the boxes that had filled the first room—probably five or more times their size—and stacked only two high.

It was the top boxes that April wanted to be lifted down.

Coffee placed carefully on the floor, it was easy for the pair of them to lift the boxes: one, two...

For the third, they both had to reach awkwardly around it, tucked away as it was between the heavy curtains and another wall of boxes.

In doing so their fingers brushed against each other, along the far side of the box.

Only for a second—or not even that long.

Barely long enough to be noticed—but Hugh did.

Her hand felt cool and soft. Her nails glossy and smooth beneath his palm.

His gaze darted to April's, but she was too busy lifting the box to pay any attention at all.

Or too busy deliberately looking busy.

He suspected the latter. He'd noticed her reaction in his flat when she'd so briefly brushed against him. Her cheeks had blushed pink in an instant.

He'd reacted, too.

It was strange, really, for his blood to heat like that from such an innocent touch.

He hadn't expected it.

Not that he hadn't continued to notice April's attractiveness. It would be impossible not to. She was beautiful in a classic, non-negotiable way—but beauty was not something Hugh should be paying much attention to when it came to a woman working for him.

So he'd made sure he hadn't.

Except for when she'd stood beside him at the sink a few nights ago, when his thoughts had been jumbled and unfocused. Then the shape of her neck, of her jaw, the profile of her nose and chin...

Yes, he'd noticed.

But, more, he'd noticed her empathy. And her sympathy. Even if he had welcomed neither.

Nor welcomed his attraction to her.

He didn't want complications. Right now—getting this house cleaned out—or ever.

His lifestyle was planned and structured to avoid complications.

Even when he dated women it was only ever for the briefest of times—brevity, he'd discovered, avoided the complications that were impossible for him: commitment, cohabiting, planning a future together...

Relationships were all about complications, and to Hugh complications were clutter.

And he was determined to live a clutter-free life.

But today contact with April's skin had again made his blood heat and his belly tighten.

He should go.

They'd moved the box to where April had directed, so Hugh headed for the door.

'Don't forget your coffee,' April said.

He turned and saw she held the two mugs in her hands—the one for him printed with agapanthus.

He should go—he could make his own coffee downstairs. There was nothing to be gained by staying, and as always he had so much on his to-do list today.

But he realised, surprised, that the boxes that surrounded him weren't compelling him to leave. At some point the tension that had been driving him from this house had abated.

It was still there, but no longer overpowering. Nor, it seemed, was it insurmountable.

So he found himself accepting his mug from April. A woman who, with no more than her smile and against all his better judgement, had somehow compelled him to stay.

He hadn't been supposed to stay.

April had honestly expected Hugh to take his coffee and head on down to his basement apartment.

But instead he'd taken his mug and approached the first box she'd planned to go through—its top already sliced open, the flaps flipped back against the thick cardboard sides.

For a moment it had looked as if he was going to start looking through the box. He'd stepped right up beside it, his spare hand extended, and then he had simply let it fall back against his jean-clad thigh.

Now he brought his mug to his lips, his gaze, as usual, impossible to interpret.

'You really don't like these boxes,' April said. Her words were possibly unwise—but they'd just slipped out.

Hugh Bennell intrigued her. And not just his looks—or his touch, however accidental. But who he was and what all these boxes meant to him.

The boxes, of course, intrigued her too.

He shot a look in her direction, raising an eyebrow. 'No.'

And that was that. No elaboration.

So April simply got to work.

Hugh walked a few steps away, propping his backside against the only available arm of the sofa. Boxes were stacked neatly on the seat cushions beside him.

This box was full of clothes. A woman's. April hadn't come across women's clothes before, and the discovery of the brightly coloured silks and satins made her smile and piqued her interest.

She held a top against herself: a cream sheer blouse with thick black velvet ribbon tied into a bow at the neck. It was too small for April—smaller even than the sample size clothing she'd used to have sent to her by designers before she'd given up on starving herself.

'Was this your mum's?' April asked, twisting to face Hugh.

She absolutely knew it wasn't her place to ask him, but she just couldn't *not*.

It was too weird to be standing in this room with Hugh, in silence, surrounded by all this stuff that meant something to him but absolutely nothing to her. And *she* was the one sorting through it.

Hugh didn't even blink. 'All clothing is to be donated,' he said.

'That wasn't why I was asking,' April said.

She tossed the shirt into the 'donate' box in the centre of the room. Soon after followed a deep pink shift dress, a lovely linen shawl and a variety of printed T-shirts. Next April discovered a man's leather bomber jacket that was absolutely amazing but about a hundred sizes too big.

Regardless, April tried it on. Felt compelled to.

*Was it disrespectful to try it on?*

Possibly. Probably.

But Hugh was about to donate it all, anyway. *He* was the one who insisted it was all junk, all worthless.

Maybe this was how she could trigger a reaction from this tall, silent man?

It was unequivocally a bad idea, but she spent her days unpacking boxes and her evenings stacking shelves. Mostly in silence.

Maybe she was going stir crazy, but she needed to see what Hugh would do.

She just didn't buy it that he didn't care about this stuff. So far his measured indifference had felt decidedly unconvincing.

She *had* to call his bluff.

'I'm not paying you to play dress-up,' Hugh pointed out from behind her.

His tone was neutral.

She spun around to show him the oversized jacket. 'Spoilsport,' she said with a deliberate grin, catching his gaze.

If he was just going to stand there she couldn't cope with all this silence and gloom. Her sisters had always told her she was the *sunny* sister. That she could walk into a room and brighten it with her smile.

It had always sounded rather lame—and to be honest part of her *had* wondered what that said about her in comparison to *clever* Ivy or *artistic* Mila. Was it really such an achievement to be good at smiling?

It had been a moot point in the months since Evan had left, anyway.

Until now. Now, this darkly moody man felt like a challenge for sunny April.

Acutely aware that this might all backfire horribly, but incapable of stopping herself in the awkward silence, she playfully tossed her hair in the way of a supermodel.

'What do you think?'

What would he do? Smile? Shout? Leave?

Fire her?

Hugh's shake of the head was barely perceptible.

But…was that a quirk to his lips?

Yes. It was definitely there.

April's smile broadened.

'Fair enough,' she said, shrugging her shoulders and then tossing the jacket into the 'donate' box. 'How about this?' she asked, randomly grabbing the next item of clothing in the box.

A boat-neck blouse, in a shiny fabric with blue and white stripes. But too small. Which April realised…too late.

Hands stuck up in the air, fabric bunched around her shoulders on top of her T-shirt, April went completely still.

'Dammit!' she muttered.

She hadn't been entirely sure of her plan, but becoming trapped in cheap satin fabric was definitely not part of it.

She wiggled again, trying to dislodge the blouse, but it didn't shift.

Her T-shirt had ridden up at least a little. April could feel cool air against a strip of skin above the waistband of her jeans.

Mortified, she struggled again, twisting away from where she knew Hugh stood, feeling unbelievably silly and exposed.

'Stay still,' he said, suddenly impossibly close. Behind her.

April froze. She was blindfolded by the stupid top but she could sense his proximity. His height. His width.

His fingers hooked under the striped fabric, right at her shoulders. He was incredibly careful, gently moving the fabric upwards. Her arms were still trapped. It was almost unbearable: the touch of his fingers, his closeness, her vulnerability.

She wanted him to just yank it off over her head. To get this over with.

*No, she didn't.*

The fabric had cleared her shoulders now, and he moved

closer still to help tug it over her arms, where the top was still wrapped tightly.

Now his fingers brushed against the bare skin of her arms. Only as much as necessary—and that didn't feel like anywhere near enough.

He was so close behind her that if she shifted backwards even the slightest amount she would be pressed right up against him. Back to chest.

It seemed a delicious possibility.

It seemed, momentarily, as she was wrapped in the temporary dark, a viable option.

And then the blouse was pulled free.

April gasped as the room came back into focus. Directly in front of her were heavy navy curtains, closed, obscured by an obstacle course of cardboard boxes.

She spun around.

'Thank you—' she began.

Then stopped.

Hugh was still so close. Closer than he'd ever been before. Tall enough and near enough that he needed to look down at her and she needed to tilt her chin up.

She explored his face. The sharpness of his nose, the thick slash of his eyebrows, the strength of his jaw. This close she could see delicate lines bracketing his lips, a freckle on his cheek, a rogue grey hair amongst the stubble.

He was studying her, too. His gaze took in her eyes, her cheeks, her nose. Her lips.

There it was.

Not subtle now, or easily dismissed as imagination as it had been down in his basement apartment. Or every other time they'd been in the same room together.

But it *had* been there, she realised. Since the first time they'd met.

That focus. That…intent.

That *heat*.

Between them. Within her.

It made her pulse race and caused her to become lost in his gaze when he finally wrenched his away from her lips.

Since they'd met his eyes had revealed little. Enough for her to know, deep in her heart, that he wasn't as hard and unfeeling as he so steadfastly attempted to be. It was why she'd known she couldn't be responsible for the disposal of his mother's memories.

And maybe that was what had obscured what she saw so clearly now. Or at least had allowed her to question it.

Electricity practically crackled between them. It seemed ludicrous that she hadn't known before. That she'd ever doubted it.

Hugh Bennell *wanted* her.

And she wanted him. In a way that left her far more exposed than her displaced T-shirt.

But then he stepped back. His gaze was shuttered again.

'You okay?' he asked, his voice deep and gravelly.

*No.*

'Yes,' she said, belatedly realising he was referring to the stripy top and not to what had just happened between them.

Way too late she tugged down her T-shirt, and blushed when his gaze briefly followed the movement of her hands. Then it shifted away.

Not swiftly, as if he'd been caught out or was embarrassed. Just away.

He didn't look at her again as he went over to the box April had been emptying.

Without hesitation he reached in, grabbing a large handful of clothing and directly deposited it into the 'donate' box. Then, with brisk efficiency, he went through the remainder of the box: ancient yellow newspapers to the recycling pile, a toaster with a severed electrical cord to the bin, encyclopaedias with blue covers and gold-edged pages on top of the clothing in the donation box.

April had been boxing books separately, but she didn't say a word.

The donation box was now full, already packed with yesterday's miscellanea, and Hugh lifted it effortlessly.

April followed him into the foyer and directed him to where she'd like the box left, ready for the next visit by the red-and-white charity collection truck.

'Thank you,' she said.

He shrugged. 'I just want this stuff gone.'

She nodded. 'I'd better get back to work, then.'

Finally her temporary inertia had lifted, and reality—the most obvious being that it was her job to empty these boxes, not Hugh's—had reasserted itself.

Although amidst that reality the crackling tension between them still remained.

April didn't know what to do with it.

Hugh seemed unaffected, but April knew for certain that he wasn't unaware.

'These clothes aren't my mum's,' he said suddenly. 'I have no idea who they belong to. I have no idea what most of this stuff is, or why the hell my mum needed to keep it all so badly.'

April nodded again. His tone had hardened as he spoke, frustration fracturing his controlled facade.

'She was more than all this stuff. Much more.' He shook his head. 'Why couldn't she see that?'

Hugh met her gaze again, but April knew he'd asked the most rhetorical of questions.

'I'll get this stuff out of your house,' she said. She promised.

'*Her* house,' he clarified.

And then, without another word, he was gone.

# CHAPTER FIVE

HUGH HADN'T SLEPT WELL.

He'd woken late, so he'd been too late to join the group he normally rode with on a Wednesday, so instead he'd headed out alone. Today that was his preference anyway.

Because it was later, traffic was heavier.

It was also extremely cold, and the roads were slick with overnight rain.

London could be dangerous for a cyclist, and Hugh understood and respected this.

It was partly why he often chose to ride in groups, despite his general preference for solitude. Harried drivers were forced to give pairs or long lines of bikes room on the road, and were less likely to scrape past mere millimetres from Hugh's handlebars.

But other times—like this morning—his need to be alone trumped the safety of numbers.

Today he didn't want the buzz of conversation to surround him. Or for other cyclists to share some random anecdote or to espouse the awesomeness of their new carbon fibre wheels.

When he rode alone it was the beat of his own pulse that filled his ears, alongside the cadence of his breathing and the whir of the wheels.

Around him the cacophony of noise that was early-morning London simply receded.

It was just him and his bike and the road.

Hugh rode hard—hard enough to keep his mind blank and his focus only on the next stroke of the pedals.

Soon he was out of inner London, riding down the A24 against the flow of commuter traffic. He was warm with exertion, but the wind was still icy against his cheeks. The rest of his body was cloaked in jet-black full-length cycling pants, a long-sleeved jersey, gilet and gloves.

Usually by now the group would have begun to loop back, but today Hugh just kept on riding and riding, heading from busy roads to country lanes, losing track of time. Eventually he reached the Surrey Hills and their punishing inclines, relishing the burning of his lungs and the satisfying ache of his thighs and calves.

But midway up Box Hill, with his brain full of no more than his own thundering heartbeat, he stopped. On a whim, abruptly he violently twisted his cleats out of his pedals and yanked hard on the brakes until his bike was still. Then, standing beside his bike, he surveyed the rolling green patchwork of the Dorking valley as it stretched towards the South Downs beneath a clear blue sky. Out here, amongst woodland and sheep-dotted fields, London was thirty miles and a world away.

*What was he doing?*

He didn't have to check his watch to know he'd missed his morning teleconference. He'd miss his early-afternoon meetings too, given it would take him another two and a half hours to get home again.

Reception would be patchy up here, he knew, but still, he should at least try to email his assistant—who worked remotely from Lewisham—and ask her to clear his calendar for the rest of the day.

But he didn't.

He hadn't planned to ride this far, but he'd needed to. He'd needed to do something to ease the discontent that had kept him awake half the night—much of it spent pacing his lounge room floor.

Hugh didn't like how he felt. All agitated and uncertain.

He usually lived his life with such definition: he knew what he was doing, why he was doing it, and he always knew it was the right thing to do. Hugh made it his business to plan and prepare and analyse *everything*. It was why his business was so successful. He didn't make mistakes…he didn't get distracted.

His mother's house had always been the exception.

When she'd died he'd considered selling it. He'd been living in his own place in Primrose Hill, not far away.

But back then—as now—he just hadn't been able to.

For a man who prided himself on being the antithesis of his mother—on being a man who saw no value in objects and who ruthlessly protected his life from clutter—his attachment to the house was an embarrassing contradiction.

But he knew how much that house had meant to his mum. He knew exactly what it had represented.

For his mother it had been a place of love, after so many years of searching.

And for Hugh it had been where his mother had finally lived a life free of clutter—a life he had been sure she'd lost for ever. For more than a decade she'd been happy there, her hoard no more than a distant memory.

And so he'd kept it.

He'd ended up hoarding his mother's hoard. There was no other way to explain his three-year refusal to dispose of all that junk.

Even now, as April Spencer attempted to clean out his mother's house, he couldn't let it go.

A stranger—April—had seen that.

Why else would she be going to such lengths to save sentimental crap unless she'd sensed that he wasn't really ready to relinquish it?

And she was right. The original 'Hugh' box still remained as April had left it, cluttering up his coffee table in all its ironic glory.

He just hadn't been able to walk to the skip behind the house and throw it all away. It had felt impossible.

How pathetic.

Yesterday he'd helped April move those boxes in an effort to normalise the situation: to prove to himself that his visceral reaction to them could be overcome. Except he hadn't considered April. He hadn't considered his visceral reaction to *her*.

He hadn't considered that, while he might be able to dismiss his attraction to her as nothing when he spent only short periods of time with her, more time together might not be so manageable.

Because more time with her meant he'd seen another side of her: a mischievous forthrightness that really shouldn't have surprised him, given her refusal to follow his original instructions.

And he liked it. *A lot.*

He'd also liked it—a lot—when she'd got tangled up in that shirt.

He'd liked being so very close to her—close enough to smell her shampoo and admire the Australian tan revealed below her bunched up T-shirt. Close enough to feel her shiver beneath his touch. To hear the acceleration of her breathing.

In those long moments after he'd helped her out of the blouse it had been as intimate as if he'd actually undressed her.

It had felt raw and naked—and incredibly intense. As if, had he touched her, they would've both lost control completely. And for those long moments he'd wanted nothing more than to lose control with April Spencer.

But Hugh Bennell *never* lost control.

And so he hadn't. He'd taken a step back, even though it had been harder than he would've liked.

He'd assessed the situation: April worked for him.

His priority was cleaning out his mother's house, not fraternising with his employees.

Besides, he suspected his reaction to April was somehow tangled up with his reaction to the boxes. Because it wasn't normal for him to have such a magnetic pull towards a woman. He was generally far more measured when he met a woman he liked. In fact he always 'met' the women he dated online.

It allowed for a certain level of…well, of *control*, really. He could set his expectations, as could the woman he was speaking too. There was never any confusion or miscommunication, or the risk of having anything misconstrued.

It was incredibly efficient.

But starting with physical attraction…*no*.

Although it had been difficult to remind himself why as he'd paced his parquet floor at three a.m.

His mind had been as full with thoughts of April as with his continued frustration over the house and all its boxes.

Mostly with April, actually.

The softness of her skin. The way her lips had parted infinitesimally as they'd gazed into each other's eyes. And that urge to lean forward and take what he knew she'd been offering had been so compelling it had felt inevitable...

*No.*

And so his bike ride. A bike ride to clear his mind of the clutter his mother's hoard and April were creating.

It had been a good plan, Hugh thought as he got back on his bike.

A total fail, though, in practice, with his brain still unable to let go of memories of warm skin and knowing blue eyes as he rode back down the hill, alongside the song of a skylark caught up in the breeze.

Mila: OMG Gorgeous!

April: That's one to save for his twenty-first! :)

April typed her instant messaging response to Ivy's gorgeous photo of her son, Nate, covered in bubbles in the bathtub. It felt like for ever since she'd spoken to both her sisters together.

April: How are sales going, Mila?

Mila had recently started mass-producing some of her ceramic work to keep up with sales at her small boutique pottery business.

Mila: Pretty good. I've experimented with pricing a bit. I'm still not sure how much people value handmade. So far it seems that the hand-glazing is the key, because...

Mila went into quite a lot of detail—as Mila always did when it came to her business—and then posted some photos she'd taken in her workshop.

April had always been proud of Mila—of both her sisters. She'd always admired how Mila had been so adamant that she'd build her business without the financial support of their mother, but until now April had never really had an issue with spending her family's money herself.

In fact it had taken her until her mid-twenties before she'd realised she should be doing a lot more with her good fortune than attending parties and buying everything she liked on every fashion festival catwalk.

And so she'd started the Molyneux Foundation.

She'd deliberately chosen not to be the face of the foundation because it wasn't about her. In fact she'd asked her mother to be the patron. But there was no question that it was April driving the foundation. It had become *her* project and, along with a small team, she'd made sure the foundation had continued to grow—and for every dollar donated to the foundation Molyneux Mining matched it twice over.

April had experimented with a few different ideas for the foundation—a website, later a blog—and by the time Instagram had gained popularity April had known exactly how to monetise it best to help the foundation. She'd had her team reaching out to any company that sold a product she could include in a photo, and she'd carefully curated the images to ensure that she mixed promotional pictures seamlessly in with those that were just her own.

And it had worked. She didn't think her mum had expected it to take off the way it had when April had talked her into the two-to-one deal, but it was certainly too late now!

She was incredibly proud of all the foundation had achieved, and of her role in that. But she'd still really just considered it a little side project. She was as hands-on as needed, but it was hardly a full-time job. She'd still had plenty of time to shop and socialise—and until Evan had left her it had never occurred to her to live without the Molyneux money.

The Molyneux money to which *she* had contributed in absolutely no way at all.

And the brittleness of all that—the fact that without the Molyneux money she had literally nothing…no means to support herself…not one thing she'd bought with money she'd actually earned herself—was quite frightening.

Ivy: How's the new job going?

April: Good. Mostly. Lots of boxes.

She'd love to post a photo to show the magnitude of the hoard to her sisters, but photography was one of the many things expressly forbidden by the confidentiality agreement she'd signed. Along with any discussion of the contents of the boxes.

April: My boss is interesting.

She'd typed that before she'd really thought about what she was doing.

Ivy: Oooh! Interesting-interesting? Or INTERESTING-interesting? ;-) ;-) ;-)

April: Both.

She'd never been good at keeping secrets from her sisters.

Mila: Photo?

April: No. I can't even tell you his name. But he's tall. Dark hair, dark eyes. Stubble. What do you call it…? Swarthy?

Mila: I've always liked that word

April: But he's my boss.

Ivy: From an HR point of view, that's not really a problem unless there is any question of a power imbalance. And I doubt nepotism is an issue in your current role.

Mila: It's handy having a CEO in the family.

April: I'm not going to do anything about it, anyway.

Mila: WHY NOT?

Ivy: WHY?

April: It's not the right time. I need to be single for a while. Right? Isn't that what you're supposed to do when your husband walks out on you?

Mila: I don't have a husband ;-)

Mila *did* have a very handsome, very successful boyfriend who adored her, however. Everyone knew they'd get married eventually.

April: Not helpful.

Mila: Sorry. Too soon?

Too soon to be teased about her situation?

April: No. I'm not curled up in the corner sobbing or anything.

She welcomed a bit of levity—she had right from the day that Evan had left her.

Plus, she was well past that now. Now she slept easily—no thoughts of Evan whatsoever. Working fourteen-hour days possibly also helped.

Ivy: I think being single for a while is a good idea.

Ivy was always good for keeping things on topic.

Mila: But you can still be single and do interesting things with an interesting man ;-) ;-)

Ivy: Exactly.

There was a long pause as her sisters clearly awaited her response.

This was not what she'd expected. She'd expected words of caution. Now the possibilities had short-circuited her brain.

Mila: April?

April: I don't know what to do.

Ivy: But you know WHO to do!

Mila: Ha-ha-ha!

April: Can you post some more photos of Nate?

Mila: Boo. You're no fun.

Ivy had taken the bait, though, and bombarded them with three adorable photos in quick succession. The conversation swiftly moved on, for which April was extremely grateful.

But that night it was Hugh Bennell who crowded her dreams.

April was almost finished for the day when Hugh opened the front door. The charity truck had just left, taking away the latest boxes full of donated things.

It had left the foyer almost empty, with only a neat stack

of flattened boxes near the door and the 'Hugh' box sitting on the bottom step of the grand stairway.

'Hello!' April said, smiling as he stepped inside. She hadn't seen him since the stripy blouse debacle, but had already determined her approach: regardless of her sisters' opinion, she was going to remain strictly professional.

Even *considering* another approach made her...

Well. It didn't matter. It was too soon after Evan, and Hugh was her boss. These were compelling supporting arguments for professionalism.

No matter how compelling Hugh himself might be, simply by walking through the glossy black door.

April had just sent him her summary email, but was doing a quick sweep-up of the dirt that the charity man had tracked inside before going home.

'Hi,' he said, shooting only the briefest glance in her direction before striding for his box. It was the first day since that afternoon in his basement that she'd had anything to add to it, and of course she'd let him know.

Hugh picked up the box in the swiftest of motions and then immediately headed down the hallway—which led through the kitchen, the utility room and then outside to the skip.

April had assumed he'd come and check the box after she'd gone for the day, so she wasn't really prepared for this.

'Wait!' she said, before she could stop herself.

He stopped, but didn't turn. 'Yes?' he asked. His tone was impatient.

She knew she shouldn't have said anything.

'Nothing—sorry,' she said.

*There. Professional.*

Then, somehow, she was jogging up the hallway. 'Wait... please.'

Again he stopped immediately at the sound of her voice.

This time he turned to face her.

She'd run up right behind him, so he was really close, with only the open box between them.

She reached inside. She'd found a lot of sentimental things

across two boxes today: a large pile of ancient finger paint-ings and children's drawings—all labelled 'Hugh' with a date in the mid-nineteen-eighties—and all of his school reports, from preschool through to Year Thirteen.

But it was some photos that she picked up now, in a messy pile she'd attempted to make neat. But that had been impos-sible with the collection of different-sized photos: some round-edged, others standard photo-sized, some cut out small and weathered, as if they'd been kept in someone's purse.

'These are from your first days of school,' she said.

Hugh didn't even look at them. He shrugged. 'I don't care.'

But he wasn't meeting her gaze, he was just looking—April thought—determinedly uninterested.

'I don't believe you.'

*That* got his attention.

'I beg your pardon?' he said, sounding as British as April had ever heard him.

'I don't believe you don't care,' she said, slowly and clearly. As if there was any chance he'd misunderstand.

His gaze was locked on hers now. 'I don't see how that matters.'

April fanned the photos out as if they were a deck of cards. 'Look,' she said, giving them a shake. 'These are photos of you in your school uniform. For each year there's a photo by yourself, with your school bag. And another with your mum. These are *special*.'

'They're not,' he said. He nodded at the box. 'Please put them back.'

April shook her head. 'No.'

'No?'

'No,' she said firmly, her gaze remaining steady.

It would seem she'd thrown her professionalism out of the window.

She'd get extra shifts at the supermarket if he fired her and the temp agency blacklisted her. Or clean toilets. Whatever. She just couldn't pretend that she agreed with this.

'You're making a mistake.'

His eyes narrowed. His voice was rough. 'You've got no idea what you're talking about.' He turned away from her and continued down the hallway. 'I'll just throw them out tomorrow.'

'Do you hate her?' April blurted out the words to his rapidly retreating back.

Faster than she'd thought possible he was back in front of her. *Right* in front of her. He'd dropped the box at some point and there was now no barrier between them.

His presence crowded her, but she didn't take a step back.

'*No!*' he said. Not loudly, but with bite. Then he blinked, and belatedly added, 'That is none of your business.'

His words were calm now, but—again—deliberately so.

'I know,' she said, because of course it was true. But she just couldn't stop. 'You know, I don't have any photos of myself with my mum like this,' she said conversationally. 'I know that because my sisters went through all Mum's old photos when I had my thirtieth birthday party, for one of those photo-board things.' She swallowed, ignoring Hugh's glower. 'I have a couple from my first day of school in Year One, but that's about it. And I have hardly any photos of myself as a kid with my mum. It was different twenty-five years ago—people didn't take as many photos. And it was usually Mum who *took* the photos anyway, rather than being in them.'

Hugh didn't say anything.

'I'd love photos of me like this with my mum. In fact I have more photos of me as a kid with my dad—again, because Mum was the photographer. And I don't even *like* him. But I love my mum.' She knew she was rambling, but didn't stop. 'So it's all backwards, really.'

'You don't like your dad?' Hugh asked.

April blinked. 'No. He left when I was five. I hardly saw him, growing up, and I have nothing to do with him now.'

Hugh nodded. 'My father did something similar,' he said. 'I never saw him again.'

He didn't elaborate further.

'That sucks,' she said.

His lips quirked. 'Yeah.'

'But your mum obviously loved you?'

She could see his jaw tense—but then relax. 'Yes,' he said. 'She did.'

'That's why she took all these photos.'

The tension was instantly back. 'The number of photos my mother took—and, trust me, within this house there are *thousands*—is not a reflection of how much she loved me, April. I'd still know she loved me if she hadn't taken even one. They're just *things*.'

April shook her head vigorously. 'No. They're not. They're memories. They're irreplaceable. What if you ever have kids? Won't you want to—?'

'I'm never having kids. And that is *definitely* none of your business.'

She didn't understand. She didn't understand any of this.

But he'd turned, retrieved the box from the floor. He faced her again, gesturing with the box for April to dump the photos inside.

But she couldn't. *She could not.*

'Why are you doing this?' she asked, still holding the photos tight.

For the first time the steady, unreadable gaze he'd trained on her began to slip. In his gaze—just briefly—there flashed emotion. Flashed pain.

'I don't have to explain anything to you, Ms Spencer. All I want is for you to empty this house. That's it. Empty the house. I don't require any commentary or concern or—'

'You want an empty house?' April interrupted, grasping forcefully on to a faint possibility.

He sighed with exasperation. 'Yes,' he said.

'Well, then,' she said, with a smile she could tell surprised him. 'I can work with that.'

'Work with what?' His expression was wary.

'Getting this stuff out of your mother's house.' A pause. 'Just not into a skip.'

'A storage unit solves nothing. This isn't about relocating the hoard. I want it gone.'

Again she smiled, still disbelieving, and now she was certain she was right. 'You're the CEO of an international software company, right?' she said.

His eyes narrowed, but he didn't respond.

'So why didn't you think to just scan all this? You could even put it all in the cloud, so you don't even have a physical hard drive or anything left behind. It would be all gone, the house would be empty, and…'

*And you won't do something you'll regret for the rest of your life.*

But she didn't say that. Instinctively she knew she couldn't. She couldn't give him something to argue with—that he could refute with, *You've got no idea what you're talking about.*

Which would be true. Or *should* be true. But it wasn't. And, no matter how weird that was, and how little she knew about this man, she was certain she was right.

When she looked at Hugh Bennell—or at least when he *really* looked at *her*, and didn't obscure himself behind that indecipherable gaze—she saw so much emotion. So much… *more*. More than she'd see if he didn't care.

She was sure there were people out there who truly didn't care about photos and old school report cards and badly drawn houses with the sun a quarter crescent in the corner.

But one of those people was definitely not standing before her.

His gaze wasn't shuttered now. In fact she could sense he was formulating all matter of responses from disdain, to anger, to plans for her immediate dismissal.

As every second ticked by April began to realise that she was about to be fired.

But that was okay. At least she'd—

'That is a possibility,' he said suddenly. As if he was as surprised by his words as she was.

April grabbed on to them before he could change his mind. 'Awesome! I can even do it for you—it won't add much time…

especially if you can get one of those scanners you can just feed a whole heap of stuff into at once. And maybe I can take photos of other stuff? Like if I find—'

'I'll organise the equipment you need.'

He stepped around April, carrying the box back into the foyer. He dropped it onto the bottom step and April added the pile of photos on top.

She wanted to say something, but couldn't work out what. 'Hugh—'

'It's late,' he said. 'You should go home. See you tomorrow.' Then, just like that, he left.

# CHAPTER SIX

THE NEXT AFTERNOON Hugh set up the scanner on the marble kitchen benchtop.

April was just finishing up the second reception room. He could hear the sound of the radio station she listened to above the rustle and thud of items being sorted.

When he'd interrupted her earlier to announce his presence she'd been singing—rather badly—to a song that he remembered being popular when he was back at high school.

She'd blushed when she'd seen him. The pinkening of her cheeks had been subtle—but then, he'd been looking for it, familiar now with the way she seemed to react to him.

He reacted too. As he always did around her. Even when she'd been standing before him, hands on hips, acting as self-designated saviour of old photos, evidence of his lack of artistic ability and irrelevant school reports.

Even then—as he'd struggled with the reality that the distance down that hallway to the skip had been traversed on feet that had felt weighted to the ground with lead—and *hated* himself for it—he'd reacted to her.

He'd reacted to the shape of her lips, to the way she managed to look so appealing while her hair escaped from its knot atop her head, and to the shape of her waist and hip as she leant against that broom…

And then he'd reacted to her imperious words, admiring her assertiveness even as he'd briefly hated her for delaying him. He'd needed to get that stuff out of the house. Quickly. Immediately. Before he succumbed to inertia like with the other box, which—while no longer on his coffee table—still taunted him from the back of the cupboard in his otherwise spotless spare room.

But then he had succumbed to April's alternative. At least temporarily.

*If it keeps a good employee happy, then what's the problem? I can just delete it all once she finishes.*

That was the conclusion he'd decided he'd come to.

He finished hooking up the scanner to the laptop he'd previously provided for April, then waited as the software was installed.

Footsteps drew his gaze away from the laptop screen.

April stood across from the kitchen bench, smiling again. *Sans* blush.

She looked confident and capable and in control—as she always did in all but those moments between them he refused to let himself think about.

Again, questions flickered in his brain. Who was she, really? How had she ended up working here?

But that didn't matter. Their relationship was purely professional.

*Really?*

He mentally shook his head.

*It was.*

Belatedly he realised she was holding those damn photos. 'Shall we get started?' she asked.

This was when he should go. From her CV, he knew April was computer savvy—she'd work it out.

Instead, he held out his hand. 'Here, let me show you.'

They sat together, side by side at the kitchen bench, on pale wooden bar stools, scanning the photographs together.

They'd quickly fallen into a rhythm—Hugh fed the photos through the scanner and then April saved and filed them.

Initially she'd attempted to categorise the photos, but Hugh wouldn't have any of that. So April simply checked the quality of the scan, deleted any duplicates and saved them into one big messy folder.

Based on the decor of his flat, April would bet that Hugh usually carefully curated his digital photos. He'd give them meaningful file names, he'd file them into sensibly organised folders, and he'd never keep anything blurry or any accidental photos of the sky.

But she got why he wasn't doing that today: he was telling himself he was just going to delete them all one day, anyway.

Was it weird that she could read an almost-stranger so easily? Especially when he was so deliberately attempting to reveal nothing.

Possibly.

Or possibly she was just spending too much time with young backpackers she had nothing in common with, pallets of groceries that needed to be stacked and walls of cardboard boxes? And now she was just constructing a connection with this man because in London she had no connections, and she wasn't very good at dealing with that?

That seemed more likely.

But, even so, she *liked* sitting this close to him. Liked the way their shoulders occasionally bumped, when they'd both act as if nothing had happened.

Or at least April did.

What was the reason she'd given her sisters for not...*doing* anything with Hugh?

Ah. That was right. She was still technically married.

And what would she do anyway? She'd had *one* boyfriend. *Ever.* She'd kissed one boy—slept with one man. Evan. That was it. Plus, Evan had pursued *her*. In the way of high school kids. With rumours that had spread through English Lit that Evan *liked* April. Like, *liked*, liked her.

She was ill-equipped to pursue a darkly handsome, intriguing, damaged man.

But what if she turned to him? Right now? And said his name? Softly...the way she really wanted too? And what if he kissed her? How would his lips feel against hers? What would it be like to kiss another man? To be pressed up tight against another man...?

'April?'

She jumped, making her bar stool wobble.

'You okay?'

She put her hands on the benchtop to steady herself. 'Yes, of course.'

He looked at her curiously. Not anything like the way he had that day of the stripy top.

Another of those damn blushes heated her cheeks. It was ridiculous—she was never normally one to blush.

'In my first day-at-school photos, from Year One, I'm always with my sisters. I'm the middle child. That means I'm supposed to have issues, right?'

She was rambling—needing to fill the tense silence. In addition to never blushing, she *never* rambled. She had sparkling, meaningless conversation down to an art—she'd been to enough charity functions/opening nights/award galas to learn how to speak to *anyone*. Intelligently, even.

Not with Hugh.

'My big sister is a typical first child. *Such* an over-achiever. I get exhausted just thinking about all she does. Although my baby sister has never really felt like the baby. She's kind of wise beyond her years—she always has been. But that fits with something I read about third-born children—they're supposed to be risk-takers, and creative, which totally fits her.'

She paused, but couldn't stop.

'You know what middle children are supposed to be? Like, their defining characteristic? *Peacemakers*. I mean, come on? How boring is *that*?'

She was staring at the laptop screen and all the photos of cherubic child-sized Hugh.

'You're not boring,' he said.

April blinked, hardly believing he'd been paying attention.

'Thank you,' she said. She rotated the latest photo on the screen and dragged it over to the folder she'd created.

'I can see the peacemaker thing, too. Just not when it comes to my old school photos.'

April grinned. 'Nope,' she said. 'Especially when I wish *I* had photos like this. My mum worked really hard when we were growing up. She was often already at work when it was time for us to go to school.'

'What did she do?' Hugh asked.

She swallowed. 'She worked in an office in the city,' she

said vaguely. *As CEO of Australia's largest mining company.* The words remained unsaid.

Thankfully, Hugh just nodded. 'My mum had lots of different jobs when I was growing up. We didn't have a lot of money, so she often juggled a couple of jobs—you know, waitressing, receptionist…she even stacked shelves at a supermarket for a while, when I was old enough to be alone for a few hours at night.'

This was the longest conversation they'd ever had.

'*I* do that!' April exclaimed. 'After I get home from this job.'

'Really?' he asked. 'Why?'

April shrugged. 'So I can get out of the awful shared house I live in in Shoreditch.'

His gaze flicked over her—ever so quickly. April ignored the way her body shivered.

'Aren't you a bit old to live in a shared house?'

She narrowed her eyes in mock affront. 'Well, yeah,' she said. 'I'm thirty-two. But I made some dumb decisions with a credit card and I need to pay it off.'

She was choosing her words carefully, keen to keep everything she told him truthful, even if she wasn't being truly honest with him.

But then, her family's billions really shouldn't be relevant. That, after all, was the whole point of this London 'adventure'. Even if it *had* made a dodgy flatshare detour.

'What kind of dumb decisions?' he asked.

The question surprised her. She hadn't expected him to be interested. 'Clothes. Eating out. Rent I couldn't afford. No job. That kind of thing.'

He nodded. 'When I first moved out of home I rented this ridiculous place in Camden. It was way bigger than what a brand-new graduate needed, and my mum thought I was nuts.'

'So you racked up lots of debt, too?'

'No. I'd just sold a piece of software I'd developed for detecting plagiarism in uni assignments for two hundred and fifty thousand pounds, so the rent wasn't a problem,' Hugh replied. 'But I did move out because all that space was really echoey.'

April laughed out loud.

'And—let me guess—you didn't move into a shared house?'

His lips quirked upwards. 'No. I can't think of anything worse.'

'You *do* realise your story has nothing in common with mine, right?'

He shrugged. 'Hey, we both made poor housing choices.'

'Nope. No comparison. One of my housemates inexplicably collects every hair that falls out of her head in the shower. Like, in a little container that she leaves on the windowsill. I…'

'I'll pay off all your credit card debt if you stop your sentimental junk crusade.'

It wasn't a throwaway line. He said it with deadly seriousness.

April tilted her head as she studied him. 'I know—and you know—that if you really wanted this stuff gone it would already be gone. Some random Aussie girl nagging you about it wouldn't make any difference.'

He slid off his stool, then walked around to the other side of the kitchen bench. She watched as he filled the kettle, then plonked it without much care onto its base. But he didn't flick the lever that would turn it on.

He grabbed April's mug from the sink, and another from the overhead cupboard, then put both cups side by side, near the stone-cold kettle.

'Do you want to talk about it?' she asked. She could only guess at whatever was swirling about in his brain. His attention was seemingly focused on the marble swirls of the benchtop.

His head shot up and their gazes locked.

*'No.'*

'Cool,' April said with a shrug. 'I don't need to know.'

Although she realised she *wanted* to know. Really wanted to.

April slid off her stool, too. She skirted around the bench, terribly aware of Hugh's gaze following her. She didn't *quite* meet his gaze. She couldn't. Even as thoughts of discovering what was really going on in Hugh's head zipped through her mind, other thoughts distracted her. About discovering how Hugh might feel if his lovely, strong body—hot as hell, even in jeans and jumper—was pressed against hers. If, say, he kissed her against the pantry door just beside him...

*Stop.*

This was Ivy and Mila's influence, scrambling her common sense. It wasn't how she really felt. She'd *never* felt like this.

She reached past him, incredibly careful not to brush against him, and switched on the kettle.

She sensed rather than saw him smile—her gaze was on the kettle, not him.

'Let me help you,' she said. 'Stop trying to convince yourself you want something you don't actually want. At all. Stop pretending.'

Too late, she realised the error of her 'help him with the kettle the way she'd help him with his stuff' metaphor. She'd ended up less than a foot away from him.

Or maybe it hadn't been an error at all.

'Okay,' he said. His voice was deep. Velvety.

April looked up and their gazes locked.

It was like the stripy blouse moment all over again. But more, even.

She was suddenly unbelievably aware of her own breathing—the rise and fall of her chest was shallow, fast. And the way her belly clenched, the way her nails were digging into her palms to prevent herself from touching him.

'I'll stop pretending,' he said.

His gaze slid to her lips.

She closed her eyes. She had to, or she couldn't think.

The way Hugh was looking at her...

'April...?' he said, so soft.

Was that his breath against her lips? Had he moved closer so he could kiss her?

She refused to find out.

Instead, she stepped away. Two steps...three.

'Good!' she said. 'Great! Let's make time to go through the stuff I find each couple of days, okay?'

Hugh wasn't thinking about the boxes. 'What?'

April nodded sharply. 'Okay, I can finish up here. Thanks for your help.'

He was gone a minute later—just as the kettle whistled to say that it had boiled.

Later, as she walked to the supermarket, all rugged up in scarf and coat, Hugh's words echoed in her brain.

*I'll stop pretending.*

But *she* wouldn't stop pretending. She couldn't.

For now she was April Spencer, not April Molyneux.

The thing was she had no idea what was pretend any more.

Hugh sat at his desk, typing a message to an old friend from university.

Ryan had completed the same computer science qualification that Hugh had, although he'd made his money in a completely different field—internet dating. Ryan's innovative compatibility matching algorithm had been game-changing at the time. But his friend had long since sold the empire he'd built, and now ran an extremely discreet, exclusive online dating agency, using a new—Ryan said better—matching algorithm.

This had come in handy for Hugh.

Ryan's system was cutting-edge, and Hugh honestly couldn't fault it. He'd liked every woman he'd met through Ryan's system—even if he hadn't been attracted to them all. Or them to him.

After all—there still wasn't an app that could guarantee that.

He didn't date often, but when he did he was very specific. He liked to meet at quiet, private restaurants where it was easy to converse without distraction. He'd go to the movies, or to a show. He didn't go to bars or pubs—there was too little order and too many people talking. He couldn't think.

If things went well, after a few dates he might sleep over at his date's place. But he never lingered long the morning after. Or stayed for breakfast.

Usually, at some point later, he'd be invited to a party, or to a family event.

He always said no.

At such events he would become 'the boyfriend'. And he didn't want that.

Understandably, usually things ended then.

A couple of times he'd met women equally happy to avoid a relationship. Those arrangements had lasted longer, until eventually they'd run their course too.

Of course he was always clear that he wasn't after a relationship, and he was never matched with anybody who specifically wanted to settle down. However, it would seem that the 'wanting a relationship' and 'not wanting a relationship' continuum was not linear. And everyone's definition of where they stood along that line varied. Wildly.

So a woman who started off not wanting a relationship might actually want a bit of clarity around her relationship with Hugh. Or an agreement of exclusivity.

And exclusivity, to Hugh, was an indicator of a relationship—not that he had ever dated more than one woman at once, however casually.

So at that point he was out.

He got it that he was weird when it came to relationships. Women always eventually asked him about his stance. But it wasn't easy for him to define.

He knew, intellectually, that it originated from his mother's serial dating. She had been quite openly on a quest to find her Mr Right after the disappearance of his deadbeat father. He'd become used to the cycle of hope and despair that each new boyfriend would bring, and he'd decided he had no wish to experience that for himself.

But—and this had been his original theory—the risk of a relationship ending in despair was surely reduced if you approached dating with comprehensive data on your side. If you were matched appropriately—your values, your interests, your goals—then surely you minimised risk.

And this, in his experience, was true. He had never experienced the euphoric highs or the devastating lows of his mother's relationships. When he dated it was…*uncomplicated*.

But that was where his stance on relationships became much more about *him*. Because, despite all this data-matching and uncomplicated dating, he still didn't want a relationship.

It was a visceral thing. When he woke up in a woman's bed—he never invited them to *his* place—his urge to leave was not dissimilar from the way the bloody boxes that filled his mother's house made him feel.

*Trapped.*

It all came back to the same thing: to Hugh, relationships were clutter.

Ryan: I'll send you the link to our latest questionnaire—we've tweaked things a little so you'll need to answer a few more compatibility questions.

Hugh: No problem.

Ryan: Then the system will automatically send you a shortlist. Same as always—if the women you say yes for also say yes then you're set.

Hugh: Great. Thanks.

But it was weird… He'd been keen to talk to Ryan, but now he was losing enthusiasm. He'd been so sure that it was the six or more months since his last date that had triggered his interest in April. And today he'd almost kissed her.

Hugh: What's your current success rate with your matching algorithm?

Ryan wouldn't need time to look this up—he knew his company inside out.

Ryan: Almost one hundred per cent. We rarely have a customer receive no matches.

That wasn't what Hugh had meant.

Hugh: So one hundred per cent go on at least one date?

Ryan: Yes. And over ninety per cent of users rate their first date experience with a score of eight or above. We're very proud of that stat.

Hugh: Second date?

Ryan: We don't track activity beyond the first date.

Hugh: Long-term relationships? Engagements? Marriages?

Ryan: Lots. There are many testimonials available.

He pasted a link, but Hugh didn't click on it.

Hugh: Percentages?

Ryan: We don't have that data.

Hugh: Could you guess?

He could just imagine Ryan sighing at his laptop screen.

Ryan: Low. Easily under ten per cent. Under five per cent, probably. Which makes sense when you consider that each user gets matched with multiple people. But anyway our job is the introduction. The rest is up to the couple. But, mate, why the interest? Do we need to update your profile to 'Seeking a long-term relationship'?

Hugh: No. Just—

He stopped typing.

Just *what*?

Why was he suddenly questioning the method he'd been following for ten years? Especially when he'd contacted Ryan today to follow that exact method again. Nothing different. No changes.

He finished the sentence:

Hugh: No. Just wondering.

If Ryan had been a close friend—the kind of mate who knew when you were talking out of your backside—he would've questioned that. But he wasn't a close friend. Hugh didn't have close friends. The habits of his childhood—of keeping people at a distance, and certainly away from his home—had never abated.

Hugh asked Ryan a few more questions—just being social now. About his new house, his new baby…

After several baby photos, Ryan wrote: We should catch up for a beer. Somewhere quiet, of course.

Hugh: Sure.

And maybe they *would* organise it. But, in reality, ninety-five per cent of their friendship was conducted via video-conference or instant message. And that suited Hugh just fine.

Later, he answered the new compatibility questions.

He hesitated before submitting them.

Why?

*Because his subconscious was cluttered with thoughts of April Spencer.*

Particularly the way she'd looked at him that afternoon in the kitchen. Particularly the way her lips had parted when she'd closed her eyes.

But Ryan's algorithm would never match him with April.

April was vivacious and definitely sociable. She had an easy sunniness to her—he found it difficult to imagine that many people would dislike April. He imagined her surrounded by an ever-expanding horde of friends and family, living somewhere eclectic and noisy.

While he— Well, he had a handful of friends like Ryan. A handful he felt no need to expand. No family.

She was a traveller…an adventurer. She must be to be her age and working at this job in London. Meanwhile, he'd lived nowhere but North London. And he rarely travelled—save for those essential meetings when he'd first expanded his company internationally. Now he insisted all such meetings took place via video-conference.

He was intensely private, and unused to having his decisions questioned.

She questioned him boldly, and she'd told him about her family and her absent father without the slightest hesitation.

And somehow he'd revealed more to her than to anyone he could remember.

So, no, they wouldn't have been matched.

Apart from the added complication of her working for him, their obvious incompatibility could not be ignored.

He was attracted to her—that was inarguably apparent. She was beautiful. It was natural, but it didn't mean anything. April Spencer was all complications. He didn't *do* complicated.

What he needed was a date with a woman who knew exactly what he was offering and vice versa. And who was like him: quiet, private, solitary. No ambiguity. No confusion. Just harmless, uncomplicated fun.

He clicked '*Submit*'.

A minute later he received an email confirmation that his responses had been received.

Now he just needed to wait to be matched.

# CHAPTER SEVEN

APRIL SAT CROSS-LEGGED in bed. It was Sunday, and her room-mate had headed out for brunch, taking advantage of an un-seasonally warm winter's day.

Loving my new nails! So pretty. What's your go-to shade for summer? #diymanicure #mint #glam #THEnailpolish

April studied her nails after she'd scheduled her post to appear at about this time the next day, Perth time—eight hours away. She'd painted them the lovely minty green that THE had supplied, along with their generous Molyneux Foundation donation. Her assistant, Carly, had priority-mailed the bottle overnight all the way to London—at a ridiculous cost that April planned to pay back to the Molyneux Foundation. But it had had to be done.

It was getting increasingly complicated as each week went by to be both April Molyneux and April Spencer. To be truthful, she hadn't really planned this far ahead, and while her absences at social events had so far been attributed to her marriage breakdown, that excuse wouldn't last for ever.

So far her Instagram account had supported the narrative of a fragile divorcee-to-be with carefully curated images. Yesterday she'd posted one of the photos she'd taken with Carly just before she'd flown to London. In that image—despite her blow-dried hair and designer-sponsored dress, apparently going for dinner with her sisters—she fitted the brief well.

She *had* looked fragile. Because she had been.

When that photo had been taken she'd been barely a month on from that devastating evening at the beach.

At the time, April hadn't seen it. Maybe because she'd become used to seeing herself like that in the mirror: her gaze flat, her smile not quite convincing.

She'd been wearing heaps of make-up to hide the shadows beneath her eyes, to give colour to her cheeks. Without it she'd looked like death. And not in an edgy, model-like way. But really crap. Like, *my husband has just left me* crap.

She didn't, she realised, look like that now.

*When had that happened?*

She dismissed the thought. It was more important that it had—that Evan and all he represented no longer dominated her psyche.

She wiggled her nails, liking the way the sun that poured through the windows made them sparkle. She'd flung open the curtains both for better light for her photos and to revel in experiencing actual sun in London.

Her sponsors were also tricky. But Carly was doing well: scheduling long into the future, where possible, and being creative with everything else. After all, it wasn't essential that April appeared in every photo. She'd even roped Mila into one—with her sister admirably hamming up her mock-serious pose as she'd modelled long strands of stunning Broome pearls. This nail polish was the first product that had definitely required April to model it. It had been specified by the company, and her hands had featured in too many photos to risk that an eagle-eyed follower wouldn't notice a substitution. Not that she would have considered it anyway...

But April knew that this couldn't continue for ever.

The thing was, she'd assumed she'd have everything worked out already.

She'd imagined writing an inspirational post—maybe at her desk at her Fabulous Job In London. She'd talk about overcoming life's challenges. About realising that she needed to stand on her own two feet and chase her dreams.

And she'd write that she'd done it all by herself, without using her family name to leap to the front of the queue.

*Ugh.*

That would've been rather sickening, wouldn't it? As if someone as privileged as her was in any position to present herself as poster girl for grit and determination.

Well, she certainly couldn't post a little snapshot of her life right now. It had been an effort to photograph her hands without accidentally including a glimpse of the peeling walls, or the cheap laminate floor, or the battered beds and bedside tables. She'd actually ended up using a pretty plum velvet cushion she'd retrieved from one of Hugh's 'donate' boxes to lay her manicured fingers artistically across—after asking permission from Hugh via email, of course.

Take anything you want, he'd said.

Hugh…

He hadn't come up to the main house on Friday. There'd been no need with nothing for him to sort through.

Which was for the best, she'd told herself. Firmly.

And yet her realisation that there was no need for her to see Hugh that day had been tinged with both relief and disappointment.

She'd finished up in the front reception room and was now up the stairs, working on the front guest bedroom. It wasn't quite as packed with boxes as the first two rooms, although it was definitely a marginal thing. The first few boxes had been full of beautiful manchester—a word she'd discovered was actually a term for bedlinen used only in Australia and New Zealand when she'd provided her summary to Hugh and subsequently confused him.

See? She was learning so much from her move to London. April grinned. Just not exactly what she'd expected.

Sitting, as she was, on the cheapest doona—*duvet*, she'd learnt, in the UK—she'd been able to find at her local supermarket, she questioned her decision not to take one of the beautiful, soft vintage white linen covers she'd found on Friday.

But she couldn't. As hard as she was trying to live as if she wasn't, she *was* an heiress—with a mammoth trust fund. Someone shopping at the local charity shop deserved an expensive doona cover far more than she did.

*What was she doing?*

In London? Living in this dodgy shared house? Working for Hugh?

Based on her current progress, in another month she would have paid off her credit card. Only another month of two jobs, rice, beans, two-minute noodles and tins of soup.

And then what?

Would she quit her night job? Start applying for jobs back in her own field—or at least her field of study? Eventually move out of this place to some place on her own?

She didn't know.

If she did that she'd definitely need to shut down her social media profiles. There was no way she could continue to use them for the Molyneux Foundation all the way over here.

The idea felt unexpectedly uncomfortable.

Because, surely, her social media profile represented all that had been excessive in her life? Shouldn't she be glad to be rid of it? Glad that she'd be leaving that version of herself behind?

But...

It also represented how successful she'd been—how well she'd connected with her followers and how seamlessly she'd incorporated her sponsors. It represented how much money she'd raised for the foundation by being social media savvy and putting all that Molyneux privilege to good use.

She had over a million followers, and she'd worked hard for every single one of them.

It was only logical reasoning to suppose that those followers were unlikely to care about her new, unglamorous life, but that didn't make the idea of deleting her accounts seem any more appealing.

She wasn't entirely sure what it said about her, but she wasn't ready to give her followers up.

Not yet, anyway.

On Tuesday, April found more photos to add to the 'Hugh' box.

This time it was a bunch of birthday photos, all stuffed

into a large white envelope that had become deeply creased and soft with years of handling.

She carried it downstairs to the kitchen, leaving it on the kitchen bench while she turned on the kettle for her morning tea break.

The photos she'd scanned with Hugh still remained in the 'Hugh' box, atop the benchtop. They hadn't worked out the finer details after he'd left so abruptly, and she hadn't seen him since. Was she supposed to keep on scanning the photos she found? Or would he? Or would he not even bother now and just keep the photos…?

She should just put them into the box and let Hugh decide.

Instead she found herself pulling up one of the bar stools and settling down with both her coffee and the envelope before her.

Even as she slid the photos out she questioned what she was doing. There was no need to *look* at the photos, really. And so to do so felt…not quite right. But that was silly, really. It was her *job*, after all, to go through everything in this house. That was what she was doing.

And so she did look.

Like the images from Hugh's first days at school, these birthday shots were across all of Hugh's birthdays. The envelope was chock-full of them—several from every year. The classic 'blowing out the candles' shot, breakfast in bed with unwrapped presents and always a photo of Hugh with his mum. The very early ones also featured his father.

His mum, of course, had been stunning. April had thought so when she'd first seen her in those school photos. She'd had dark hair and eyes, like Hugh, but her face had been rounder and her eyes and lips had looked as if they always smiled, not just in photos. She'd worn her long hair mostly loose, and had alternated year to year from having a fringe and growing it out.

These photos were different from the school ones, though, which had all been taken outside Hugh's kindergarten or primary school. These were taken indoors. And not all in *this* house, which surprised April.

For some reason she'd assumed this was the house where Hugh had grown up, but the photos showed she was wrong. Silly of her, really, given she'd known his mum hadn't had much money, and Islington was decidedly posh.

April took a sip from her coffee, and then shuffled back to the beginning again.

Outside, it had started raining, and the occasional fat droplet slapped against the kitchen window.

The first photo had a chubby Hugh sitting on his mother's lap, reaching out with both hands for a birthday cake in the shape of a lime-green number one. Standing at his mother's shoulder was—April assumed—his father. A tall man, but narrower in the shoulders than Hugh, he had dark blond hair. He was handsome, but his smile looked uncomfortable.

They sat at a dining table with a mid-nineteen-eighties swirly beige laminate top. Behind them was a sideboard with shelving above it, neatly filled with books, trinkets and brass-framed photographs.

For Hugh's second birthday the cake photo was again taken at the same table. This time Hugh looked as if he was deliberately avoiding the camera, his gaze focused on something out of the picture. Again, he was with his mum and dad. There were more things now, on the shelves behind Hugh and his parents: more brass-framed photographs, more books. But still neat.

For his third birthday Hugh had had a cake in the shape of a lion, with skinny, long pieces of liquorice creating its eyes, nose and whiskers. There was no dad in this one, and while the table and sideboard were still the same the paint on the walls was now blue, not beige. There was less on the shelves—only a few photos. A new house? Or new paint?

April checked the other photos from his third birthday—yes, definitely a new house. His breakfast in bed was no longer beside a lovely double sash window, but instead one with a cheap-looking frame, probably aluminium.

His mum, though, still smiled her luminous smile.

When Hugh had turned four, the birthday parties had clearly begun.

There was Hugh playing pass the parcel, sitting on top of an oriental-style rug with his friends. Or playing pin the tail on the donkey. This photo was a wider shot, showing Hugh from the side, blindfolded and with his arm outstretched. Beyond him was a small kitchen, where a row of parents stood, some observing their kids, others chatting to each other.

The room was very neat, the kitchen bench clear but for trays of party food. In fact in all these early photos every room was tidy. April knew that careful angle selection could make the messiest room appear tidy, but she didn't believe that was the case here. There wasn't one cardboard box, or any pile of useless random things to put inside one, anywhere to be seen.

*When had it started?*

April flipped ahead through the photos, trying to work it out.

In the end it was that sideboard behind the dining table that told the story.

In front of that blue-painted wall it gained items year on year. At first neatly. More books, more photos, more trinkets, a small vase, a snow globe. But each item had definitely been carefully placed.

By the time Hugh had reached age seven the shelves were stuffed full. So many books jammed in horizontally and vertically. Photos in mismatched frames along the top. A few more trinkets…fat ivory candles. A carved wooden horse.

But still neat. *Organised* chaos.

By Hugh's ninth birthday it was just chaos.

Books were randomly stacked with pages outwards. The vase had been knocked over and damaged, but it still remained on its side in multiple pieces. Paper had now appeared on the shelves: envelopes with plastic windows, sheets of paperwork…piles of magazines.

In the background of a blurry photo of kids dancing— musical statues?—April spotted a cardboard box. Just one.

Beside it was a stack of newspapers, and beside that a stack of books.

But in the photo of Hugh and his mum together she was still smiling. Her hair was still lovely, her eyes sparkling. Hugh was smiling too, looking up at his mum.

April's throat felt tight and prickly.

It seemed impossible, given she'd now spent weeks surrounded by the hoard, but until now she hadn't really thought about the actual compulsive hoarding that must have occurred for this house to be in this state.

Maybe because the house was very neat—for a house full of boxes. And April associated hoarding with those unfortunate people you saw on television documentaries, with rotting food and mountains of rubbish. Vermin. This place wasn't like that.

But that didn't mean accumulating all this junk was normal.

April went back to the photos. For Hugh's tenth birthday there had been no party. Possibly he just hadn't wanted to have one, but April doubted it.

There weren't any party photos the year after, or any of the years after that.

Instead it was just pictures of Hugh and his mum and—in the background—more and more boxes…

'Boxes suck as party decorations.'

Hugh's voice made April jump.

Her stool wobbled dramatically, and his hand landed firmly at her waist, steadying her.

She was wearing a chunky knitted jumper with a wide neck. The wool was soft against his fingers and the shape of her waist a perfect fit against his palm. But he made sure his hand dropped away the instant the chair was still.

A moment after that April practically leapt from her seat, turning to face him.

'I didn't hear you,' she said, unnecessarily.

Her gaze roamed over him—just briefly. He was wearing

his normal uniform of sorts: jeans, T-shirt, hoodie, trainers. Completely unremarkable.

And yet he sensed April's appreciation. She liked how he looked.

Although hadn't he known that since he'd helped her out of that stripy top? He'd certainly appreciated how April looked from the moment he'd first seen her.

Today was no different.

She wore light-washed jeans, and her jumper was pale lemon, oversized and slouchy, revealing much of her golden shoulders and a thin silver chain at her neck. Her dark hair was scraped back from her face in a high ponytail. It was neater than normal—probably because it was early in the day, and all those rogue strands hadn't had the opportunity to escape.

He gave himself a mental shake. It wasn't important. Wasn't he supposed to be annoyed with her?

That was what he'd meant to do when he'd walked into the kitchen to find April so absorbed in those photos that she hadn't heard his approach. He'd meant to ask her, *What the hell are you doing?*

Although, he reflected, that *would* have been a dumb question.

She was looking at photos. *Duh.*

But why? There was no need any more. The photos were *his* responsibility now. And something about having her look through them felt…almost intimate. Crazy when a few days ago she'd done the same thing with his school photos and he hadn't cared.

Or at least hadn't *let* himself care. He'd still been telling himself the photos were worthless and meaningless to him, after all.

But that hadn't been true.

So maybe that was why his instinctive reaction was anger—anger that she'd been looking at images he now accepted meant something to him. Just what they meant he could work out later. They were his, and they were private photos. None of her business.

But by the time he'd gone to speak he hadn't been angry at all.

*Boxes suck as party decorations.*

'You stopped having birthday parties,' April said, reading his mind.

'Yeah,' Hugh said.

He stepped closer to the bench, picking up a bundle of the photos she'd been studying with such concentration. He'd dump them in the box to take down to his flat. He would go through the photos later. It had been nice of April to offer to help him, but it wasn't necessary.

'I didn't notice at first,' he said. 'You know…all the clutter, I mean. I was a kid. It was just my house. When I was old enough to tidy I kept my room pretty neat, but the rest of the house… I don't know. Like I said, it was just my house.'

Hugh hadn't intended to continue the conversation. *At all.* And yet—he continued.

'The other kids didn't notice either. Why would they? Their parents may have, but I wouldn't have known, and Mum never would've cared.'

'Really?' April asked with raised eyebrows.

Hugh shook his head. 'No. At first it wasn't that bad, and my mum had always been pretty forthright about people accepting each other for who they were. She figured if the house was a bit untidy what was the big deal?'

'But you didn't like it?'

'No,' he said. 'And it just got worse. And as kids get older they notice things. I had a friend over one day after school, before it got really bad, and he had a box fall on him while we were playing. He was fine, but I remember his mum talking to my mum in this really low, concerned voice, asking if she was okay and if she'd like some help. My mum didn't like that. She laughed, I remember, and said she'd just had a busy week and really needed to get all the stuff to the charity shop.'

He was flipping through the photos, but not looking at them.

'That was a lie. I knew she was never going to do that. Although I suppose maybe she was telling herself that she would one day. I don't know. But—anyway—my mum never lied. Ever. And that combined with the other mum obviously thinking something was wrong... Well, then I knew something was wrong. So I didn't have anyone over again.'

April hadn't moved from where she stood. She just watched him, letting him speak.

'Things got worse after that. Mum was always really sociable. I remember when I was really little that she'd have these elaborate dinner parties where she'd always try something fancy out of this fat hardcover cookbook she'd get from the library. But they stopped, too. She'd still go out and see her friends—we had a nice neighbour and I'd go and stay with her and watch TV—but the house was just for us. Us and the damn boxes.'

'That must have been hard,' April said.

Her words were soft. Kind. That was the *last* thing he wanted. Kindness. Pity. He didn't know her. Why was he telling her this?

'I was fine,' he said, his words hard-edged. 'I managed.'

She stepped close to him now and reached out her hand, resting it just below his elbow.

Instinctively he shook his arm free. 'What are you doing?'

She looked surprised—at her action or his, he couldn't be sure.

April swallowed. 'Sorry. I...' There was a pause, then she straightened her shoulders. 'I wanted to touch you,' she said. 'I thought it might help.'

He shook his head. 'It was a long time ago,' he said. 'I'm fine.'

'A long time ago?' she prompted, her forehead wrinkled.

Hugh ran a hand through his hair. 'I mean since I had to live like that. Mum—' He hadn't intended to explain, but he couldn't stop himself. 'When she met Len I was in the Lower Sixth, and she got better. She got the help she needed—did this cognitive behavioural therapy stuff, got in a professional organiser—and then, when she married Len, we moved here.

She was good for a long time. It only started again when Len died, and—honestly—I did all I could. *Everything* I could think of to stop it happening again, to stop her filling the emptiness she felt after my father left and Len died with *stuff*. Objects she could cling on to for ever, that would never leave her—'

Her hand was on his arm again. His gaze shot downwards, staring at it. Immediately she removed her touch.

'I'm sorry, I—'

'It's okay,' he said. 'I don't mind. It felt good.'

She placed her hand on his arm again.

Her touch through the fabric of his hoodie was light against his skin. Her fingers didn't grip…they were just there.

'I'm a hugger,' April explained, her gaze also trained on her hand. 'I can't help it. I hug everybody. Happy, sad, indifferent. Hug, hug, hug.' She sighed. 'It's sucked, really, not having anyone to hug since I've been in London.'

'You want a hug?' he asked, confused.

Her head shot up and she grinned. 'No!' she said. 'I was just explaining.' She nodded at their hands. 'The touching thing. Because I'm guessing you're not a hugger.'

A rough laugh burst from his throat. 'No,' he said. 'I'm not a hugger.'

Her lips curved upwards again. 'I thought so.'

He rarely touched anyone except by accident. When would he? He had no family. A handful of friends. He worked remotely. He was resolutely single. And when he dated touch was about sex. Not this—not reassurance or comfort. This was touch without expectations.

It should be strange, really, to find comfort in the touch of a woman he was attracted to. The few times they'd touched before had been fleeting, but charged with electricity. And, yes, that current was still there. Of course it was.

But what she was offering was straightforward: her touch was simply to help him calm his thoughts and to acknowledge the uncomfortable memories he'd just shared.

It was working, too.

His gaze drifted from her hand to the photos he still grasped. On top was a photo taken of him in bed the morning of his tenth birthday. He'd just unwrapped his present: a large toy robot that he'd coveted for months. His mum had used the timer on her camera, propping it on his dresser, and she sat beside him, her arm around him, his superhero pillows askew behind them.

He and his mum were both smiling in the photo, and Hugh smiled now. A proper smile at a happy memory.

'Thank you,' he said.

For making him keep the photographs. For listening.

'My pleasure,' said April.

Then she squeezed his arm and her touch fell away.

'Wait,' he said.

# CHAPTER EIGHT

HUGH'S VOICE WAS LOW. Different from before.

April went still. Her hand fell back against her thigh, already missing his warmth.

He stepped towards her, close enough that she needed to tilt her chin up, just slightly, to meet his gaze.

He studied her intently. 'Why did you leave behind all the people you used to hug?' he asked.

Her gaze wavered.

She put on a smile. 'Early midlife crisis,' she said.

Best to keep it simple.

'No,' he said. 'Why are you here? Why are you working for me?'

She shrugged. 'I told you the other day. Credit card debt.'

He looked her dead in the eye. 'I don't believe you.'

*Ah.* He was echoing her own words…the way she'd been challenging him.

She hadn't expected the tables to turn.

She twisted her fingers in the too-long sleeves of her jumper…the fabric was all nubbly beneath her fingertips.

She wasn't used to being secretive. She did, after all, document her life for millions of strangers. But this was different.

Hugh didn't talk the way he just had about his past very often. Ever, maybe. April knew that—was sure of it. She understood what he'd revealed to her. How big a deal it was for him. So he deserved her honesty—she knew that.

But her reticence wasn't just about hiding April Molyneux from a man who thought her to be April Spencer—it was more than that. There was something about Hugh—something between them that was just so different. So intense.

Until today they'd only teased the very edges of that intensity, and neither had taken it any further.

They'd both resisted temptation. The temptation to touch. To kiss.

Right now—with these questions, this conversation—it wasn't as primal as before, although all that continued to simmer below the surface. But it was still a connection. And it still felt raw. As if sharing any part of herself, even her past, was only the start of a slippery slope.

It would lead to more. Much more.

And that was as tempting as it was frightening.

*Frightening?*

What was she scared of?

She didn't answer her own question. It didn't matter. Because she hadn't come all the way to London to be scared of anything.

'My husband left me,' she said.

Silence.

She'd expected him to recoil. Because surely *this* wasn't the conversation Hugh Bennell wanted to have with her?

Instead, he nodded. 'Are you okay?' he asked simply.

She smiled. Genuinely this time. 'Yes,' she said with confidence. 'Now. Sucked for a bit, though.'

He smiled too.

'I needed a change. So here I am. Unpacking your boxes and stacking supermarket shelves. Trust me, it's not as glamorous a midlife crisis as I'd expected.'

'What happened?' he asked. Gently.

'We fell out of love,' she said. 'Him first, but me too. I just hadn't realised it. So I'm okay. Not heartbroken or anything. But it was still sad.'

'Not heartbroken?' he prompted.

Her gaze had travelled downwards, along his jaw and chin. Now it flew upwards, locking with his.

'What do *you* think?' she asked.

Her gaze was heated. Hot. Deliberately so.

Nope. Definitely not scared any more.

'No,' he said, his voice deliciously low. 'I don't think you are.'

And just like that weeks of tension, of attraction, of *con-*

*nection* were just—*there*. No glancing away, no changing the subject, no pretending it didn't exist.

It was *there*. Unequivocally.

*Oh, God.*

His eyes were dark, and intensely focused on her. He'd moved closer again, so that only centimetres separated them, and there was no question about what he wanted to do next.

He leant closer. Close enough that his breath was hot against her cheek and then her ear.

'I want to kiss you,' he said, and the low rawness of his voice made her shiver.

How did he know? April thought. That she needed that? That she needed a moment? That despite the crackling tension between them doubts still tugged at her?

Could she trust her instincts after what had happened to her marriage? She'd got it all so very wrong. And, even more than that, could she actually kiss another man?

It had been so long—so very, very long...

'Kiss me,' she said, because she couldn't wait another moment.

Although it turned out she had to.

His lips were at her ear, and he didn't move them far. Instead he pressed his mouth to the sensitive skin of her neck, at the edge of her jaw. Suddenly her knees were like jelly, but strong hands at her waist steadied her.

The sensation of his lips against her neck and his hands against her body was *so good*, and April's eyes slid shut as a sigh escaped from her mouth.

Her fingers untangled themselves from the sleeves of her jumper and reached for Hugh blindly, hitting the solid wall of his stomach and sliding up and around to the breadth of his back.

Hugh dotted her jaw with kisses that were firm but soft. And glorious. But not even close to enough. More than almost anything, she wanted to turn her head to meet his mouth with hers—but she didn't. Because, even more than she wanted that, she wanted this anticipation to last for ever. This promise of Hugh's kiss that, she realised, had been growing from the moment they'd met.

But he was definitely going to kiss her now—this mysterious man who was so different to anyone she'd ever met—and the wonder of that she wanted to hold on to. Just a few seconds longer.

By the time his mouth reached hers April felt about as solid as air. His hands pressed her closer, and then her own hands drew his chest against her breasts.

His mouth was hot against hers, and confident.

If she'd been tentative, or if her brain had been capable of worrying about her kissing technique or other such nonsense, his assuredness would have erased it all.

But, as it was, April didn't feel at all unsure. In fact, Hugh made her feel that this kiss was about as right as anything could get.

His tongue brushed a question against her bottom lip and her own tongue was her crystal-clear answer. Her hands slid up his chest to entwine behind his neck and in his hair, tugging him even closer.

Their kiss was as intense as every moment between them, and as volatile. He kissed her hard, and soft, and voraciously. As if he could kiss her for ever, and as if they had all the time in the world.

But April was impatient.

She took the lead now, kissing him with everything she had and more. More than she'd thought she was capable of: with more passion, less control.

This was raw and passionate and…near desperate.

April wanted to be as close as she could be to him. She wanted him pressed up hard against her. She wanted to feel his solidity and his strength.

She wanted to feel his *skin*.

Her hands drifted down his back, skimming wide shoulder blades and the indentations of his spine. And then they slid beneath jacket and T-shirt to land at the small of his back. Against smooth, gorgeous, hot skin.

His hands followed a similar path, and his touch made her sigh into his mouth as it moved against her back, her stomach, and then upwards—against her ribs to the underside of her—

Something vibrated and Hugh went still.

He broke his lips away from hers, but not far. She could feel him breathe against her mouth as he spoke.

'My phone,' he said. 'I'm sorry.'

'Me too,' she said, all husky.

His smile was crooked. 'Yeah…'

Then he stepped away, and her skin felt bereft without his touch.

He fished his phone out of the back pocket of his jeans. It appeared to have been a notification vibration, not a call, and he turned slightly to scroll through his phone.

When he turned back to her, he just looked at her for long moments. At her still slightly askew jumper, at her lips that felt swollen, at her eyes that she knew were inviting him to pick up exactly where they'd just finished.

But he didn't.

Instead, he said, 'That probably shouldn't have happened.'

April blinked, her brain still foggy. 'Why?'

'Because you work for me. And your husband just left you.'

She shrugged. 'You definitely didn't take advantage of me,' she said. 'And the husband thing—that's my problem, not yours. Nothing about what just happened was a problem for me.'

Mila and Ivy's encouragement fuelled her. For all her misgivings up until their kiss, she didn't regret it one bit now. She felt amazing: alive, and strong, and sexy and feminine…

'I don't want a relationship with you, April.'

*Ouch.*

It shouldn't have hurt, but it did.

'And you thought the desperate divorcee must be keen to jump straight into another relationship?' Her tone was tart. She didn't give him time to respond. 'And also, that if I did, I'd want a relationship with *you*? That's rather presumptuous.'

April crossed her arms.

His forehead crinkled as he considered her words. 'I suppose it is,' he said. 'I apologise.'

April nodded sharply. 'Just to be clear—the *last* thing I want is a relationship. I was with my ex for a long time—I need to just be me for a while. That being said, I really liked what we just did. I'd like to do it again.'

She didn't know where this bravado came from. She was practically propositioning Hugh Bennell. In fact, she definitely was. She was *propositioning* him.

Because that kiss… She'd never experienced anything like it. She'd never felt like this before and heat continued to traverse through her veins simply from the memory of his mouth against hers. His body against hers.

'I'd like to do it again, too,' he said. His gaze was steady and his words measured—as if he'd carefully considered her proposal before constructing his answer. 'But, I'd also like to be clear. I date, but that's it. I never take it further. I'm never anyone's boyfriend. I'll never be someone's husband. You need to be aware of that before this goes any further.'

April found herself fighting a smile in response to his seriousness. 'That seems a bit extreme,' she said. '*Never?* Really?'

'Really,' he said.

He didn't elaborate. He still looked at her with a determinedly serious expression.

'Well,' April said, smiling now, 'I must say my experience of marriage wasn't ultimately positive, so maybe you're onto something.'

His lips quirked now. 'It would seem so.'

'Okay,' she said. 'I can deal with that. No relationships. *Deal.*'

As she'd told Hugh, it was exactly the right thing for her. Quite honestly, the last thing she wanted was to leap from one relationship into another. But for some silly reason, Hugh's rejection of anything more with her still stung.

There was another noisy buzz as his phone, now on the kitchen bench, vibrated again.

'I need to go,' he said. 'I have a meeting. Can we do dinner? Tonight? I can email you the details.'

He was in business mode now, as efficient as his instructions and his emails.

'Sure,' she said. 'But I only have a few hours before my second job.'

He paused, looking up from his phone. 'How much extra would I need to pay you so you could quit that job?' he asked.

'Ah,' April said, 'that sounds like a conflict of interests. I don't think HR would approve of that.'

'I own the company,' Hugh pointed out. 'And I don't like rushing dinner.'

'Well, then, *I* don't approve,' April said firmly. 'Let's keep this professional.'

Hugh stepped closer—much closer. He leant down and spoke just millimetres from her lips. 'Sure,' he said, 'except for making out in the kitchen.'

Long minutes later they came up for air, and April lifted her fingers to her thoroughly kissed lips as Hugh finally walked away.

'Agreed,' she said, as the front door clicked shut.

The conference call was endless.

Hugh sat back in his chair, letting the wheels roll him back a small distance from his desk.

He'd docked his laptop, so the other attendees' faces were displayed on the large slender screen before him. Everybody else allowed their faces to be shown, so Hugh could see each of them: the red-headed product manager in Ireland, his gaze focused on his keyboard, the dark-haired user experience manager in Sydney, her attention focused on the slides that the senior developer, also in London, was showing them…

The developer was talking directly into his camera as he discussed some of the technical difficulties his team was currently encountering, his purple dreadlocks draped over his shoulders.

Of course, Hugh's face didn't appear.

Hugh still insisted upon that, despite the recommendations of the digital collaboration expert he'd engaged to improve the effectiveness of his widely dispersed team. Yes, he could see how a video feed might—as the consultant had advised—improve both rapport and communication, but no matter how large his company became he was still in charge. Hence—no cameras. For him, anyway. Even now, so many years later, old habits died hard. Because, of course, it wasn't about *him*. He didn't care if his colleagues saw him and his slightly too long hair and three-day-old beard.

It was about his *house*. Everyone on the conference call was in their home. This meeting had a backdrop of contrasting wallpapers and paint colours, of artwork and photographs, of bookcases and blinds and curtains.

Hugh wasn't going to contribute his home to that landscape. He didn't let anyone into his home. In any way. Ever.

*Except April.*

It seemed April had become the exception to several things. Such as his structured approach to dating.

It had been timely that he'd received an alert from Ryan's dating app mid-kiss with April. It should've been a reminder that he already had a tried and true approach to meeting women. And that kissing an employee in his mother's kitchen was *not* his modus operandi.

Instead, he hadn't even bothered to open the profile of the woman he'd been so carefully matched to.

After all, he'd just experienced a kiss that made his pulse beat fast and his body tighten simply by the act of thinking about it. It had been all-consuming: a hot, intense phenomenon of a kiss. Which was, after all, the point. He dated. He liked women. He wanted to meet women who liked him. And he definitely wanted that spark of attraction. April ticked each and every one of those boxes. Except the spark was more like a bonfire.

So—why not?

If the parameters were made as clear to April Spencer as he always made sure they were with other women, what was the problem?

Logically, none.

Although somewhere right at the edge of his subconscious doubts did twinge.

But they were easily overcome. At the time he'd simply had to look at April to forget anything but his need to touch her again. Now he just needed to recall the shape of her waist and the heat of her skin beneath his palms.

When he did that there was no need to analyse it further.

# CHAPTER NINE

APRIL HAD NEVER been more grateful for an unexpected delivery in her life. But she only had a minute to photograph her new peep-toe, sky-high ankle boots before heading out through the door.

Taking these lovelies out to dinner! #highheels #peeptoes #CovetMyShoesCo

She had hardly anything to wear, what with her nonexistent social life since arriving in London, but her new shoes teamed with black jeans and her dressiest shirt made her look marginally more glamorous than she did when unpacking cardboard boxes.

At least she'd recoloured her hair the week before, so there was no hint of her blonde roots. And she'd left her hair down, although there had been hardly any time for her to attempt some loose curls with her straightening iron. Back in Perth, she put more effort into getting ready to go to the supermarket.

Part of her was a little disappointed that she didn't have the time—or the money—to really go all out for Hugh. A lot disappointed, actually. But then—did it matter? Hugh hadn't seem bothered by her dusty, messy-haired *dishabille* that morning.

Plus, it wasn't as if she needed to impress him. They'd both been pretty clear about what they wanted: each other. For a short time.

That was it. No complications. No relationship.

It should be...freeing.

But it wasn't. Instead this felt very much like a first date to her. A first date full of nerves and anticipation and possibilities.

April knew she couldn't think like that. It wasn't what Hugh was offering, and it wasn't what April wanted.

*It wasn't.*

She meant that with every cell in her body—except for that little chunk of her heart that had ached when Hugh had so summarily rejected her.

She supposed *I don't want a relationship with you, April* had too many echoes of Evan's *I don't love you* rejection not to hurt, at least just a little bit. She wouldn't be human if it didn't. Surely?

So it didn't mean anything.

She was strong and independent and single—and she had a date with Hugh Bennell.

April grabbed her scarf and coat, and headed for the Tube.

Hugh had booked the same table he always booked.

He figured that while April might not have been matched with him by any computer algorithm, really tonight was no different from any other date.

*Except for the fact she was his employee, and that he'd already kissed her...*

*No*, he told himself firmly. There was nothing different or special *whatsoever* about tonight.

It was just a date.

And so they were at his favourite restaurant. A very nice restaurant, with white linen tablecloths and an epic wine list. Importantly, it valued the privacy of its customers, and kept tables well-spaced and the lighting intimate. He'd had many very pleasant dates here, with great food and robust conversation.

'This is lovely,' April said from across the table. She held a glass of sparkling water in her hand, and her long hair cascaded over one shoulder in chocolate waves. 'I wish I had more time to enjoy it properly. To be honest, I just thought we'd go to a pub.'

She started work at nine p.m., so they didn't even have two hours before she had to leave.

'I don't like pubs,' he said truthfully.

'Really? But London does them so well. There's a pub near your place I've been wanting to try for ages. But I'm such a Nigel now, I haven't had the opportunity.'

'Nigel?' Hugh asked.

'No Friends. You know? Nigel No Friends? Or is that another Australianism I didn't realise was one?'

Hugh grinned. 'Like Billy No Mates?' he prompted.

'Exactly,' April said, looking pleased. 'Seems being a loser is universal.'

He laughed out loud. 'I don't believe for a second that you don't have friends,' he said.

'Well, I *do* have friends,' April said. 'Just not here. And I've been working too much to meet anyone. Not that I particularly wanted to—especially at first. I just wanted to be on my mopey lonesome.'

'Not any more?'

'No,' she said firmly. 'I guess I'm a pretty social person usually. I'm always out—catching up with friends for coffee or lunch. Going to parties or—'

Her voice broke off, and he raised an eyebrow in question.

'Or…ah…the movies, or a bar, or whatever.'

Her gaze had slid downwards, was now focused on her bread and the untouched gold-wrapped pat of butter. She seemed suddenly uncomfortable.

But then she was refocusing on him, and the moment was gone as if it had never happened. 'So, once I get rid of this night-job nightmare, I'm hoping to finally get to explore London. So at the moment you're basically my only friend, as my housemates seem convinced I'm bordering on elderly at my advanced age—'

'I don't like pubs,' he repeated.

April blinked. 'Really?' she asked again, only now seeming to realise that he hadn't elaborated on that. 'Why?'

He shrugged. 'I don't like people. And pubs are full of them.'

'No,' April said simply. 'Not true.'

'It *is* true,' Hugh said, with deliberate patience and the hint of a smile. 'They *are* full with *lots* of people.'

She shook her head. 'No, the bit about you not liking people. You like me.'

'You're not everyone,' he said.

His gaze slid over her as he reminded himself exactly how *not everyone* April Spencer was. She'd apologised when she'd arrived for her—as she'd described them—'casual clothes'. But personally Hugh thought she looked incredible, in skinny jeans that highlighted the curve of her hips and a colourfully abstract printed silk blouse that skimmed her breasts and revealed her lovely neck and collarbones. She'd painted her lips a classic red and her eyes were smoky and...

*Narrowed.*

Hugh sighed. 'Okay. I don't like people I don't know. Or hanging out with people I don't know in one, dark cramped place.'

'Okay,' she said. 'Then how do you meet people?'

'Women?' he clarified.

She might have blushed, but the lighting meant he couldn't be absolutely certain.

'Sure,' she said. 'Or men. Anyone. Just people.'

'Women—except you—I meet online. I prefer to set my expectations up-front, and there is no better way than in writing. And as for new mates—well, I've got friends from uni I'm still in touch with. That's enough. And I cycle with a group that lives locally, but that's not a social thing.'

'I *like* meeting new people,' April said, not surprising Hugh at all. 'Everyone has a story to tell, you know? Although I'm close to my sisters, so I've never really gone out of my way to find new *close* friends.'

She paused, looking thoughtful.

'I hadn't thought about dating yet—or online dating, I mean. When I met Evan we communicated with folded-up notes via our schoolfriends—not smartphones. But, yes, I can see the appeal of online. Seems very efficient for identifying deal-breakers. Although,' she said, leaning forward slightly,

'I've always kind of liked the idea of meeting someone random at a bar or in a pub. You know—the intrigue of it. Discovering little bits and pieces about them, revealing little bits about you, working out if you actually like each other or not. I never got to do that because I was with Evan since high school.'

'But it could be a total waste of everyone's time,' Hugh said. 'The odds aren't high that you'll meet the person of your dreams one random night at a random pub.'

'Why not?' April said as their meals were served. April had ordered gnocchi, garnished with thin slices of parmesan. In front of Hugh was placed a steak. 'Don't you believe that some people are destined to meet?'

'No,' he said firmly. 'If you want to meet Mr Perfect and you find him at the pub, that's great. But it's just luck—not destiny. Online dating takes the luck out of it.'

April looked sceptical. 'I don't know about that. Perfect on paper is different to perfect in person. You can't guarantee chemistry.'

Hugh sliced off a small piece of steak, smothering it in mashed potato and mushroom sauce. 'In my experience the matching algorithm of the app I use does a pretty good job. And it also means that when there *is* chemistry it's with someone who wants the same things as you. There isn't much point having great chemistry if you both want completely different things.'

There was a long pause as they both ate, and April's concentration was aimed at her dinner plate.

'And you don't want a relationship ever? Why?' she asked.

He swallowed, barely tasting the delicious food. 'Isn't that a bit personal for a first date?'

April glanced up and looked determined. 'I told you that my husband left me because he didn't love me enough. We've been plenty personal.'

'"Enough"?'

She hadn't mentioned that word before, and he watched as she winced—but quickly hid it—when he repeated it.

She shrugged and put on a smile. 'Our love wasn't like in

movies and books, apparently. I didn't elicit that level of emotion in him, it would seem. He met someone else who did.'

Her words were light, but he could see it still hurt her to say them.

'What a—' Hugh began, but then stopped. What was he going to say? *What a tosser?* For not loving April more?

He couldn't say that. After all, he was no better. He wasn't offering her anything: not a relationship, and certainly not love.

If her ex-husband was an idiot, what was *he*?

A realist. Not someone caught up in imaginary stories and Hollywood fairytales.

But he knew he didn't want to hurt April. So she deserved the truth.

'I'm happier on my own,' he said. 'I don't feel any urge to share my life with anyone.'

'But you date?' she prompted. 'You just said that you meet women online.'

He nodded and reached for his bourbon. 'That has absolutely nothing to do with sharing my life.'

'Ah,' April said. 'So it's just about the sex.'

Hugh coughed on his drink. But her directness made him smile. 'Well, I also just *like* women, and spending time in the company of women.'

'Just not in pubs, and you never share any of your life with them?'

'Yes,' he said. 'That pretty much sums it up.'

April tilted her head, studying him carefully. Her gaze drifted across his hair, his nose, his lips, then downwards across his off-white open-necked shirt, along the shape of his arms to his wrist and his heavy, stainless steel watch.

She met his gaze again. 'You're weird,' she said.

Hugh laughed. 'I've been told that before.' He shrugged now. 'But it's who I am. Take it or leave it.'

He'd said that casually, with no real intent. But he could see April turning it over in her mind. Really *he* should be turning it over in *his* mind. She was clearly emotionally vulnerable, for all her brave words.

He believed her when she said she wasn't ready for a relationship. But she definitely wasn't ready to be hurt again.

And he'd hurt women before, despite all his signposting and expectation-setting. With those women he'd reconciled the situation with an almost 'buyer beware' lack of emotion. Although of course he hadn't *liked* it that he'd caused anyone pain. In his quest to avoid the complications of relationships the last thing he wanted was to cause the kind of despair he'd observed in his mother's many failed relationships.

But with April—he'd kissed her before telling her any of this. He'd invited her out for dinner before she'd had a chance to catch her breath after that crazy hot kiss in the kitchen.

She'd be smart to walk away. *He* should walk away. This was already far more complicated than any other date he'd been on.

But he didn't.

And she didn't.

'Tell me about your company,' she said, 'What's actually involved in creating a new app? I've always wondered…'

And so they changed the subject, and the conversation became as pleasant and robust as on every other date he'd had at this restaurant.

For a short while.

Then it became easy and rambling, as April told him about a camping trip to northern Western Australia with her sisters as a child, and he told her about how he'd discovered cycling a few years ago and now had seen more of the UK on his bike than he'd ever thought possible. They talked about nothing serious—certainly nothing as serious as divorce or relationships.

As their desserts arrived, and April started to tell him about an amazing frozen dessert she'd had once in a food court in Singapore, she realised the time.

'Oh, crap—I'm late,' she said urgently.

And then she was up, her bag slung over her shoulder and

her coat over her arm, leaving her half-eaten dessert. She was a few steps away from the table before he knew what was happening.

A moment later his hand was on her elbow, slowing her.

Then he kissed her.

It was supposed to be quick—he knew she was late. But it wasn't.

They both lingered. It wasn't a passionate kiss—they were standing in the middle of a restaurant and he hadn't forgotten that. But his lips tasted hers for long moments, and then their gazes tangled wordlessly after their mouths had parted.

'I need to go,' she whispered.

So Hugh returned to his table to eat his parfait alone.

The next day was Saturday.

April had slept in, and the late-rising December sun had already been in the sky for at least an hour.

Her roommate lay curled up in a multi-coloured duvet bundle on her bed, her slow, deep breathing indicating she was still sound asleep.

Quietly April retrieved her phone from where it was charging, and propped herself up in bed to scroll through her Instagram and Facebook feeds.

The ankle boots had been a hit, and she had hundreds of 'likes' and comments. She replied to a few before opening up her instant messenging account, which had a little red circle on it indicating she'd missed a heap of messages.

All from her sisters.

They'd caught up for lunch in Perth while she'd been sleeping, and had sent a photo of them both—and baby Nate—sitting cross-legged on a patchwork quilt at King's Park, towering trees and a playground in the background.

Mila: Wish you were here!

Neither of her sisters was currently online, but April typed a reply anyway:

April: I miss you all so much!

Her roommate rolled over in bed. April had nothing against Fiona personally, but she *hated* not having her own space.

She started a new message.

April: I have so much to tell you. Something happened with Mr Mysterious...

But then she stopped and deleted everything she'd just written.

It felt...too soon.

*For what?*

She put her phone down and headed for the bathroom before the rest of her late-rising housemates woke up.

Under the sting of hot water she closed her eyes, remembering that kiss in the restaurant.

She'd spent a lot of time remembering it as she'd unloaded pallets at the supermarket and stacked shelves until one a.m.

For some reason it was that last kiss that she kept replaying. It hadn't been as sexy as their first kiss but it had been... Unexpected. And differently unexpected from that first remarkable unexpected kiss in the kitchen.

Because she knew how intensely private Hugh was. Yet he'd kissed her in a room full of strangers.

What did it mean?

*Nothing.*

She squeezed face-wash onto her palm and scrubbed her face much harder than necessary.

*No.* He'd explained that when he dated he was clear about what he wanted. That was all it was.

A few minutes later, with a towel wrapped around her, she made a phone call. After all, she could be clear about what she wanted, too.

'Hugh Bennell,' he answered, in his amazing low and sexy voice.

'I know that I was only supposed to use this number in an

emergency,' April said, remembering his instructions on the day they'd met. 'But this *is* an emergency.'

'What's wrong?' he asked, sharply.

'I need someone to have all-day breakfast with me at the best all-day breakfast place in London.'

She could sense his smile. 'And where is that?'

'I don't know,' she said. 'I'll look it up and let you know where to meet me?'

'Done,' he said. 'See you soon.'

April was smiling as she typed *Best all-day breakfast London* into her phone.

Based on reviews, and reasonable proximity to where they both lived, April had chosen a simple corner café in Clerkenwell that had red gingham curtains on the windows and white-tiled walls inside covered with black-framed old newspaper articles.

She ordered coffee while she was waiting for Hugh, and spent way too much time trying to select a table—*where to sit if your date doesn't like random people?*—before just grabbing a table by the window. She still felt very much like a tourist, and welcomed the opportunity to overlook a classic London streetscape. Hugh could always suggest they move if he wasn't comfortable.

While she waited she scrolled through the remaining photos from her shoot back in Perth, trying to work out which to use next. She only had five more left, so if she really stretched it out maybe five weeks before she needed to sort out what she was doing.

Or at the very least reveal her new hair colour.

Although even now she was losing followers—and definitely losing engagement. Her research had shown that optimum post frequency for follower growth was, on average, around one point five posts a day. Since her move to London she was down to about a post every two days. And, as she was rationing the shoot photos, very few had her physically *in* them—or at least all of her—and she knew that photos of her coffee, or her feet, or her fingernails, or the book she was reading, or shots of the sunset—*thanks, Carly*—were never going to be high-performing posts.

It wasn't great. Not for her 'April Molyneux brand'—for want of a better phrase—and certainly not for the foundation. Her follower numbers were critical when it came to enticing brands to work with her. She couldn't afford for those numbers to continue to drop.

'Blonde?'

It was Hugh—behind her. Absorbed in her phone, and her thoughts, April hadn't heard him approach.

'Oh!' she said, automatically pushing the button to make her phone screen black. 'Hi! Is this table okay? I know there are people around, but it's such a nice view...'

She was talking fast, mentally kicking herself for letting him see the photos.

'It's fine,' he said, pulling out a chair. 'It's just crowded places that I don't like. This is fine.' He gestured towards her phone. 'Can I have a look? I can't imagine you blonde.'

April couldn't think of any plausible reason not to show Hugh. Reluctantly, she handed the phone to him. 'It was just a silly photo shoot that a friend did with me. It was supposed to make me feel better after Evan.'

That excuse worked, as the photos had been taken in different outfits, and all over Perth.

Hugh nodded as he flicked through the images, and April prayed that she wouldn't receive a message or an email or notification—because if he inadvertently opened up an app her real name would be plastered all over her social media accounts.

But thankfully he simply handed her phone back after what was probably less than a minute.

'Blonde is nice,' he said, 'but I like you brunette.'

So did April. Colouring her hair had been more symbolic than a fashion statement, but she was so glad she'd done it. Her natural hair colour was a pale brownish blonde, but she'd been highlighting it for years. The dark chocolate colour she had now was flattering—and strikingly different. But then, wasn't *she*? Sitting here, in this café, watching London pass by, she didn't feel anything like the woman she'd been before Evan left her.

'Thank you,' she said, and slid a menu across the table towards him.

She already knew what she was going to order, and she needed a moment to think.

She'd just lied to Hugh. A white lie, possibly—because, technically, it *had* been a photo shoot. Just not only for herself. But for her million followers.

*Did it matter?*

Last night at dinner, despite a few near misses, it hadn't been too difficult to avoid revealing who she was. Because, really, her family's fortune wasn't relevant first date conversation.

And it wasn't as if she was hiding the important stuff: he knew she was getting divorced, he knew a bit about her family—skimming over the details—and now he knew she'd happily eat breakfast for every meal.

And—really—did she owe him any more than that? In this relationshipless, life-sharing no-go zone, did her billion-dollar trust fund, million social media followers and socialite lifestyle make any difference? Especially when he thought she was a penniless backpacker?

*Yes*, said her gut.

*No*, reasoned her brain.

'I know what I want,' Hugh said, nodding at his menu.

In the midday sun that streamed through the window he squinted a little. He even did that attractively, somehow. And with his stubble-less jaw—he'd clearly shaved—he looked so darkly handsome that April's heart skipped a beat.

'Do you?' he asked.

'Mmm…' she said. Then blinked, and swallowed. 'Yes,' she said more firmly. 'I do.'

He went to stand, but April put her hand on his arm. 'No,' she said. 'I'll order. This is my treat.'

So she went to the counter to order breakfast that she really couldn't afford, waiting in line behind a couple. They were older than April, and looked blissfully happy: the man's hand was wrapped loosely around the woman's waist, his thumb hooked into her belt loop.

April glanced back at their table and went still when she realised Hugh was watching her. His gaze was intense. And appreciative. It made her feel hot and liquid inside.

A sharp but low-pitched word drew April's attention. The happy couple were arguing about something in harsh staccato whispers that continued as they walked back to their table.

Now, *that* looked complicated.

Relationships *were* complicated.

So why complicate things by revealing the truth?

She ordered their breakfast and walked back to Hugh, table number in her hand.

He smiled at her, and she smiled back.

Yes. She definitely knew what she wanted.

Hugh.

Without complications.

# CHAPTER TEN

AFTER LUNCH HUGH played tour guide as he and April spent the afternoon walking through London. They chatted as they ambled the mile from Clerkenwell to St Paul's Cathedral, then headed across the Millennium Bridge and along the Thames. Beside the river they stopped occasionally to lean against the stone and iron barrier and watch the boats float by, for April to take photos of the sparkling silver skyscraper skyline beyond Canary Wharf, or for April to ask questions about the height of The Shard or how often Tower Bridge opened to allow ships through.

This wasn't his usual Saturday.

He'd gone for his early-morning group cycle ride as normal, and had been reading the newspaper at his dining table when April had called.

Usually he'd spend the rest of his Saturday maybe lifting weights in his spare room, or binge-watching something that looked interesting. Later, he'd work. He always did at the weekend.

So, nothing critical.

But still... After he'd agreed to meet April so readily he'd felt uneasy. Maybe because it hadn't even occurred to him to say no.

He'd told April he liked spending time with women, which of course he did. But at dinner. At night. On a date.

Not casually. Not wearing jeans and trainers and without an actual plan.

So he'd decided he'd just have breakfast with April, then go home. That would be okay—no different from the night before.

Instead here he was. Willingly being her tour guide after she'd asked him so sweetly—with a big smile and those gorgeous eyes. And he was in no hurry to get home.

In fact he was having fun.

And having fun with April was so easy. He only felt uneasy when he reminded himself that he should be. Which was crazy, right? April had said he was weird, and he knew he was. But he wasn't a masochist.

He was having fun, and he and April were on exactly the same page. He needed to get over it—and himself—and just go with the flow.

He reached out, grabbing her fingers as she walked beside him. He tugged at her hand, pulling her to the side of the footpath and then pulling her towards him.

Hugh kissed her thoroughly, his hands at her back and her waist and hers tangled in his hair.

'Wow,' she said when they came up for air.

He murmured against her ear. 'I realised I hadn't kissed you today,' he said.

That he'd waited so long seemed impossible.

He felt her smile as he kissed her jaw. 'Where did you learn to kiss like that?' she asked on a sigh.

'Rachael Potter in the Upper Sixth asked if she could practise on me,' Hugh said, grinning against the skin of her cheek. 'She was a year older than me—an older woman. At the time it was the most thrilling moment of my life. Although I wasn't to tell a soul, of course.'

April stepped back, still meeting his gaze. 'Why not?'

'Because—as we determined last night—I'm weird. As an adult, I'm fortunate that people just consider me a little idiosyncratic. In high school I was just plain strange.'

'But why would people think that?'

Hugh shrugged and started walking again, his hands stuffed into his coat pockets.

'It's like I told you—I didn't want anyone to know about the house. As a young kid it was just easier to not have any friends. It wasn't until uni—you know, when playdates aren't really expected—that I had friends again.'

'That's sad,' April said. 'I'm sure most kids wouldn't have cared.'

Hugh raised his eyebrows. 'I was already the nerdy computer kid. I wasn't about to sign up as the kid with the crazy mother. And I definitely wasn't going to let my mum be thought of like that.'

They kept on walking. Around them it was dusk, and the trees that lined the Thames were beginning to twinkle with hundreds of blue lights that grew brighter as the sun retreated.

'Not that it made any difference,' Hugh said, minutes later. 'Kids still whispered about my mum. And about me. Maybe some kids would've been fine with it, but I didn't let anyone close enough to find out. I was moody—and resentful that I had to look after my mum.'

'Look after her?' April asked.

They were still walking, and Hugh kept his gaze on the concrete footpath.

'Yeah,' he said. 'Eventually it was more than just *stuff* that Mum was collecting. There were piles of rubbish. Piles of dirty laundry. I had to create a safe passage for her to get to bed each night. I had to make sure her bed was clear of crap and her sheets were clean. I did all the shopping…the cooking. I remembered to do my homework. I packed my own lunches.'

'She wasn't well,' April said.

'No,' Hugh said with a humourless laugh. 'And I was too young to really understand that. I'd researched hoarding at the library, and I'd tried to help—but even though I kind of got that it must be some sort of anxiety disorder, I wasn't really sympathetic. All I saw was that she managed to go to work each day. She managed to socialise, to continue her quest to find the perfect man, and yet we lived in this absolute horror story of a house that *I* had to keep liveable even as she brought more and more crap inside it.'

April remained silent, letting him speak.

He stopped again. They stood beneath a cast-iron lamp-post with dolphins twined around its base—one of many that lit the South Bank.

'So, yeah…' Hugh said. 'Rachael Potter didn't want anyone to know she was kissing the weird, friendless geek with the crazy mother.'

April reached out and held his hand. 'What happened to her?' she asked. 'To your mum?'

He'd known this question was coming.

He swallowed, angry that his throat was tight and that his heart ached and felt heavy.

'Cancer,' he said. 'I always thought her hoarding would kill her, but I was wrong. It was unexpected—quick and brutal—and she told me in the hospital that she wanted to come home to die. I thought that was bizarre—that she would want to be in the house that represented all she'd lost when Len had died, illustrated with box after box. But she did, so I organised to have her room cleared, to make it safe for a hospital bed to be delivered.'

He swallowed, staring at their joined hands.

'But it was already too late. Before the first box was moved she died.'

Suddenly April's arms were around him.

She was hugging him, her arms looped around his neck, her cheek pressed against his shoulder. She hugged him as he stood there, stiff and wooden, his hands firm by his sides.

She hugged him for long minutes until—eventually—he hugged her back. Tight and hard, with her body pressed tight against him.

He wasn't a hugger—he'd told her that. Even if he was, he'd had no one to hug when his mother had died. At the time it hadn't mattered. It hadn't even occurred to him that he might need or want someone to hug, to grieve with.

As always, it had just been him.

Eventually they broke apart. He turned from April, wiping at the tears that had threatened, but thankfully hadn't been shed.

When he caught April's gaze again, her own gaze travelled across his face in the lamplight, but she said nothing.

He didn't want to be standing here any longer.

'Want a drink?' he asked.

April blinked, but nodded. 'Let's go.'

* * *

They headed up a series of narrow cobblestoned lanes, Hugh still holding April's hand. His strides were long, and April had to hurry to keep pace with him.

He hadn't said a word, and April wasn't really sure what to say.

Then he stopped in front of a small bar. Beyond black-framed windows April could see exposed brick walls and vintage velvet couches.

'Want to try here?' Hugh asked.

She was confused. 'You don't like bars.'

He grinned. 'I don't like *people*. It's still early—hardly anyone's here.'

She followed Hugh inside. The bar's warmth was a welcome relief. It wasn't entirely empty, but only two other customers were there: two women in deep conversation, cocktails in hand.

At the bar, April ordered red wine and Hugh bourbon. April chose one of the smaller couches, towards the rear of the rectangular space, and ran her fingers aimlessly over the faded gold fabric as Hugh sat down. With Hugh seated the couch seemed significantly smaller—their knees bumped, in fact, his dark blue denim against her faded grey.

Not that April minded.

'So,' Hugh said, 'tell me about *your* first kiss.'

His tone was light, and the pain she'd glimpsed in his eyes beneath the lamppost had disappeared.

'Well,' she said, 'I was six. Rory Crothers. Kiss-chasey.' She sighed expansively. 'It was *amazing*!'

Hugh's lips quirked. 'Doesn't count,' he said.

She widened her eyes. 'You mean Rachael Potter *didn't* just give you a kiss on the cheek?'

'No,' he said. Straight-faced.

'Ah…' April said. 'So we're talking *tongue* kissing, then?'

Hugh gave a burst of laughter. 'Yeah,' he said. 'Definitely tongue kissing.'

The look in his eyes was smouldering—and April knew it had *nothing* to do with young Miss Potter.

Something suddenly occurred to her, and she leant forward, resting her hand on Hugh's thigh. 'Am I flirting with a guy in a pub?' she asked.

He grinned, obviously remembering their conversation from the night before. 'Just like you always wanted.'

She smiled. 'This is just as fun as I'd imagined.'

Hugh's eyes flicked downwards to her hand on his thigh. 'Yep,' he said.

Someone had turned up the music, and the beat reverberated around them. As they'd been talking a handful of customers had walked in, were now standing in a group only a few metres away from them.

She nodded in their direction. 'Still okay?' she asked.

He nodded.

'Well,' April said, returning to his original question, 'this is going to sound really sad, but if we're only counting tongue kissing, then Evan was it. I was sixteen, and he kissed me on my front doorstep when I was his date for his high school ball.'

'So I'm only the second guy you've kissed?'

She nodded.

He took a long drink of his bourbon. 'I know you said you met in high school, but I hadn't really considered what that actually meant.'

April tilted her head quizzically. 'It means I met him in high school.'

'You were with him half your life. You grew from teenager to adult with him. That's a really big deal.'

'None of this is news to me,' she said dryly, then sipped her wine.

'And he left *you*?'

April blinked. 'What is this? Remind-April-Of-Crap-Stuff-That's-Happened Day?'

She sounded hurt and defensive, which she didn't like.

Hugh was silent, and she knew she didn't have to answer

his question if she didn't want to. He'd be okay about it. But for some reason she started talking.

'He left me,' she began, 'and I've been telling people I didn't see it coming, but that's a lie.'

April paused, this time taking a long drink of her wine.

'We were having problems for years—even before we got married. It's probably why we took more than ten years to get married, actually. But it was nothing serious—just issues with communicating. Different expectations about stuff—when we'd have kids…that type of thing. So we went to counselling and we tried talking about it. I guess for me, after such a long time, ending it just didn't feel like an option. Evan had been part of my entire adult life, and I couldn't imagine life without him. So I didn't. But obviously Evan had no issues with imagining his life without *me*.'

April watched her fingers as she drew lines in the velvet of the couch.

'I was really keen to have a baby, and we started trying pretty much as soon as we got married—three years ago. But that was all my idea. Evan just went along with it. Maybe that's when he started wondering if things could be different—I don't know.'

Her hair had fallen forward and she tucked the long strands behind her ears as she looked back up at Hugh. Over his shoulder, she saw that more people had entered the bar, and now more couches were occupied than empty.

'I thought he was the love of my life right until the end. I mean, relationships are *supposed* to be hard at times, so I didn't see any red flags when we were having problems. I probably should have. But, yeah, Evan was right. We didn't have that epic, all-consuming love that you see in movies.' She looked at her glass, swirling the deep red liquid but not drinking. 'Although,' she said, 'I think now I realise that I always loved him more than he loved me.'

That last bit had come from nowhere, and April went still as she realised the truth of what she'd said. A truth she hadn't allowed herself to acknowledge before.

'Do you still love him?'

Her gaze flew from her glass to meet Hugh's. He was looking at her with…*concern*? With *pity*?

She sat up, removing her hand from his leg.

'Why?' she asked. 'Would you prefer it that I still do?'

'That wasn't why I was asking,' he said.

April didn't understand why she'd reacted this way, but anger out of nowhere shot through her veins. 'If I still loved him you wouldn't have to worry about the poor, rejected divorcee getting too attached to you, would you? That would keep things neater.'

'April—' he began.

But she wasn't ready to listen. The still raw pain of Evan's rejection was colliding with Hugh's pity. Pity from yet another man who didn't want a relationship with her.

'Why do you care, anyway? What do you know about love, Mr Never-Had-A-Relationship?'

'I care,' he said.

But that was just too much.

She put her glass down on a low table, then stood up and headed for the door.

After a few steps she realised just how crowded the bar had become. There was no clear path for her to take.

She turned back to Hugh, who—as she'd known he would—had followed her. He was only a step behind her. As she watched, a heavy-set bloke turned and accidentally banged his beer against Hugh's arm, spilling the liquid down Hugh's jacket. The man apologised profusely, and a moment later April was at Hugh's side as he reassured the other man and waved him away.

April was standing right in front of Hugh now. They were surrounded—a big group must have entered the bar together—and suddenly the space had gone from busy to absolutely packed. The air was heavy with the smell of aftershave and beer.

Hugh's jaw was tense beneath the bar's muted lighting.

'Are you okay?' she asked.

Hugh's expression was dismissive. 'I'll get it dry-cleaned. It was just an accident.'

'No, not that,' she said. 'I mean—you know—all the people?'

'It doesn't matter. Why did you walk away?'

Someone tapped on April's shoulder and asked to squeeze past, which moved April closer to Hugh.

She lifted her chin. 'I don't want you feeling sorry for me,' she said. 'I'm fine. I don't need your pity.'

'I don't *pity* you, April,' he said, low and harsh in her ear. 'But you've been hurt badly. This might not be a good idea.'

He meant *them*.

'You want to end it?'

'No.' He said it roughly. Firmly. His gaze told her he still felt every bit of the sizzling connection between them. 'But I should.'

'Ah…' April said, nodding slowly. 'You're being *noble*.'

'Well—'

She cut him off. 'Thanks, but no thanks. I didn't sign up for you to be my knight in shining armour, Hugh. I get to make my own decisions. And, if necessary, my own mistakes.'

'You also didn't sign up for my relationship quirks.'

'You mean all your relationship rules and expectations? I get that you don't like it that I haven't followed your rules, but you've been crystal-clear. No relationship. I get it, Hugh, and I'm going to be okay. I'm not fragile. You're not going to break me.'

*Or her heart.*

She wouldn't allow it.

Another clumsy patron bumped into April's back, pushing her into Hugh's chest. Her forearms landed flush against him, her hands splayed across his shoulders.

According to Hugh, she had a choice here: one was to push her arms against him and walk away. But that wasn't an option for April.

She'd spent months in a fog, questioning so much about her life and all that she'd once taken for granted. Everything was different for her now: her present *and* her future. Her life would not unfold the way she'd always expected it to.

But she didn't question this.

She knew now why she'd reacted so strongly to Hugh's concern, and to what she'd perceived as his pity. She *never* wanted someone to be with her unless she was the person they most *wanted* to be with. Her marriage hadn't been perfect, but she'd still not wanted anyone but Evan. And Evan had aspired to something more.

God, that *hurt*.

So she didn't want Hugh to feel sorry for her. She wanted him to *want* her.

And he did.

Right now he wanted to be with no one more than her. She believed that with every cell of her body: with every cell in her body that was now hot and liquid, thanks to the way his chest, belly and legs were pressed so close against hers. So what if he only wanted her *right now* and not for longer?

It didn't matter—because she *knew* that right at this moment she didn't need to worry about not being 'enough', or to worry if the man she was with was wondering if there was something—someone—*more* out there for him.

Right now Hugh wanted *her*. Just her. No one else.

It might not be about love or relationships or a future together, but it still felt good. Great. The best, even. It still felt like exactly what she needed. And, yeah, she definitely wanted Hugh more than anyone. She could barely think with him this close to her.

Her hands relaxed and shifted, one moving up to his hair. Her body softened against him. She loved how hard and solid every inch of him was. His hands, which had been at his sides, now moved. They slid across her hips to her back.

April stood on tiptoes to murmur against his lips. 'You know, there's something else I've always wanted to do in a pub,' she said. 'Kiss a hot—'

He silenced her with his mouth, kissing her thoroughly—with lips *and* tongue.

Yes, this was a *proper* kiss: sexy and playful, deep and soft and hard.

When her eyes slid shut April forgot about where they stood, forgot about the crowd, and she couldn't hear the music or the blur of conversation around them. It was just her and Hugh—the hot stranger she'd always wanted to kiss in a bar.

Although after today he didn't feel like a stranger. They'd had some big conversations. They'd shared each other's pain. Surely *that* didn't follow Hugh's rules…

But beneath Hugh's mouth, his teeth, his tongue, her ability for coherent analysis no longer existed. Instead she just got to feel—the strength of his shoulders, the heat of his mouth. And to react as she took her turn to lead their kiss, to explore his mouth and to lose herself in delicious sensation.

And then, just as Hugh's hand slid beneath her shirt and jacket, the heat of his touch shocking against the cool skin of her waist, yet another person bumped into them.

Hugh dragged his mouth from hers to speak into her ear. 'Can we get out of here?'

'Please,' she said.

And, holding Hugh's hand, April navigated them through the sea of bodies and noisy conversations finally to spill out onto the cobblestones outside.

Hugh tugged her a few metres away from the doorway into the shadows of a neighbouring shopfront, the shop now closed in the evening darkness.

'Still hate pubs?' April asked, breathless as he backed her up against the wooden door.

'Intensely,' he said, his breath hot against her skin. 'But I really like this.'

And then he kissed her again.

# CHAPTER ELEVEN

'DO YOU THINK it's a form of claustrophobia?' April asked as they were driven through London in the back seat of a black cab.

'The pub thing?' Hugh said, relaxing into his seat.

Streetlights intermittently lit the car's interior as they drove, painting April in light and shadow.

'No,' he continued. 'If anything it would be ochlophobia, which is a fear of crowds. But "fear" is too strong a word. Intolerance of crowds is more accurate.'

He'd researched his dislike of bustling, enclosed spaces, much as he'd researched his mother's hoarding. It hadn't been much of a leap to realise that if his mother had an anxiety-related disorder then possibly he did too.

But the label wasn't a comfortable fit. And certainly his issues were nowhere near as extreme as his mother's.

Tonight, for instance.

He *never* would've walked into that bar if it had been busy when they'd arrived. And, truthfully, while he'd been aware of the small space filling and people growing rowdier, the longer he and April had talked, the less it had bothered him.

His focus has been on April. Solely on April.

Later, as the crowds had buffeted them both, the familiar cloak of tension had wrapped around him. He had definitely wanted out of that bar, as rapidly as possible. But then April had asked if he was okay. And then it had become about *her* again—about his clearly unwanted concern for her—and then, soon after, about his need to touch her.

When he'd kissed her he wouldn't have cared if he'd been surrounded by a million people—he wouldn't have noticed. He'd been entirely and completely focused on April and on kissing her.

Surely if he truly had a phobia he wouldn't have been able to just forget about it like that? Just for a kiss?

In the rare times he'd found himself in a crowded space in the past fifteen years he certainly wouldn't have expected a kiss to have distracted him from the way his throat would tighten and his heart would race. But a kiss *had*.

*Or maybe it was April?*

He didn't let himself spend any time considering that.

'It isn't even crowds in general,' Hugh said, talking to silence his brain. 'I can go to the movies, to the theatre, without much problem. I generally go outside during intermissions, and I never wait around in the foyer before a show, but once I'm in my seat I'm fine, because it's an ordered, organised crowd. Also, I generally have a date if I'm going somewhere like that, so I'm not expected to converse with random people. Something else I don't enjoy. That's why the café today was fine—there wasn't a mass of people and I was there with you.'

'So you need white space?' April said.

He hadn't thought of it quite like that before, but the analogy worked.

'Like in your flat,' she said. 'That's like one big ocean of white space.'

His lips quirked. 'Yes,' he said. 'I suppose it is.'

The antithesis of the home he grew up in.

The cab slowed to a stop outside an uninspiring town house with a collection of dead weeds in a planter box at the front window. They'd arrived at April's place—a destination they'd chosen after having had a group of passing teenagers wolf-whistle as they'd been mid-kiss within that shop doorway and April had whispered, 'I should go home.'

He still felt the stab of disappointment at those words. But she was right to slow things down—even if it was the last thing he wanted to do.

He asked the cab driver to wait as he escorted April to the door. A sensor light flicked on and then almost immediately fizzled out, leaving April to search around in her handbag for keys in almost pitch-darkness.

'I hate this house,' April said when she eventually slid the key into the lock. 'Like, with a deep and abiding passionate hatred, you know?'

'So you're not going to invite me in?' he asked with a smile.

'No,' April said. 'Because I am certain two-day-old pizza remains on the coffee table and the fridge stinks like something died in it. And because I have a roommate—literally. And also because I'm trying to be sensible.'

But it seemed whenever Hugh was this close to April, being sensible just didn't feel like an option. So he kissed her again.

She kissed him back in a way that confirmed what he already knew—that April didn't want to be particularly sensible either.

'Do you want to—?' he began.

*Come back to my place.*

What was he *doing*?

'Do I want to what?' April asked. Her words were a husky whisper.

'Nothing,' he said firmly, stepping away. 'Nothing.'

He *never* invited a woman back to his place. It was, as April had so accurately said, his white space. Unadulterated with clutter or complications. *Any* complications.

He was halfway back to the cab before he'd even realised he was retreating.

'Hugh?'

'Bye, April,' he said, knowing he should say more, but unable to work out what.

He didn't give her a chance to respond and slid into the back seat of the cab, then watched her step into the townhouse, turn on the light and close the front door behind her.

Hugh knew he'd just reacted poorly. That he was being weird. But then, that was what he did. It was who he was.

He didn't have unexpected, amorphous day-long dates with women who worked for him. All of today had been exceedingly weird for him. It just hadn't felt weird at the time. At all, really—even now.

Being with April had felt natural. Inviting her to his place—*almost*—had felt natural, too.

But as the cab whisked him home he felt more comfortable with his decision with every passing mile. He'd been right to halt his rebellious tongue and his rebellious libido.

This thing with April was definitely breaking *some* of his rules. But not the important ones: No sleepovers at his house. No relationships.

Those rules were non-negotiable.

And those rules would never be broken.

April: I have some news.

Mila: Yes?

Ivy wasn't online, but April messaged both her sisters so Ivy could comment later if she wanted. She needed their advice.

It was Sunday morning, her roommate was once again sleeping in and this wasn't a conversation she wanted to have in the kitchen, with her other housemates listening in. So instant messaging it was.

She snuggled under her doona and typed out a brief summary of the past forty-eight hours. It seemed completely impossible that it had been less than two days since Hugh had kissed her—it felt like for ever ago.

She closed her eyes as the memory of his lips at the sensitive skin beneath her ear made her shiver.

April: So what do you think?

She'd just described the way Hugh had practically run from her front doorstep after she'd been certain he intended to invite her back to his place.

Mila: I think he was just following your lead. You slowed things down, so he did too.

Mila's interpretation seemed logical, but April wasn't so sure.

April: I didn't want to slow things down. But it seemed the right thing to do.

Honestly, until those teenagers had whistled at them, slowing things down had been the absolute last thing on her mind.

Mila: Why?

April: Because I don't know anything about dating. Isn't there some protocol about what number date you sleep with someone on?

Ivy: No.

April grinned as her sister announced her appearance. Ivy's now husband had started as a one-night stand.

Ivy: But seriously. Do whatever feels right for you. This guy has made it clear that he doesn't want commitment, so you don't owe him anything. Do what you want, when you want. Date numbers are meaningless.

April: But the way he just left made me feel like he was having second thoughts.

Mila: Maybe he is.

April: Ouch!

Mila: Just ask him if you're not sure. What do you have to lose?

April: My job, I guess.

But she didn't really think so. Hugh wouldn't fire her—he'd just make sure their paths didn't cross.

Ivy posted a serious of furious emoticons.

April grinned.

April: No, don't worry. I'm one hundred per cent sure he wouldn't fire me.

Ivy: Good. I didn't think your taste in men was that bad.

April: It's not bad, just limited.

To two guys—one she'd married. She felt utterly clueless.

Mila: Exactly! So just ask him if he wants to help you expand your experience or not. Then you'll know.

Ivy: Good euphemism. And good plan. You don't want to waste time on a guy who isn't interested.

Ivy was right. On her bad days, April already felt she'd wasted almost half her life with Evan.

April: But what if he says no?

She paused before she sent the message.

She already knew what her sisters would say: they'd reassure that he wouldn't, or tell her that if he did it was his loss, not hers, or that if he did he was an idiot…blah-blah-blah.

Which would be lovely of them, but it wouldn't make a difference, would it?

Of course not.

If Hugh rejected her, then it was going to hurt. There was no sugar-coating that.

She deleted the words, thanked her sisters for their advice and then they chatted awhile longer.

Later, she responded to some comments on the latest post to her Instagram account—one of those blonde images from months ago.

For the first time she felt a little uncomfortable doing so. Until now her double life hadn't been impacting anyone: her family and those close to her knew exactly where she was and what she was doing. She'd felt a little guilty hiding such a big move from her followers, but she'd justified it with her confidence that they would understand when she eventually made her grand reveal. As for her suppliers and sponsors—well, she was ensuring that she was showcasing their products just as she would if she was living her life as April Molyneux, so there was no issue there.

So it was just Hugh that was making her feel this way.

*You don't owe him anything.*

Mila's remembered words helped April dismiss her concerns. She was over-complicating a situation that was supposed to be uncomplicated. Nothing had changed since she'd made her decision at the breakfast café.

There was no need to tell him.

On Monday, April decided to be very civilised—and, she imagined, very British—by inviting Hugh for a cup of tea. She sent him a text message practically the moment she arrived at the house:

April: Cup of tea? I'm just boiling the kettle.

Hugh's response was to simply walk in the front door a couple of minutes later.

'Good morning,' he said.

'Morning,' said April. She'd made—she hoped—a subtle effort in her appearance. She was still dressed for work, in jeans, a button-down shirt and sneakers, but she'd made a more concerted effort with her hair and make-up. Her ponytail was sleek, her make-up natural but polished.

Her intent had been to give herself a boost of confidence.

In reality it made everything feel like a very big deal. After a whole Sunday convincing herself it was anything but.

'I'm sorry about how I left,' Hugh said from across the marble countertop.

April nodded, then held out a small box full of teabags she'd found in one of the cupboards, so Hugh could select the type he wanted. April was more of a coffee girl, and she dumped a generous teaspoon of coffee granules into her Dockers mug as she waited for Hugh to elaborate.

'I panicked, I think,' he said.

April's gaze leapt to his. She didn't think that Hugh was a man who often admitted to panic—of any kind.

'Saturday was…unusual for me. You told me in the bar that you weren't following my rules, but the thing was I wasn't either. And I didn't like that. I *don't* like it, really.' He swallowed. His hands were shoved into the pockets of his jeans. 'So I'm sorry I didn't call or text yesterday. I was still panicking.'

She nodded. 'Okay.'

'The thing is, I decided on my cab ride home on Saturday that I needed to slow things down—put some space between us. By last night I'd decided that the best possible thing to do was to end this. Immediately.'

April's stomach dropped, leaving her empty inside. It turned out she *hadn't* been prepared for this possibility. Not at all.

The kettle was bubbling loudly now, steam billowing from its spout. Suddenly, though, Hugh had skirted the counter and was standing right beside her.

'But that would've been idiotic,' he said.

April continued to study the teabags, not ready to risk Hugh seeing what she could guess would be revealed in her eyes.

'And besides, I realised it was impossible the moment I received your text. I'd been kidding myself. I don't want to end this.'

'Okay,' April said again.

She did meet his gaze now, and tried to work out what he was thinking. What exactly did he mean?

His expression wasn't quite unreadable. But equally it told her little. Not like when they'd walked along the Thames. Or even at other little moments scattered throughout that Saturday as she'd told him more about her relationship with Evan, or just before they'd kissed in the centre of that crowded bar.

'Same deal, though? No relationship?'

Deliberately she'd phrased her question lightly. As if that was what she wanted, too.

*Wasn't it?*

'Of course,' Hugh said.

Then, before she could attempt to read anything more into his gaze or his words, he kissed her.

Softly at first, and then harder, until he lifted her off her feet to sit her on the bench. Then the kiss was something else altogether…it had intent. It was a promise of so much more.

But, wrenching her mouth away from his, April said breathlessly, 'I have to work, Hugh.'

And when he might have told her that it didn't matter, that he was her boss, he seemed to realise he shouldn't say any of that, and that it was critically important to her that he didn't.

She *was* supposed to be working. And for a woman who'd never worked a proper day in her life until recently, it was probably strange that she found that so important. But she did. Working for a living wasn't just some rich girl's fancy to April—it was real…it was her life.

She slid off the counter and walked Hugh to the front door. She stood on tiptoes and kissed him softly, sliding her hand along his jaw. His sexy stubble was back, and she loved the way it rasped beneath her fingertips.

'See you later,' she said.

And she knew she would.

# CHAPTER TWELVE

THE REST OF the week was torture.

Delicious torture, but torture nonetheless.

Despite Hugh's best efforts, April was determined to be the most diligent of workers. He thought he understood—possibly—why she felt that way. While the fact that he was technically her boss was mostly irrelevant to him, April clearly felt differently. Which was admirable, really, but also…frustrating.

By Monday afternoon April had quite a collection of things in the 'Hugh' box, having hit a bit of a mother lode of potentially sentimental items in the corner of the almost completed first bedroom.

Most of it was school stuff: finger paintings, honour certificates, ribbons from school athletics competitions. Plus yet more photos—these in battered albums, and mostly of his mother as a child.

The finger paintings went to recycling, and the ribbons to the bin. One certificate in particular he kept—he remembered how, aged about eight, he'd run his thumb over the embossed gold sticker in the bottom right-hand corner with pride. The rest he chucked. He kept his mother's photo albums.

'Penmanship Award?' April asked, dropping down to kneel beside him.

She'd cleared about ninety per cent of the boxes in the bedroom, so she'd been able to open the heavy curtains. Light streamed into the room, reflecting off hundreds of dust motes floating merrily in midair.

'It was a fiercely contested award,' Hugh explained with mock seriousness. 'But in the end I won with my elegant $Q$s.'

'Wow!' April said. She was so close their shoulders bumped. She met his gaze, mischief twinkling in her eyes. 'I've always rather admired your $Q$s myself.'

'Really?' Hugh asked.

He leant closer, so their foreheads just touched. Her grin was contagious, and he found himself smiling at her like a loon.

'Yeah…' April breathed.

A beat before he kissed her, Hugh whispered, 'When have you seen my *Q*s?'

'Oh,' April said, 'I have a remarkable imagination.'

Hugh's eyes slid shut. 'Trust me,' he said, his words rough, 'I do too.'

Minutes later, with her lips plump from his kisses and her shirt just slightly askew, April slid from Hugh's lap and stood.

'Looks like the 'Hugh' box is sorted for the day,' she said.

'So I'm dismissed?' he said.

She shrugged, but smiled. 'Something like that. See you tomorrow.'

On Tuesday he brought lunch.

They sat on the staircase, brown paper bags torn open on their laps to catch the crumbs from crusty rolls laden with cheese, smoked meats and marinated vegetables.

'Tell me about where you live in Australia,' he asked.

And so April spoke of growing up beside a river with black swans, of camping in the Pilbara and swimming in the rock pools at Karijini. She spoke of where she lived now: in a house where she could walk to the beach—a beach with white sand that stretched for kilometres, dotted with surfers and swimmers and the occasional distant freighter.

'So why come here?' he asked.

Today it was raining, with a dreary steady mist.

'Because,' she said as she wiped her fingers with a paper napkin, 'London was far away. From Evan and my life. And it was different. I imagined a place busy where Perth was slow; and cool where Perth was hot. Perth is isolated geographically—here the world is barely hours away. I needed a change, and I needed it to be dramatic.'

She neatly rolled up her paper bag, being sure that the crumbs remained contained.

'Although,' she continued, 'I imagined walking into my dream job—which, of course, didn't happen.'

'Why not?'

She rolled her eyes. 'Because generally environmental consulting firms want experience, not just a thirty-something with a degree from a decade ago.'

'Why didn't you use your degree?' Hugh asked, confused. 'If that was your dream job?'

'Because…' she began, then paused. She started folding her rolled-up paper bag into itself, her gaze focused on her task. 'Because I travelled a lot,' she said quickly. 'And maybe it wasn't my dream job, after all.'

She stood up and offered her hand for Hugh's paper bag. He handed it to her, and followed her into the kitchen, where she shook the crumbs out into the bin before adding the paper bags to the recycling.

'You okay?' he asked.

She nodded, and then his phone vibrated in his jeans pocket: a reminder he'd set for a meeting he needed to attend.

'I need to go,' he said, and then kissed her, briefly but firmly, on the lips.

'Bye, Hugh,' she said.

On Wednesday Hugh took her to the British Museum.

Initially she'd said no.

'Consider it a team building day,' Hugh said, firmly. 'It's a sanctioned work event, okay?'

She wanted to argue. After all, she'd been playing the professional card hard—and consistently—all week.

'It's great there on a weekday,' Hugh said. 'Not too busy. And it's such a big place that even school groups and tourists don't make it feel crowded.'

Crowds didn't bother her. It was still a no…

'I liked playing tour guide the other day. Let me do it again.'

*Oh.*

That got her—his reference to their day together…a day she knew he'd both enjoyed and felt uncomfortable about.

Those damn rules. Yet he wanted to do it again.

'Okay,' she said.

On the way, as they sat in the back of another black cab, she wondered—yet again—what exactly she was doing.

She was fully aware that her determined professionalism was something of a cover. Yes, it was important to her to complete the job she'd been hired to do, and to actually *earn* the money that Hugh was paying her. She wasn't going to slack off just because she got to kiss her boss during her tea breaks. Tempting as that was. But also her professionalism was giving her time.

After work she had only a few hours before her job at the supermarket started—and, as their truncated dinner had proved, that wasn't enough time to do much.

It certainly wasn't enough time to do anything more than kiss Hugh. Well, technically it was, but it seemed by unspoken agreement that both she and Hugh were waiting until the weekend before taking things further. When they would have all the time in the world.

The tension this delay was creating was near unbearable. Every touch and every kiss was so weighted with promise that the weekend felt eons away—an impossible goal.

But waiting was good, too. It gave April time to think. To process what was happening.

To process who she was now.

When she'd decided to move to London she'd wanted to discover who she was without Evan. She hadn't worked that out yet, but she did know that she didn't ever want her identity so tied up with a man again.

Not that that was what was happening with Hugh. This thing with Hugh would never be more than what it was—which was fleeting. A fling. And even if it wasn't—even if Hugh *had* wanted more—April knew she couldn't lose herself in 'Hugh and April' the way she had in 'Evan and April'.

Not that it was Evan's fault that had happened. It had been

a product of youth and inexperience and an utter lack of independence—and maybe confusing independence with wealth.

It had been *her* fault—*her* error. And she couldn't make it again.

She was different now. As April Spencer she'd proved to herself that she could live alone, and survive without her family's money. Without Evan.

But the way she was around Hugh…that pull she felt towards him…that intensity of attraction and the way it overwhelmed her when he touched her, when he kissed her…

She needed to adjust to this sensation, and she needed time to acknowledge it for what it was: hormones and chemical attraction. Nothing more.

And definitely nothing that she would or could lose herself within.

She would not allow it.

The cab came to a stop beneath a London plane tree, sparse with leaves in gold and yellow. As Hugh paid the driver April slid out onto the footpath. She stood beside the fence that surrounded the museum—an impressive, elaborate cast-iron barrier—through which she could see tourists milling in the museum forecourt. A brisk breeze fluttered the leaves above her, and April hugged her coat tight around herself.

Then Hugh was in front of her, looking both enthusiastic and just slightly concerned, as if he wasn't sure he'd made the right decision to bring her here.

But April smiled. 'Lead on, tour guide!' she said with a grin.

Hugh smiled right back—with his mouth and with his eyes. *Damn, he was gorgeous.*

She definitely hadn't got used to that.

Side by side they entered the forecourt, and as April's gaze was drawn to the mammoth Greek-style columns and the triangular pediment above, she shoved everything else from her mind.

This thing with Hugh—each day with Hugh—was not

complicated. It was about fun and attraction. *Only.* She had nothing to worry about.

In that spirit, she grabbed his hand as they were halfway up the steps to the museum's entrance. He stopped, and on tiptoes she kissed him.

'This is fun,' she said. Because it was, and because it was a useful reminder. 'Thank you.'

He grinned and tugged her up the remaining steps.

*Yes. Fun and nothing more.*

It ended up being rather a long lunchbreak.

After they'd wandered through artefacts from the Iron Age, and then lingered amongst the Ancient Egyptians, Hugh now stood alone in the Great Court—the centre of the museum—which had a soaring glass roof constructed of thousands of abutted steel triangles. April had darted into the gift shop for postcards for her mother and sisters.

Hugh's phone vibrated in his back pocket, but a quick glance had him sliding it back into his jeans. It was just work, and for once he wasn't making it his priority.

With April no longer by his side it was easier for his brain to prod him with a familiar question: *Why had he brought April here?*

But his answer was simple. Just as April had said on the museum steps: because it was fun. There was no need to overthink it.

He'd wanted to get April out of that dusty, cluttered house and into the London that he loved. He'd been to this museum a hundred times—he loved it here. Even as a teenager he'd come. He'd been attracted to its scope and its space, and to the way people spoke in low voices. Plus, of course, all the exhibitions. It was such a simple pleasure to lose a day discovering relics from a different time and place.

'Can we get a selfie?' April asked, appearing again by his side.

Her bag was slung over her shoulder, and she was digging about within the tan leather for—he assumed—her phone.

She retrieved it with a triumphant grin, and he watched as she opened the camera app.

'No,' he said.

'Pardon me?' she asked, her gaze flying to his.

But before he could respond her phone clattered to the floor, finishing near his left foot.

'Dammit,' she said, and crouched to reach it.

But Hugh had already done the same, and now held the phone in his hand. In its fall, the phone had somehow navigated itself to April's photo gallery, and the screen was full of colourful thumbnails: April's hands, shoes that looked vaguely familiar, even a photo of the dinner she'd had with him last week.

'When did you take that?' he asked, pointing at the picture of her meal.

They were both sitting on their heels. April had her hand outstretched for her phone.

'Can I have my phone back, please?' she asked, and her tone was quite sharp.

Hugh met her gaze as he handed it back. 'Of course,' he said.

'Thank you,' she said, her eyes darting to her phone, her fingers tapping on its screen.

He'd only had her phone a few seconds, and it was hardly as if he'd been scrolling through its contents. He'd simply looked at what it was displaying—nothing more. But April seemed uncomfortable, her shoulders hunched and defensive.

'Are you okay?' he asked.

But she ignored him. 'I took it when you went to the bathroom,' she said, answering his original question.

Now she looked up at him and smiled, and the moment of awkwardness passed.

'I wouldn't have picked you as one of those people who takes photos of their food,' he said.

'One of *those* people?' she teased. 'Who are *those*?'

He shrugged. 'You know—the people who feel compelled to document every tedious moment of their existence.'

'Well,' she said, 'sorry to disappoint you, but sometimes I *do* take photos of my food. Or of my shoes, my outfit, or the view, or whatever I'm doing. Like now.' She grinned, waving her phone. 'So I guess I am one of *those*. *Can* we take that selfie?'

'Hmm…' he said.

She moved closer, bumping his upper arm with her shoulder. 'Come on,' she said. 'They're just photos. They aren't hurting anybody. Why do you care if I or anyone else likes taking photos?'

'I don't,' he said.

'You just disapprove?'

He looked down at her. She was smiling up at him, her face upturned, her hair scraped back neatly from her lovely cheeks.

'No,' he said. 'I just don't get it. Why bother?'

Now it was April's turn to shrug. 'Why not? It's just sharing happy moments with other people, I guess. Or unhappy moments, I suppose.'

A shadow crossed her face—so quickly that he decided he'd imagined it.

'So it's not a narcissistic obsession with self or a compulsive need to elicit praise and garner acceptance from others?' he asked, but he was teasing her now.

'Nope,' April said with a smile. 'It's just sharing a whole heap of photos.'

*Sharing.*

An echo from their first dinner together seemed to reverberate between them:

*I don't feel any urge to share my life with anyone.*

'Hugh,' April said, seriously now, 'I want to take a photo of us together. But just for me. I'm not going to post it on social media anywhere. I'm not going to share it with anyone.'

His instinct was still to ask why and to continue to resist. He'd never taken a selfie in his life, and had never intended to.

But he already had his answer. April wanted it for herself. It was a happy moment she wanted to document.

'Okay,' he said.

He'd surprised her, but then she smiled brilliantly and wrapped one arm around him quickly, holding the phone aloft, as if she was concerned he'd change his mind.

'Smile!' she said, and he did as he was told, looking at the image of April and himself reflected back in the phone's screen.

She took a handful of photos, and then held her phone in front of them both as she scrolled through them. One was the clear winner—they both wore broad smiles, their heads were tilted towards each other, *just* touching. The sun that poured through the glass roof lit their skin with a golden glow, and behind them the staircase that wrapped its way around the circular reading room at the centre of the Great Court served as an identifier for where they were.

'Perfect,' April said.

'Can you send me a copy?' Hugh said, although he'd had absolutely no intention of asking.

April blinked and smiled, looking as surprised as he felt. 'Of course,' she said.

Hugh cleared his throat. 'We'd better go,' he said.

April nodded, and together they left the museum.

On Thursday Hugh didn't come up to the main house.

He sent her a text, just before lunch, explaining that he had back-to-back meetings—something about bug fixes and an upcoming software release.

Not that the details mattered. The key point was that she wasn't going to see him that day.

April set her phone back in place, returned it to the radio station she liked to listen to and got back to her boxes. She was in a new room now—Hugh's mother's, she suspected, but she hadn't asked.

*Why doesn't he want to see me today?*

April shook her head to banish such a pointless question. He needed to work—that was all. There'd been no expectation that they were to meet each day.

Far from it.

Later that night, after she'd got home from the supermarket, April approved Carly's planned schedule of posts for the following week. Carly had also noted how low they were on blonde-haired April Molyneux photos, and had asked, gently, if April had made any plans for once they'd run out.

*No.*

But she knew she needed to.

She was now more than halfway through cleaning out Hugh's house and her credit card debt was nearly paid off. Decisions definitely loomed: What job next? And where? London? Perth? Somewhere else entirely?

And what would she do? Because, as she'd told Hugh, she now knew her heart wasn't in what she'd thought would be a magnificent environmental consulting career.

And what about Hugh?

Again April shook her head, frustrated with herself.

There was no *What about Hugh?*

Hugh was not part of her decision-making, and he was not part of her future.


On Friday Hugh brought lunch again.

Although it grew cold, forgotten on the kitchen counter, as April and Hugh made up for lost time.

Later, Hugh closed his eyes, breathing heavily, his cheek resting against the top of April's head. April, pressed up against the closed pantry door, was taking in long swallows of air, her breath hot against his neck. His hands lay against the luscious skin beneath her shirt...her hands had shoved his T-shirt upwards to explore his back and chest.

'What, exactly,' he managed, his voice gravelly, 'are we waiting for?'

'Time,' April replied, and he sensed her smile. 'Tomorrow.'

He groaned.

'Tomorrow,' she repeated, pushing gently against his chest. 'I need to get back to—'

'Work,' he finished for her. 'I know.'

\* \* \*

Finally it was Saturday.

A cab was arriving at three p.m. to collect April.

Hugh was once again playing tour guide—but a mysterious one today, having only hinted at their destination with a dress code: a bit fancy…no jeans.

Another package had arrived from Perth from one of her suppliers: stunning hand-painted silk dresses that would have been perfect if it hadn't been December in London.

So April had spent the morning searching for a more season-appropriate dress along the High Street and at the many vintage clothing shops that Shoreditch had to offer. In the end she'd chosen a mix of modern and vintage—a new dress with a retro feel, in a medium-weight navy blue fabric with a full skirt, short sleeves and a pretty peekaboo neckline.

She'd also bought new stockings and heels, and spent more money than she had in weeks. Although she realised, as she walked out of the store, bags swinging from her fingertips, that this was the first outfit she'd ever bought with money she'd earned herself.

The realisation was both a little embarrassing and also incredibly satisfying.

Right on time, Hugh and his cab arrived.

She rushed to the door with her coat slung over her arm and swung it open.

Hugh was wearing a suit of charcoal-grey and a tie—something she'd never imagined him wearing. He looked *amazing*—his jaw freshly shaven, his hair still just too long and swept back from his face. His eyes were dark, and he was silent as his gaze slid over her from her hair—which she'd curled with her roommate's curling wand—to her red-painted lips, and finally down to her dress and the curves it skimmed.

He stepped forward and kissed her—hard. 'You are stunning,' he said against her ear.

April shivered beneath his touch.

Twenty minutes later they arrived at The Ritz Hotel. The

building was beautiful, but imposing, stretching a long way down Piccadilly and up at least five or six storeys.

Inside, Hugh led her into the Palm Court—a room with soaring ceilings decorated in sumptuous shades of cream and gold. Tables dotted the space, each surrounded by gilded Louis XVI oval-backed chairs, and everywhere April looked there were chandeliers, or mirrors, or flowers, or marble. It was opulent and lavish and utterly frivolous.

'What do you think?' Hugh asked.

'I *love* it,' she said.

Hugh smiled.

They were seated at a corner table. Around them other tables' occupants murmured in conversation to the soundtrack of a string quintet.

'I thought you might like to experience a traditional British afternoon tea,' Hugh said.

A waiter poured them champagne.

'You thought correctly,' April said. 'Although I wouldn't have thought this was really your thing.'

'It's not,' Hugh said. 'So this is a first for me, too.'

*'Really?'* April said, quite liking the idea that this was new to them both.

Hugh nodded. 'Surprisingly, a reclusive computer science nerd doesn't take himself to afternoon tea at The Ritz.'

April took a sip from her champagne. 'I wouldn't say you're a total recluse,' she said. 'You have to interact with people to run your company, even if not face-to-face. You spend time with me. And with the other women you date.'

Her gaze shifted downwards, to study the clotted-cream-coloured fabric of the tablecloth.

'Selectively reclusive, then,' he said. 'Generally I prefer my own company.'

'So I'm an exception?' April said, unable to stop the words tumbling from her mouth. What was she even *asking*?

'Yes,' he said simply.

But before he could elaborate the three tiers of plates housing their afternoon tea arrived, and the moment was lost. Or at least April decided it was best not to pursue her line of questioning as she didn't like what it revealed. Not so much about Hugh, but about her.

She didn't need to be special, she reminded herself. *This isn't about special. It's about fun. Special is irrelevant.*

Afternoon tea was lovely.

They ate delicate sandwiches that didn't have crusts; scones with raisins and scones without—both with jam and cream, of course—and pretty cakes and pastries with chocolate and lemon and flaky pastry.

They talked easily, as they always seemed to now, in a way that made their first kiss seem so much longer than eight days ago.

Today their conversation veered into travel. April had, of course, done a lot—Hugh very little.

April buried uncomfortable feelings as she deftly edited the stories she told him. She didn't lie, but rather didn't mention details—like the fact that she'd often travelled in the Molyneux private jet, or that her grandfather had once owned his own private island in the Caribbean. Instead she told him only about the experiences: the Staten Island Ferry, the junks in Halong Bay, a cycling tour through the French countryside. Which were the important bits, really, anyway.

She took a long drink of her champagne.

'Why haven't *you* travelled more?' she asked. He'd travelled to the US—Silicon Valley—and that was about it.

'I run my business entirely remotely, so I don't need to interact with people or leave my house,' he said. 'If I did travel the world, wouldn't that seem more surprising?'

April studied Hugh as he drank his champagne. The isolated man he described did not align with the man she'd shared the week with.

'But you love the museum,' she said. 'And that's all about learning and discovering new things. You brought us here today. And you ride your bike. Don't you ever ride somewhere new?'

He nodded. 'Of course I do.'

'So are you *sure* you wouldn't enjoy travelling? You just need to avoid crowds—but that wouldn't be too hard with a bit of planning. There are these amazing villas in Bali…' She paused a split second before she said *where I've stayed.* 'That I've heard of where you have your own private beach. It would be totally private. You'd love it.'

'Would I?' he asked, raising an eyebrow.

'I think so,' April said. 'We could explore the nearby villages and swim in—'

Too late she realised what she'd said, and her cheeks became red-hot. She'd done it again—mistakenly stumbled into a fanciful world where she was special to Hugh—where with her he broke the shackles of the insular world she suspected his mother's hoard had created.

'I mean, *you* could. Of course.'

'Of course,' he said, and when he met her gaze his expression was as frustratingly unreadable as it had been when they'd first met.

The tension between them had shifted from charged to awkward, and April rushed to fix it.

'I can't wait to travel again,' she said, possibly slightly too loudly. 'My credit card is almost paid off, so once I finish working for you I'm going to start saving for my next adventure. I've never been to Cambodia, and I've heard that Angkor Wat is really amazing.' She was talking too quickly. 'Plus, accommodation is really cheap, which is good. And I've heard the food is fantastic. A friend of mine was telling me about Pub Street, which is literally a street full of restaurants and pubs, so you'd probably hate it, but I—'

She talked for a few more minutes, grasping at random remembered anecdotes from her friends and things that she'd read online. She didn't really care what she said—she just wanted to fill the silence.

'So you've got it all sorted?' Hugh asked, and his gaze was piercing now. 'Your plans after you stop working for me?'

'Yes—' she began, and then she took a deep breath. She was sick of all these half-truths. 'No,' she said. 'I have no idea. I have no idea where I'll work or what I'll do. And if I travel—who knows when?—I am as likely to go to Siem Reap as Wollongong or Timbuktu.'

She swallowed, her gaze now as direct as Hugh's. She couldn't tell what he was thinking, but he was studying her with intent.

'In fact,' she continued, 'about all I know right now is that I'm sitting here with you, the hot, charmingly odd British guy I met at work, who is absolutely perfect as my rebound guy. I know that you make me laugh, and I know that you love to show me London as much as I love you showing me.'

She lowered her voice now, leaning closer. Her hand rested on the tablecloth. Hugh's was only inches away.

'And I absolutely know that I *really* like kissing you,' she said. 'I also know exactly where this night is headed. So... um...' Here her bravado faltered, just slightly. 'I'd really like to just focus on the things I know tonight. If that's okay with you?'

Hugh's hand covered hers, his thumb drawing squiggles on her palm.

'Do with this information as you wish,' he said, his voice low, 'but *I* know that I have a key card in my pocket for a suite upstairs.'

His words were so unexpected that April laughed out loud in surprise. But it was perfect. As simple and uncomplicated as their non-relationship was supposed to be. It was what they both wanted—right now and tonight.

Tomorrow, or after she'd finished working with him, or after Hugh had walked out of her life—in fact *anything* in the future—she had absolutely no clue about. But that didn't matter—at least, not right now. As she sat here in this remarkable room, with this remarkable man.

'Let's go,' she said, lacing her fingers with his.

# CHAPTER THIRTEEN

IT WAS DARK when Hugh awoke, although a quick check of his phone showed that was due to the heavy brocade curtains rather than the hour. In fact, it was midmorning. Usually by now he'd already be home from his Sunday morning bike ride, showered and about halfway through the newspaper, and probably his second cup of tea.

Right now he had no urge to be doing any of those things.

April lay sleeping beside him, her back to him. His eyes had adjusted to the darkness and now he could see the curve of her shoulder, waist and hip in silhouette beneath the duvet. She was breathing slowly and steadily, fast asleep.

He sat up so he could observe her profile and the way her dark hair cascaded across the pillow. She was beautiful. He'd always thought that, but she seemed particularly so right in this moment.

It was tempting to touch her—to kiss the naked shoulder bared above the sheets and to wake her. But they'd already kept each other awake for most of the night, and she needed her sleep. She was working two jobs, after all.

It had actually been her job stacking supermarket shelves that had inspired him to choose The Ritz. He'd already known he'd need to book a hotel room—April's house was clearly not an option and his definitely was not. A hotel had been the obvious solution for where they'd spend the night together. Clearly he would always have selected somewhere nice. *Very* nice. But The Ritz—The Ritz was a whole other level.

And he'd liked the idea of choosing somewhere so grand and iconic, to give April a London experience she otherwise wouldn't have experienced on a box-emptying, supermarket-shelf-stacking income. Something to remember after all this had ended.

Afternoon tea had been offered by the reservations office

when he'd rung to book, and he'd known instantly that April would love the idea. He'd surprised himself by very much enjoying himself too, getting as caught up in the pomp and ceremony as April had.

Hugh's stomach rumbled—a reminder that they'd skipped dinner. Although he certainly hadn't minded the trade-off. He wouldn't have passed on one touch or one sensation for literally anything last night.

It had been nothing like he'd ever experienced. More than just sex. And, considering sex had always just been sex to him, that was...

*Unexpected*, Hugh supposed.

Although really had anything that had happened between Hugh and April in the past week or so in any way indicated that when they made love it would be anything but raw and intense and intimate?

*No.*

He'd told himself as he'd driven in that cab to collect her that tonight would be it: one night with April and then they'd go their separate ways. It would be simpler that way, he'd decided. He'd simply give April his word that he would keep out of her way at work.

But that had been just as big a lie as telling himself that making love to April would just be sex.

April stirred, maybe under the relentless stare of Hugh's attention, and rolled onto her back. But she didn't wake. Now she was just simply closer to him, an outflung hand only centimetres from his hip.

In her sleep, she smiled.

April was always smiling, he'd discovered, and when he was with her he smiled too.

*He wanted more than one night.*

He needed it.

Hugh had never watched a woman sleep before. His usual protocol was a swift exit the morning after, and he'd always done so with ease. He'd never simply enjoyed lying in bed with a woman, watching her sleep: he'd never felt compelled to.

And *compelled* was the right word when it came to April. In fact since he'd met April so much of what had happened had felt almost inevitable—and certainly impossible to resist.

Not that he was complaining.

But if he wanted another night with April—in fact, many nights—what did that mean?

Did he want a relationship with her?

As he considered that question he waited for the familiar claustrophobic sensation he'd always associated with the concept of relationships: that visceral, suffocating tightening of his throat and the racing of his heart. Similar to the way he felt in pubs, or bustling crowds, or when he was surrounded by his mother's hoard. As if he was trapped.

But it didn't come.

April stirred again, reaching towards him. Her hand hit the bare skin of his belly and then crept upwards, tracing over the muscles of his stomach and chest with deliberate languor.

'Good morning,' she said softly, and he could hear that smile she'd worn in her sleep. 'Please don't tell me we need to check out anytime soon.'

'We have until two p.m.,' he said. 'Hours. But we should probably eat.'

Her hair rustled on her pillow as she shook her head. 'Later,' she said firmly as she sat up, and then she pushed against his shoulders so he was lying beneath her.

As her hair fell forward over her shoulders to tickle his jaw and she slid her naked body over his he said, 'That works for me.'

'I thought it might,' she said, smiling against his lips.

And then she kissed him in a way that sent all thoughts of anything at all far, far from his mind.

He wanted April. Now, and for more than one night.

The details he'd work out later.

April discovered that walking out onto Piccadilly after check-out, wearing the dress she'd worn the day before and with a biting wind whipping down the street, worked as a seriously effective reality check.

She wrapped her arms around herself, rocking back and forth slightly on her heels.

*What now?*

Hugh stood beside her. He hadn't shaved today, and she'd already decided that the way he looked right now was her favourite: the perfect amount of stubble, dishevelled hair and bedroom eyes.

They'd left their hotel room for the first time that day when they'd walked to the reception desk to pay. In fact it had been Hugh reaching for his wallet that had been the first fissure in their little 'April and Hugh' bubble of lust.

'Oh—' she'd said, with no idea what she'd actually planned to say next.

He'd looked at her reassuringly: *he had this*. Which of course he did—he was wealthy. A billionaire.

But she wasn't used to a man paying for her. Yes, Hugh had bought her dinner and lunch before, but April had bought him breakfast, and had insisted on paying for their lunch at the British Museum. It had felt as if they were equals.

It was just that she knew how much hotels like this cost per night—she'd stayed at many of them. Not The Ritz, for which she was immensely grateful—she couldn't have stomached pretending if she had. And she'd paid for many of those rooms. With Molyneux money, of course, not her own. Evan had never paid—it would have been crazy. His income was a mere drop within the Molyneux Mining money ocean.

For the first time she wondered if that had been problematic for Evan. Maybe it had? She'd refused to let him pay whenever he'd tried...

Well, there was her answer.

Anyway, April thought she understood money now. Or at least appreciated it more. So Hugh paying thousands of pounds for a night with her made her in equal parts thrilled and flattered and terribly uncomfortable.

*He didn't even know her real name.*

But then he'd leant forward and kissed her cheek before murmuring in her ear, 'I had a wonderful time last night.'

And that had been such an understatement—and his lips against her skin such a distraction—that worries about money or her name had just drifted away.

Until she'd been hit by the bracing cold outside.

She turned to Hugh. He was already looking down at her. Was he about to say something?

She could guess what it would be: something to reiterate the insubstantiality of their non-relationship, to re-establish this supposedly uncomplicated thing or fling they were doing or having.

Then later—maybe in a few days—he'd end it. He'd finally wake up to the fact that he was, in fact, doing what he'd so clearly told her he didn't want: he was sharing his life with April.

She mentally braced herself for it, simultaneously telling herself it would be for the best anyway. No point imagining their incredible evening had been anything but sex. Even though it had felt like so much more.

But what would *she* know, anyway? She hadn't even realised that her husband didn't love her any more. She hadn't even realised that he hadn't loved her enough *ever*.

Hugh didn't say anything. He was just looking at her with a gaze that seemed to search her very soul.

'So what happens now?' she blurted out, unable to stand not knowing for a moment longer.

'Well,' he said, 'I thought we might go past your flat so you can pick up a change of clothes. Then, if it's all right with you, we could go and grab some groceries for dinner. At my place.'

That was about the last thing April had expected Hugh to say, and it took her a minute to comprehend it.

Another gust of wind made her shiver. She saw Hugh reach towards her—as if to somehow protect her from the cold—but then he stopped and his hand fell back against his side.

Her gaze went to his. He was studying her carefully. Waiting.

It hadn't, she realised, been a throwaway casual invitation.

While she might not know, or *want* to know, exactly how his rule-defined dating worked with other women, she knew absolutely that what he was doing now was outside that scope.

How far, she couldn't be sure. But it was far enough that April glimpsed just a hint of vulnerability in his gaze.

*He didn't even know her real name.*

She needed to tell him.

But as swiftly as she'd considered it Mila's words thrust their way into her brain to override it: *You don't owe him anything.*

'April?' Hugh asked.

She was taking far too long to answer a simple question.

'That sounds great,' she said eventually. She managed a smile. 'So does that mean you're cooking me dinner?'

Hugh's lips quirked as he waved down a cab, but he didn't answer her question. He probably was. Why else would he need groceries for their meal?

*You don't owe him anything.*

But of course she did.

She owed him her honesty.

But if she told him, this would be over.

They climbed into the back seat of the London cab and immediately Hugh reached for her hand. He drew little circles and shapes on it again, like he had during afternoon tea. And again his touch made her shiver and her blood run hot.

It also made her heart ache.

She needed to tell him.

Just not now.

She wasn't ready to give him up, or to give up how he made her feel.

Not just yet.

He did make her dinner.

It was nothing fancy—just a stir fry with vegetables, cashews and strips of chicken. But April seemed to like it, which was good, given he hadn't cooked for anyone other than himself since he'd moved out of home. He didn't mind cooking, actually—it was a skill he'd learnt by necessity when his mother had been at particularly low points, and had been cultivated when his curiosity for varied cuisine had been hampered by his reluctance to socialise much or to have takeaway delivered to his home.

But, anyway, it hadn't really been about cooking the meal, had it? It had been about inviting April into his home. To sleep over, no less.

Not that April was aware of the significance.

After dinner, she asked for a tour of his flat.

As he opened each bedroom door he felt that familiar tension—as if he was worried that behind the door would be a hoard he'd somehow forgotten about.

Of course each room was spotlessly tidy.

April didn't comment on his severe minimalism: there was nothing on the walls, there were no photo frames or shelves… no trinkets. Had she guessed why?

Probably. It wasn't too difficult to work out why the child of a compulsive hoarder might loathe anything hinting at clutter.

The last room he showed her was his bedroom.

Right at the rear of his flat, it had French doors that led into a small garden courtyard, although currently pale grey curtains covered them. The room wasn't large, but there was ample space around his bed, and a narrow door led to the en-suite bathroom.

It was as unexciting as every other room he'd shown her, with nothing personal or special about it. But still…bringing April into *this* room felt different. More than the anxiety he'd felt at each door. Those moments had passed. *This* sensation persisted.

This room—generic as it might be—was unquestionably his private space. He wanted April here—he knew that. But it was still difficult for him. He'd been so intensely private for so long that to be showing April his house and his room—it was a big deal. He felt exposed. He felt vulnerable.

Again he wondered if April realised how he was feeling. She'd walked a few steps into the room and now turned to face him. She'd changed at her place, and now wore jeans, a T-shirt and an oversized cardigan. Her hair was still loose, though, all tumbling and wild. He could see something like concern in her gaze.

'Hugh—' she began.

But he crossed the space between them, and silenced her with a kiss. He didn't want questions or concern or worry right now: hers *or* his. April was here, in his bedroom. And he was kissing her.

That was all that mattered.

# CHAPTER FOURTEEN

APRIL WOKE UP before Hugh on Monday morning.

He lay flat on his back, one arm on his pillow, hooked above his head. The other rested on his chest, occasionally shifting against his lovely pectoral muscles as he slept.

She should have told him.

On Piccadilly…outside The Ritz. Or probably the first time he'd kissed her, actually. Definitely last night, when he'd walked her into this room and she'd suddenly realised what a massive deal it was to Hugh. It had been written all over his face: a mix of determination and alarm and hope that had made it clear that *this* was most definitely not in the scope of his non-relationship rules.

But he'd wanted her enough to break his own rules. He'd *trusted* her enough to allow her into the sanctuary of his home. She'd realised, too late, that the young boy who'd never invited his friends over to play had grown up into a man who never had overnight guests. Who never let people into his house or into his life.

It seemed obvious now—from the eccentricity of the confidentiality agreement she'd signed to the way he'd insisted on only email communication when she'd started work—even though he lived only metres away. And his aggravation when she'd turned up at his doorstep in her aborted attempt to resign.

Somehow he'd let her beyond all his barriers—both tangible and otherwise.

Yet she'd been lying to him the whole time.

Hugh was smiling now. He'd woken, caught her staring at him. He captured her hand to tug her towards him, but she didn't move.

Belatedly he seemed to realise she was dressed. His gaze

scanned her jeans and shirt, her hair tied up in a loose, long ponytail.

He sat up abruptly. 'What's going on, April?' he asked.

'Do you want to get dressed?' she asked.

It felt wrong that she was clothed while he was naked.

His eyes narrowed. 'No,' he said.

Where did she begin?

'Can I ask you a question?' she asked.

'What's going on, April?' he said again, this time with steel in his tone.

'I just need to know something. Just one thing and then I promise I'll tell you.' She didn't wait for any acknowledgment from Hugh, certain she wouldn't receive it anyway. 'I just want to know the last time you had a woman sleep over.'

He blinked, and his expression was momentarily raw: she'd hit a nerve. That, in itself, was all the answer she needed. But she could practically see him thinking, determining how he would answer her or if he would answer her at all.

Then—heartbreakingly—she realised he'd decided to be honest.

'Never,' he said. 'I've never wanted a woman to sleep over before.'

Hugh wasn't trying to be unreadable now. He'd clearly made a decision to cut through the pretence that had over-laid their relationship. And why wouldn't he? For Hugh, in-viting her into his home—and therefore into his life—was the point of no return. He probably felt he now no longer had anything to hide.

And yet she'd been hiding all this time.

'Okay,' she said, struggling to force any words out and hating herself more with every passing second.

'Is that what this is about?' he asked. 'About what we're doing?' His mouth curved upwards. 'I know I've talked about rules and no relationships, but you, April…with you, maybe—'

'Stop, Hugh,' she said. She couldn't bear to hear him say anything like that: words that would tell her she was special and words that she wanted so desperately to be true.

She'd been so caught up in her lies that she hadn't allowed herself to think how she'd feel if Hugh actually *wanted* to be with her. If he had feelings for her. Like she had feelings for *him*.

*What feelings?*

She shook her head—at Hugh and at herself. None of this mattered because none of it would be an option once she'd told him the truth.

April took a deep breath. 'Hugh,' she said finally, 'I need to tell you something. Something I should've told you at the beginning but thought it was okay not to, I thought it was okay to keep it secret because we weren't actually *in* a relationship, you know? It was just kissing, or sex, or just dinner, or the museum, or afternoon tea… Which, I suppose, when you say them all together, sounds pretty much like a relationship, right?'

Her smile was humourless. But she needed to say this now, because she knew instinctively she wouldn't get to explain later.

Hugh just watched her. He sat there motionless, tension in his jaw and shoulders, but otherwise perfect and glorious in his nonchalant nakedness—the sheets puddled around his waist, the light from the bedside lamp making his skin glow golden.

He said nothing. Just waited.

She swallowed. 'The name on my passport is April Spencer, but for as long as I can remember I've gone by April Molyneux. I'm the second eldest daughter of Irene Molyneux, and I'm an heiress to the Molyneux Mining fortune.'

Hugh recognised her mother's name—she could see it on his face. Most people did…she was one of the richest people in the world.

'When Evan left me I realised that I've never been truly independent. That I've never been single, never had a real job and that I've never lived off anything but Molyneux money. So I got on a plane with practically nothing and came to London to—'

'To play a patronising, offensive, poor-little-rich-girl game.' He finished the sentence for her.

'Hugh—'

But he ignored her, ticking his words off on his fingers as he spoke. 'Live in a shared house, work on minimum wage and pretend to live in the real world. I get it. Then, once you're tired of living like an actual real person, walk away. Feel fleetingly sorry for all those genuine poor people who don't get that choice as you fly home in your private jet. I'm sure you have one, right?'

'That's not what I'm going to do at all—' she began.

But he wasn't prepared to listen. 'So I was just part of the fantasy? A story to share with all your friends when you got home, along with humorous anecdotes about life in the real world. That was what that selfie was for, right?'

April shook her head vehemently. 'No. I didn't plan any of this,' she said. 'How could I? I never expected to kiss my boss. I certainly never expected this week…then this weekend. Hugh, these past two nights with you—they are like *nothing* I've ever experienced. Please understand that. There was nothing false about that—'

'Except the person I thought you were doesn't exist,' he said.

'Of *course* she does, Hugh. The woman you've been with is *me*, regardless of my surname or my family's money. These past few months I think I've been more me than I ever have in my life. *Especially* with you.'

Now Hugh shook his head. 'I'm *so* pleased I was such a helpful, if unwitting assistant in your journey of self-discovery, April.' His tone was pancake-flat.

He turned from her as he slid out of bed. She watched as he retrieved his boxer shorts and pulled them on, and then his jeans. She probably shouldn't have been watching him, but she couldn't stop herself.

Maybe she'd been secretly desperately hoping that this would somehow all be okay—that he'd brush off the specifics of her past and accept her for the woman she'd been with him.

*Yeah, right.*

Now she knew for certain. Knew that this was it—this was her last few minutes with Hugh…at least like this. He wasn't going to invite her into his room, and more importantly into his life, ever again.

So she looked. She admired the breadth of his back, the curve of his backside, the muscular thighs and calves honed from thousands of cycled kilometres. When he pulled his T-shirt over his head she admired the way his muscles flexed beneath his skin. And then she closed her eyes as if to capture the memory of a naked Hugh she would never see again.

'Who *are* you, April? What do you *actually* do if you're not a backpacking traveller?'

Her gaze dropped to her fingers. They were tangled in the hem of her untucked shirt, twisting the fabric between them. She still sat on his bed, reluctant to move and take that first physical step towards walking away.

'I…ah—' she began, then stopped her repentant tone. *No.* She was *not* going to apologise for who she was—or who she had been. She didn't know which just yet. 'I have a heavy social media presence,' she said.

Hugh rolled his eyes, but she ignored him.

'I use my public persona as a wealthy jet-setting socialite to gather followers—currently I have just a little over one point two million, although that has dipped a little since I've been here.'

She met his gaze steadily.

'I use my platform to attract suppliers and companies that I respect and admire to offer product placement opportunities in exchange for donations to the Molyneux Foundation, which is a charitable organisation that I founded. Last year the foundation made significant contributions to domestic violence and mental health organisations, and while since I've left Perth I've realised that there is far more that I could be doing, I'm still incredibly proud of what I've achieved so far.'

If Hugh was in any way moved by what she'd said he didn't reveal it.

'I'm not some vacuous socialite. At one stage I was—and I own that. And until recently I had no comprehension of the value of a dollar, or pound, or whatever. But I've learnt a lot and I've changed. I'm never going to take my good fortune or my privileged existence for granted ever again.'

Hugh's hands were shoved into the front pockets of his jeans. If she didn't know him she'd think his pose casual, or indifferent. But she did know him, and she knew that he was anything but calm.

'I've been poor, April,' Hugh said, his voice low and harsh. 'After my father left we were on benefits, on and off, for most of my childhood. We were okay...we always had heat and food...but it wasn't easy for my mum. She struggled—you've seen her house. *She struggled.* It wasn't a game.'

'It was never my intention to trivialise another's experiences, Hugh.'

'But you *did*, April. Can't you see that?'

April was getting frustrated now. 'What would you have preferred? That I continued to live off my mother's money for the rest of my life?'

'No,' he said, and his tone was different now. Flat and resigned, as if he'd lost all interest in arguing. 'But I also would've preferred you'd told me your name.'

It was a fair comment, but even so April couldn't bite her tongue. 'But why *would* I? You were offering me absolutely nothing, Hugh. A kiss, sex, but absolutely not a relationship. You may scoff at my so-called journey of self-discovery, but I needed it. Desperately. For *me*. Why would I jeopardise that for a man who couldn't even stomach the idea of officially dating me? I'm so sorry I lied, Hugh, but this wasn't just about you.'

'So I'm just collateral damage?'

April slid off the bed, unable to be still any longer. 'No, of course not, Hugh. You are *so* much more.'

'More?' Hugh prompted. 'What does *that* mean?'

April blinked. She hadn't answered her own question what felt like hours earlier: *What feelings?*

'What would I know, Hugh?' she said honestly. 'I've been with one other man before you and I totally got that one wrong. All I know is that for you to invite me into your home, and for me to be telling you my real name, there *must* be more. More than either of us expected.'

She was standing right in front of him now. If they both reached out their hands would touch. But that wouldn't be happening.

'It doesn't matter,' Hugh said. 'Not now.'

'No,' April said. 'I know.'

For a while they both stood together in silence.

Finally April stepped forward. On tiptoes, she pressed a kiss to Hugh's cheek.

'I'm sorry,' she whispered in his ear, just as he'd murmured so intimately to her on so many other occasions. 'But I promise you I meant what I said. I was more *me* with you than I've ever been. In that way I never lied to you.'

Then she collected her packed overnight bag from a side table and headed for the door.

'Just finish up today,' he said, sounding as if it was an afterthought. 'I'll pay you your two weeks' notice. Donate it to the Molyneux Foundation—I don't care. But I don't want to see you again.'

April nodded, but didn't turn around.

Tears stung her eyes. Pain ravaged her heart.

Oh. *Finally* she recognised those feelings.

What they represented. Only they were different this time. Amplified by something she couldn't define, but distinctly new, distinctly *more* than she'd experienced before.

What she was feeling was love.

# CHAPTER FIFTEEN

*One week later*

HUGH SAT DOWN at his desk and set his first tea of the day carefully onto a coaster.

It was raining, and the people walking along the footpath above him were rushing across the wet pavement.

As always, he checked his to-do list, which he'd prepared the night before.

Except—he hadn't.

The notepad instead listed yesterday's tasks. Mostly they were ticked off, but the remainder had definitely not been transcribed into a new list for today. There was a scrawl in the corner which he'd scribbled down during yesterday's late-afternoon conference call…but it was indecipherable now that he'd forgotten its context.

Also, surely he'd received an email about something he needed to action today? He *always* added such tasks to his list. He liked everything to be in one place.

He opened up his email, searching for that half-forgotten message in his inbox. Unusually, the screen was full of emails—many unread. Time had got away from him yesterday, so he spent a few minutes now, filing and then responding to the emails that had been delivered overnight.

Just as he remembered he was supposed to be looking for the email with information about today's action, a little reminder box popped up in the right-hand corner of his screen: he had a conference call in five minutes.

He had a moment of panic as he wondered what was expected of him at this meeting—he was completely unprepared—but then he remembered. It was a pitch for a totally new app concept—something he would need to approve before it could begin formal analysis, research and requirements-gathering.

So he was fine. He hadn't forgotten to prepare because he hadn't needed to.

He took a long, deep breath.

*What was wrong with him?*

He was all over the place: an impossibility for Hugh Bennell. He was always structured, always organised, always in control.

*Except when he wasn't.*

Hugh dismissed the errant thought. He *was* in control. He was just…temporarily out of sorts. His mother's house was still half full of her hoard, following the termination of April's employment. The weight that had lifted as he'd watched the hoard being dismantled and exiting the house had returned. Oppressive and persistent.

*The termination of April's employment.*

As if that was really what had happened.

Again the little reminder box popped up—this one prompting him to enter the meeting. He clicked the 'Join' button and immediately voices filled the air around him as people greeted each other, punctuated by electronic beeps as each attendee entered the virtual meeting room.

As always, everyone in the meeting appeared in a little window to the right of his screen. Some were talking, some had their eyes on their computers, a few were looking at their phones. Of course there was, as usual, a generic grey silhouette labelled 'Hugh Bennell' in place of the live video feed of himself.

He wasn't chairing this meeting, so he sat back as the group was called to order and the agenda introduced. First up was a staff member he didn't recognise: a junior member of the research and development team.

She was young, looked fresh out of uni, with jet-black hair and stylishly thick-rimmed glasses.

She was also nervous.

She was attempting to be confident, but a nervous quiver

underscored her words. She was sharing her screen with the group, showcasing mock-ups and statistics along with competitors' offerings that didn't cover the opportunity she suggested *they* could capture. But she was still visible in a smaller window, deliberately glancing to her camera as she spoke, as if she was attempting to make eye contact with the group.

Or with the *rest* of the group. She couldn't meet Hugh's gaze, because black electrical tape still covered his camera lens. But of course *he* was the one she was presenting to. He was the one who had the power to approve or reject her idea. He'd listen to the other heads of department to gather their thoughts, but ultimately it was up to him.

The woman presenting knew that, too.

And she was presenting to a faceless grey blob.

He reached forward and peeled the tape off the camera. A moment later he clicked the little video camera icon that would connect his camera feed to the rest of the meeting.

A second later, the presenter stopped talking.

She was just looking at him, jaw agape.

The rest of the group seemed equally flummoxed.

Hugh shrugged, then smiled. 'I'm nodding as you speak,' he said, 'because you're doing a good job. I thought it would help if you could see that.'

'Yes,' she said, immediately. 'It definitely does. Thank you.'

Then she started talking again, her voice noticeably stronger and more confident.

Later, once he'd approved the new app concept and wrangled his email inbox and to-do list back into order, he headed into the kitchen for another cup of tea.

*Why, after so many years, had he turned on his camera?*

Why today? And—more importantly—why was he okay about it? It should have felt significant. Or scary, even. After all, he'd been hiding behind that tape for so very long.

Instead it just felt like exactly the right thing to do.

He had nothing to hide. He wasn't about to invite all his

staff over to his place for Friday night drinks or anything—
ever—but still…

Revealing himself to his team, even in this small way, had
to be a good thing. Revealing himself *and* his house.

It felt good, actually. Great, really. As if part of that weight
on his shoulders had lifted.

Because nothing had happened. Nothing bad, anyway.
Something good, definitely. The vibe of the meeting had
shifted with his appearance—there'd been more questions
and more discussion. It had felt collaborative, not directive
as he'd so often felt in his role.

The risk had been worth it.

Unlike other risks he'd taken recently.

The kettle whistled as it boiled and he left his teabag to
brew while he headed for the spare room, so he could cross
off that forgotten emailed task he'd eventually added to his
to-do list. It hadn't even been work-related in the end—it had
just been a reminder to check if he still had the original pedals
from his mountain bike, as one of the guys from his cycling
group needed some.

However, it wasn't the container of bike parts his gaze was
drawn to when he opened the cupboard door, but the simple
cardboard box that sat, forgotten, on the floor.

The original 'Hugh' box. Complete with two faded photos of him with his mother, a crumpled birthday card, an old
film canister and that awful finger-painted bookmark he'd
made in nursery.

He picked up the bookmark and turned it over and over
aimlessly with his fingers. It was just a bookmark. It wasn't
anything special. He didn't remember his mother using it,
but she would have—just as she'd used or displayed all of his
primitive artwork and sculptures when he was growing up.

The bookmark didn't stand out as special, or different. Or
worth keeping, really.

But April had asked the question anyway. Despite his
clear directions, despite his prickliness and impatience when
it came to the hoard he'd so long refused to deal with. And by

asking the question April had confronted him with the hoard. She'd forced him to engage and to make decisions.

She'd sensed that he needed to. That if he sat by passively as the hoard disappeared he would be left with a lifetime of regret.

And she'd been right.

He wouldn't keep everything. He might not even keep the bookmark. But he realised now that he needed to make choices. That he needed to pay attention to his mother's treasures and identify his own.

Because there *were* some there. Reminders and mementos of the mother he'd loved with all his heart. And without April they would have been gone for ever.

He bent down and picked up the box. He carried it back into the kitchen, placing it on the benchtop as he fished the teabag out of his mug. He sat on one of the bar stools, staring at the box, thinking as he drank.

He'd spent the week angry because the one woman he'd ever let into his life didn't actually exist. April Spencer had been a fraud, and no more than a facade for a spoiled, rich, selfish woman who enjoyed playing games with people's lives.

But that wasn't true. That wasn't even close to true.

Yes, she'd lied. And it still hurt that the one woman he'd ever trusted could have treated him that way.

But—as she'd asked him—what other choice had she had?

He'd been up-front with all his rules and regulations, and with his immovable view on relationships. And, given he'd spent so much of his life building up barriers between himself and the world, was it fair to be surprised that April hadn't immediately torn down her own?

He recognised what she was doing with her April Spencer persona now: she was being an authentic, independent version of herself, without the context of her wealth or her family which he realised must colour every interaction in her life.

They weren't so different, really. They were both hiding a version of themselves.

April had been hiding the *old* version of herself—the

moneyed, privileged socialite, out of touch with reality. Yet he'd met the *real* April: the woman who'd challenged him, who'd made him laugh, and who had made him want to get out of his house and into the real world just so he could share it with her.

The woman who'd cared enough about a still grieving, complicated stranger to save a child's bookmark when it would have been so much easier to throw it away.

Yes, she'd hidden her old self—but she couldn't have been more honest when it counted.

*He*, however, had been hiding for a lot longer than April. Hiding in his house, in seclusion, behind self-imposed rules and regulations and the piece of tape obscuring his camera.

He'd been hiding his true self until April came along.

He realised now—too late—that everything important in their relationship remained unchanged despite April's disclosure. April Molyneux or April Spencer—she was still the same woman.

The woman he loved.

He picked up his phone.

The interview had felt as if it would never end.

April sat at a narrow table that looked out over the Heathrow runway, her boots hooked into the footrest of the tall stool she sat upon.

Her impatience wasn't the interviewer's fault, however.

'Thank you,' April said, briskly. 'I look forward to reading it.'

'It' being the glossy magazine that was included in Perth's Saturday newspaper. This was a great opportunity for the Molyneux Foundation—she needed to remember that.

The interviewer thanked her again, and then finally hung up.

Phone still in hand, April rubbed her temples. She felt about a hundred years old—as if this week, like the interview, would never, ever end.

But of course it would. No matter how hard each day was,

inevitably it eventually faded into night and a new day would begin. She'd learnt that when Evan had left her.

She'd learnt it again now that…

She closed her eyes. God, how could she possibly compare *one week* with Hugh to fifteen years with Evan? It shouldn't be possible.

And yet she hurt. Badly.

On that awful Monday she'd been a zombie as she'd finished up as well as she could upstairs, sorting through half-finished boxes, leaving detailed hand-over notes for whoever Hugh hired next.

She hadn't cried then. She'd thought maybe she shouldn't. After all, it had only been a week. Surely it wasn't appropriate to cry after such a short period of time?

April had no idea if there were rules about such things.

But in the end, she *had* cried. Silently, curled up in her single bed under her cheap doona, horrified at the prospect that her roommate would hear her.

Crying hadn't really helped, but she was still glad she had.

The next day—before she'd told her sisters what had happened—she'd gone for a walk. She'd walked to the supermarket where she'd stacked shelves even that very night before and resigned.

Then, outside the shopfront, with the large red-and-blue supermarket logo in the frame, she'd taken a selfie.

And uploaded it to Instagram.

I have so much to tell you! #london #newjob #newhair #new-beginnings

And so she'd taken control of her account, sharing with her million-odd followers over the next forty-eight hours what she'd *really* been doing these past few months.

She'd caught the Tube to take a photo of the glitzy apartment she'd originally rented, she'd printed out all her polite 'we regret to inform you that you weren't our preferred candidate' emails and asked a random person on the street to take her photo as she waved them in the air. She'd shared the balance of her embarrassing credit card debt, and then she'd taken a photo of her scratchy, terrible bedlinen, and shared a recipe for a tomato soup and pasta 'meal' that had helped her spend as little as possible on food.

She'd shared how it had felt to be rejected for so many jobs—how it had felt not to have the red carpet laid out for her as it had been so often in her life. She'd shared her shame at her lack of understanding in her privileged life, and the satisfaction she had felt from earning her very first pay-cheque.

She'd posted about being lonely—being *alone*—for the first time in her life. About learning how to clean a shower, and discovering muscles she'd thought she never had as she'd stacked supermarket shelves.

And she had apologised for not telling her followers any of this earlier, and written that she hoped they would understand. She had told them that she had needed to do this—had needed to be April without the power of her surname carrying her through her life. That she had needed to do it on her own.

What she hadn't shared was Hugh.

She placed her phone back on the table, belatedly noticing a missed call notification.

*Hugh had called her.*

The realisation hit her like a lightning bolt.

But why?

He must have called during her hour-long phone interview, but he hadn't left a message.

Should she call him?

She twisted in her seat to check the flight information screen.

There was no time. Her flight was boarding soon—she needed to head for the gate.

As she strode through the terminal she wondered why he would have called. It had been a week since she'd last seen him, and they'd spoken not a word. Why would they? Hugh couldn't have made it any clearer: *I don't want to see you again.*

So why call?

A silly little hopeful part of her imagined he'd changed his mind, but she immediately erased that suggestion.

Hadn't she learnt anything? She'd already worked it out that first night, as she'd wrapped herself in her doona, that it was just like with Evan. Hugh simply hadn't loved or even *wanted* her enough to see beyond her past and her good fortune in being born into one of the wealthiest families in the world. To see who she actually was—the woman she had been with *him*.

She arrived at the gate.

Boarding hadn't yet started, and other passengers filled nearly all the available seats. With surely only a few minutes before boarding, April didn't bother searching for a seat. Instead she opened up Instagram, intending to respond to some of her latest comments. This past week her followers' 'likes' and comments had exploded. It would seem that her riches-to-rags experience had struck a chord. Of course now she needed to harness that engagement and monetise it for the foundation. Hence the interview and—

'April,' said a low, delicious voice behind her.

She spun round, unable to believe her eyes.

'What are you doing here?' April asked Hugh.

He shrugged. 'I needed to talk to you. When you didn't answer your phone I came here. Thanks to that selfie you posted I knew where to find you. Had to buy a ticket I won't use, though, to get to the gate—which was annoying.'

'*You* follow my feed?'

He shook his head. 'No. Not my thing. But it came in useful today.'

April needed a moment to wrap her head around his unexpected appearance. She used that moment simply to look at Hugh. At his still too long dark hair, his at least two-day-old stubble, his hoodie, jeans and sneakers.

He looked as he had nearly every time April had ever seen him.

He also looked utterly gorgeous.

*She'd missed him.*

'What are you doing here, Hugh?' she asked again, wariness in her tone.

'I'm here,' he said, capturing her gaze, 'to apologise for my behaviour.'

April took a deep breath, attempting to process what he was saying.

Over the PA system, a call was made for all business class passengers to board.

'Is that you?' Hugh asked. 'Because I'll get on that plane if I need to. I can't let you leave like this.'

April shook her head. 'No,' she said. 'I can only afford economy seats on my new income. I've got a few minutes.'

'New income?' he prompted.

'Yes,' she said dismissively. 'I'm Chief Executive Officer of the Molyneux Foundation. It's about time I took it seriously, I figure. Fortunately the board agreed.' She paused. These details didn't matter right now. 'Hugh, what exactly are you apologising for?'

'For overreacting,' he said. 'You may not have told me your name from the start, but now I know you were always the real April with me. I guess—'

His gaze broke away from hers and drifted towards the pale, glossy floor.

'I was upset, of course. I trusted you, and that was a big deal for me. When you told me your real name I felt like that trust was shattered. As if you'd been laughing at me the whole time—as if it had been a game.'

'None of this was ever a game for me,' she said quietly.

Hugh was looking at her again now, searching her face. His lips curved upwards. 'I know,' he said. 'I was the one with the rules—not you.'

He was holding his phone in one hand, and he absently traced its edges with his thumb as he spoke.

'I think maybe,' he said, 'I was looking for a reason to justify my lifelong stance on relationships. I've always hated the idea of being trapped within one, of being controlled by one. My mother's hoarding began after my father left her, and I watched her search for love over and over. But she chose the wrong men and they left. That's when she started keeping everything—surrounding herself with things while she was unable to keep the one thing she desperately wanted. Love.'

He swallowed.

'I didn't want to be like her…to *feel* like her. All that pain… all that disappointment. It was all clutter to me, making life more difficult and more complicated. Without love I was in control of my life. And if I walked away from you then I'd be back in control. I would've been right all along.'

Around them people were beginning to line up for the gate, responding to a call that April hadn't heard, with her focus entirely on the man before her.

'But of course,' Hugh said, 'it turns out I was wrong.'

Finally April smiled. Until now she hadn't dared to believe where this was heading.

'This week I *haven't* been in control. I've been a right mess, actually. Life hasn't gone back to normal—or if it has it isn't a "normal" that's enough for me any more. Not even close. Not without you.'

April closed her eyes.

'April, I want to share my life with you.'

Her eyes popped open and for a minute they stood in silence. Around them the terminal bustled. A small child dragging a bright yellow suitcase bumped into Hugh as he hurried past, sending Hugh a furtive glance in apology.

Very late, April realised they were surrounded by a jostling crowd of people.

'Are you okay Hugh?' she asked, suddenly concerned. 'With all these people?'

'Seriously…?' he said. 'I can deal with any crowd when I'm with you.'

But April saw the way he gritted his teeth as the passengers swarmed around them.

'Nice try, Hugh,' she said, grabbing his hand. 'Very romantic. But we're in the way, anyway.'

She tugged him several metres away, so they stood before the floor-to-ceiling windows that looked out onto the runway. The plane that would take April home to Perth sat waiting patiently.

'April?' he said.

She readjusted her handbag on her shoulder, trying to work out what to say. Joy was bubbling up inside her now, and she was desperate to launch herself into Hugh's arms. But instead she dropped his hand.

'April?' he prompted again, raw emotion in his eyes.

'I want to share my life with you, too, Hugh,' she said. A beat passed. 'I think.'

'You *think*?'

April nodded. 'In fact,' she said, 'I'm pretty sure I'm falling in love with you. But the thing is how can I be sure? We were together little more than a week.'

'*I'm* sure,' he said, with no hesitation.

*He loves me*, April realised—and that realisation almost derailed her resolve.

He meant it too. It was obvious in the way he was looking at her—as if right now nobody else in the world existed.

It was an intoxicating sensation.

'I'm not,' she said firmly. 'And I want *so* badly to believe that you are, but I won't allow myself to. Not yet.'

She registered, absently, the final call for her flight.

'I was with one man for fifteen years, Hugh. I loved him and I thought he loved me. But I was wrong. Love is… complicated for me right now. I really don't know what I'm doing, and I definitely don't trust my judgement. I think I need time to work that out—to be just April for a while, and make sure that I'm not leaping from one relationship to another simply because being in a relationship is what I'm familiar with.'

To Hugh's credit, he seemed to take no offence at that.

'So you just need time?' he said. His gaze was determined.

Ah, April realised. He was confident—not offended.

She smiled.

'Yes,' she said. She searched her brain for a time frame—for a number that felt right to her. 'Six months.'

He nodded immediately, and April would have loved him a little more just for that—if she'd been allowing love to enter the equation, of course.

'Okay. I can work with that. Gives me enough time to sort out the house and work out any logistical issues.'

April's eyes widened. 'Logistical issues?'

He grinned. 'So I'm ready to move, should you decide you still want me. You know I like to be prepared.'

'You do,' she said, and she was smiling now.

'Are there any rules and regulations?' he asked, teasing her, but he was serious too.

God, there was so much of Hugh in that moment—his rigidity and sense of fun intersecting.

'Of course,' April said. 'Loads. I'll work them out and email them to you.'

She knew he'd like that.

'A question,' he said, as they both heard April's name being called over the PA and both flatly ignored it. 'Are there rules about kissing?'

'Most definitely,' April said, 'but they don't start until I get on that plane.'

And just like that he was kissing her. Her arms were tight behind his neck...his arms were an iron band around her body. It was a kiss that told of their week apart, of mistakes and regrets and hope and...

Hugh broke their mouths apart to trail tiny kisses along her jaw to her ear.

'I *know* I love you, April,' he said, his words hot and husky and heartfelt.

*I love you too*, April thought. But she wasn't even close to ready to say the words.

Instead she kissed him again.

Then, when she heard her name being called one last time, she said goodbye.

# EPILOGUE

*One year later*

APRIL'S BARE TOES mingled with the coarse beach sand, and she felt the January sun hot against her skin.

Before her stood her sister Mila and her partner, Seb. Mila's *husband*, Seb, actually—as of about thirty seconds ago. Her sister wore a bright red dress and the most beautiful smile as she stared up at the man April knew Mila had loved for most of her life.

The sun just touched the edge of the blue horizon as the small group watched the celebrant say a final few words. The beach was otherwise deserted—the small, isolated cove surrounded by towering limestone cliffs, and with oversized granite rocks interrupting the white-tipped waves.

It was a tiny wedding: just Mila and Seb; Seb's parents; Irene Molyneux; Ivy and her husband, Angus; and their son, Nate.

And April and Hugh.

Hugh wrapped his arm around April and kissed her temple. She could feel his lips curve into a smile against her skin.

The ceremony over, the group headed for picnic blankets laden with hors d'oeuvres and bottles of champagne. Candlelit lanterns dotted the space, waiting for dusk and the opportunity to flicker in the dark.

April hung back and looked up at Hugh as the sun continued to descend beyond them.

The last beach wedding she'd attended had been her own— to Evan. It had been in Bali, with hundreds of guests—so very different from the wedding they were attending today.

But still today had triggered memories.

Not of Evan, but of how she'd felt that day. Her joy and anticipation at marrying Evan. And her love for him.

She *had* loved her ex-husband. On that day on that beach in Nusa Dua she had thought it impossible to love anybody more.

But she'd been wrong.

And on that night in London a year ago, at Heathrow Airport, she'd found it impossible to trust her judgement when it came to love. After months of berating herself for not realising that her husband hadn't loved her, love had seemed to her like a complex, complicated and impossible concept. A concept she hadn't yet been equipped to handle.

And she'd been right. She had needed those six months. To heal after the end of her marriage. To establish herself in her new role at the Molyneux Foundation. And to live independently of both any man and of her fortune.

She'd also needed the time to work through what she'd learnt while she'd lived in London about her life of excessive privilege and her ignorance of the reality of the world—despite all the charity events her socialite self had attended.

Really, it had taken those six months to love *herself* again. To be proud of what she'd achieved and continued to achieve at the Molyneux Foundation. To let go of the shame of her years of excess.

And to forgive herself for loving a man for fifteen years when he hadn't loved her the same way.

Because she'd realised that love existed even if it wasn't returned. Her love for Evan had been valid, regardless of his feelings. And that love would remain important and special—a love she couldn't regret.

She'd also realised that love grown over a week could be even more powerful than love cultivated over half a lifetime. And that she *could* trust in that love. That she could believe in it and that it could be real and true.

Her rules and regulations for Hugh regarding those six months had been simple: there was to be no contact.

None at all.

It had been hard, and it had felt impossible, but it had been necessary.

Her week-old love for Hugh had been just as strong—

stronger, actually—after all that time, when she'd woken on the morning of her six-month deadline to an email from Hugh.

He was in Perth, and he would be having all-day breakfast at a café on Cottesloe Beach at lunchtime that day. He would love her to join him. If not he would continue his Australian holiday alone, and wish her well.

And so she'd taken herself and her love for Hugh to breakfast.

And his love had been waiting for her. No pressure, no expectations.

'I love you,' April said now, on this beach, as the setting sun painted the sky in reds and purples.

'I love you too,' Hugh said, and kissed her again.

When they broke apart his gaze darted to the rapidly setting sun.

'You'd better hurry with that photo,' he pointed out. 'The light is about to go.'

April grinned. Hugh might not participate in any of her photos, but she now had his full support and understanding of the business of social media.

Today she wore black South Sea pearl drop earrings, and a generous donation from the company that made them was awaiting after a suitably glamorous photo.

She fished her phone out of her clutch and handed it to Hugh. A sea-breeze made the silk of her dress cling to her belly and her legs, and she fiddled with the fabric as she planned her pose. She needed to be careful—

But then Hugh was standing beside her again, holding the phone aloft to take a selfie of them both.

'Hugh...?' she asked, confused.

He grinned. 'I figure a close-up might be easier. That wind doesn't seem to realise you've got a bump to hide.'

Only for a few more weeks. And at the moment her followers were more likely to think her a bit plumper than usual, not pregnant, but even so...

'But with you?'

Another smile. 'It's about time I become more than the

"mysterious new boyfriend" people are talking about, don't you think?'

'Are you sure?'

He nodded. 'I've got nothing to hide, April. Not since I've met you.'

And so, as the sun made the ocean glitter and the breeze cooled their summer-warm skin, Hugh took the photo. A photo of the two of them on a beach—and of the earrings, of course—but mostly of their love. For each other and for the baby they'd created together.

It was a love that April knew was more real than any love she'd ever experienced. A love for the man she loved more than she'd thought possible, and a love for her that had taught her she would always be enough—and more—for the man she loved.

Later, after the sun had set and they were sitting together on the beach in the candlelight, April posted the photo to her followers.

There's someone I'd like to meet... #love #romance #happilyeverafter

\* \* \* \* \*

*If you really enjoyed this story, check out*
*THE BILLIONAIRE FROM HER PAST*
*by Leah Ashton. Available now!*

*If you're looking forward to another romance*
*featuring a billionaire hero then you'll love*
*THEIR BABY SURPRISE by Katrina Cudmore.*

# MEET THE FORTUNES

**Fortune of the Month:** Jayden Fortune

**Age:** 36

**Vital Statistics:** Tall, sexy cowboy. Former military with a penchant for adventure and pretty girls.

**Claim to Fame:** He is one of three equally gorgeous triplets. Oh, and he may be the son of a billionaire.

**Romantic Prospects:** Jayden has never had a problem attracting the female of the species. If anything, he's had trouble fighting them off.

"I traveled all over the world with the army, and I used to think I'd never come back to quiet old Paseo. But I'm older now—hopefully a little wiser, too—and there's something to be said for 'home, sweet home.'

Not a lot happens in Paseo, usually. Who'd believe that a stunning city girl would get stuck here on the road to nowhere—and that we'd wind up trapped in a storm cellar together with no lights, no phone service and plenty of sparks? Ariana got under my skin right from the start. We're different, all right, but I feel like she's perfect for me. Or maybe a little *too* perfect? Just what is it that Ariana is hiding?"

\* \* \*

**The Fortunes Of Texas:**
The Secret Fortunes—
A new generation of heroes and heartbreakers!

# WILD WEST
# FORTUNE

## BY
## ALLISON LEIGH

MILLS
BOON

First Published in Great Britain 2017
By Mills & Boon, an imprint of HarperCollins*Publishers*
1 London Bridge Street, London, SE1 9GF

© 2017 Harlequin Books S.A.

Special thanks and acknowledgement to Allison Leigh for her contribution to The Fortunes of Texas: The Secret Fortunes continuity.

ISBN: 978-0-263-92303-2

23-0617

Though she's a frequent name on bestseller lists, **Allison Leigh**'s high point as a writer is hearing from readers that they laughed, cried or lost sleep while reading her books. She credits her family with great patience for the time she's parked at her computer, and for blessing her with the kind of love she wants her readers to share with the characters living in the pages of her books. Contact her at www.allisonleigh.com.

For Susan and Marcia.
Nobody keeps our Fortune world
together better than the two of you!

## Chapter One

"Girl, this is not good."

Ariana Lamonte made a face as she looked out the windows of her car. She hadn't seen another vehicle for more than an hour. Grassland whipped in the wind all the way to the horizon in every direction. The same wind rocked her little car where she was parked on the dirt shoulder, and sent the thick clouds overhead racing across the sky. "Not good at all," she repeated to herself.

She fished her cell phone up from the passenger side floor by the charging cord tethering it to her dashboard. Using the GPS on the phone always drained the battery quickly, so she'd at least been prepared on that score when she'd set out from Austin that morning. But she sure wished she'd been better prepared with the address she was seeking. There was a dot blinking on her phone screen, right atop a barely discernible line that indicated the laughable excuse for a road on which she sat.

But that was it. No town. No other roads.

Nothing. Nada.

For the third time, she checked her notes and verified the address she'd put into her GPS app. Everything matched.

Which meant she ought to be sitting in the middle of a place called Paseo, Texas.

Instead, she was sitting in the middle of…

"Grass," she muttered, looking out the windows again. "Nothing but grass and more grass." And she'd wasted nearly an entire day getting there.

The wind howled and her car rocked again. She studied her phone for a moment. The GPS dot blinked back at her, but there wasn't a strong enough cell signal to even make a phone call or send a text message. Not that she particularly wanted to advertise to anyone that she wasn't really home in her apartment where she was supposed to be working on an assignment for the magazine.

Instead, she'd set out on yet another wild goose chasing down facts for the real life story behind Robinson Tech's founder, Gerald Robinson. The real life story that would prove once and for all that Ariana Lamonte wasn't just an internet blogger who'd more or less stumbled into print journalism. That she deserved her own spot on the map.

Preferably a better map than the one her GPS was currently providing.

She dropped the useless phone on the passenger seat and opened the thick pink notebook on the console, clicking her pen a few times before sighing and drawing a line through the address as she thought about Gerald Robinson.

For one thing, he was a tech industry giant. A household name well beyond the city limits of Austin, Texas, where Robinson Tech was based and where Austinites tended to follow his family like the Brits followed the Royals.

On the surface, the billionaire had everything. Money. Power. Success. He was the father of eight children thanks to his long-standing marriage to a woman who didn't seem outraged at all over the fairly recent revelation that he'd also fathered more than a few illegitimate children during that marriage.

But what made the situation particularly interesting to Ariana was that Charlotte Prendergast Robinson had also been resolutely closemouthed since the truth came out a year ago that the very *identity* of the man she'd married was a fiction. Gerald Robinson was a creation of Jerome Fortune. A black-sheep relative of an immensely wealthy, immensely powerful family who'd all believed Jerome to be dead.

Half the world had collectively gasped when that came out.

But not Charlotte. It was as if there was nothing on earth capable of shocking or surprising Gerald's wife.

Though that wasn't exactly accurate, either. If it weren't for Charlotte, Ariana wouldn't be trying to find Paseo.

She flipped a page in her notes, chewing the inside of her cheek as she studied Charlotte's photograph. Presumably, she enjoyed the perks of her position so much that she'd rather stand by her husband's side than publicly express even the slightest hint of outrage and possibly hinder those perks.

But would they really be hindered?

Charlotte was clearly the injured party in the Robinson marriage. Ariana had found no record of the couple ever having a prenuptial agreement. Their marriage predated Robinson Tech's astronomical success. Success that hadn't been hurt in the least by Gerald's scandals. If anything, the company was stronger than ever. If Charlotte chose to walk away from a philandering husband, she'd be walking away with at least half of their fortune. The luxurious lifestyle to which she was accustomed wouldn't be changed in the least.

And it wasn't as if the children she and Gerald had together would necessarily be affected. They were all accomplished adults in their own rights. Ariana had profiled many of them, as well as some of Gerald's illegitimate offspring, in her series, "Becoming a Fortune," for *Weird Life Magazine*.

As she'd gotten to know them, she'd formed the opinion that Charlotte was hardly the most loving mother in the world. The woman seemed more involved with her charity work than she was in their lives—even when they had been much younger. Admittedly, none of them had derogatory things to say about their mother. They were too classy for that. But Ariana still sensed there *was* some curiosity regarding their mother's steadfast loyalty to their father.

And Ariana was pretty curious, too. Particularly after she'd managed to get a moment alone with the excessively private woman at one of Charlotte's recent fund-raisers. All Ariana had asked her for was a little clarification about a newspaper article she'd found at the Austin History Center. Not once had Ariana seen the woman look even remotely rattled until she'd grabbed Ariana's arm, escorting her personally from the function with the warning that she was not going to treat kindly anyone digging up useless old dirt about Paseo.

So far, Charlotte had said, she'd tolerated Ariana's vacuous magazine series, but it would be an easy matter for her to have a "little talk" with the local magazine about the harassment her family was receiving at the hands of Ariana. After all, she and the publisher sat on a few boards together.

Ariana could have argued the harassment point, but

she'd chosen to leave instead. The tacit threat about her job would have been more worrisome if not for the fact that she had bigger fish to fry than the magazine where she worked. Now she had a book deal. The kind of deal where Ariana could really make her mark as a biographer.

But she hadn't left empty-handed. Because not once had Ariana ever mentioned Paseo in any of her pieces. She hadn't even heard of the name before. It hadn't been in the article Ariana had uncovered. That had simply been a decades-old society feature about Charlotte and Gerald's wedding.

And Ariana wasn't even certain now that Mrs. Robinson had meant the *town* of Paseo. It could just as easily be a person's name. Maybe the name of a company...

Ariana looked out the window again. Not that the town seemed to exist outside of a map.

Which meant she'd have to go back to the drawing board where Gerald's life was concerned. She wanted to tell the story that no one else had already told.

Yes, Gerald had been born as Jerome Fortune. Yes, he'd cut his ties with his real family so decisively that he'd even faked his own death. Then he'd effectively disappeared from all existence until one day springing forth as Gerald Robinson. And soon after, he'd made Charlotte Prendergast his bride.

It ought to have been a grand love story. Gerald and Charlotte went on to have eight children together, for heaven's sake. There'd been countless articles and news stories about them. Yet now it came out that Gerald had consistently strayed. Even during the earliest years of their marriage, he'd been off Johnny-Appleseeding with other women.

Was it simply a character flaw? He wasn't the first brilliant, powerful man to have a weakness for women. Or was there something deeper? Another secret that motived him?

What had really happened between Jerome's "demise" and Gerald's explosive success in the tech field?

That was a big black hole into which her book would shine a good, long light.

And that was why she was sitting on the side of the road in the middle of Grassland, USA.

She rubbed her face and wished she hadn't finished her Starbucks coffee two hours earlier. It would take her hours to get back to Austin. She'd do better to just keep plowing onward. She knew she had to be close to the state line by now, which would put Oklahoma City much closer.

A decent hotel bed. A lot of fresh coffee. Then she could hop on the interstate and drive back to Austin in the morning. It would still take five or six hours, but at least she'd be driving faster than the snail's pace she'd had to use during today's wasted trek. She'd be home in plenty of time to finish up her article about the grand opening of Austin Commons, Austin's newest multiuse complex scheduled for the end of the month. She wouldn't even have been assigned the story if the project's architect hadn't been Keaton Whitfield. He'd been one of her first "Becoming a Fortune" subjects.

She sighed and tossed aside her notes, peering through the windshield again. The clouds were angrily black, and lightning flashed in the distance.

A sharp crack on the side window made her jump so hard she banged her elbow on the steering wheel.

The sight of a man standing on the road right next to her car, though, made her nearly scream.

She reared away from the window, slamming her foot on the brake and jabbing the push-button start.

"Whoa, whoa, whoa," the man yelled through the window. From the corner of her eye she saw him tip back his black cowboy hat. "Don't run me over, honey! Just checking that you're all right."

Hesitating was stupid. Every single thing she'd ever read or written about a woman's personal safety told her that. Her heart was lodged somewhere up in her ears, pounding so loudly she felt nauseated.

The wind ripped, yanking the hat off the man's head, and she heard him curse before he jogged after it.

She could have driven off right then, but the sight of him chasing after his hat, reaching down more than once trying to scoop it up as it rolled and bounced along the road, kept her in place.

That, and the sight in her rearview mirror of a shaggy brown-and-black dog hanging its head out the window of the dusty pickup truck parked behind her.

Did ax murderers tie bandanna kerchiefs around their dogs' necks?

"Get a grip, girl." She put the car in gear but kept her foot on the brake. The guy finally caught his cowboy hat and jammed it back on his head as he strode back toward her car.

This time, when he leaned down to look in her window, he kept his hand clamped on top of his hat, holding it in place. "Got a bad storm coming, ma'am. I can give you directions if you're lost."

"I'm not lost."

He squinted his clear brown eyes at her, clearly skeptical.

Her heart was back in her chest again, pounding harder than usual, but at least in the right sector of her body. She need only hit the gas to drive off.

And she'd already wasted a whole day…

She surreptitiously double-checked that her doors were locked and squinted back at him. If he was an ax murderer, he was a fine-looking one. And what his rear end did for his plain old blue jeans was a work of art. He wouldn't have any difficulty getting a woman to follow him most anywhere.

Not her, of course. She was too smart to get bowled over by a stranger just because he happened to be—as her mama would have said—a handsome cuss. If he was an ax murderer, he was going to have to work a little harder than that.

She reined in her stampeding imagination and wondered if she should give writing fiction a try, since she was so far doing such a bang-up job on the biography.

Despite common sense and caution, she rolled down her window. Her hair immediately blew around her face. She grabbed her phone and held it out for the stranger to see the map displayed on the screen. "I'm looking for a town called Paseo. Paseo, Texas," she elaborated just in case she *had* crossed into Oklahoma without knowing it.

He ducked his head when another dirty gust blew across them. "What kinda business you got there?"

She squinted at him. "Well, that's *my* business, isn't it?"

He yanked off his hat, evidently tired of trying to keep it in place. The wind chopped through his brown hair and pulled at the collar of his gray-and-white plaid shirt, revealing more of his suntanned throat. "Gonna be my business if I have to haul your toy car here out of a ditch when this storm gets worse." He thumped the top of her car with his hand. "You want Paseo, you almost found it. Up the road a ways, you gotta cross a small bridge and then you'll see the sign. But you'd better get your pretty self going before those clouds open up. This isn't a road you want to be on in a storm."

"So you live around here?"

"Yes, ma'am." He stuck out his hand toward her. "Jayden Fortune."

The phone slipped out of her fingers.

He caught it. "Whoa, there. Looks too expensive to be tossing around on the highway." He held it toward her.

"Not much of a highway," she managed as her mind spun with excitement. Could it be so easy? *Fortune?* "There are more dirt ruts than pavement."

The corner of his mouth curled upward. "Well, we're not exactly looking for strangers around here. Which—" he ducked his head against a gust of wind accompanied by a crash of thunder "—pleasant as this may be, *is* what you are."

She was blinking hard from the dust blowing into her eyes. "My name is Ariana Lamonte. From Austin. I'm working on a magazine article." It was true. Just not the whole truth.

"A magazine article about Paseo?" He snorted, looking genuinely amused. "Don't want to disappoint you, ma'am, but there isn't a damn thing interesting enough around these parts to merit something like that."

"I don't know about that. Considering a Fortune lives here." She yanked her hair out of her eyes, holding it behind her head so she could see him better. If this man was one of Gerald's illegitimate offspring, then he'd be the first one she'd encountered who already *knew* he was a Fortune. Or maybe he wasn't even illegitimate. She'd already entertained the idea that Gerald could have had a family before his Robinson one. There were certainly enough missing years in his life to allow for one. And it would definitely account for Charlotte's antagonism toward Ariana bringing up the past.

Could there have been another wife? Maybe one whom Gerald had never even bothered to divorce before he'd married Charlotte Prendergast?

The wheels in her head spun fresh again as she gave Jayden a closer look.

"The name Fortune doesn't mean I possess one," he was saying. His smile was very white, very even, except for one slightly crooked cuspid that saved him from looking a little too perfect. Maybe there was a resemblance to Gerald Robinson. Or maybe that was just hopeful thinking on her part.

He rested his arm on top of her car and angled his head, his gaze roving over her and the interior of her car. He glanced over the empty coffee cups and discarded fast-food wrappers lying untidily on the floor as well as the thick notebook laden with news clippings and photographs spread open on her passenger seat.

"Only thing I'm rich in is land, and land round here isn't all that valuable, either. So what's interesting enough about Paseo to bring a reporter like you all the way from the big city?"

Her car rocked again and several fat raindrops splattered on her windshield. "I'm not a reporter for the local news or anything. I'm a journalist."

"There's a difference?"

"If I was a news reporter, I'd probably have a better salary," she admitted ruefully. She casually closed the notebook as she reached behind her seat and grabbed the latest edition of *Weird Life Magazine* and passed it through the window. A photograph of Ben Fortune Robinson—Gerald's eldest son, who was the Chief Operating Officer of Robinson Tech—was on the cover. "I'm not just writing an article. I'm working on an entire series about the members of the Fortune family, actually, for *Weird Life Magazine*. You have heard of Gerald Robinson, right? Robinson Tech? His real name used to be Jerome Fortune." She watched

Jayden's face. But the only expression her admission earned was more humor.

"Then you're really gonna be disappointed," he drawled, barely giving the magazine a glance before giving it back to her. "I'm not related. My last name might be Fortune, but only because my mom made it up."

The sky suddenly opened up in earnest and he shoved his hat back on his head. "Storms around here're pretty unpredictable, ma'am. Last year we had hail that damaged the town hall so badly it looked like a bomb had hit it. Might be best if you come with me."

She rolled up the window, stopping shy a few inches, but rain still blew in. Just because he had the last name Fortune—which she wasn't ready to attribute to coincidence no matter what he said—didn't mean she planned to get into his truck. The weather hadn't worried her before, but the rain was coming down so hard now, she could barely see out the windshield. "I'll follow you."

He was already drenched, rain sheeting off the brim of his hat. He looked like he was going to argue, but then just tilted his head. "Suit yourself."

She closed the window the rest of the way and switched on her windshield wipers, watching through her rearview mirror as he yanked open his truck door. Even the bandanna-wearing dog had ducked back inside the cab of the truck.

The car rocked again, whether from the vibration of another violent thunderclap or the wind, she couldn't tell. "Not good, Ariana," she muttered. "Not good at all."

The truck passed her, and even through the curtain of rain between them, she could see Jayden Fortune looking at her.

A shiver danced down her spine.

Okay. So not *all* not good.

She gave him a thumbs-up sign and steered back onto the road to follow him.

Less than a mile had passed before she was starting to wish she'd taken his offer and left her car on the side of the road. It might have washed off in the deluge but at least she wouldn't have been in it. As it was, she'd nearly driven off the side of the road twice, her wheels slipping and spinning in the slick mud.

Her knuckles white, her windshield wipers going full blast, she followed as closely as she dared. She didn't want to lose sight of his taillights, but she was also afraid of running right into the back of his truck.

"Times like this make you want to be a waitress again," she muttered, then screeched a little when she felt her tires sliding sideways again. Her heart in her throat and her father's lectures spinning inside her head, she finally regained traction only to see Jayden's truck had turned off the highway and those red taillights were getting fainter by the second.

She couldn't tell where the road was that he'd turned onto, but she followed him anyway, her chest knocking the steering wheel and her head hitting the headrest as she bounced down a small hill.

"Next time just get in the dang truck," she said loudly when water splashed up over the hood of her car, dousing her windshield with mud.

The only saving grace was the force of the rain that washed away the mud and allowed her a moment to see the road—yes, it *was* a road—in front of her and Jayden's taillights still ahead.

She exhaled loudly, focusing on them like a lifeline as they drove onward. It felt like they'd been driving for miles when the rain suddenly eased up, and she spotted buildings nearby that soon became distinct enough to identify as a two-story house and an enormous barn.

"Thank you, God," she breathed, unclenching her fingers as she pulled up next to where Jayden had parked. She jabbed the ignition button and her car went still.

She hadn't even had time to unbuckle her seat belt when she saw him streak from his truck to the side of her car again, yanking open the door.

"What—"

"Hurry up."

Ariana automatically reached over for her phone that had once again fallen onto the passenger side floor.

"Leave it." His voice was sharp and her hackles started to rise.

She deliberately closed her hand around the phone before straightening in her seat once more. Annoyed or not with his tone, she still needed to explore this whole Fortune thing. And a girl usually got further with honey than she did with vinegar. "I appreciate your—"

"Sweetheart, in gear. *Now.*" He grabbed her arm, practically hauling her out of the car.

Horror mingled with annoyance as she struggled against his iron grip, nearly tripping before she found steady footing. If it weren't for her high-heeled boots, he would have towered over her. As it was, her forehead had a close encounter with the faint cleft in his sharp chin. "I don't know who you think you are, but—"

"I'm the guy who's trying to get us to cover."

She dragged her blowing hair out of her eyes again. "Are you going to melt in the rain? Seems to me you're already soaked through."

"No, but I don't want a house coming down on those ruby slippers of yours." He gestured and her mouth went dry all over again at the sight of the funnel cloud snaking downward from the clouds.

"Oh, my God!" She grabbed his wet shirtfront. "That's a tornado? Is it coming this way?"

"Let's not wait around to see, okay?" His hand was like iron as he pulled her along with him—not toward the nearby stone-sided house surrounded by a wraparound porch, but well off to the side of it in the direction of the barn. He stopped halfway there, though, letting go of her long enough to lean down and pull open a storm-cellar door angled into the earth. "Get in."

She looked nervously from the house to the barn, then stared into the black abyss below the cellar door. Ax murderer? Tornado? It was no time to weigh odds, but she couldn't help herself.

"Sweetheart, I'll carry you down those steps myself if you don't get your butt moving." He whistled sharply, making her jump. But the bandanna-clad dog simply trotted past her, brushing against Ariana's leg before sniffing the ground in front of the cellar entrance. "Steps, Sugar," Jayden said and the dog hesitantly took a gingerly step down into the darkness. "She's mostly blind. Don't trip over her on your way down. There's a handrail. Use it."

A blind dog.

She couldn't have made up such a detail if she'd tried.

She held her arm around her head, trying to keep her hair from blowing in his face as well as hers as she took the first step beyond the wooden door. "Is that, uh, that door going to keep out a tornado?" The wood was faded nearly gray and looked to be a hundred years old. It was a fitting complement to the steep stairs, which seemed to be carved from stone.

"Guess we'll see, won't we." He was right on her heels, pulling the door closed as he followed her.

"I've never been in a tornado." Or gone down into a dark storm cellar with a blind dog and her handsome cuss of an owner.

"I have. There's usually a flashlight right here by the door, but I'll find one soon as I can. The walls are stone, but the floor's dirt. You'll feel the difference when you get to the bottom."

She did, but was glad for the warning. She felt as blind as Sugar and leaned over to pet the dog, who seemed to plant herself immediately in front of Ariana's shins. Then she felt Jayden brush against the back side of her as he, too, reached the base of the steps.

She straightened like a shot.

"Sorry," he murmured. His hand cupped her shoulder as he sidled around her. "No electricity down here."

She wasn't so sure about that. Both her butt and her shoulder were tingling from his brush against her, even after his touch left her and she heard him moving around.

A deafening clap of thunder made her jump. Sugar whined and she knelt down to rub her hand over the shaggy dog, all the while looking up at the wooden cellar door. She had some serious doubts about that door. "Was that tornado a few years back in Paseo? Are we even still near Paseo?"

"My address says so." She heard a few clanks, and then a narrow but reassuring flashlight beam shone across the floor as he moved back to her side. "Here." He handed her the sturdy, metal flashlight and retreated once more to what she could now see were shelving units lined up against two walls. "And there *was* a tornado around here a few years ago, but I wasn't here for it. Shine that up here, would you?"

"Sorry." She immediately turned the flashlight in his direction again. But she'd seen enough of the rest of the cellar to know that it was larger than she'd expected. Her vivid imagination was conjuring any number of creepy crawlies hanging out in the far corners of the dirt-floored cellar.

She realized her flashlight was trained squarely on his extremely excellent rear end and angled it upward where his hands were. "So where were you, then?"

"Two years ago? Germany. The close-up brush I had with a tornado was further back than that. In Italy."

He spoke with a distinct Texas drawl that said he'd grown up here. "World traveler?"

He shot her a grin over his shoulder. "Courtesy of the United States Army, ma'am."

She was glad he quickly turned back to his task. His grin was positively lethal.

She sat down on the bottom step and rubbed Sugar's warm head when the dog rested it on her lap. It was hard not to keep looking up at that cellar door. It was hard not wondering what unmentionable creatures they were disturbing in the dirt cellar with their very presence. "You don't look like a soldier." She jerked the flashlight upward again and jumped at another crack of thunder.

"I'm not anymore. You don't look like a reporter."

"I told you. I'm a journalist."

"Working on a magazine article. I remember."

Which brought her mind squarely back to her purpose for being there in the first place. She blamed the fact that she'd been even momentarily sidetracked by the storm.

She jerked the flashlight—and her gaze—away from his butt when he turned with a lantern in his hand. She'd seen ones like it pictured in the advertising section of *Weird*. She herself, however, had never had any personal experience with the things.

Primarily because her idea of roughing it meant being somewhere without a handy Starbucks.

Or traveling to a tiny map-dot called Paseo, Texas, where cell phone signals were apparently unheard of.

Along with the lantern, he'd also found a box of kitchen matches. But instead of lighting a match by scraping it against the box, he just scraped his thumbnail over the top. Then he set the flame to the lantern, and a moment later, another source of light countered the gloom. He set the lantern on the floor near her feet. "Turn off the flashlight. Might as well save the batteries."

She turned it off before handing it to him. He stepped around her, going up a few stairs before tucking the flashlight between the wall and the handrail near the door. "That's where we usually keep it." She leaned to one side for him to go past her again as he came back down.

Then he picked up the lantern, holding it high as he looked around the rest of the room, making a satisfied sound as he headed into one of those far corners. When he came back into the small circle of light, he was carrying a puffy, orange sleeping bag that he flipped open a foot from her toes.

Her alarm level started rising again. "We're, uh, not going to be down here all day, are we?"

"Probably not." He set the lantern on the floor next to the brightly colored bag and disappeared into the shadows again. He came back with another sleeping bag, though he left this one rolled up and tossed it down on the one he'd spread out. "There used to be a small table and a couple chairs down here. Don't know what happened to them. But we might as well be a little more comfortable while we're here." Suiting action to words, he knelt down and stretched out on one side of the opened sleeping bag and propped the rolled-up one behind his head.

Then he patted the area beside him. "C'mere, girl."

Her mouth went dry.

Then she felt her face flush when Sugar sniffed her way along the edge of the sleeping bag before circling a few times next to Jayden's hip and lying down.

Of course he'd meant his dog.

"Room for you, too," he said.

She pressed her lips together in an awkward smile and shook her head. She was twenty-seven years old. Hardly inexperienced when it came to men. But lying on the floor next to a soaking wet stranger—even a handsome cuss of one—was not exactly in her wheelhouse.

Though it had been over a year since she'd broken up with Steven—

The thought blew away when the cellar door suddenly flew open.

Dirt and debris rained down the stairs and she shot off the step where she'd been sitting. She would have collided with Jayden, who'd bolted upright to his feet, if not for the quick way he set her aside.

She wrapped her arms around her midriff, but that didn't really help the quaking inside her. She didn't know how it was possible, but the sky outside was even blacker than before. So black that she almost questioned the time of day, even though logic told her it was still afternoon. "Can I help?"

He was halfway up the stairs, reaching out of the cellar opening to grab the door that kept slamming against the ground. "Stay there." His voice was terse.

It seemed the nerves inside her stomach had found a whole new set of hoops to toss around.

The wind was whipping down the stairwell so violently that it blew his shirt away from his back like a maniacal parachute. The end of the sleeping bag flipped up and over her boots. Her hair felt like it was standing on end and Sugar shot off to hide in one of the dark corners.

She sat down on the sleeping bag and patted her hands together. "Come here, Sugar. It's okay." After a moment, the dog slunk back. Her tail was tucked. Her pointed ears were nearly flat against her head. She was more terrified than Ariana. She put her arm around the dog, wanting to bury her face in the dog's silky fur.

Then Jayden finally won his battle with the door and it slammed shut with such force that even more dust came down, settling over his head.

He secured the latch again and jammed the flashlight through it as well.

"Is that going to hold it?"

"It'll hold the latch." He came back down the stairs. "Whether the door holds together is another matter."

Sugar whined.

Ariana wished she could, too.

"Hey." He crouched down next to them both. "Don't worry. Everything's going to be fine."

The door blew again, metal and wood seeming to scream against the pressure.

"You don't know that," she told him.

"You're too pretty to be so pessimistic." He put his arm around her and his dog.

She didn't move away. Because, whether she wanted to admit it or not, just like Sugar obviously did, she felt safer with him right there even though the wetness of his clothes seeped through hers.

Still… "There's a tornado out there," she said, as if she needed to point that out to him.

"Not yet. At least I didn't see the funnel cloud again. Hopefully, it's just one hellacious storm."

Right on cue, thunder shook the very walls. She couldn't help flinching. "I never liked thunderstorms, either," she admitted.

His hand squeezed her shoulder. "I don't know. This one's not so bad."

She huffed out a disbelieving laugh. "Right."

"It brought you, didn't it?"

## *Chapter Two*

Jayden felt Ariana stiffen next to him and wished he'd said just about anything else.

That was the problem with his propensity for voicing blunt truths.

He pushed to his feet. He was soaked to the skin but he ignored the annoyance. "If I remember, there ought to be some stuff to eat and drink down here. Interested?"

She rubbed her hands up and down her arms. "If it's a hundred years old like that cellar door, I don't think so."

He chuckled as he went over to the shelves. They were crammed with everything from tools to packing boxes that had been there since before his mom had ever set foot in Paseo. Which dated them more than thirty-six years, since he and his brothers hadn't yet been born. In the years he'd been gone in the army, the shelves had only gotten more jumbled.

"The door's old," he allowed. "But not a hundred years

old. It's just the Paseo sun that makes it look that way." He pushed aside a stack of newspapers. Who kept old newspapers these days? To him it was sort of like saving string.

Outside, the thunder had settled into a continuous rumble. He hadn't lied to the lovely, young Ariana Lamonte. Aside from that one sight of the funnel cloud, he hadn't seen it again when he'd been fighting with the damn cellar door. But he still wasn't inclined to leave the safety of the cellar just yet, either. Not when the sky had that ominous blackish-green hue. Just because he hadn't seen a funnel didn't mean there wasn't one. And he had no desire to tangle with a tornado.

As far as storm cellars went, this one was pretty old. Back in the day, it'd been used more as a root cellar than anything. Nowadays, it was the place where old crap—like thirty-plus-year-old newspapers—went to die.

He didn't find the box of crackers he'd been hunting for, but he did find an old radio. He switched it on.

"Is that a radio?"

He didn't want to dash the hopefulness in Ariana's voice, but truth was truth. "There are only a few radio stations with a strong enough signal to reach Paseo. Television's even worse. Hated it when I was young."

"That's what cable and satellite dishes are for."

He chuckled. "No cable out here. And satellite was *way* too expensive. At least it used to be." They had satellite television now, primarily so his mom could keep up with Grayson's rodeoing when she wasn't traveling with him. But when the weather was bad, the first thing it did was lose its signal. He held up the radio that emitted only static no matter how many times he turned the dial. He turned it off again and stuck it back on the shelf.

"And no cell phone signal, either," she said. "Which I discovered for myself already."

"Nope. No cell signal." He shrugged and moved a cardboard box full of toys he vaguely remembered from his childhood. If he was really lucky, he'd find some old towels.

"Any internet?"

"The library in town has it. They're only open on Wednesdays, last time I checked." Admittedly, that had been a good year ago, when he'd been ironing out leftover details from leaving the service.

"This is Texas," she muttered. "Not a third-world country."

He smiled faintly. "We are kind of off the grid," he allowed. "But I've traveled the world. Seen the best and more often the worst of people along the way. So I've come to appreciate Paseo's peacefulness."

The cellar door shuddered again.

"Usual peacefulness," he amended, resuming his search for the crackers. From the corner of his eye, he watched Sugar cuddle up close to Ariana.

The dog was ordinarily wary as hell around strangers. But he couldn't exactly blame Sugar.

The reporter—*journalist*—had curves just meant to be cuddled up close against. She had rich brown hair that reached halfway down the back of the artsy black-and-white sweater she wore open over a clinging gray top. Her snug jeans showed off shapely thighs before they tucked in impractical knee-high red boots. They ought to have looked ridiculous, those boots. Like they belonged on a fashion runway. On her, though, they were just plain sexy. Combined with darkly lashed brown eyes that had sucked him in the second she'd turned them his way out on the highway, Ariana Lamonte definitely made an impact.

And her presence now was only serving to remind him just how long it had been since he'd enjoyed an attractive woman's company.

He'd hooked up a time or two right after things ended with Tess in Germany, but that was it. Grayson had told him he was turning into a hermit and suggested he meet some of the buckle bunnies always following him around. Jayden had bluntly told his brother to stuff it.

He finally spotted the old-fashioned metal container that held a sealed box of saltine crackers. "Ah. Success."

For all he knew, they were the same ones he'd put there when he was eighteen, but he was hoping they'd been refreshed somewhere along the way. He pulled the tin off the shelf, as well as the dusty bottle sitting behind it—definitely not his doing when he'd been eighteen. He'd been a hell-raiser, but even he hadn't had the nerve to keep a bottle of whiskey in the cellar right under his mom's nose. She'd have tanned his hide, regardless of his age. He'd never met a fight he didn't like—except when it was against his mom.

Carrying both the tin and the bottle, he went back to sit on the sleeping bag.

Sugar lifted her head and shuffled over to him, curling up against his thigh and going back to sleep.

"How old is she?"

He rubbed the dog's ruff. "About three. I brought her back from Germany with me when I got out of the army." He left out the part that he'd basically stolen her from his master sergeant. The man had gotten Tess. As far as Jayden was concerned, he hadn't deserved to have the dog, too.

"Was she born blind?"

"No." He ignored her curious expression and peeled open the cracker box. Fortunately, it looked relatively new. And the outer metal box had done a good job keeping bugs from getting at the cardboard inside.

The storm was howling worse than ever outside. Rain had started lashing against the door and he hoped to keep Ariana distracted from it as much as he could. "Here."

He set a sleeve of crackers on the sleeping bag between them and wiped off the dusty bottle with his wet shirttail. "No glasses, I'm afraid." He held the bottle closer to the lantern so she could see the label he'd exposed. "You are legal, right?" For all he knew, she could be a twenty-year-old journalism student.

She let out a soft, sexy laugh and leaned forward to take the bottle. Her fingertips brushed his. He wasn't sure if that made more of an impression on him than the way her long, tangled hair formed a curtain around her. "More than legal," she assured him. "I'm twenty-seven."

Older than she looked, which was a relief. "I've got nine years on you."

"Not exactly a generation gap," she offered drily. She twisted off the cap from the bottle of whiskey, took a sip and promptly coughed. "Potent," she finally managed. She set the bottle next to the crackers and peeled off her sweater.

The clinging shirt beneath possessed no sleeves. Just two narrow straps over shoulders that gleamed ivory-smooth in the lantern's light. His gaze started to drift over the shadowy cleavage also on display beneath her collection of thin gold necklaces, and he grabbed the whiskey bottle for himself.

Hell of a time for that dead feeling inside him to be shocked back to life.

"Potent," he agreed after he took a healthy swig. The liquor burned all the way down, joining the heat already pooled inside him.

Fortunately, she seemed to take his comment at face value and fiddled with her cell phone. "I couldn't function without the internet," she said. "How do you stand it?"

"Just fine," he drawled. "What do I need it for?"

"Keeping up with the world?"

He smiled slightly. "Hear everything I need to know at the feed store in town." It was an exaggeration, but not that much of one since he, personally, wasn't all that inclined to ever turn on the television. Not when every time he did, all he saw were politicians arguing and neighbors shooting neighbors. He'd seen enough of that in the service. "What do *you* need the internet for?"

She'd been sitting cross-legged and she shifted, straightening out her legs, too. "My job, for one thing. Research. Filing stories." Her lips twitched. "Keeping up with the world."

"I kept up with the world plenty thanks to fifteen years with the army."

She set aside her phone and lifted her hair off her neck with both hands. "It's warm down here."

And getting warmer. He wasn't entirely certain that his clothes hadn't started steaming. "Blame it on the whiskey." Personally, he was blaming it on *her*.

"It's June but the rain still ought to cool things off." She twisted her hair, managing to tie it into a knot atop her head. She inhaled deeply and Jayden did blame the whiskey then, because he should have looked away from the lush curves pushing against that thin excuse for a shirt, but he didn't.

And the heat inside his gut just increased.

The only thing that distracted him was the thumping of the cellar door as the storm buffeted against it. It sounded like it was hailing, but in the lantern light, he could see the glimmer of rain dripping through the slats of the wood door.

If he'd met Ariana Lamonte under just about any other circumstance, he wouldn't hesitate to pursue the attraction. But she was in his storm cellar. Essentially under his protection.

Which changed the rules entirely.

Or should.

"So what do you do in Austin when you're not chasing around stories for your magazine?"

She shrugged a shoulder. "The usual. I have friends. Parents." As if she realized the spare details were hardly the way to keep a conversation going, she pushed to her feet and paced the short distance to the shelves, arching her back a little as she stretched. Then she bent over in half, her bracelets jingling softly, and pressed her fingers against the dirt floor.

He damn near swallowed his tongue.

The knot in her hair wasn't holding up. As he watched, it seemed to uncoil in almost slow motion. Then she straightened again, caught her hands behind her back and stretched once more.

He closed his eyes, stifling an oath. "Grow up there?" He had to raise his voice over the noise from outside.

"In Austin? Born and raised. Same as my mom and dad before me. I love the city. I have an apartment that overlooks the skyline. Ridiculously expensive, so I barely have it furnished, but I can walk or ride my bicycle to work if I want. I can get most anywhere I want, really, without even taking out my car."

He looked at her again and was both relieved and chagrined that she'd stopped stretching and was pacing once more. "Except here," he said drily.

Her lips curved. They were full and luscious, like the rest of her. Not overblown. Just…right.

Exactly right.

"Except here," she agreed. "What about you? Did you grow up in Paseo?"

"Born and raised," he parroted. "Right here on this very ranch."

She propped her hands on her hips and looked at him. "And your parents?"

He wasn't accustomed to telling strangers his business. But she was easy to talk to. And it kept her from turning to see the water that had begun streaming down the steps.

The cellar had stone walls and a dirt floor. He'd never known it to flood more than a foot. Still, if it got worse, he was already figuring they'd have to leave the shelter. In a flood, being inside the house higher up was better than being below ground. If there really were tornadoes in the area, they'd have to take their chances. His mom's bedroom closet in the house would be the best bet. First floor. Interior room.

There wouldn't be much space for the two of them. It would definitely be close quarters—

"Never knew my father," he said, pulling his thoughts away. "My mom was pregnant when she came to Paseo."

Her expression shifted a little. "So your *mom* is a Fortune?"

"Not one of *those* Fortunes," he reminded her. "The ones you've been writing about for your magazine. Like I said. The name's just a coincidence. So if that's what brought you to Paseo, you've wasted a trip. My mother's definitely not related to them."

She tilted her head slightly. "It's not that common a name."

"It's the one my mom decided on when she was making a fresh start here. She wanted a new life. A new identity. Said my brothers and I were the only fortune she needed. Thus the name. I'm pretty sure she was running from the guy who'd gotten her pregnant. She could have chosen any surname she wanted." He raised his voice over a crack of thunder. "Always figured Fortune was better than Smith."

Ariana jerked to attention at his words. *His mother had been running?*

"It's just thunder." Jayden's deep voice was calm. The kind of voice to inspire trust. "It can't hurt you."

"The lightning that causes it can." Much as she disliked thunderstorms, she was glad to blame her reaction on it. "So why do you think she was hiding from him?" she asked casually, concealing her intense interest. Gerald Robinson had a history of being a womanizer. But not a violent one. Even now, in his seventies, he was a compellingly attractive man. She'd only had a few brief encounters with him—he was *not* a proponent of her magazine articles, to say the least, and had no idea about the book of course—but it wasn't difficult to understand how women had flocked his way. But none of the women—even his wife—seemed to hold his heart.

Some said that Gerald Robinson didn't really have one.

But maybe he'd had one and left it in Paseo.

"Was your mother afraid of your father?"

"I probably should have phrased it differently." He adjusted the rolled sleeping bag behind him, stretching out even more fully on the one spread beneath him. He tore open the sleeve of crackers and fed one to Sugar. "I think she was running from a broken heart. And that's it."

Another frequent refrain when it came to the women in Gerald's past. The only heart that seemed to have not broken along the way belonged to his wife.

Then she realized what else Jayden had said. "You have brothers?"

He'd uncapped the whiskey again and held up two fingers as he took a sip. When he was finished, he held the bottle toward her.

Even though she knew she oughtn't, she took the bottle

again and this time managed not to choke on the alcohol as it burned down her throat.

But she dropped the bottle completely when a loud crash vibrated through the very walls, making even the metal shelving shudder and squeal.

She froze, forgetting entirely her interest in his brothers, and warily looked up at the low ceiling, half-afraid it was getting ready to collapse in on them. It was covered in wood. But above that, she really had no idea what was there. Except earth and that awful, awful howling wind. "That was not thunder."

He'd sat up, too, and shook his head. He righted the whiskey bottle she'd dropped. "No, it wasn't." He went up the stairs and pried the flashlight out of the metal latch where he'd jammed it. Only then did she realize the stairs were flowing with water.

"Are you sure you should go out there?"

"No, but I want to know what the hell that noise was. I'm not worried about the house—nobody is here but us—but I've got horses in the barn." He pushed up on the cellar door and swore.

Her stomach curled in on itself nervously. "What's wrong?"

"Something's blocking the door." He put his shoulder to it and heaved.

The door that had blown open from the wind now stayed stubbornly closed.

She felt like choking on a whole new lump of misgivings. "So we're trapped?"

"I wouldn't say that."

She picked up the lantern and carried it with her up a few steps until she was just below him. In the light she couldn't see the faintest glimmer of anything between the wood slats. She could, however, see the muscles standing out in his arms as he pushed futilely against the door. And she could also see the stream of water pouring steadily down the stone steps. How it was getting around whatever blocked the door was a mystery.

But water had a way of going where it wanted.

Take the Grand Canyon, for example.

"What *would* you say, then?"

His answer was curt. And unprintable.

Her mouth went dry. She backed down the wet steps.

He followed her and took the lantern from her fingers that had gone numb. "Don't look like that."

"Like what?" She wrapped her arms around herself. It was humid and warm in the cellar but she suddenly felt cold. How much water would the dirt absorb before it started to fill the cellar? "You just said nobody was here but us."

"Not for a few days."

She gaped. "A few *days*? So someone will find our bodies sooner or later?"

He set the lantern on the ground and put his arms around her. "You do have an imagination, don't you?"

She nodded against his shoulder, breathing in the warm, comforting scent of him. "My teachers always told me that was a good thing. But this is not at all how I expected this day to go."

"Me, either." His hands slid down her spine. "We'll get out of here before we're reduced to *bodies*. The cellar has never flooded much more than ten, twelve inches before."

The details were not a comfort. "I don't know how to swim."

"You're not going to need to," he promised.

She tilted her head back, looking up into his face. It really was a cussedly handsome one. From the cleft in his chin to the straight brows over his level gaze. "My mother

will never forgive me for not giving her grandchildren."
Karen Lamonte had been going on about it ever since
Ariana had broken off with Steven.

His eyebrows shot up and the corner of his lips lifted.
"Pretty sure that's not going to be decided here and now,
sweetheart."

She really didn't know what was wrong with her. She'd
never particularly been prone to panic before. But she'd
also never found herself stuck in a storm cellar in a town
nobody could seem to find except for those who actually
lived there, in the company of a man who might or might
not be another son of Gerald Robinson, but who definitely
had an overwhelming appeal for her personally.

And focusing on Jayden was far preferable to thinking about what could happen if that water kept coming
down the stairs.

"You have a scar," she murmured inconsequentially
and touched the faint white line above his eyebrow. "Right
there."

"Bar fight." His lashes drooped and she knew instinctively that he was looking at her lips.

Without conscious thought, she moistened them. His
fingertips were tracing her spine, setting off all manner of
sensations inside her. "Are you, ah, in a lot of bar fights?"

"One or two. I stopped more of them." He shifted slightly,
pulling her in closer till her breasts were pressed against
his chest. "I was an MP in the army."

Her breasts were pressed against his chest. "MP?" Her
voice was little more than a whisper.

"Military Police." His head dropped toward hers. "Former badass Sergeant First Class Fortune at your service."
As he said the words his head lowered toward hers. His
breath fanned her mouth as he said, "I'm going to kiss
you, you know."

Heat flushed through her veins, collecting in her center. Her head felt heavy as she looked up at him. Any hope of maintaining a professional distance had gotten washed away. "Former Sergeant, I sure hope so," she breathed.

One of his hands left her back to slide along her jaw.

Her lips parted and she drew in a deep breath. She felt the way he went still when she slid her hands around his neck. His thumb brushed over her lower lip and she couldn't help the soft sound that rose in her throat.

"Damn," he murmured. And then his mouth found hers.

His kiss didn't feel damned. If anything, his kiss felt glorious.

And if she was going to go in a storm cellar, at least she was going to go like this.

He lifted his head way too soon. His eyes were dark and unreadable in the dim lantern light, but the searching in them felt as real as the moisture leaching from his clothes into hers.

She pulled his head down. "If you're going to kiss me," she said as she caught his lower lip between hers and lightly tugged, "*kiss* me."

He groaned, kissing her even more deeply. His hands traveled down her back, down her hips, her rear, pulling her up and into him. He was hard and her head whirled even more. All she wanted to do right then and there was twine herself around him and he seemed to know it because he yanked his mouth away from her and lifted her right off her feet.

"Put your legs around me."

She didn't need the request. She was already linking her boots behind him and wishing there weren't two layers of denim between them. She couldn't do anything about that at the moment, but she could do something about his shirt. She yanked it upward, hearing a few buttons scatter before he let out a low, groaning laugh and managed to pull it off his head.

She pressed her open mouth against his collarbone, tasting the moist, salty heat of his skin. He cradled her backside as he crouched down, finally lowering her onto the sleeping bag. One corner of her mind wondered if the thing was floating in water yet, but that didn't stop her from reaching greedily between them for his belt.

He jerked and caught her hands in his, pinning them above her head against the sleeping bag.

"Don't tell me you want me to stop." In any other world, she'd have been shocked by her own boldness. But this wasn't any other world. The only world that existed was contained in a flooding dirt cellar from which they had no way out. She angled her hips against his. "I can feel what you want."

"Yeah?" His hair brushed her cheek as he kissed the side of her neck. "Does that mean I have to hurry?" His mouth burned along the curve of her shoulder. Over the thin strap of her camisole and down to where her achingly tight nipples pushed against the cotton fabric. "You're not wearing a bra."

Was there any point in explaining the built-in shelf bra? "Maybe you do need to hurry, if we're going to be flooded in this cellar."

"We're not getting flooded," he said again.

"How do you know?"

"Because I know." Still holding her wrists above her head with one hand, he peeled down the top of her camisole with the other, until she felt his breath on her bare breasts. She was coming positively unglued, anticipating the brush of his mouth, the slide of his tongue—

But instead of tasting her, he lifted his head a little. "What is that?" He reached for the lantern, pulling it near so he could look more closely at her exposed breasts. "A butterfly?"

She groaned, twisting beneath him. "Yes, it's a butterfly." All of an inch big in pale pink and black, tattooed on the upper curve of her right breast when she'd been twenty-one. She still couldn't free her hands, so she arched her back, rubbing her rigid nipples and the tattoo against his hard chest. "You were in the army, Sergeant Fortune. Surely you've seen tattoos before." In the scheme of things, her little butterfly was hardly a record breaker. Neither was the floral curlicue on her left shoulder blade.

His teeth flashed. "Sweetheart, I've seen things that would turn your hair white." He ducked his head and kissed the point of her shoulder. Then the butterfly.

Heat flowed under the surface of her tingling skin and she bit back a moan when his lips finally surrounded her nipple. Even though she twisted her wrists, halfheartedly trying to free them, he kept them bracketed. She pressed her face against the top of his head. "Jayden, please," she breathed.

In answer, he pushed his thigh between her legs and palmed her other breast.

Pleasure rocketed through her and she cried out.

Jayden made a low sound. Utterly male. Utterly triumphant. Then his mouth was on hers again, and her wrists were finally free, and he rolled over, pulling her over him.

Noise seemed to rage beyond the storm cellar, but she was far more aware of her heart pounding loudly inside her head, of the low sounds coming from Jayden, of the clink of his belt when he finally loosened it. Breathless, she braced one hand on the floor, reaching to undo her own jeans with the other. But instead of dirt, her hand sank into mud. "Jayden, the water—"

"I know." He cursed and kissed her hard again while the pounding outside the cellar door got even louder.

Then suddenly, he went still. "Wait." He sat up, dumping her somewhat unceremoniously onto her butt as he stood. Instead of finishing the job of undressing, though, he fastened his belt and headed up the stairs. He pounded on the door. "Nate," he yelled. "That you?"

Ariana hoped she wasn't hearing things when she heard a faint, indecipherable response.

"Yeah, we're stuck," Jayden yelled, pressing his head close to the wood.

Once again, her adrenaline seemed to want to blow the top of her head right off. She wiped off her muddy hand and scrambled up the few steps behind him. "Who's out there?"

"My brother Nathan. So you, uh, might—" He gestured and she flushed, realizing her camisole was bunched around her waist.

Suddenly embarrassed, she turned and tugged the stretchy fabric back where it belonged, hiding her still-tight nipples and the butterfly tattoo. She would have put on her sweater for good measure, except when she picked it up from where she'd left it bunched by the base of the stairs, it was soaking wet.

As was her cell phone.

She grimaced. It was supposed to be waterproof, but she wasn't sure that meant it could withstand sitting in several inches of water. She was drying it off the best she could against her jeans when Sugar started barking, pacing back and forth across the sleeping bag, leaving muddy paw prints all over it.

"Sugar, come here." Ariana reached out so the dog could sniff her hand and then closed her fingers around the bandanna to hold her still. "Good girl." She tucked the phone in her back pocket and looked back at Jayden. "I can't hear what your brother is saying. What's blocking the door?"

"Your car."

*"What?"*

"It's on its side." He pressed his ear against the door again. "Yeah," he shouted. Then he looked back at her. "He's hooked up the winch from my truck to drag it off."

She hadn't even had the car for three months yet. She'd bought it outright with her book advance. Her savings account wasn't quite sucking air, but it was close. What if she had to pay for car repairs? "Is it going to be damaged very badly?"

"I doubt the winch will do anything worse to it than the wind that turned it on its side in the first place."

She grimaced, knowing it had been a foolish question.

Jayden was listening again at the wood panels, and then he backed down the steps, sliding his arm around her waist to pull her away as well. "Sugar, come on." The dog moved also, sitting against his leg, thumping her tail and looking up at him with an adoring expression on her pointed face. "Just to be safe," he told Ariana and brushed his lips over her temple.

She closed her eyes for a moment, fighting the strong urge to put her arm around him, too.

"Relax," Jayden said. His long fingers squeezed her hip. "Everything's going to be fine. We're getting out."

She smiled weakly. She was relieved about that. More than she could say. But it also meant that getting carried away like she had with Jayden *Fortune* could not happen again. Not when she was far from convinced his name was merely a coincidence. Getting personally involved with someone she was writing about was out of the question.

"I thought you never had any doubt about us getting out."

"I didn't." He gave her a quick wink, and then they both went silent as they heard what could only be the sound of her car being dragged away from the cellar door.

A few moments later, the door was opened from the outside. Rain pounded through the opening and then a drenched man appeared, shining a heavy-duty light down on them. "Well, well, bro. Glad to see you still like bringing the pretty girls to see your underground bachelor pad."

Ariana flushed. She had no right to feel jealous of what Jayden had done in the past or would do in the future with anyone. But that didn't stop her from feeling it anyway.

Jayden grabbed her hand and started up the stairs. "Be careful," he warned her. "The stones are slippery as hell."

She found that out quickly enough when Sugar slipped and lost her footing. Jayden immediately let go of Ariana to pick up the dog and carry her up the rest of the stairs.

Grabbing hold of the handrail, Ariana followed. She was soaked even before she accepted the hand that Jayden's brother offered when she reached the top of the stairs.

"Out you go," Nathan said, practically lifting her right out onto the ground. "You guys all right?"

Ariana nodded. Even though it was pouring buckets and it was nearly dark, the sky no longer had that terrible, angry black look, as if it were ready to explode. "Thank you." He'd set the big flashlight on the top of her car—make that the *side* of her car, because she saw right away that it was, indeed, lying on its side. "How could this happen? Was it a tornado after all?" She looked up into Nathan's face, and now that the flashlight wasn't shining in her face, she nearly did a double take. "You're twins?"

Nathan grinned. "Triplets, actually. But I'm the best-looking one of the lot."

Jayden let Sugar jump to the ground. The dog, mostly blind or not, raced immediately across the muddy ground toward the house. "I'll disagree with that," he said, reaching out to give his brother's hand a pump. "But I'm glad as hell that you're the most unpredictable of us. Thought you were still in Oklahoma City."

Nathan shrugged, offering no explanation.

Ariana took the flashlight to shine it over her car.

Not only was it sitting on its side, but half the windows were broken out. The copy of the magazine was gone. Worst of all, though, her thick notebook was nowhere in sight.

She'd had nearly a year's worth of research packed in that notebook. It had contained everything that her laptop—which was sitting safely in her apartment back home—did not. And the thought of losing it was almost overwhelming.

"It's not so bad," Jayden said. "We'll get it turned right side up and replace the windshield—"

She nodded and blinked her eyes hard.

"Hey." Nathan took the flashlight from her nerveless hand. "I'm used to being waterlogged, but maybe we could get out of the rain and take this inside the house."

"Getting out of the rain sounds good," she agreed.

She followed the two men who were so alike that they were two peas in a pod. And evidently, there was a third pea from that pod as well.

Multiple births ran in Gerald Robinson's family. His two eldest sons with Charlotte were twins.

Ariana didn't need her notes to know that.

She didn't need her notes to know a lot of things.

But she honestly couldn't recall from her biology classes whether multiples happened from the mother's side or the father's. Which meant she needed to do a little research.

The very thought of it energized her.

Her car would get fixed. And her notes could be recreated. When it came to some things, she had an excellent memory for detail.

Maybe Paseo wasn't turning out to be a wild-goose chase after all. She'd just found three more sons of Gerald Robinson. *Possibly* three more sons.

That in itself was huge.

But Jayden and his brothers were also thirty-six. Which meant if Gerald was their father, they were his eldest heirs.

Was that the reason Charlotte Robinson had shown her fangs to Ariana?

Because she knew?

## Chapter Three

"Still dead?"

Jayden nodded as he hung up the wall phone. The dead line wasn't surprising, considering the weather. He didn't particularly care, except it meant if their mom heard about the storm, she might be concerned.

He pulled a mug from the cabinet and tossed Sugar a treat that she snagged when it landed on her bed, then sat down at the kitchen table across from his brother.

From over their heads, they could hear the sound of a shower running.

"She's a looker," Nathan said.

It took no effort at all to imagine Ariana standing beneath the running water.

It took considerable effort to squelch the inevitable result of that image. He grabbed the coffeepot his brother had set in the center of the table and filled his cup. "True enough." He considered warning Nathan off, but decided against it. His brother would probably make something of it.

"Didn't mention you were having company when I talked to you last week."

"Didn't know I was going to have company."

"Sure about that? You guys were looking pretty cozy down in the cellar. Makes me wonder if my timing couldn't have been a little better."

Jayden ignored the devilry in his brother's eyes. What he and Ariana had been doing in the cellar was none of Nathan's business. "She's a journalist from Austin," he said. "She came to Paseo for some magazine she works for."

Nathan gave a bark of laughter. "Paseo? What the hell is interesting around here?"

"She's writing about the Fortune family. The real one. With all the money over in Austin."

Nathan made a face. "Only one in the money around here is Grayson and he doesn't even use our last name. Disappointing for her, I guess. What's she been doing? Going through all the Texas phone books looking up anyone with the last name Fortune?"

Jayden sipped the coffee. Grimacing, he got up to get some milk from the refrigerator. Usually, he liked his coffee black, but Nathan made the worst coffee in the world. "I don't know how she knew about us. Doesn't matter, anyway. I told her the truth. Mom made up the name when she had us." He dumped milk into the mug, then added a spoonful of sugar. "When did you get back from OK City?"

"Ten minutes before I saw that dinky red car sitting on its side."

Jayden was the eldest of his brothers by a matter of minutes. "You shouldn't have been driving in this weather."

Nathan gave him a look. "Dude."

"I don't care if you used to be a SEAL or not. It was

stupid." He glanced up at the ceiling when the sound of the shower cut off.

He'd put a clean towel in the bathroom for Ariana to use. About now, she'd be running the pale blue terry cloth over that sexy little butterfly. Then, when she was all nice and dry, she'd be pulling on a pair of his sweatpants and one of his T-shirts.

He buried his nose in his coffee mug, taking a big swig of the nasty stuff. He choked it down and it was almost enough to overpower the images in his head. He should have found something for her to wear from his mother's closet. It would have made more sense. And he wouldn't be thinking about her skin, bare and soft, beneath his own clothes.

Banishing the image, he asked his brother, "Did you notice any other damage around the place?"

"Barn's damaged on the north side, but the roof's intact. Horses were restless, but okay. Haven't checked anywhere else. I saw your truck. When I realized you weren't in the barn or the house—" His brother didn't finish. Just shrugged.

He didn't need to finish. Nathan had come looking for Jayden. Period. Everything else could wait.

Through the window over the sink, he could see Ariana's car. The wind was finally gone, but the rain showed no sign of slowing. Rivers of water had formed, crisscrossing the saturated ground around the storm cellar.

Well beyond the cellar was the barn. Only the corner of it was visible from where he stood. He was glad the barn roof was okay. But even gladder that the horses were okay. Property damage was bad enough without adding damage to their livestock.

"We'll need to check the rest of the stock," he said.

"I've spent enough time in the water for today. I never

saw any cows flying through the air, so I figure it can wait until the rain lets up."

His brother hadn't been joking. Still, Jayden found himself smiling a little. "Weird, isn't it?"

"What?"

"You went to the navy. I went to the army. Neither one of us wanted to be here."

"And we both came back," Nathan finished the thought.

Jayden knew why he'd come back. So far, though, Nathan wasn't saying much about his reasons. Since he himself didn't feel inclined to talk about his military separation, his brother's similar silence didn't strike him as particularly unusual.

"We should check and make sure there are no broken windows in the house."

"That your way of getting rid of me so you can go on about entertaining your…journalist?"

He'd never known not having brothers. But there were moments when the idea was more than a little appealing. He lifted a brow and looked over the coffee mug.

Nathan didn't bother hiding his amusement. "Hey. I think it's great. About time you showed some of the old Jayden spirit." But he pushed away from the table anyway. Like Jayden, he'd already changed into dry jeans and a shirt. "I'll check this floor. You can check upstairs."

It hadn't been Jayden's plan to go upstairs anytime soon. Keeping a little distance between him and Ariana didn't sound appealing, but he knew it was only smart.

She'd been panicking in the storm cellar. Before he'd fallen for Tess, he'd been no saint when it came to women. But taking advantage of the situation with Ariana like he had was all sorts of wrong.

Not that he had even been thinking real straight at the time. Soon as she had tried undoing his belt, his resistance had been laughable. And when she'd come apart the way she had—

"Jayden?"

He jerked slightly, realizing that his brother had left the kitchen and Ariana had entered it. And the way she was looking at him made him suspect she'd been there for more than just a second.

He dumped the rest of the undrinkable coffee down the sink, trying not to dwell on the way the V-neck of the white undershirt he'd loaned her hung off one of her bare shoulders. On her, the shirt was loose, thank God. Way too loose to give any hint of the gorgeous breasts he knew were beneath.

"Shower okay?"

Her wet hair was slicked back from her face and twisted in a thick braid down the center of her back. "Yes, thank you." She held up the towel in her arms and he realized she'd wrapped it around her wet clothes. "Do you have a washer and dryer I could use?"

"Sorry. I should have thought of that already." His wet clothes were still lying in a heap on the floor in his bedroom.

"Why?" Her face was shiny and clean, yet she still had the thickest, darkest eyelashes he'd ever seen. And they surrounded the brownest gaze he'd ever fallen into. "We've both had a little distraction lately." She moistened her lips. "What with the, uh, storm. So—" She lifted the bundle slightly.

"Laundry room's back here." He led the way from the kitchen to the mudroom in the back where the washer and dryer sat. "Grayson bought 'em for my mom a few years ago, so they're fairly new." His neck went a little hot. Like he was bragging or something.

She slid around him and pulled open the washing machine. "Grayson?"

"My other brother. He's gone a lot. Rides rodeo."

She chuckled. "There's a famous rodeo rider who goes by just Grayson."

At his silence, she looked up at him.

His neck felt even hotter.

"Wait a sec. Your brother?" She looked astonished. "He's *The* Grayson?"

"Guess you've heard of him."

"Well, yeah. One of my coworkers does a blog for *Weird Life* entirely devoted to rodeo. She never stops talking about it."

"Blog?"

"Online journal. You know."

"I guess. Never been particularly interested in that sort of thing. And around here…no internet."

"Except for at the library."

He smiled slightly. "Right." He reached above her head to open the cabinet. "Soap and stuff. Use whatever you need."

She shook her wet things out of the towel into the machine. Thin excuse for a shirt. Jeans. One red sock. One blue sock. A tiny scrap of something white that caught on the edge of the machine before she flicked it inside with the towel and hastily closed the door.

He looked at her bare feet below the rolled-up legs of the sweatpants he'd provided. For some reason, he'd expected her toenails to be painted some bright, shocking color. But they were naked. No color at all.

And who knew why, but the sight of her entirely naked feet turned him on all over again.

God, he was a head case.

"I should check for storm damage upstairs," he said

abruptly. And take his own damn shower. An icy one. "You need anything else?"

She looked a little startled. "I appreciate everything you've already done," she said swiftly. "I'll be fine. Do what you need to do." She tugged at the neckline of the shirt, pulling it up her shoulder where it promptly slid right back down again. "Go."

"Look, about what happened—"

She shrugged, which sent the shirt sliding even farther. She reached up to snatch the oversized bottle of laundry soap from the cupboard. "There's no reason to talk about it. We're two consenting adults—" Her eyes rounded and she gave him a quick look. "And *unattached* adults...right?"

"I sure hope so." Tess hadn't been unattached at all. She'd just neglected to share that fact with Jayden.

Ariana looked away from him again, nodding. "So, no harm, no foul. It's not like we, uh, actually—" She broke off and cleared her throat slightly. "You know."

Not for lack of wanting, he answered silently. Particularly after she'd writhed against him the way she had, making the sexiest sounds he'd ever heard. Sounds that were sure to haunt his sleep for some time to come.

"I mean, I don't sleep with men I don't know," she added. She filled the soap dispenser and jabbed a few buttons on the front of the fancy machine. "I imagine you're more discriminating than that, too."

He took the heavy soap bottle from her and replaced it in the cabinet. "I don't sleep with men I don't know, either."

"Sweetie," she drawled sweetly without missing a beat, "if you swing both ways, I'm not going to judge."

He let out a bark of laughter. "Do *you*?"

Her face was rosy, belying her seemingly bold expression. "As a matter of fact, I don't, but—"

"Neither do I," he assured her. "I like women." Despite

his better intentions, he moved closer to her. Crowding her back against the machine. Standing close enough to smell the minty toothpaste on her breath and inhale the warmth from her smooth skin. "Particularly the one I'm looking at right now."

Her lips parted like she was struggling to breathe. He knew she wasn't, though, because he could feel the rise and fall of her breasts against him just fine.

"You smell like toothpaste."

"I didn't use your toothbrush or anything." Her voice was faint. "I…made do without."

He wasn't sure he'd have cared all that much if she had used his toothbrush. "Sweetheart, I was in the army a long time. I know all about making do. I am a little sorry my brother found us when he did," he murmured. "Another hour—"

*"Hour?"* She pressed her lips together again and looked away. Her cheeks were even redder.

"Okay." He smiled slightly. "Fifteen minutes."

She let out a breathy laugh and shook her head. She crossed her arms between them. He didn't have the heart to tell her that only plumped up her creamy, butterfly-kissed breasts, making them plainly visible for him within the neck of the loose shirt.

"I thought you had things you needed to do," she prompted.

He nodded. "Things I should do." Because he couldn't resist, he grazed his knuckle across that small butterfly. "Things I want to do."

She inhaled sharply. Her eyes met his.

A noise from the kitchen startled them both.

"There you are." Nathan stepped into the mudroom with a bland look that didn't fool Jayden for a second.

His brother always did have a twisted sense of humor. And impeccably annoying timing.

"Window in Mom's room needs to be boarded up," he said, pulling out the toolbox from where it was stashed in a bottom cabinet. "I wiped up the water already, so hopefully the wood floor'll be okay."

Ariana had looked down at her feet. She shifted slightly.

Jayden stifled a sigh. "Plywood's in the barn. I'll get it." If he didn't have a cold shower, he guessed the still-falling rain outside would do the job just as well.

Ariana chewed the inside of her lip, staring at the screen of her cell phone.

It was useless. She could get it to turn on, but it just as quickly turned itself right back off. And she didn't know if that was because the battery was dead or because of the soaking it had gotten in the storm cellar.

She tossed it onto the nightstand and threw back the sheet, pushing off the bed. It was his mother's room, Jayden had told her. She'd protested, but he'd insisted. Deborah Fortune was gone for the week, anyway. Off with Grayson. Evidently she acted somewhat as his third brother's manager when he was touring.

Then Nathan had chimed in with that strangely unholy innocent look he seemed to possess, saying that Ariana could either use their mother's room or she could use Jayden's.

She could envision sleeping in Jayden's bed all too easily. Which was—as she had to keep reminding herself—completely out of the question.

So Mrs. Fortune's bedroom would have to do.

Even though Ariana wanted to, she couldn't look out the window, because the two men had already boarded it up, along with several more around the house. Then, after they were satisfied with their makeshift repairs, Jayden had dumped a loaf of bread and a collection of sandwich meats on the table for supper.

Now it was the middle of the night.

The rain had finally stopped. The house was dark and quiet.

And she was ensconced in the bedroom of the woman who might have been—if the article from the Austin History Center was on the mark—the cause of the broken heart Gerald had supposedly been nursing when he'd met Charlotte.

She paced around the bedroom.

It wasn't large. There was the bed, modestly sized and covered with a faded quilt. Below the boarded-up window was a set of dresser drawers. A tall, narrow chest stood against another wall. There was a lamp on the single nightstand, and that was it. Plenty of framed photographs were scattered around—all of them featuring her sons.

It was easy to pick out which ones were Jayden. The army uniform helped when he was wearing it, but even without it, Ariana was already able to tell him apart from his brothers. It wasn't just the scar on his brow or that slightly crooked cuspid. It was an attitude that sat on his shoulders.

She picked up the largest photo of the three brothers. They were just summertime kids, grinning into the camera. Skinny, bare chests and lanky legs stretched out beneath swimming trunks. But even then, that attitude seemed to shine from the boys' faces.

Jayden's was challenging.

She was pretty sure it was Nathan on the left of Jayden. In one sense looking like butter wouldn't melt in his mouth and in another sense like he held that stick of butter behind his back. Which left Grayson as the boy on Jayden's right. Smiling head-on into the camera with a smile that already packed a lot of wattage.

What had their life been like, growing up in Paseo? Three sons with no father. On a ranch that was basically in the middle of nowhere. In a house that was certainly comfortable but by no means lavish.

Without question, it had to have been the very antithesis of what it had been like for Gerald and Charlotte's children, growing up at their palatial estate in Austin.

She set down the picture frame and pressed her lips together.

The idea of hunting around Deborah Fortune's bedroom for some hint that she'd known Gerald before he'd become Gerald had already occurred to Ariana. And she'd dismissed it.

For one, she wasn't that unethical. For two, she figured the odds were minuscule anyway of Jayden's mom keeping something around that would identify her sons' father, since she had never told them who he was in the first place.

Ariana picked up her phone again and tried once more to power it up. Not that it would do her any good, anyway. If there wasn't a strong enough signal to make a phone call, there certainly wasn't a strong enough signal to send an email or get online.

Feeling frustrated and hemmed in, she left the phone on the bedside table and quietly opened the bedroom door, stepping out into the dark hall. Deborah's room was on the main floor of the house. The rest of the bedrooms were upstairs and she was fairly certain Jayden and his brother had gone to bed some time ago.

Still, she didn't want to chance disturbing anyone as she crept barefoot down the hall toward the faint light coming from the kitchen. It was empty when she got there, though the light over the stove had been left on just as Jayden had said it would be. Sugar's bed was empty and the room was cooler than it had been earlier. Probably because of the breeze she could feel drifting through the wooden screen door.

Feeling thirsty, she took one of the mugs hanging below an upper cupboard and filled it with water. She stood there at the sink and drank it, looking out at the sight of her tipped-on-its-side car.

She still didn't want to think about all of her research notes being lost. If they'd scattered in the wind, the rain would have surely ruined them.

She chewed the inside of her lip, then abruptly set the mug in the sink and quickly returned to the bedroom. Her clothes were dry from when she'd laundered them earlier, but she was still wearing the oversized T-shirt Jayden had loaned her. It practically reached her knees and she'd justified that it served as a good nightshirt.

But mostly, she just hadn't wanted to take it off, enjoying too much the feel of his shirt against her.

She made a face at the dampness still clinging to her suede boots when she pulled them on. She'd already decided not to snoop through Deborah Fortune's room, and opening the woman's closet to see if there were some shoes to borrow felt almost as invasive. So Ariana's own damp boots would have to do.

She walked on her tiptoes back to the kitchen and, as quietly as she could, let herself out of the house through the wooden screen door.

The air smelled wet, and the breeze tugged at her hair and the hem of the T-shirt around her thighs. There wasn't much moonlight, but as her eyes adjusted, she could tell that the layer of clouds overhead had broken up enough to let an occasional star shine through.

Hoping that she wouldn't step in a big puddle of mud, she picked her way to the car, slowly circling it until she was standing by the roof.

Not entirely sure what to expect, she set the flat of her hand on the roof and gave a cautious push.

If the car had been likely to tip back onto its wheels or, heaven forbid, roll right onto its roof, it probably would have done so when Nathan had pulled it away from the cellar door using the winch on Jayden's truck.

She put her other palm against it and slowly leaned her weight against it.

No movement.

The heels on her boots gave her extra height, so it was easy enough to see and reach the car door handle. Getting the door to open, however, wasn't easy at all. No matter how she pulled or pushed, she couldn't get the darn thing to open more than an inch. The only solution would be to climb up on the top—

"You don't have the right leverage."

She snatched her hand back from the car at the sound of the voice behind her and whirled around to see Jayden sitting on the kitchen porch step.

He was shirtless, and he looked like he'd been sitting there for some time.

She dropped her hand from where she'd pressed it to her pounding heart. "How long have you been sitting there?"

"Long enough."

Which told her nothing.

"What's so important inside the car?"

"Nothing." Her heart still pounded. Only now it had a distinctly guilty quality to it that she hated. It was her car, after all. If she wanted to look inside it, wasn't that her right? "I just, uh, couldn't sleep. Couldn't stop thinking about my car."

"So you figured you'd go for a drive?"

She was glad it was dark. It would hide her hot cheeks. Of course, that same darkness hid the expression on his face just as well. "I suppose it's silly of me, but I never thought to ask my insurance company whether my coverage extends to, well, *weather*. No pun intended."

He stretched out his long legs and crossed his ankles.

Unlike her, he hadn't put on boots. Or any other type of footwear, for that matter.

His feet were as bare as his chest. Logically or not, it made her tend to think he hadn't expected to encounter her, either. "What's got *you* up in the middle of the night?"

"Couldn't sleep."

Unlike her, he didn't offer a reason or an excuse and the silence that followed felt awkward. She moistened her lips and swallowed. Then the breeze tugged again at the hem of the T-shirt and she pushed it down. "I must look ridiculous."

"My mom's got shoes in her closet. You could've borrowed something better suited to tramping through the mud."

"I know." She really didn't want to explain her reasoning. "I'm imposing enough already." He also hadn't disagreed that she looked ridiculous. Given the circumstances, she had no right whatsoever feeling vaguely offended. "I should've given you back your shirt and sweatpants after I got my clothes out of the dryer."

"What's stopping you?" He splayed his fingers across his bare abdomen. "God knows I can't go another minute without that T-shirt."

Heat went from her face straight to her stomach. She wondered what he would do if she pulled it off right then and there and handed it to him.

But then again, she didn't really wonder.

She knew exactly what he'd do.

And even though there was an aching, soft spot inside her that wanted that very thing, she turned on her heel again and looked at the car. "I thought about climbing up on top of it so I could get the door open."

"What stopped you?"

She propped her hands on her hips and shook her head. "Afraid I'd tip the car over."

"I doubt it would tip. When Nathan hauled it away from the cellar door, it dug into the mud pretty well."

She hadn't thought about that. "So, you think I *could* climb up—"

He made a sound.

She looked over her shoulder at him again. "What?"

He rubbed his hand over his head, then pushed to his bare feet. He braced his arm against one of the thick wooden posts supporting the overhang of the porch roof. "Just because you could doesn't mean you should. The car's not going anywhere. The insurance policy or whatever you're so anxious to look at is not going anywhere. We'll get the car back on its tires when it's daylight and then we'll see about getting it fixed."

"Is Paseo even large enough to have an automotive repair shop?" The damage might not have affected her ability to drive it, but she couldn't go anywhere with the windshield in the state it was in.

"There's a guy who does work."

She chewed her lip, managing to keep her "Is he qualified?" contained within her own thoughts. She didn't think she was a snob and she certainly didn't want to sound like one. Even if she did have some doubts about the availability of services around here. How could she not?

"You're right. There's nothing that can't wait until daylight. Do you suppose the phone lines might be working again by then?"

"Might be. We're remote, which makes a working phone

line pretty important to everyone in the area. You have someone you need to call?"

"Sooner or later. I do have people who'll wonder where I am." Her parents. Her work, particularly if she couldn't deliver her piece about the grand opening of Keaton's office complex.

She pushed his shirt back down again when it fluttered around her thighs and walked back toward the porch. The entire house was perched on a stone-covered foundation that was at least two feet high. If she'd bothered putting on her jeans—or the sweatpants he'd loaned her—she could have stepped from the ground straight onto the porch without using the three stairs he was blocking.

But she hadn't put on her jeans. Or the sweatpants.

And the only things she had on beneath the shirt was the skin she'd come into the world with plus a pair of seriously skimpy white panties that she'd be embarrassed for her mama to know she'd ever bought.

Which he would most certainly see if she took that two-foot-high stretch.

Instead, she put her boot on the first step. Then the second. The third.

He still didn't move.

She swallowed and had to force the words through her tightening throat. "Excuse me."

He shifted to one side, though he didn't move entirely out of the way. Instead, he lifted his hand and put one finger beneath her chin.

She froze in place, her nerve endings suddenly fizzing. He stood so close to her that she could feel the warmth emanating from his bare skin. Could smell the same scent of soap on him that was on her own skin.

"I can think of one thing that can't wait until daylight," he murmured.

She waved her hand a little desperately at the house. "Your brother—"

"Sleeps like the dead. A skill he learned with the teams. Nothing wakes that guy up these days." He pressed her chin up an inch.

She was having the hardest time breathing. If she leaned forward, she could touch her mouth to the hard line of his collarbone. Taste that warm, smooth skin one more time. "Teams?"

"Navy SEAL."

"My dad was in the navy for a few years. Surprised your other brother isn't air force."

He smiled slightly. His fingertip lifted another inch. "So about that thing that can't wait."

Her lips tingled, already anticipating his kiss. "Yes?"

His finger slid down her throat. It seemed to linger over the pulse she could feel throbbing there, then slid farther, slowly tracing down one side of the V neckline to the lowest point in the valley between her breasts, then even more slowly up the other side and back to her pulse again.

She shifted from one foot to the other, feeling herself leaning closer to him. If her pulse beat any harder she might well pass out. "Jayden."

His head dropped toward hers until his lips were a breath away from hers. "The shirt."

"Hmm?"

"Turns out I can't go without it after all."

She knew he wasn't serious about the challenge, because she could feel the curl of his smile against her mouth.

But it was enough to bring her to her senses.

At least a little.

Because she'd rarely been able to resist a challenge. And this one—right or wrong—was too irresistible to ignore.

She pulled back a few inches and gave him a long look

before turning away from him. She reached out and pulled open the screen door. But before she let it close, she tugged the shirt off her head and tossed it over her shoulder at him.

She heard his muffled exclamation as the door closed between them.

## Chapter Four

"Sleeping beauty finally awakens."

Ariana smiled ruefully at Nathan's greeting and let the screen door close behind her as she walked out onto the porch. The sun was bright and warm and halfway to noon and the sky was entirely cloudless, as if it were completely innocent of the mayhem it had so recently caused. "I didn't intend to sleep so late," she admitted. "I can't remember the last time I slept until ten in the morning."

Jayden's brother was leaning over the opened hood of her car. Jayden himself, however, was nowhere in sight.

Considering the outrageous way she'd walked away from him in the middle of the night wearing nothing but her panties and boots, his absence—however brief it might be—felt like a good thing to her.

She squinted against the sunlight and went down the steps, crossing to her car. "How hard was it to get it back on four wheels?"

Nathan shrugged. He was wearing a dark T-shirt and disreputable-looking cargo shorts. "Bitty car like this? Not hard. We can be glad the twister didn't carry it farther than it did."

"It *was* a tornado, then? How'd you find out?"

"Phone line's fixed. Neighbors have been calling all morning wanting to talk about it."

"I hope nobody was hurt."

He shook his head. "But it ran along the highway for a good while. Ripped the heck out of the highway bridge just outside of town. Tore down a farmhouse back the other way."

She swallowed.

"All things considered, we got off lucky." He focused on the car again. "This thing's got one of those hybrid engines."

She nodded even though it hadn't been a question. Rather, judging by the face he was making, it was more of a condemnation.

That was okay. Her father thought her choice of vehicle was ridiculous, too. But then, aside from his four years in the navy right out of high school, he'd spent his life working for a gas company. She made a mental note to check in with her mother as soon as she could and gestured at the car.

"It's quite a mess, though." She stated the obvious. Mud was caked against the passenger side of the vehicle, pressed into every crevice from the wheel wells of the two flat tires to the door handles to the cracked windows. She walked around to the driver's side. It was cleaner, but not by much. At least the windows and tires looked to be intact.

She pulled open the door. She'd never had the chance to lock it when Jayden had pulled her to the storm cellar the day before, and it opened easily at her touch.

She swiped a few inches of dirt off the seat the best she could and sat down behind the steering wheel.

"Couldn't find your key," Nathan said.

"It takes a keyless remote. I keep it in my purse."

"That's what we figured. We looked."

Her nerves tightened. She'd been so preoccupied with her notes. "I hadn't even thought about my purse." No purse. No key.

And how on earth was she supposed to get back home again without her key? Without her wallet? Her money? Her everything?

"You never know," he said. "With a tornado? Sometimes things get found hundreds of yards away."

"Like my purse?"

"Stranger things have happened." He was silent for a moment. "But I probably wouldn't get my hopes up, if I were you."

"Great." She couldn't see him because of the upraised hood in the way. She felt under her seat, then the passenger seat and came up with nothing but a crinkled receipt from the coffee she'd bought before leaving Austin the morning before.

She got out and opened the rear door. There was glass on the seat and the floor from the back window.

But nothing else.

Trying not to succumb to the panic bubbling around the base of her stomach, she sat back behind the wheel again and leaned over to paw through the glove box. At least there, among a jumble of receipts she needed for her expense report at work, she found her insurance policy information right where it belonged in its little plastic sleeve.

It was one sign of normalcy. As was the wrapped chocolate bar also sitting there.

Coffee was a daily necessity. Just thinking about her

lack of it was almost more than she could stand. Which meant if ever there was a time for emergency chocolate…

She pulled out the candy bar and peeled back the wrapping, took a bite off the corner and let it sit on her tongue to dissolve.

"Not the healthiest of breakfasts."

She jerked upright, banging her elbow on the console, and looked at Jayden, standing next to her opened door with Sugar by his side. Unlike his brother, he was dressed in faded jeans and a white T-shirt.

For all she knew, the same white T-shirt from the night before. On him, the plain white cotton seemed stretched to capacity across his wide shoulders.

She swallowed the melting bite and swiped her mouth just in case she'd been oozing chocolate bliss. She broke off another corner and offered it to Jayden while she reached out to let Sugar sniff her fingers and accept a few pats. "Never knock chocolate."

"Or accept candy from strangers." He smiled slightly as he took the small wedge. "But then, can you really be considered a stranger after everything?" His voice dropped a notch and his eyes were wicked. "I mean, I have seen two of your tattoos." He popped the chocolate in his mouth, seeming to savor it. "Makes me wonder if there are more."

She flushed, but figured she deserved to after her behavior the night before. "There aren't," she said briskly.

She rewrapped the chocolate bar and closed it once more in the glove box. But she kept hold of the insurance card and got out of the vehicle. Sugar was working her way around the car, sniffing at the tires. "I'm going to need to use your phone." She wiggled the plastic-covered card between her thumb and forefinger. "I don't think they'll pay for a towing company all the way back to Austin, but it doesn't hurt to ask."

At that, Nathan pushed the hood down and it shut with a noisy bang. "Don't need to tow it anywhere except to Charlie's." He propped his hands on his hips, not seeming to care that there was grease on his fingers.

Jayden was nodding. "And you don't need to hire a towing company for that. We'll just hook 'er up and take care of it ourselves."

A mental image formed of her poor car being dragged along behind Jayden's pickup by a rope. "I don't want to cause you any more work."

"No work," he assured her.

She lifted her eyebrows and gestured toward the barn behind them. "Really? So that wall over there on the barn is supposed to look all caved in like that?"

"She's got you there." Nathan started toward the house. "But before we do anything, I need more coffee."

Amen to that. Coffee sounded good to her, too. Ariana swung her arm, following Nathan's progress toward the two-story house with its patchwork of boarded-up windows. "It looks like you and your brother are facing a lot of extra work already without worrying about my car."

Jayden's arm brushed hers as he pushed the car door closed. "Do you know how to make coffee?"

It wasn't exactly the kind of response she'd expected. "Of course. Who doesn't?"

"Nathan," he muttered. "I don't know what the hell he does to it." He wrapped his warm hand around her bare elbow and drew her around the car. "You take over coffee and I'll be happy to tow your car all over the state if necessary. It's a fair trade. Trust me."

It was a warm summer morning. Much too warm for the sweater she'd been wearing the day before. But at least if she'd been wearing it now, his hand wouldn't be in direct contact with her skin, setting off all sorts of little fires beneath the surface.

He evidently took her agreement for granted, because she didn't even have a chance to respond before he called his brother's name.

Nathan had just opened the screen door and he looked over his shoulder at them.

"Ariana offered to make it," Jayden said quickly.

She did?

She looked from Jayden's blithe expression to smile brightly at his brother. "It's the least I can do." And all of this talk about coffee had her coffee buds jangling more than ever, anyway. She quickened her step and Jayden's hand fell away before she darted up the stairs and through the screen door that Nathan was still holding open.

Her shoulder brushed against him as she slipped past him. "Excuse me." The two men looked identical. But there was zero effect when it came to Nathan.

To her way of thinking, it was irrefutable proof that physical chemistry wasn't only about looks.

One portion of her mind wondered if there could be an interesting blog about that as she stopped in the middle of the kitchen. There wasn't a coffeemaker visible on the scarred butcher-block counters. "Just point me in the right direction."

In answer, Jayden opened a cupboard and pulled down a huge can of ground coffee that he set on the counter. And Nathan plucked an old-fashioned coffeepot from the sink.

He sniffed the inside, then set it next to the can of coffee. "Go for it."

So much for a coffeemaker.

She eyed the pot. It was tall, white and blue. "My grandmother used to have one like that." Her grandma's hadn't been blackened around the base, though. Nor on the inside, as she saw when she picked it up and looked in. "But then, when she was alive, I wasn't anywhere close to coffee-drinking age."

"Long as it doesn't taste left over from when your grandma did make it, we're in for an improvement," Jayden murmured. "Make as many pots as you want."

"You don't like my coffee, *you* fix it," Nathan said, looking annoyed.

"*I'll* fix it," she said quickly. She'd never once made coffee without a coffeemaker, but she wasn't going to let that stand in her way. She'd simply Google—

The thought screeched to a halt.

Without internet, she wouldn't be looking up how to do anything at all. Not on Google or any other search engine. "Just go on and do your thing and I'll bring it when it's brewed."

Nathan immediately pushed open the screen door again. "Sounds good to me," he said as he left. She heard his whistle and Sugar's answering bark.

Jayden didn't go so quickly, though. "You sure you don't mind—"

"I'm not exactly a guest. If it weren't for the weather, you wouldn't be saddled with me at all."

"Don't hear me complaining, do you?"

She chewed the inside of her lip, wallowing a little in pleasure.

"Seems to me my brother and I are the ones benefiting all around." He peeled the plastic cover off the coffee can and the smell of ground coffee filled the room, tantalizing her taste buds. "But you've got a crunched car and nothing for that magazine article of yours."

At the reminder, her pleasure stepped right into a pothole, tripping all over itself.

She set her insurance card on the counter. Until she

had more information one way or the other about Jayden and his brothers' "made up" Fortune name, she needed to focus on more immediate matters.

Like coffee.

"On the other hand, I wasn't alone and out on the road when my car decided to tangle with the wind." She had to wait out the sudden tightening in her chest. "And for that, I have you to thank," she finished huskily. "Seriously, Jayden. Who knows what might have happened if you hadn't stopped to check on me. Thank you."

He waited a beat. Then two. And when he spoke again, his voice was low and impossibly deep. "My pleasure."

She moistened her lips.

Nathan's impatient shout from outdoors felt like a bucket of cold water being thrown in her face.

And judging by Jayden's rueful expression, she was pretty sure he felt the same. He angled his head toward the screen door. "I'd better make sure he doesn't tear down half the barn while he's at it."

She nodded quickly. "Of course. I'm not a guest, remember?"

His beautiful mouth twitched. "Maybe not. But you're sure the prettiest thing the wind's ever blown in."

"You're the pretty one." The words came out before she could stop them.

His eyebrows shot up. He let out a short bark of laughter, and shaking his head, he followed his brother's path out the screen door.

The second it banged softly back in place, Ariana exhaled shakily and leaned back against the counter. "Not good, girl," she whispered to herself. "Objectivity is key. So you can't go falling for someone you're writing about."

*And if you're* not *writing about him?*

She shook off the notion. The storm had complicated

things for her, but she still had a book advance to earn. She'd do well to remember it.

Then she turned and stuck the coffeepot under the sink faucet.

She didn't know how to make coffee in it, but she was pretty certain that she wanted the thing to at least be clean inside when she started. Then she'd just use the old-fashioned rotary-dial phone hanging on the wall to call and ask her mom what to do with it.

Her car didn't need to be dragged by a rope behind Jayden's truck after all.

Turned out the brothers had a flatbed trailer on which they loaded her car later that day. And the trailer was hauled behind Jayden's truck.

When he'd asked if she wanted to accompany him for the drive into town, she'd eagerly agreed.

Only because of her curiosity about Paseo in general, of course.

Not because sitting beside him in the front of his pickup truck going anywhere at all was too tempting to pass up. No, not at all.

Nor did she feel like a teenage girl on her first real car-date with the high-school quarterback, either.

She could feel a wry smile determined to work its way loose and turned to look out the side window as they drove down the highway. Once again, all she could see for miles was grass, grass and more grass. It undulated this way and that in the breeze in a mesmerizing manner. One way, nearly golden. The other, nearly green. Then *swoosh*, back again.

"What're you thinking about over there?"

Nothing that she felt compelled to admit. Yet she still couldn't wipe off the smile that she knew was on her face as she looked back at him. He'd tossed his hat on the dashboard and his short hair was ruffling in the warm air blowing through his opened window. "Just thinking that there is sure a lot of open space."

"Yep."

Looking at him was too enjoyable to stop. "What made you decide to leave here and go into the army?"

"The opportunity to leave." He had a few laugh lines radiating from the corners of his eyes. She'd noticed the faint lines when his expression was serious because they were slightly lighter. Which made her think he spent a lot of time outdoors either laughing in the sun or squinting in it. Right now, his amusement evident from the glint in his eyes to the slant of his lips, she figured the odds were about even, either way. "Like you said. Lots of open space around here."

"Too much?"

"For a restless eighteen-year-old kid, yeah."

"You enlisted right out of high school?"

"I wanted to. My mom had a fit. She insisted on college first."

"Where'd you go?"

"TJC."

Tyler Junior College, she deciphered.

"You?"

"University of Texas."

"Journalism, I'm guessing."

She shook her head. "Advertising at first, actually. Only I never quite fit."

"Why not?"

"I don't know. I guess I wasn't comfortable enticing people to want what you're selling even if you don't happen to believe in it yourself."

"And you think journalism is more ethical?"

"I don't think there's anything unethical about either.

As long as it's done with integrity. Advertising is an interesting mix of science and art. But the further along I got in school, the less satisfying it felt."

"Journalism satisfies you?"

"It's getting there." Her book deal certainly didn't hurt on that score. "I like writing," she said honestly. "I like people. I like learning about their lives and interests and understanding what makes them tick."

"Surprised you didn't switch to psychology, then."

She chuckled. "I minored in sociology. That's close enough for me. What'd you study in Tyler?"

His smile widened. "Girls." He shrugged. "Criminal justice. But only because I had to pick something."

She was surprised, though she probably shouldn't have been. He'd told her already that he'd been an MP in the army. But she had no idea if that was something a person sought out or if it was assigned. "Did you want to be a cop?"

"No. I just wanted out of Paseo. TJC was as good as any other place and it was affordable. It was far enough from home that I finally got the dirt out from under my nails and the smell of hay off my skin. And the second I graduated with an associate degree, I trucked on down to see the recruiter. Two years later than I'd originally wanted."

"Do you feel like your time at Tyler was wasted?"

His smile kicked up again. "Nah. There were the girls, after all."

She laughed and realized they were slowing. Since they'd gotten on the highway, they hadn't passed a single other car. "Was there anyone serious?"

"Not serious enough to keep me from enlisting."

"And after that? You were in the army for fifteen years." She caught the look he gave her. "What?"

"Good memory."

"I like to think so, but you told me that just yesterday when we were in the storm cellar."

"Yeah, but a lot's happened since then. Seems longer than just a day."

Heat flowed swiftly in her veins from thinking about how much had happened. It wasn't just the storm. It was *him*.

"Well, I don't worry that you're an ax murderer anymore," she admitted.

His concentration was forward as he turned off the highway onto a narrow paved road, but he shot her a quick look. "Ax murderer?"

"You never know." She raised her eyebrows right back at him. "A complete stranger on a remote Texas road? Blockbuster slasher movies have been made on less." When her mother had heard about the situation, she had been nearly apoplectic until Ariana told her that Jayden and his brother were *The* Grayson's brothers.

Evidently the fact that Karen had heard of the rodeo rider lent some legitimacy to Ariana's situation.

"Maybe I figured *you* were an ax murderer," Jayden countered.

She shook her head immediately. "Statistics are all wrong. Eighty-seven percent of murders are committed by men."

"Should I be alarmed that you can pull that stat out of your head?" He shot her an amused look. "You don't have to tell me what men are more capable of doing. But trust me. Women don't get a pass, either."

"Didn't say that they did."

"So if you were so worried I was the next character out of a horror flick, why go with me at all?"

"Sugar. What can I say?" she added at the expression

that earned from him. "You'd tied a bandanna around her neck for a collar."

"Because crazed people never have dogs?" His tone was dry. "Frankly, I was glad that you had the sense to show some caution." He'd reached a run-down-looking house. He propped his arm over the top of the steering wheel and peered through the windshield. "Should have shown more, probably."

She looked skeptically from him toward the house. It was surrounded by a chain-link fence behind which a growling white pit bull was racing back and forth along the rut it had worn among the weeds. "Where you're concerned or where this place is concerned?"

Unlike Jayden's stone-fronted home, which had a comfortable and welcoming demeanor, this place practically shouted "stay away."

"If I had a sister, I'd want her to assume every man wanted something from her they shouldn't."

"I'm not your sister."

His gaze dropped to her mouth for a moment. Then he grabbed his hat off the dash and planted it low over his forehead and pushed open the truck door. "Thank God for that," he said as he climbed out.

She started to open her own door but stopped when she realized he was coming around to open it for her. "The only man who always opens my door for me is my father," she said as she hopped out.

"I'm not your father."

She couldn't stop her smile. "Thank God for that."

The frenzied dog's growling had graduated to barking, and the racket drew a short, skinny man wearing denim overalls and a stained ball cap from around the side of the house. "Betsy, shut up," he yelled and the dog's barking immediately subsided to a yip. She reared up on her hind legs and hung her front paws over the top of the fence.

Ariana almost wished she'd stayed inside the truck. "She's not going to jump the fence, is she?"

The man in the overalls had reached them. "Nah," he drawled. "Less'n you give her a reason to." He stuck out a hand that was missing half a forefinger toward Jayden and grinned as they shook briefly. He had a lined, weathered face that could have put him anywhere between fifty and eighty. "She's got a real soft spot for Sugar."

"Last time I brought her with me to see Charlie, it took us a whole day to track them down," Jayden said. "Learned the hard way that I had to leave her at home whenever I come here." He introduced her. "Ariana Lamonte, meet Charlie Esparza."

"Fool pooches were halfway to the next county." Charlie doffed his cap, revealing a shock of white hair that he dipped in her direction in a vaguely quaint, courtly manner, even though he was a good head shorter than she was. "Pleased to make your acquaintance, miss. Sorry it's because of that tornado." He looked back at Jayden. "Glad to hear things weren't torn up too bad over at your place."

"Nothing we can't put back together again with a few days' time. Unlike the Ybarras' house. Figured we'd stop by there on our way back home," Jayden told him. "See how they're doing."

That was news to Ariana, but obviously not surprising to Charlie, who nodded. "'Spect they'll have a lot of people callin'. Damn shame about their farmhouse." He gave Ariana an apologetic look. "Pardon my French, miss."

She couldn't help her bemusement. "Ariana, please."

"That's a real pretty name, miss."

"Thank you."

"Watch out for Charlie here." Jayden clapped the man

on the shoulder. "Besides his considerable skill at flirting, he's been fixing up everything on wheels around these parts ever since I was a kid."

"Since before you wrecked your first car, that's for sure." He replaced his ball cap and walked to the trailer and her car. "Looked a lot worse than this little doll, if I remember rightly."

"And I was driving that old Mustang for another couple years."

"Until he wrecked it again," Charlie told Ariana in an aside.

"I've never even had a fender bender," Ariana admitted. "What caused your accidents?"

"Fool-headedness," Charlie said before Jayden could.

She looked from the older man to Jayden. He'd reached one hand over the fence to pet Betsy's head. Gone were the ferocious teeth she'd been baring, and instead, her long tongue hung out of her triangular face as she panted. It almost looked like the dog was smiling.

"Racing a friend out on the highway." He rubbed the dog's floppy ears and Betsy's eyes rolled in pleasure. "Fool-headedness, just like Charlie said."

"The first wreck or the second?"

Jayden's lips twisted wryly. "Both." He gave the dog a final pat, much to Betsy's obvious dismay, and moved over to the car as well. He propped his hands on his lean hips. "So what do you think, Charlie?"

In answer, the man nimbly climbed up on the trailer, working his way around the car. "Gonna take some time. Parts for these hybrids are harder to come by than some."

She may not have had experience with vehicular accidents, but she did have some dealing with auto repair shops since the car she'd owned before this one had broken down more often than it had run. "Where do you do the work, Mr. Esparza?"

"Charlie," the man corrected her, hopping down to the ground next to her. "Back in the garage." He gestured vaguely in the direction of the house. "Drive 'er on back," he told Jayden. "We'll get 'er unloaded."

"I have insurance," she said quickly. "They'll want an estimate before they'll pay for work. And I don't know if Jayden told you, but I can't find the key—"

Charlie waved off her words. "Sure 'nough, miss. We'll get all that official stuff taken care of. And I can get a replacement key just like the rest of the parts, no problem. Just takes time, like I said. Don't worry yourself none. Everything'll be fine." He looked at Jayden. "Pull up by the back bay," he said and started walking away.

Jayden opened Ariana's door again and she climbed in.

Then he drove around the run-down-looking house and she spotted the garage. It was easily four times the size of the house and not run-down in the least. "Wow."

"Yeah." Jayden clearly understood her surprise. "What Charlie doesn't put into his house, he puts into the garage. It's his one true love. Guy does everything from bodywork to building cars from the ground up."

He backed the trailer up to one of the several oversized garage doors. They were all closed, but as Charlie neared, the one behind them began opening and Ariana could see inside the cavernous space that already housed a sports car with its hood up, a fancy-looking boat on a trailer and a half-dozen motorcycles in various stages of assembly.

"Looks like he does more than just cars. There's enough water around here for a boat?"

"If you don't mind a bit of a drive." He got out of the truck. "Charlie's got an office inside on the other side of that tire rack if you want to go over and wait while we get your car unloaded."

She'd already taken her insurance information out of the glove box. Aside from the clothes on her back, at the moment, the insurance information and her still-inoperable cell phone comprised all of her personal effects. With both in hand, she walked through the spotless garage into the office. It had a glass door and she could see Jayden and Charlie make quick work of unloading her small car. Then the two men started toward the office, stopping along the way to check out one of the motorcycles.

Ariana couldn't hear what they were saying, but she couldn't help but chuckle at the sight they made. Physically, the two men couldn't be more different. But their expressions as they lovingly examined the bike were exactly the same.

She was still smiling when they pushed through the glass door. Charlie shuffled around to sit behind a metal desk that had only a single in-box sitting on its surface, squarely aligned in one corner, while Jayden sauntered to where Ariana was sitting in one of the black-and-white-checked chairs lined against the wall beside a small, also spotless, restroom.

Ariana had to admit that Charlie's garage was the cleanest one she'd ever been in.

"What're you sitting there smiling about?" Jayden pulled off his cowboy hat as he sat beside her and hooked it over his bent knee.

"You guys drooling over that Fat Boy out there."

He raised his eyebrow. "You know your Harleys?"

"I did a blog a year ago on men's love affairs with their motorcycles." It had actually been about men's love affairs with their toys superseding their love affairs with their mates, but that was beside the point.

She could smile about it now. Which meant the cathartic blog had done its job. Hadn't hurt that her readership had skyrocketed, either. That was when her editor at *Weird Life* had first assigned her to interview an up-and-coming architect from London named Keaton Whitfield...who also happened to be the illegitimate son of Gerald Robinson.

And her series "Becoming a Fortune" had been born.

Jayden's booted toe was bobbing in her peripheral vision and her sense of well-being wilted.

The series might have become the delight of the magazine's readers, but it wasn't always to the delight of her subjects whether they were one of Gerald's legitimate *or* illegitimate progeny. She'd also never exposed anyone as being one of his offspring. By the time she'd interviewed Keaton—and subsequently, his half sister Chloe Elliott— they'd already learned elsewhere that Gerald was their biological father. They'd had time to adjust. Sort of.

"Miss?"

The same couldn't be said for Jayden and his brothers, though. The truth—if it was the truth—would blindside them.

Ariana realized that Charlie was speaking to her. She looked over at him, dragging her thoughts into the present.

"You all right?" Jayden's head was angled as he studied her from those steady brown eyes.

It was never her intention to cause harm in her writing. But it was her intention to be truthful.

And some truths were harder to swallow than others.

"I'm fine," she lied. "Just got to thinking about what a hassle it's going to be replacing my driver's license and everything else in my wallet. I don't even have my credit card with me to pay the insurance deductible to Charlie."

Jayden's hand covered hers and squeezed. "You're not worried about that, are you, Charlie?"

"Nah." Charlie had pulled a paper form onto his desk

and she could see that he'd completed some of it. Now he extended the pen he'd been using toward her. "Only need your signature, miss, and we'll settle up the score later."

Jayden squeezed her hand again. "Sound good?"

"Sounds good," she repeated dutifully and reached for the pen.

She just wished she were certain that settling the score with Jayden wasn't going to cost her more than whatever she ended up owing for her car.

# Chapter Five

"There you have it." Jayden braked in the middle of the road and gestured at the cluster of buildings ahead of him. "Downtown Paseo in all its glory. Bet you've never seen anything quite like it. Outside of a spaghetti Western, at any rate."

He was determined to put the smile back on Ariana's face. The smile that had been absent since she'd signed the paperwork in Charlie's office.

The smile that was still absent as she looked through the windshield of his truck at the town he called home.

"I've never seen anything quite like it," she agreed. "What's the population?"

"Last census had us just over a couple hundred. Of course, that includes the surrounding ranches." He took his foot off the brake. "Let me give you the tour. Don't blink now. If you do, you'll miss it."

That, at least, earned a twitch of her lips.

It was progress.

"That's the town hall." He gestured to a square brick building that was under construction.

"It's still being repaired from the hailstorm last year. You mentioned it," she reminded him when he showed his surprise.

He kept forgetting her attention to detail. She had a singular ability to listen and listen well.

It wasn't a trait he was all that used to when it came to women. Or at least when it had come to Tess, he supposed.

Fortunately, Ariana wasn't Tess.

"The construction isn't from those repairs, though that did take a while. What they're doing now is expanding to accommodate the library." He pointed to the RV sitting in the town-hall parking lot as he slowly trolled past the building.

"That motor home is the library? It's a bookmobile?" She looked at the vehicle with a hopeful expression. "I wish this was one of the days it was open. I could sure stand a little time with the internet."

"Thought you called your boss before we left."

"I did. But I've also got to get the ball rolling on replacing my driver's license and such."

He shook his head. "Ball is still going to have to wait. Library's not open on Saturdays. And it's not exactly mobile. The RV is just a shell. Doesn't run."

She made a face. "Well, that's my luck lately. So, is the existence of a library new around here?"

"Nah. But it used to be just a wall of books in the gas station. The RV was donated by the Ybarra family a few years back. Same Ybarras who just lost their farmhouse."

He poked his thumb in the direction of said gas station. "You can get your gas and your groceries there. Or if you're feeling in a festive mood, you can sit down in the Mexican restaurant they run in the back."

A humorous light filled her chocolate-brown eyes and the twitch on her lips had turned into a soft curve. She didn't have on a lick of makeup but she couldn't have been prettier if she'd tried.

"Sounds tasty," she drawled.

"Don't knock it until you've tried it. Rosa—she owns all three businesses—makes some mean carnitas. Better than I've had anywhere else."

"I'd offer to take you in return for giving me shelter during the storm, but—" She spread her hands and the bracelets around her wrist sparkled. "I have no way to pay."

He grinned. "Play your cards right, and maybe I'll take *you.*"

"Careful. You'll turn my head with such fancy offers." Smiling fully, she pointed at another building.

"Hardware store," he provided. "Sells bits of everything from farm equipment to bolts of fabric."

Her eyebrows immediately went up. "How about a cell phone charger?"

He doubted it. "Let's check and see. I need to stop anyway and order the replacement window glass we need cut."

She smiled winningly and quickly unclipped her seat belt, hopping out before he had a chance to get around to her side. He followed her into the store and couldn't help but chuckle at the amazed expression crossing her face.

"I'll go ask about the charger," he offered, but she was already setting off for the nearest aisle. He couldn't imagine what would be so interesting about stove parts and cast-iron cookware, but he followed her through the aisles anyway.

Watching her explore fascinated him. She stretched up to look at a dusty copper bracelet display and crouched down a few steps later to examine a metal water trough. When he plucked a wind chime off the shelf, she gave him a surprised look. "Wind chimes with little fairies on it?"

He didn't care about the fairies. He cared about the tones it made. "We lost the set of wind chimes that usually hangs by the kitchen door. They help orient Sugar when she's outside."

Her eyes softened.

They made it around the entire store, never having encountered another person. Much to his surprise, though, she had found a section of electronics and had pounced on one package in particular with glee.

Until she'd rolled her eyes and shook her head, muttering to herself as she put the package back on the shelf.

It didn't take a genius to figure out why. He handed her the package. "You can owe me if it makes you feel better."

She told him it did, and she clasped the package to the front of her thin excuse for a top as if it were precious and carried it there through the rest of the store, not setting it down until they reached the checkout counter at the front. "Is there anyone even here?"

He'd begun wondering that himself. Admittedly, Paseo wasn't a hotbed of crime when it came to shoplifting. But there was usually someone around the store, either the owner, Harvey, or one of the local kids he hired. "I'll check the stockroom." He headed to the back of the store again, pushing through the swinging door there and calling Harv's name.

The two teenagers getting busy on a camping mattress in the back sprang apart.

Jayden gave the boy—Harvey's grandson—a look. "Kind of hard to watch the store when your eyes are closed, son."

The kid flushed, though Jayden privately gave him props for trying to shield his nearly naked girlfriend from view.

"Need some window glass cut." He pulled a folded paper from his pocket and set it on the shelf just inside the swinging door. "Those're the measurements. I'll be back tomorrow to pick them up."

He returned to the front of the store, dropped a fifty-dollar bill on the counter for their two items and steered Ariana out of the store.

"I can't believe someone would leave the store open like that without anyone there," she said as they climbed into his truck once more.

"Someone was there," he said wryly. He tossed the wind-chime box in the backseat. "Just…otherwise engaged."

She looked up from peeling open her cardboard package.

"Sex," he elaborated as he pulled a U-turn on the empty street. There were other highlights the town possessed besides a town hall and a hardware store, but it was getting late and the clouds on the horizon had started climbing high in the sky with what would likely become another thunderstorm before too long. And he still wanted to get by the Ybarra place. "Two kids in the storeroom making the slow day pass by a lot more quickly."

He watched her cheeks flush. Which was interesting, because in their limited but eventful time together, Ariana had not struck him as being either shy or prudish. "Never made out in the back of a store when you were a teenager?"

She rolled her eyes, shaking her head. "Never worked in a store when I was a teenager."

"So, what *did* you do when you were a teenager?"

"Daydreamed." She gave him a wry smile, looking vaguely chagrined. "Babysat. Helped out at the front desk at the dental office where my mom still works." She lifted her shoulder. "Cheerleading."

"No kidding?"

She did a sort of rah-rah thing with her arm. "Go Cougars."

"Suppose you dated the captain of the football team, too."

"Briefly." She pulled the contents from the box and held up the car adapter. "Do you mind?" When he shook his head, she leaned forward and plugged it into the cigarette lighter, then sat back and attached it to her cell phone. "Whoahoa!" She held up her phone. The surface of it was black, but a small light on the corner was blinking. "We have liftoff."

She was clearly delighted, so he didn't remind her how useless he figured the thing was in their corner of the world.

She rolled down her window, propping her elbow in the opening, and her long hair streamed away from her face. "Anyway, the quarterback's name was Scotty. We lasted all of two weeks."

"What ended the great romance?"

"Juliette Wysocki. My next-door neighbor, head cheerleader and chief easy-pants of the school." She waited a beat. "Not that I held a grudge or anything."

He laughed. "Easy-pants, huh?"

"Better than calling her Empress of Slutville. Though I'll tell you that particular shoe is one she's still wearing." Her eyes danced as she looked at him. Then she seemed to realize that her long hair was blowing across his shoulder and she gathered it together, holding it in one hand.

He'd been a long way from complaining about it. Ariana had amazing hair. Thick. Lustrous. He couldn't look at it without wanting to wrap his hands in it.

He dragged his mind out of that particular puddle.

"So you lost out to Juliette's seductive ways. What happened then?"

"I swore off boys for the rest of the year, graduated *almost* at the top of my class—that honor went to Simon Mendivil—went to New York City on a two-month internship and came back home to start UT a few weeks later."

"What'd you think of New York City?" He could imagine her there.

"Vibrant. Crowded. *Way* too expensive. Have you been?"

He nodded. "Always on my way to somewhere else, though."

"Well, while I was there, I shared a one-bedroom apartment with four other girls. Cozy, to say the least."

"What was the internship for?"

"Working at an advertising firm. It was interesting and I was even offered a longer-term stint, but I couldn't afford to stay on the pittance I was earning, and I didn't have time enough after hours to get another job. So—" She shrugged. "I came back home." She peered through the windshield. "That's not another storm, is it?"

"Supposed to be the tail end of the season for storms, but I figure anything's possible. Clouds are pretty far off yet." He flipped through the radio dial, finding a handful of talk shows in Spanish, a fuzzy country station and a pregame for the Astros. No weather at all. He turned the volume down, but left the baseball station on.

She was chewing her lip.

He reached over and caught her hand. "Don't look so worried. Watching the rain from our front porch is one of the most peaceful things in the world."

"So long as it's only rain," she said.

But she'd stopped torturing her soft lower lip.

And she'd left her fingers curled around his.

Even though Nathan had said the tornado had torn down a neighbor's farmhouse, until Ariana saw it for herself through Jayden's windshield as he slowly rolled to a stop in front of it, she had no real conception just how devastating the sight would be.

"Oh, my God," she murmured. She couldn't tell if the house had been a single story or a multistory. She couldn't tell if it had been painted white or yellow or purple.

If it weren't for an avocado-green refrigerator with the door half torn off lying on its side in the midst of the pile of sticks and lumber and debris, she wasn't sure she would have even known it had ever been a house.

Someone's home.

"That poor family."

Jayden's expression was solemn as he pushed open his door. "You want to come or wait here?"

Beyond the group of camper trucks and SUVs clustered together, she realized that someone had erected a pop-up canopy midway between the remains of the house and a tall white barn, and there was a group of people milling around it. "I'd like to come if I won't be intruding."

"When it comes to Paloma and Hector Ybarra, nobody is an intruder."

She pushed open her own door. "They're the owners, I take it?"

"Yes. Be careful," he warned. "Don't get close to the house."

She nodded and went around the back of the truck to join him on the far side. He pulled a five-gallon jug of water out of the truck bed that she hadn't even noticed before and propped it on his shoulder before taking her elbow as they walked toward the tent. Which was good, since Ariana could barely tear her attention away from the destruction of the house and she nearly tripped over a broken roof tile in her path.

It didn't matter how many news stories she'd ever watched about tornadoes and the damage they caused. It was positively eerie seeing the house leveled, while a couple hundred yards away, the barn looked blissfully untouched.

"Jayden." A diminutive white-haired woman broke away from the group under the tent and approached them. She was smiling and her arms were held wide. "What a welcome sight you are. I see you brought us more water."

Jayden let go of Ariana and set down the heavy water container to hug the tiny woman. "*Lo siento*, Paloma."

"Ah. Thank you, *mijo*. But it is a house. Hector and I are the home." She patted his cheek, looking past him with bright brown eyes to Ariana. "And who is this?"

Jayden's gaze moved over Ariana, setting off a sweet warmth inside her. "A new friend. Ariana Lamonte, this lovely lady is Paloma Ybarra. One of my most favorite people on earth."

Ariana held out her hand and found it clasped warmly between both of Paloma's. "I'm so sorry to meet you under these circumstances, Mrs. Ybarra."

"Better to meet than not to meet, isn't that right, Jayden?" She smiled up at Ariana. "Come and meet my Hector." Still holding Ariana's hand, she also grabbed Jayden's arm and tugged them toward the canopy. She called out something in Spanish and a teenage boy trotted past them to take the water and add it to the collection of supplies that Ariana could see under the canopy.

"Graciela is here," Paloma was telling Jayden. "She and Tomas arrived this afternoon." Her eyes bounced back to

Ariana. "My daughter and her husband. They live in Mexico City. Tomas is an attorney there."

"She definitely moved up from the likes of me," Jayden said with a smile. His eyes met Ariana's over Paloma's head. "Graciela was the girl who got away."

"He is teasing you, Ariana," Paloma assured her. "Jayden was only a boy when my daughter finished high school."

"Yeah." They'd reached the tent and Jayden gave Ariana a quick wink. "The unattainable older woman." He moved away from Paloma and Ariana to kiss the cheek of a strikingly beautiful, dark-haired woman who threw back her head and laughed throatily over whatever it was he said.

Even with that wink of his, Ariana still felt a curl of jealousy. She clamped down on it witheringly.

Oftentimes when people were displaced from their homes because of some disaster, local charities lent aid. But in such a remote area as Paseo, Ariana had a feeling those services were probably hard to come by.

"Mrs. Ybarra, do you and your husband have some place to stay?" Admittedly, she hadn't seen all of the businesses in Paseo, but considering its size, she doubted there was a motel of any sort. "Do you have more family in the area?"

"Graciela is our only child." Paloma patted Ariana's hand. "But Hector and I have each other." She gestured toward the barn. "We have shelter." She nodded toward Jayden, who was working his way through the dozen or so people there, greeting them all. "We have friends. We are very blessed."

Ariana wasn't sure how many people would feel so blessed when confronted with similar circumstances.

Because Paloma didn't let go of her hand, she found herself pulled along, being introduced to everyone. "This is Jayden's new *friend*," Paloma would say. Emphasis on the *friend*. As if it weren't all that ordinary to be introducing a female fitting that particular category when it came to Jayden Fortune.

Someone started moving the folding lawn chairs, and before Ariana knew it, she was sitting in one squarely between Hector and Paloma with a plate of coleslaw and corn bread on her lap and a bottle of beer in her hand. Paloma's husband mostly smiled benignly at everyone, Ariana included. Whatever he didn't have to say, his wife more than made up for it as she chattered on about Paseo, about the weather, about God and the Devil and just about everything in between.

"He was a wild one, your Jayden," Paloma said after finally pausing to draw breath.

Ariana had been fascinated by everything Paloma had said. But she really needed to correct this misapprehension about her and Jayden. "Mrs. Ybarra, Jayden's not my—"

"Never deliberately chased a fight," Paloma said right over Ariana's attempt to correct her. "But he never turned away from one, either. Oh, how his mama used to worry about him. He's told you about his mama, *si*?"

Ariana glanced his way. She had the feeling he'd just as easily stand out among five dozen people as he did in this small gathering. And as if he felt her attention, he turned his head and looked at her.

His lips tilted up and the lines beside his eyes crinkled.

Her nerve endings fizzed.

Lord, the man did have a smile.

Then he turned back to the three teenagers he was speaking with—Hector's second and third cousins who were both named Arturo and who also lived in Mexico—and Ariana belatedly focused on Paloma. She casually set the beer bottle on the ground next to her boot. "Jayden's mother? He, uh, he hasn't said a lot." *Just that Deborah supposedly made up the surname of Fortune.* She ignored the voice inside her head.

"Raised those boys all on her own." Paloma hadn't waited

a beat. "Course, she had a little help early on from the Thompsons. Earl and Cynthia. Deborah was a comfort to them, sure enough, after they'd lost their only daughter that horrible way just a few months before." Paloma nodded as if all of these were details that Jayden's *friend* undoubtedly already knew. "But even in tragedy there is blessing. Earl and Cynthia took in Deborah when she was in a bad way. Traveling like she was, so pregnant and all. And my, they loved those little babies when they were born a little while later. If it hadn't been for them, I'm not sure what Earl and Cynthia would've done. And vice versa. They had someone to pass on their ranch to, and those babies had a safe and happy place to grow up in." She set her wrinkled hand on top of Ariana's and patted it gently. "Life tends to work out the way it's supposed to if we don't let ourselves get in the way." Then she pushed herself off the chair, because another car had driven up and she was heading toward it.

"My wife likes you," Hector said in a low, raspy voice.

"She's lovely," she told Hector truthfully. "But I have the feeling your wife would like everyone she meets." Paloma obviously would find something good to say about anyone. Even the Empress of Slutville. She shoveled some coleslaw in her mouth and popped her plate into the opened trash bag that Graciela's handsome husband was offering to everyone. "Mr. Ybarra, I don't want to intrude, so please tell me it's none of my business if you like. But where will you and Mrs. Ybarra be staying?" All of their relatives seemed to have come from miles and miles away. Which also had her wondering where they would stay.

"Right here, girl." His arm encompassed the devastated house, the temporary canopy and the barn all in one.

"But it's going to rain again soon." The clouds on the horizon were nearing and they were obviously carrying rain.

Hector looked amused. "Roof on the barn's still sound. Was last night. And will be tonight."

"You're sleeping in the barn?"

"Unless it's clear. There's nothing like sleeping under a Paseo sky." His eyes shifted to Jayden for a brief moment. "Ask him. He'll tell you the same." He looked back at Ariana. "Been living on this land since I was born. Not going to leave Paseo just because of some wind and rain. Stole my wife from her family in Mexico when she was just seventeen. Been married more 'n fifty years now and every night of that's been spent here on this land whether we were under what used to be that roof or not."

She smiled at him. "Mr. Ybarra, I write for a magazine in Austin. Nothing you would have even heard of here in Paseo, but I'd really like to do a piece about you and your wife."

His bushy gray eyebrows shot up. "The heck you say!"

"I think our readers would be inspired by your story."

He laughed and shook his head. "If that ain't *loco*. Long as you don't say something untrue, I guess I don't see the harm. Paloma'll be real pleased, I'm sure."

"Hector," Jayden drawled as he stopped in front of them, "you married the prettiest woman already. Then Graciela didn't wait for me to get out of short pants before she married Tomas. So don't be smiling like that at the next beauty to come along."

Ariana laughed at that. She had never made the mistake of considering herself beautiful. She was reasonably passable when she had a bag of armor to brighten up her face and plenty of hair products to tame her unruly, long hair. But that was okay, because she was generally comfortable in her own skin. A trait that made the people she talked with more comfortable in theirs.

"Mr. Ybarra has agreed to let me write a story about him and his wife for *Weird,*" she told Jayden.

"Weird?" Hector looked suddenly alarmed. "What kinda magazine is that?"

She smiled reassuringly. *"Weird Life Magazine,"* she clarified. "It's a lifestyle magazine published in Austin. It's named after 'Keep Austin Weird'—the town's unofficial slogan. Trust me, you have nothing to worry about."

He looked somewhat appeased. "You vouch for your girl, Jayden?"

It felt like a rope suddenly sneaked its way around Ariana's throat.

"Sure I do, Hector." Jayden grabbed her hand and pulled her to her feet. "Nathan and I will come by tomorrow and help with some of the cleanup. You and Paloma can talk yourselves hoarse with Ariana then."

The older man pushed to his feet and shook Jayden's hand. Then he bowed slightly over the one Ariana offered, as if he weren't particularly accustomed to shaking women's hands.

Paloma was in the clinch of a sausage-curled woman wailing about the tornado when they started to leave. Paloma just spread her hands behind the woman's stranglehold and smiled as she caught their eye. Then she patted the woman's back. "It's all right, Molly," they heard her soothe. "Don't upset yourself this way."

"I think Paloma must be a saint or something," Ariana said in a low voice once she and Jayden returned to his truck. "I'm pretty sure I wouldn't be up to comforting someone else if my house was a pile of kindling around my feet."

"They're good people." He pulled open the passenger door for her and she climbed up inside. "You really want to write a story about them?"

She nodded. Her gaze went from the destroyed house to

the canopy. "I really do." She picked up her cell phone. It still looked like it was charging, though nothing happened when she pressed the power button. "Hopefully, this thing will be working again and I can record the interview and take some photographs of them. Whether I can use it as a phone or not, it has a really good camera."

She'd love to take a photograph of Jayden, too, but she kept that tidbit to herself. Particularly considering she wasn't sure if she wanted it for personal reasons or professional.

"I'm surprised you didn't have a laptop or something with you. But you never mentioned one getting lost in the storm."

She waited until he got behind the wheel. "I only use my laptop when I actually get down to the business of writing. I had one crash on me once without a backup—my fault entirely—but it made me superstitious, I guess. I take most of my notes by hand."

"So you're not tied quite so much to technology as I had you pegged," he drawled.

She smiled and turned her hands upward. "We'll see."

He worked their way around the collection of haphazardly parked vehicles and it dawned on Ariana that, while Hector and Paloma slept in the barn, many of their callers were probably sleeping in those campers.

A fact that Jayden confirmed when she voiced it. "Unless it's clear out and they'll move their sleeping bags under the stars."

She couldn't help but smile, thinking of what Hector had said.

"So what other kinds of stories do you write? Besides your Fortune thing and guys' fixations on things that go zoom."

She grabbed her hair before it could start blowing

around too much from the opened windows. She was already going to have a heck of a time getting a comb through it. "I mostly do human interest stories." That was entirely true. Even her bio on the magazine's website said so. It just didn't say a thing about her current pursuit into one man's secretive past.

She shifted in her seat, pulling the shoulder belt a few inches away from her chest because it felt strangely tight.

"Mostly?"

She reminded herself that she wasn't really hiding secrets. Jayden already knew about her "Becoming a Fortune" series for the magazine. And when it came to her book, she'd deal with the facts as she learned them.

She realized she still hadn't answered him and shifted again. "I still do a weekly blog on the club scene around Austin. That's pretty much how I started out. With the blog, I mean. I check out popular venues. Grand openings. New concerts. New shows. That sort of thing. I was supposed to do a place called Twine last night. I have a couple of friends who bartend there. Surprisingly enough, my editor hadn't reassigned it to someone else when I called in yesterday."

"Lot of competition among the writers?"

"Enough to keep you on your toes." Enough to know that her book deal would add considerable weight when it came time to negotiate her next contract with *Weird Life*. "So you had a crush on Graciela? She's very beautiful."

"That's a quick change of subject."

"What can I say? People interest me, obviously."

"That's all it is?" A small smile played around his lips as he shot her a quick look. "Professional interest?"

He charmed her way too easily.

"I'm not going to answer that," she said calmly.

His laugh was low.

It still managed to send shivers straight down her spine that didn't ever really stop, not even when they arrived back at his ranch almost an hour later.

They did beat the clouds back to the ranch, but not by much. Nathan and Sugar met them when Jayden drove up and it started to rain as the two men unhitched the trailer.

Hovering around watching them only meant getting wet or getting in their way, so she headed back to the house. She plugged her phone into one of the kitchen outlets and left it on the counter to charge, then went into the bedroom and sat on the bed to pull off her boots.

Mismatched stockinged feet freed, she dropped the boots on the floor and lay back on the mattress, wiggling her toes and rotating her ankles. "Oh, yessss."

"I suppose it would be wrong of me to take that as an invitation."

She looked to where Jayden was standing in the open doorway. His shirt was speckled with raindrops. And she had to fight the strong urge to hold out her hand to him in invitation.

Instead, she rolled onto her side and propped her head on that hand just to make sure it didn't do something it shouldn't.

"Unless you're offering a foot massage," she said drily, "yes, it would be very wrong." She leaned over and picked up one of her bedraggled-looking boots. The red color had turned patchy and the suede itself was flattened and shiny. "Aside from the sad state of the suede, these boots weren't quite made for walkin'. At least not anymore."

"They have kind of taken a beating."

"That's one way to put it. I don't know if they shrank after getting wet, but they sure fit tighter now than they did before yesterday's storm." She let the boot drop back onto the floor next to its mate and swung her legs off the bed and stood.

Lying there didn't feel all that wise. It was too easy for her mind to skip down seductive paths.

"That's why you pretreat suede," he said, walking past her to open the closet door. "So it doesn't shrink. Doesn't stain, either." He gestured at the interior of the closet. "Find something in there that'll be more comfortable. Shoes. Clothes. Whatever. I doubt anything of my mom's clothing is going to be too small for you. She's taller 'n you. And she wouldn't mind," he added before she could open her mouth to protest. "That's what people do in these parts, in case you missed it. We look out for each other. It's a necessity when there're so few to depend on. Hell, that's how Mom came to settle in Paseo in the first place. Depending on the kindness of strangers." He gestured again at the clothing. "Find some shoes. Then come on outside. I'll get the grill going soon for supper. You like steak?"

"Couldn't call myself a Texan in good conscience if I didn't."

He grinned and left the room.

Ariana drew in a deep, needy breath that was owed entirely to the wallop packed into that grin.

Even though she still felt strange about it, she crouched down and plucked a pair of faded black tennis shoes from the neat row on the closet floor and pulled them on.

Jayden had been right. They were at least one size too large. She tied them tightly, but still had to be careful not to step right out of them as she left the room.

She found him and his brother sitting in two of the wooden rockers that were scattered along the wraparound porch. Sugar, sprawled between them, lifted her head as Ariana approached, sniffed a few times, then lowered her head again to her paws and closed her eyes.

Jayden pulled a third chair closer to him. "Sit."

She sat. She stretched out her legs and crossed them at the ankles the same way the two men were doing.

"Now just watch," he said. "And listen."

So she did.

Beyond the overhanging roof, the light rain fell. She could hear the sound of it striking the roof, pinging on the gutters, splashing on the stones. The air filled with the redolent scent of moist, rich earth.

She wasn't going to think about Gerald Robinson. About Deborah Fortune. What their relationship might have been and what, if anything, Charlotte had known about it. Not while Ariana was wearing Deborah's shoes and sitting beside two of her sons.

Ariana drew in a deep breath and let it out.

She felt Jayden's dark gaze on her and looked his way.

He smiled slowly.

Warmth—comfortable and sweet—seemed to fill her, rising right up through her from the soles of her feet to the top of her head.

He was right.

Watching the rain from Jayden's porch was about the most peaceful thing in the world.

## Chapter Six

The following day, after Jayden and his brother had already spent several early-morning hours working the cattle—whatever *that* meant—Ariana went with him again back into town to retrieve the window glass he'd ordered.

While he was busy with that, she made a beeline for the aisle two rows over from where she'd found the cell phone charger. There, she flipped through the neatly folded pile of neon-colored tie-dyed T-shirts emblazoned with *Paseo Is Paradise* that she'd seen the day before and found two size mediums at the very bottom. She took them both. Then she found a tube of lip balm and a travel toothbrush in the camping supply aisle and was just thinking wryly how lucky she was not to be needing any type of feminine supply items anytime soon when Jayden found her.

"Find everything you want?"

She nodded and followed him to the checkout counter where his panes of window glass were already waiting, padded and packed in wooden crates.

"I'm keeping a list," she said once he'd paid and was strapping the crates upright in the truck bed. To prove it, she showed him the screen of her cell phone, which had finally powered up even though she still couldn't use it to make calls. "I'll pay you back every dime."

His lips twitched and his eyes squinted against the bright morning sun. "Or we *could* work it out in trade."

"Tempting though that may be, I'm not taking that particular bait," she said drily.

She pocketed the phone, and while he finished tying down the windows, she got in the cab, deftly pulling one of the T-shirts over her head and down her chest. Watching him through the side-view mirror to be certain he was otherwise distracted, she pulled the straps of the camisole off her shoulders and worked it off through the neck of her T-shirt, then hastily shoved her arms through the sleeves just in time before he got into the truck.

He took in the bright pink, orange and green T-shirt and the camisole bunched in her fist. "You're a quick-change artist in addition to everything else?"

"It's a skill that comes in handy sometimes." She shoved the camisole in the hardware-store bag and tossed it onto the backseat next to the notepad she'd borrowed from him before they left the ranch. She often recorded interviews but was equally comfortable going old school with pad and pencil. As evidenced by the notebook she'd lost from her car. Which was still something she didn't like thinking about. "I've changed into cocktail dresses in my car before when I've had to run from one club to another for my blog."

He gave her a sidelong look that had her nerves fizzing and thoughts about anything besides him flying out the window.

"Are we stopping anywhere else?" The plan was to meet Nathan—who was bringing the front loader from the ranch—at the Ybarras' after Jayden had picked up the windowpanes.

"I doubt you'll find a pair of shorts to go with that T-shirt anywhere in town, if that's what you're hoping." A smile flirted around his eyes. "Pretty sure those shirts were left over from a fund-raiser the school had when *I* went there."

She plucked at the hem of the cheap tie-dyed cotton. If she were honest, it wasn't all that far a cry from her usual style, which admittedly leaned toward the Bohemian. "I don't care how old it is. At least it's not borrowed." That made her wonder about the Ybarras again. Their entire house had gone the *Wizard of Oz* way. Would they be dependent upon the donations of other people's clothing while they put their life back together? "I hope the Ybarras have good hazard insurance."

"I guess you can ask them when we get there."

"I imagine that I will." She chewed the inside of her cheek as she thought about the questions she planned, absently noting the half-dozen vehicles pulled up at the gas station. "Looks like there's a run on gasoline today."

He followed her glance. "Sunday-after-church grocery shopping, more like." This time, he wasn't hauling a trailer on the back of the truck, and as soon as he left behind the town, he picked up speed.

In the side-view mirror, she could see the wind blowing at the crates holding the window glass. "Who will do the window work for you?"

"You mean replacing the panes? We do it ourselves."

She watched him thoughtfully. "Did you and your brothers come out of the womb just naturally self-reliant?"

He chuckled. "It's kind of do-it-yourself 101, sweetheart."

"Maybe for some. My maintenance and repair skills reach as far as replacing the bag on my vacuum cleaner."

"If you're interested, I'll give you a lesson on glass repairs for the next time you're stuck after a tornado."

"At least I'd be of more use to the people saddled with me."

"You've said that before. And if you'll remember," he said, his voice deepening as he gave her a steady look, "I said it was my pleasure."

She was vaguely shocked to feel her skin tightening the way it was. To feel her nipples peaking under the cheap cotton shirt that was all that covered them. She wasn't a prude by any means, but she'd never met anyone besides Jayden who elicited such a visceral reaction from her.

And without so much as a single touch.

She swallowed and struggled not to moisten her lips.

His gaze dropped to them anyway. Then, for an infinitesimal moment, it dropped to her breasts before he focused again on the road ahead of them.

Feeling hot, she rolled her window down a few more inches and stared out at the passing landscape. It was all she could do not to cross her arms over her chest and squirm in her seat, and she had never been so grateful to get somewhere as she was when they arrived at the Ybarra place.

It meant she could throw her focus entirely on someone other than Jayden. At least for a little while.

It was a good idea. In theory.

But after she'd spent the afternoon talking with Paloma and Hector about their life together in Paseo—interrupted by family members and friends who presented them with pieces of personal property they'd salvaged from the tornado wreckage as they helped clean up—Ariana had to admit defeat.

To herself, at least.

No matter what she did, how truly interesting she found

Paloma and Hector to be, she was never able to completely move Jayden out of her mind.

The task certainly hadn't been helped by the fact that he was within Ariana's eyesight almost every minute of the afternoon. Even when she and Paloma and Hector left the shade of the canopy—where a camp kitchen had been set up, to Hector's delight—into the barn to show off their make-shift living quarters—complete with a portable potty, to Paloma's delight—Ariana had been able to see him through the wide-open barn doors. He sat there shirtless and sweating atop the tractor as he drove it back and forth. Slowly and inexorably and with the help of many hands, he cleared away the destruction until all that remained were a huge pile of bricks and a farmhouse-sized patch of bare earth.

Everything else had been loaded onto trailers and a roll-off Dumpster that had appeared since the day before.

If she hadn't seen it for herself, she would have found it difficult to believe that so much work could be done in such a short amount of time. And without a lot of heavy equipment. She'd captured some video of it on her phone, knowing it would be a good online tie-in for the article when she wrote it.

By the time the work was done, somebody had brought trays of carnitas and tortillas from Rosa's in town. The helpers, who had worked for hours in the hot Texas sun, tucked hungrily into the food, and although they had to be exhausted, they broke into song and dance when some-one produced some loud Tejano music. They hung around making merry until the only light there was came from the moon and the two strands of red and green Christmas lights Tomas and Graciela hung from one edge of the barn to the corner of the portable canopy.

Ariana was so moved by the whole thing she had to

break away from the crowd just so she could wipe her wet cheeks in private.

"Talk about the human spirit, eh?" Jayden—shirt back in place—found her standing in the shadows of the barn.

"Yes." Her voice was husky. "Last I saw, you were dancing with Graciela." If not for the fact that every time Graciela looked at Tomas it was with adoration in her expression, Ariana might have been eaten up by jealousy. Because Jayden most definitely was not in short pants anymore when it came to women.

"Last I saw," he returned, "you were sitting with the two Arturos eating some of Rosa's killer flan."

"I was."

He angled his head slightly. "Everything all right? I should have offered to take you back to the ranch. It's been a long day."

"Please." Teary-eyed or not, her toe was tapping inside her too-large tennis shoe in time to the rhythmic music. "Do you think I'd have taken you away for even an hour this afternoon? I didn't work anywhere near as hard as most of you did." Not to mention the hours he'd put in at his own place even before she'd rolled out of bed.

"Your interview was good?"

"Very." Somehow, the distance between them was shrinking and she wasn't sure if she could lay the blame on him. "But I think it was less an interview *I* conducted than keeping up with them as they just talked." She'd gone with her instincts, knowing the second she suggested recording them that they'd have gotten self-conscious. So she satisfied herself instead with taking a few notes that she would elaborate on when she was alone. If she needed to clarify any particular facts later on, she could.

"Do you know Paloma said she wasn't afraid when the tornado was blowing through? That she and Hector waited it out in their storm shelter playing cards?" If Ariana hadn't spent as many hours with the couple by now, she'd have found it difficult to believe. "When it was blowing over us while we were in your storm cellar, I was terrified."

He lifted his hand and tucked a lock of hair behind her ear and her heartbeat stuttered. "Guess I should have tried playing cards with you."

Her laugh sounded breathless even to her own ears. "You were plenty distracting."

His lips stretched into a smile as his head lowered closer to hers. "So were you." He slid another lock of hair behind her other ear and she felt rooted to the earth when his mouth grazed lightly over hers. "You're still distracting," he murmured.

She could hear her blood rushing through her head. But she still managed to pull back. "Jayden, this isn't a good idea."

"Afraid someone will see?" He wrapped his hand behind her back and started moving faintly to the music.

Before she could even think, she was moving along with him. She only realized he was dancing her farther away from the twinkling red and green lights when they circled around the side of the barn and out of sight entirely. "No one can see us now." His voice was low. Deep.

And she was dissolving on the inside.

"It's still not a good idea," she managed and slid out from between him and the wall of the barn behind her.

But he still held her hand and he followed, pressing close against her back. He pushed her hair away from her neck and kissed the side of her throat. His fingers were linked with hers and he pressed them flat against her belly, still swaying slightly with the music. "Sure?"

The only thing she was sure of at that moment was that she could feel every inch of him pressed against her, burning from her shoulder blades to her rear. She turned her head toward him and his lips grazed her ear.

The music carried easily in the night, but she could still hear the faint sound of his breath. And heaven knew, she could feel the warmth of it. She turned her head a little more and his lips brushed over her cheek. When she tilted her head back against his chest, they found her jawline.

She stared blindly at the stars overhead. There was a carpet of them, and they blurred together when his palm slid beneath the front of her T-shirt and pressed flat against her belly.

He had large, calloused hands. His splayed fingers stretched from below the dip of her navel to the valley between her breasts. And oh, she longed for him to move his fingers over her. It was an acute ache inside her, centering with a ball of heat beneath his palm.

"I haven't wanted a woman this badly in a long time." He pressed even closer against her and she wondered vaguely if this was what it felt like to *swoon*. Then his mouth slid from her jaw to cover hers. And for a mindless moment, her lips clung to his.

When he turned her into his arms, she hauled in a fast breath. Grasping for common sense felt like trying to hold sand in a sieve. But she shook her head, pressing her hand against his chest. "We can't."

His strong hands circled her hips, fingertips kneading. "Not here, I know."

Her head was too heavy for her neck. She let her forehead fall against his chest. He smelled of heat and sweat and smoky carnitas and the wide, wide land around them.

And she'd never been more aroused by a scent in her life.

"It's not that." It seemed to take a ridiculous amount of willpower to lift her head. To look up into his shadowy expression. "But there are reasons—"

She broke off at the pounding of footsteps. They had only a moment to step away from each other before the two Arturos came skidding around the barn, running past them, laughing hilariously as Tomas chased them, threatening bodily harm for some transgression.

The trio was long out of sight before either one of them moved. And then it was Ariana, who took another step away from him, tucking her thumbs in her back pockets as she stared down at the ground. Everything inside her wanted to move back into his arms. To forget her ethics and everything else but him.

"You told me you weren't attached," he said.

Genuinely surprised, she looked up at him. "I'm not! I don't cheat. I haven't been involved with anyone for more than a year."

"That's a long dry spell," he murmured. "Or did he break your heart?" He rubbed his thumb down her lower lip and she darn near drooled.

But she *did* have ethics. Not everyone might agree or like them, but they were hers. And if she crossed the line once with him…

So she pulled back an inch. Just enough for his hand to fall away. "I've never had a broken heart," she admitted huskily. Not even after Steven and his obsession with motorcycles. But having met Jayden, she finally had some inkling of how easily it could happen.

"Then if it's not someone else, what's stopping us?"

She exhaled. She'd never ever let herself be in this position before. "I told you I was writing about the Fortunes." She had to push the words past the constriction in her throat. Because even though that part was true, there was so much more beneath the surface that she hadn't told him. "I shouldn't be getting involved with you at all. Not…not like this."

"Try again, sweetheart. I told you the name's pure fiction. There's no 'Becoming a Fortune' for us. I thought I'd made that clear already."

She moistened her lips, swallowed hard for what felt like the tenth time and lifted her chin. "What if it's not pure fiction? What if there's actually more to your name than what your mother told you?"

In an instant, his expression went hard. So hard that she could suddenly see the military man in him.

"Is that what you're hoping? That why you're batting those big brown eyes at me, showing off your little butterfly tat? You want to seduce a story out of me?"

He could have slapped her and not shocked her more. Her teeth clenched so tightly, she could barely manage to speak. "Is that what you really think of me, Jayden? *Really?*"

He was silent for so long that she wasn't sure he intended to respond at all. "No." The admission was grudging. "But my mom's the straightest shooter I've ever known. If she says she made up the name, then she made up the name." His tone was inflexible. "Far as I'm concerned, the bastard who knocked her up could be alive or dead. I don't care either way. Pretty sure my brothers feel the same." He shoved his fingers through his hair and took a step back. The gap was only a foot and a half, maybe, but it felt so much wider. "So the sooner you take your Fortune hunting down the road and leave us the hell alone, the better."

She was shaking with anger, but she still winced.

He took a few steps away from her, back toward the corner of the barn, and she could see the silhouette of him more clearly in the faint light coming from the other side. She could see the rise and fall of his shoulders as he took a deep breath.

Then he gestured sharply with his hand. "It's late. Time we get going."

She managed to keep it together as she went to thank Hector and Paloma again for their time. They were sitting together, their fingers linked, and even though she insisted they remain where they were, they both stood and accompanied Ariana and Jayden halfway back to Jayden's pickup.

She realized Nathan must have left with the trailer and the front loader while she and Jayden had been—

She closed her eyes for a moment, then quickly walked around to the passenger side of his truck and pulled open the door before he could even try.

They drove back to the ranch in silence.

He stopped near the house, engine running. Taking her cue, she climbed out with the bag from the hardware store and her notepad.

He drove off the second she pushed the truck door closed again.

Even though she could see he was only moving the truck down toward the barn where he usually parked it, she still felt like he was driving away from *her*.

Rather than be caught watching, she quickly turned. The wind chimes that Jayden had bought the day before were hanging next to the door and they clinked musically as she went inside.

There was no sign or sound of Nathan as she walked back to her borrowed bedroom, but Sugar got up from her bed in the kitchen and padded after her.

"At least you still like me, Sugar."

She turned on the lamp and sat on the edge of the bed. The dog hopped up to lean against her, swiping her tongue over Ariana's hand.

She rubbed the dog's silky head and looked into her dark, sightless eyes. "He never did say how you went blind. But I don't think he's going to tell me now, do you?"

Sugar's tongue came out, catching Ariana's chin.

"You're a sweet girl." Ariana pressed her face against the dog's head for a moment. Then she got off the bed, changed into the robe hanging on the back of Deborah's door and went down the hall to the bathroom. She heard Jayden's footsteps on the staircase as she was hand-washing her stretchy knit cami and panties in the bathroom sink and wasn't sure if she felt more like screaming or crying.

She did neither, of course. No matter what he thought about her, she was under his roof. At least for one more night since he hadn't kicked her out.

Yet.

The bathroom downstairs didn't have a tub or a shower, so she made do with the washcloth and a sink full of water. She worked the comb she'd found in the medicine cabinet through her tangled hair and wove it into a long braid. She didn't have a band to fasten it, but the braid would hold for a little while. Then she used her new travel toothbrush, rubbed lip balm on her lips and returned to the bedroom where she hung her wet things off the closet doorknob. They would both be dry long before morning. She'd washed her jeans the night before last. She figured she could stand another day in them while she figured out just how she was going to take her Fortune hunt down the road, when she was currently stuck and dependent only on Jayden's once-good graces.

She pulled on the sweatpants he'd already loaned her and tugged the second tie-dyed hardware shirt over her head. Sugar was still lying on the bed, so after returning the robe to the door hook, Ariana left the door ajar in case the dog wanted to leave.

Then she climbed in bed with her notebook and tried concentrating enough to expand on her notes with the Ybarras. It was difficult. Because she would never be able to think of the couple without also thinking about Jayden.

She flipped to a fresh page and drew a line across it. At the left end of the line, she wrote "Jerome." At the right end, she wrote "Gerald." Then she made little hash marks along the line, dividing it into segments. She marked the point when Jerome had faked his demise. Then at the midpoint of the timeline, she wrote "Charlotte." After that, she filled in the names of all the children so far accounted for.

It made for a busy, congested timeline to the right of Charlotte.

And like it always had before, it made the area to the left between Charlotte and Jerome's supposed death look very, very empty.

She bit the end of the pen, her gaze roving around the bedroom. Then she made another hash mark in the bare zone and wrote Deborah's name above it. Quickly scrawled in Jayden and his brothers.

She sighed as she circled Jayden's name a few times.

Then she scratched her pen back and forth across the entire page as if to erase it and turned back to her notes from the Ybarras.

He couldn't sleep.

And lying there in bed, tossing and turning because he couldn't sleep, was just pissing him off.

He threw back the sheet and got out of bed, pulling on a fresh pair of jeans before stomping down the steps.

Ever since Ariana had challenged the facts as he knew them about his family name, he'd been angry. And he didn't much care if he disturbed anyone else in the house.

Petty? Maybe.

But wasn't a man's house supposed to be his castle? Or some such thing?

At the base of the stairs, he looked toward the end of the hallway where his mother's bedroom was located. The door was ajar and a triangle of gold light shone onto the hallway floor.

Ariana was still awake.

His jaw tightened and he turned away, heading into the kitchen. Sugar's bed was empty, but as soon as he yanked open the refrigerator door hard enough to make the bottles inside rattle, he heard the dog's paws on the hallway floor.

"Hey, Sugar." The dog walked over to him and leaned against his leg. "Where you been, huh?" Usually, the second he went to bed, the dog followed right on his heels. Not tonight.

He fed her a treat, then grabbed a beer and twisted off the top, tossing it onto the counter.

She followed him when he went out onto the patio and threw himself down on one of the old chairs. She propped her head on his knee, working her wet nose under his hand, and flopped her tail against the stone porch. "I wish everything was as simple as pleasing you, mutt." He patted his knee and she gathered herself, hopping nimbly onto his lap.

She was too big to be considered a lapdog. But she didn't know it. She just propped her front paws on his shoulders and stuck her nose in his face. He tolerated a few messy kisses across his forehead before angling his head away. "Yeah, I love you, too." He patted her back and she gave a sigh, finally settling her head on his shoulder where she breathed noisily against his ear. "What're we gonna do about her, huh?"

Unfortunately, his dog gave him no helpful answers.

He finished his beer and nudged at Sugar until she reluctantly hopped off and allowed him to stand. Back in the kitchen, he refilled the water bottle that kept her bowl always full and then started for the stairs.

Instead of following him, though, she trotted confidently to the end of the hall, passing through the triangle of light and nosing her way into the bedroom.

Jayden wasn't a man accustomed to hesitating. But he found himself doing so, one bare foot on the first stair tread and one bare foot still on the scarred wood floor as he looked toward his mother's bedroom.

He'd been too harsh with Ariana at the Ybarras'. But knowing it didn't make it any easier to swallow what she'd suggested.

Or swallow the fact that he had his own sliver of doubt.

He was thirty-damn-six years old.

He didn't want to think about the man his mother had always refused to discuss. Deborah Fortune was made of leather and steel. She'd had to be to raise three sons on her own in an area of Texas that people tended to forget existed.

And the only time he'd ever seen tears in her eyes had been when he was little. When he'd complained once too often about Nathan and Grayson and him not having a dad the same as other kids around Paseo did.

He exhaled roughly and pulled his foot away from the stair tread and soundlessly followed Sugar's path to the triangle of light. The dog never slept in his mom's room.

"Ariana." He pushed lightly on the door, opening it wider.

She was sprawled on her back, sweatpants hanging low over her golden-hued hips and a pad of paper lying on her belly. She didn't move even when Sugar, who'd hopped onto the bed, circled a few times as she sniffed her way around and knocked the pad aside before settling on the pillow next to Ariana's head.

He gave the dog a look. Even though she couldn't see him, he knew she'd interpret his vibes. But she only turned her head and flopped her tail a few times.

He put his fingers together, intending to snap them.

But he didn't.

Instead, he walked into the room. Silently he picked up the notepad. It was covered in almost indecipherable handwriting, but *Ybarra* was clear enough. He set it on the nightstand.

And still, Ariana didn't waken. Her lashes looked darker than ever against her cheeks. Her soft lips were parted faintly. The rise and fall of her breasts beneath the T-shirt were even.

Much as he wanted to stay there and look at her, he reached out and shut off the lamp.

Then he turned around and went to bed.

## Chapter Seven

She didn't intend to oversleep. But once again, when Ariana opened her eyes, she was dismayed to see that it was already the middle of the morning.

Maybe it had something to do with the total lack of sunlight coming into the bedroom since plywood was still secured over the window. When she was sleeping, it was fine. But now that she was awake, it made the otherwise comfortable room feel more like a cell. And a warm one, at that.

She rolled off the bed, scrubbing her face, trying to remember how late it had been before she'd stopped working and turned off the light. But she couldn't.

She picked up her notepad, feeling a little bleary-eyed as she read a few lines of her notes from the Ybarras.

Then she tossed it down on the nightstand and stuck her head out into the hallway.

She couldn't hear a sound, so she ventured into the kitchen. The blue-and-white coffeepot was sitting on the unlit stove. It was half-full and barely warm, but she filled a mug from it anyway, then nearly choked on the first sip and hastily leaned over the sink, spitting it back out.

"Good grief."

She rinsed out her mug with water, then did the same with her mouth. When Jayden had said Nathan's coffee was the worst, he hadn't been exaggerating. And obviously, the reason couldn't be attributed to the cleanliness of the coffeepot, because she'd cleaned it to spotless herself only two days ago. And it had been just as clean when she'd made a pot the day before.

She dumped the coffee into the sink and was refilling it with clean water when she spotted Jayden and Nathan through the window, unloading bales from the same trailer they'd used to haul her car. They were both dressed in jeans and short-sleeved T-shirts, with heavy gloves on their hands. The sheen of sweat on their roped arms was visible. But even from her distance and despite the straw cowboy hats on their heads, she could tell them apart.

She'd been born and bred in Texas. Had been around men in cowboy hats and jeans all of her life. Some wore them as a fashion statement. Some wore them simply because it was who they were.

These two men—whether they'd spent years in military service or not—were definitely in the latter camp.

The shrill ringing of the telephone nearly made her jump out of her skin.

She looked at it and wondered if she ought to answer it. But given Jayden's attitude the night before, she decided it probably wouldn't be appreciated.

She left the coffeepot in the sink and turned away from the window. At the moment, the men were entirely occupied. She went down the hall and grabbed up her clean clothes, the toothbrush and comb, then dashed up the stairs.

She was going to take a real shower while the taking was good, because she had no idea when the next opportunity would come.

Ten minutes later, after the fastest shower in her personal record, she was once more in the kitchen.

There was no sign of the guys through the window now, and she finished putting the coffee on the stove. The temperature in the kitchen was already excessively warm. She had no idea if the house came equipped with central air-conditioning, but it wasn't her business if it did or did not. In any case, she still wanted coffee, even if she ended up putting it on ice. And when she'd fixed it before, Jayden and Nathan had finished off the entire pot. So they obviously didn't reserve drinking the stuff for cooler temperatures, either.

She left the water to heat and returned to the bedroom and made up the bed. She found cleaning supplies and quickly cleaned the hall bathroom as well as the one upstairs. By the time she was done, the coffee water was boiling away. She mixed up the coffee grounds in a bowl the way her mother had described with an egg and a piece of the shell. She dumped the grounds into the pot, watching to make sure the water didn't boil over. After a few minutes, she pulled the pot off the heat, poured in another cup of cold water and watched the mucky mess of coffee grounds that had amassed in a froth at the top of the water sink like magic to the bottom.

"Coffee makes everything better," she murmured, standing over the pot and inhaling the aroma. "Please make some miracles now, too."

The wind chimes outside the door jangled softly and she looked over her shoulder in time to see Jayden coming through the door.

He had one finger of his leather glove between his teeth

as he tugged his hand free and he stopped short at the sight of her.

She leaned back against the sink because the impact of him pretty much in full-on cowboy mode was almost overwhelming. Her knees, quite literally, had gone weak.

"I made coffee," she said stupidly, because of course he could see that. "I hope you don't mind."

He finally yanked his hand free and slapped the glove against the other that was clutched in his fist. He didn't take off his cowboy hat. "Make it whenever you want. Already told you that."

Yes, she thought. But that was before she'd dared to suggest that his mother had lied to him.

"It's hot in here." He sounded—and looked—peeved. "Why didn't you turn on the air?"

"One, I didn't know if you even had air-conditioning." She spread her hands. "And two, I wasn't particularly inclined to snoop in order to find out. Shocking to you, no doubt. I know you want me out of your hair at the earliest opportunity."

His lips compressed. She could see a muscle work in his jaw, and for a moment, she thought he intended to say something, but then he just strode out of the room.

A moment later, she heard the distinctive clicking sound of a central air-conditioning unit coming to life.

Then he came back and shoved the kitchen door closed.

"Thermostat is in the living room." He slapped his gloves against his palm again. "Look. About last night—"

She shook her head quickly, raising her hand. "No, wait."

His eyebrow went up.

"Please," she added. "Let me say what I've, uh, got to say and then—" She broke off. They both knew what she'd been about to say. *"—and then you can kick me to the curb."*

His lips compressed again. He waved the clenched gloves. "Go ahead, then."

He didn't look particularly pleased and she wished at that moment that she were better at expressing herself verbally. But she'd always been better with the written word and that fact wasn't going to magically change right now just by wishing it.

So she just dived in.

"I shouldn't have pushed the issue about who your father is." The words came out in a rush. "You told me from the beginning that I was on the wrong scent and I should have left it at that." She wasn't going to mention her book deal. She'd decided the night before that as long as she was under his roof, she had to forget *any* kind of research about Jerome.

"Because that's what journalists do? Give up at the first roadblock?"

The accusation stung. "Do you want my apology or not?" Then she winced. "Sorry." She looked away from his face, staring into the clear brown brew inside the coffeepot. It was the exact shade of his eyes.

She looked back at him. "Look, I didn't come to Paseo specifically hunting for Fortunes to feature in my 'Becoming' series. Believe me or not, but it's still the truth. I never expected to meet someone who actually had the name. And frankly, coincidences like that are pretty suspect in my line of work! So of course I was interested."

"Except you didn't come here to find Fortunes," he scoffed.

"I *didn't*. If I had been, would I have told you right up front about my series?" She pressed her fingertip to the pain that was suddenly throbbing in her temple. "All I came here to do was try and establish whether or not Jerome Fortune had ever been in Paseo. If he had any ties here."

"Why don't you just ask him? According to you, this Jerome guy is Gerald Robinson. You know where *he* is at. Hell, everyone in the country probably knows where he is at. The guy's always in the news."

"He refuses my requests for interviews."

"Imagine that."

Her lips tightened. She reminded herself that she was the interloper. This was Jayden's home. Jayden's space.

"Why do you think he might have been here, anyway?" His voice sounded grudging.

"I don't necessarily think he was. Not for certain. I was trying to figure that out."

"Sounds like you're grasping at straws to me."

"Maybe I am." Maybe it was wishful thinking on Ariana's part. But why would Charlotte have mentioned Paseo when the only thing in the article from the Austin History Center had been about Jerome's new bride, Charlotte, healing his broken heart?

"Did you ask Hector or Paloma about him?" Jayden's voice hardened even more. "They've lived in Paseo as long as anyone has. Is that what that interview was really about?"

"What? *No!*" The pain in her temple deepened. She still hadn't gotten to the point of what she was trying to tell him. "That interview was exactly what I said it was. Nothing more. Nothing less." She lifted her chin. "I don't lie to people in order to gain their trust. And I don't manipulate situations to my advantage. Not with you. Not with the Ybarras. Not with anyone. You couldn't have shocked me more by telling me your name was Fortune than if you'd poked me with a cattle prod. I didn't plan to get stranded here any more than you did. And the second I can leave, I will." The phone rang again, making her jump.

His gaze pinning hers in place, he reached out a long arm and snatched the phone off the hook. "Fortunes," he snapped.

Then he angled his head and she could no longer see his eyes below the brim of his hat. "Hey, Mom." His tone had turned neutral. "Yeah. No. Everything's fine here." The brim of his hat lifted an inch and his eyes fixed on hers. "Just still cleaning up the mess from the storm."

She exhaled shakily and left the room.

Jayden's grip tightened on the telephone receiver as he watched Ariana walk away, her head not ducking quickly enough to hide her pinched expression.

All he'd meant to tell her was that he was sorry for being too harsh the night before. But every time he opened his mouth, he seemed to dig himself in deeper.

His mom was still speaking—something about Grayson's tour—and he focused in on her with an effort. "You'll be gone another week, then? Yeah, no problem." In fact, it was better than that. Because Ariana's car should be fixed by then and she'd be long gone before his mother came back to Paseo.

There'd be no reason for Deborah to ever even know about Ariana Lamonte and her damn Fortune hunt.

After he hung up, he went in search of Ariana.

She was sitting on the front porch with Sugar in her lap. The dog was spread across Ariana the same way she'd been on his lap just the night before.

He shoved his gloves in his back pocket and stepped out the door.

Ariana looked warily at him over his dog's head. "If you don't mind me using your phone, I'll call someone in Austin to come and get me."

His jaw tightened. "That's not necessary."

"Well, I obviously can't stay here."

"Why not?"

Her eyebrows went up. "Seriously? You don't want me here anymore. You were pretty clear about it, Jayden."

"I was frustrated." On more than one level. "That doesn't mean you have to get somebody to drive all the way from Austin to take you home."

"Well, I'm not going to ask you or Nathan to do it," she muttered. "You've already got enough on your plate as it is. You haven't even had a chance to do your own repairs around here except for boarding up the broken windows."

He couldn't argue with her on that score.

She nudged Sugar off her lap and stood. She was wearing her jeans and that skin-hugging camisole that showed off her sleekly toned shoulders and full breasts. But it was the wide brown eyes she trained on him that caused the knot in his gut.

"I can't pretend I don't have an interest in all things Fortune," she said. "But as long as I'm stuck here, I promise not to bring it up again. Not in any way. That's what I was trying to tell you before your phone rang."

"That's what you were trying to say?"

She huffed. "Next time I want to say something important, I'll send you a letter."

"What?"

She lifted her arms to her sides. "I'm better on paper!" She dropped her arms. "So can we call a truce or not? Because if not, maybe Nathan could drop me off at the Ybarras' and I can camp out with them."

"Nathan can do what, now?" The brother in question had come around the corner of the house, bearing a couple of sawhorses over his shoulder. He looked at Jayden. "Thought you wanted to get started on the windows."

"I do." It had only been a couple of days but he was already sick of feeling penned in in his own dark bedroom. It reminded him too much of sleeping in army barracks.

He looked at Ariana again and wondered when he would manage to stop feeling his gut tighten every time she blinked those brown eyes at him, or if he was going to be plagued by the problem until she left for good.

"You're not going to go camp out with the Ybarras, or anyone else, for that matter." He knew all the irritation he felt came through loud and clear. Particularly when Nathan shot him a sideways look. "Just…just go find something else to put on."

Her cheeks turned red. He wasn't sure if it was embarrassment or fury.

But she ducked her head and rushed past him, slamming the door so hard after her that the windowpanes in it shook.

So, fury then.

"I see you still have the magic touch when it comes to the ladies," Nathan drawled. "Ever thought about giving classes?"

"Shut up."

His brother chuckled as he set down the sawhorses and walked away. He was still shaking his head when he returned with the toolbox and power drill. "Well? You just gonna stand there, or are you going to give me some help here?"

"I hate having brothers," Jayden muttered.

Nathan wasn't fazed. He just held out the power drill toward Jayden. "Preaching to the choir, bro."

He grabbed the tool and stomped down the front steps and around to the plywood they'd fastened over their mother's bedroom window. He attacked the screws while Nathan set up the sawhorses and got the rest of the supplies ready for the first windowpane.

Then the two of them lifted the plywood away from the window.

Ariana was on the other side, sitting on the foot of the bed watching.

Obviously waiting.

Not only had she pulled on one of her virulent *Paseo Is Paradise* shirts, but she'd topped it with that artsy sweater she'd been wearing when they'd met.

"Is this better?" Her tone was dulcet.

A more god-awful combination of colors had never existed.

The base of his spine still tingled. His gut still tightened.

"It'll do." He slammed his hat harder on his head. At least he didn't have her hard little button nipples staring at him through that sleeveless excuse for a shirt. "Do you want to see how this is done or not?"

She stood. Her eyes were practically shooting sparks, but the smile on her face was demure. "How could I resist such a charming invitation?" She turned with a flip of hair and left the bedroom.

"She's gonna get heatstroke wearing that sweater this afternoon," Nathan warned conversationally. He laid the plywood on the horses, giving them a flat surface to work on, and then turned back to start removing the window sash. It was a large window. Even though it meant a little more prep work, glazing the window flat would be easier than doing it with the sash still in place. "Guess if she passes out, you'll have a reason to try mouth-to-mouth."

It would be about the only reason she'd let his mouth get close to hers again, Jayden figured. Not that he appreciated his brother's dig. "When did you get to be such a chatty Cathy?"

Nathan didn't answer. He just smiled slightly at Ariana

when she joined them. She'd pulled off her sweater before coming outdoors and she had her cell phone in her hand.

"Don't mind if I take a few pictures, do you?"

"Gonna write an article about home DIY projects?" Better that than some damn thing suggesting his mother had once been one of Gerald Robinson's playthings.

It made his blood boil every time he considered the possibility. The unlikely, ridiculous possibility.

"A DIY article could come out of this. You never know." Ariana had moved around to the other side of the sawhorses, as if she wanted to keep a physical separation between them.

Or maybe he was letting his imagination go berserk and she simply wanted to stand in the shade afforded by the Texas Ash that his mom had planted several years ago.

"So, Nathan," she said with annoying cheer. "Tell me about yourself. Jayden said you were in the navy. A SEAL. Was that as exciting as it sounds?"

"Don't go asking my brother a bunch of questions."

Ariana gave him a wide-eyed look. "I'm sorry, Jayden. Are *all* questions off-limits? I didn't realize." She looked back at Nathan and gave an apologetic shrug. "Clearly even navy SEALs need protection from me."

Berserk was right. "Dammit, Ariana—"

"Okay, kids." Nathan set the putty knife and screwdriver he'd been using on the makeshift plywood table. "Choose your weapons. I'm outta here." He strode off.

Ariana's lashes swept down, hiding her expression. She pushed her phone into the back pocket of her jeans.

Jayden yanked off his straw hat and swiped the sweat from his brow. He was letting good air-conditioning literally blow right out his mother's window.

"Ever been on a horse?"

Her lashes lifted. "Sorry?"

"Horse. You know. Long nose. Four hooves. Sometimes wears a saddle. A real one."

"I know what a horse is, thank you."

"So? You know how to ride or don't you?"

"No, I do not know how to ride."

"You don't swim. You don't ride. And you call yourself a Texan?"

Her chin went up a notch. "Not all Texans grow up on ranches or around horses."

"That's true. And you're a city girl if ever there was one." One who changed into cocktail dresses inside her car whenever the need arose.

"I'm not going to apologize for the way I grew up, if that's what you're expecting. Just because you're spoiling for a fight—"

"I'm not spoiling for a fight."

"Then what *do* you want?"

"Dammit, I want you!"

The bright color faded from her cheeks, making her eyes look even darker brown. A swallow worked down her long, slender throat, as if she was bracing herself for what she was about to say.

"I want you, too." Her voice was husky when she finally broke the ringing silence. "But I can't change anything. I can't change the fact that I've written nearly a half-dozen articles in my 'Becoming a Fortune' series. I can't change the—" She broke off and twisted her fingertips through her hair, drawing it off her face and neck. "I can't change anything."

"I can't change the fact that my mother chose *Fortune* for our names."

"If she'd chosen *Smith*, things would've been a lot simpler, that's for sure. I'd just be me. You'd just be you. And—"

He almost felt a click inside his head because it suddenly seemed so simple.

He stepped forward, shoving out his hand. "Jayden Smith, rancher. Nice t' meet you."

Her lips parted. Those mesmerizing eyes of hers softened.

Then she stepped forward also and slowly placed her hand in his. "Ariana Lamonte, writer. Nice to meet you, too."

He tightened his grip, fighting the impulse to draw her closer and nearly losing. But then he heard Sugar barking and he let go of Ariana's hand.

He gestured at the window. "Since we ran off the big, brave SEAL, first thing to do is get the sash out."

Her eyes clung to his for a moment. Then she suddenly rubbed her hands down her thighs, as if she, too, had made a decision. "Tell me what to do to help."

So he did.

And he quickly learned that whatever Ariana lacked in knowledge, she more than made up for in willingness.

Soon, he had the sash removed and laid out on the plywood. He and Nathan had cleared all the broken glass before they'd boarded it up with plywood. But there was still old glazing to clean away from the wood and Ariana attacked it with fervor. Once she'd scraped one section clean, he sanded it down to bare wood. When they were done, he brushed on a fresh coat of primer.

"The window sash looks practically brand-new," she said when he finished cleaning his paintbrush. "So now what? We put the glass in the grooves?"

"Putty first. Then the glass. But the primer needs to dry before we can putty." Which would only take a few hours, considering the heat. "Time for lunch."

She didn't argue.

When they went inside, the temperature was cool and comfortable. He went upstairs to wash up first, but when he got back down to the kitchen, she'd already assembled sandwiches and had them grilling on the stove.

"I hope you don't mind." She gestured at the frying pan with the slotted metal spatula in her hand.

"Toasted ham and cheese? What's to mind?" He filled a water glass and chugged it, then filled it again and took it with him to the table and sat down, watching her. The only woman he could remember ever cooking in this kitchen was his mother. "You know how to cook anything else?"

"A few things."

He nodded toward the coffeepot that was sitting on the rear burner. "You made a huge improvement over Nathan."

"If his coffee is so bad, why don't you just make it yourself?"

"Because even his bad coffee is better than having to do it myself." He grinned faintly. "Gotta have something to complain about."

Her lips twitched. "Well, that's honest, I guess." She flipped one sandwich, then the other. She glanced at him and then away. "I could do the cooking for you guys." Her suggestion sounded diffident. "You know. If I'm going to stay here. At least then I'd actually feel like I'm doing you a service in exchange for—" she waved the tip of the spatula in the air "—the roof over my head and all."

"There's no *if* about it. So is that what cleaning the bathroom upstairs was all about?"

She looked surprised.

"I'm not such a slob that I don't appreciate a clean bathroom mirror when one magically appears."

"You're not a slob at all." She lifted her shoulder and *Paseo Is Paradise* shifted softly. "For two men living on their own, this place is surprisingly tidy."

He was a grown man. He knew that openly staring at a woman's chest was against the rules of common politeness. But it was damn hard when he also knew the only thing beneath Ariana's ugly shirt was some seriously beautiful flesh.

"You forget," he said a little absently. "Nate and I were both military. Order is the rule. Grayson, now?" He shook his head. "He's another story."

"Speaking of the military—" She peeked at the bottom of one sandwich and turned off the gas flame. "And assuming this isn't an off-limits topic, after fifteen years of service, why get out?" She transferred the sandwiches to two plates, sliced them quickly in half and carried them to the table. "Why come back to this place when you'd been so anxious to leave it when you were young? Were you just burned out or what?"

"The woman I was sleeping with was engaged to my master sergeant. My boss," he translated. He wasn't sure whom he'd surprised more with the admission. He wished he could retract it, but it was already too late.

"He found out?" Her brows pulled together and she almost looked outraged. "Did he *make* you quit?"

"No." He bit into the crispy sandwich. Ariana had browned it perfectly. "*I* found out. You wouldn't think a thing like that could be kept secret so easily, but you'd be wrong." Especially on an installation where the population easily exceeded twenty thousand. "I've done a lot of things, but I don't mess around with another man's woman. Not knowingly, anyway. And I damn sure don't forgive a woman lying to me like that."

"Couldn't you have sought a reassignment? I mean, after all those years in the army, to just give it up—"

"I didn't give it up because of Tess. She was just the final straw. I gave it up because I knew I was never going to get any further." He rubbed his jaw. "Eventually, even in the army, there's a game to getting advanced and I didn't particularly like the rules." He gave her a twisted smile and the same excuse he'd given his mother when he'd shown up on the doorstep two years ago. "Besides, I was sick of wearing the uniform."

"I'm sorry." She reached across the table and lightly touched his hand. Just for a moment, before sitting back and snatching up her sandwich. "Not about the army. If you were ready for a change, you were ready. But it still can't have been easy."

"Easier than considering proposing to a woman only to learn she's already got another man's ring on her finger." What the hell was wrong with him? One compassionate look from Ariana and he was totally spilling his guts.

Her sandwich paused halfway to her mouth. "So it was more than just sleeping with her. You loved her."

He'd thought he had. He and Tess had been together for more than a year before she'd confessed the truth. But even from the first, Jayden couldn't remember her affecting him as easily as a single glance from Ariana could.

He was no stranger to lust. But that was controllable. And nothing had felt particularly controllable these last few days. Add to that the fact that he couldn't keep his mouth shut about details he hadn't even shared with his own family?

Hell. Maybe he wasn't berserk. Maybe he was having a damn midlife crisis.

"Are you still in love with her?" Ariana had set her sandwich back on her plate. She was looking down at it, picking tiny pieces off the corner.

"No." He could see that now, with a clarity he hadn't possessed even two weeks ago.

She got up from the table suddenly, but only to open the

kitchen door and let Sugar inside. "You said you brought Sugar home from Germany?"

"She belonged to Tess's fiancé." He held out his palm and the dog nuzzled against it. "He never took good enough care of her."

"Tess or Sugar?"

"I came home with Sugar, didn't I?"

She smiled faintly.

She hadn't sat back down at the table and he moved his hand from Sugar to Ariana's hip. Then he slid his hand around to the small of her back, pulling her toward him.

She didn't resist.

He pressed his forehead against her chest, and after a moment, he felt her fingers sliding through his hair. She leaned over him slightly, and he felt engulfed by her warmth.

"Sex is off the table," she whispered.

"Okay." He slid his other arm behind her. His palms fit perfectly over the curve of her rear.

She shifted and curled her arms even more around his head. "I mean it, Jayden."

"Okay." He was so hard, he hurt. But he still turned his head slightly, feeling the soft give of her warm flesh beneath her shirt.

She made a low sound as she flexed her fingers against his head. "You're killing me."

"Tell me about it," he said darkly. Ironically.

She exhaled. He felt it in the faint sway of her breasts against him as she lowered her head toward his.

"I ache," she whispered near his ear. "If you really want to know, I'll tell you all about it."

His comment had only been sarcasm. Directed squarely at himself. He hadn't expected her to take it literally.

She ran her hand along his arm, circling his wrist with

her fingers and pulling his all-too-willing hand around to the front of her. "Here." She pressed his palm against her belly. Then she pushed it even lower, right at the juncture of her thighs. "Here," she breathed.

He nearly ground his teeth together, fighting the urge to push her back on the kitchen table right then and there.

Instead, he let go of her like he'd been burned and shoved his chair so hard, it slid back more than a foot.

Her dark, dark eyes were fastened hungrily on his face. Rosy color rode her high cheekbones. And her pointed little nipples were clearly stabbing through her shirt.

He pointed at her. "You said sex was off the table."

"You said okay," she retorted swiftly, jabbing a finger in the air right back at him. "You don't get to pull out all the seduction stops and expect me not to give it right back to you!"

He nearly choked. He wasn't sure what to make of her. He wasn't sure about much of anything except that she had him twisted in knots. She had since the tornado.

He stood, muttering an oath because he had to adjust himself just so he could stand. "Be careful playing with fires, sweetheart."

She lifted her chin and raised an eyebrow. Though she didn't exactly look right at him, he noticed a fresh blush of pink on her cheeks. "Burn goes both ways, *sweetheart*."

Then she reached behind her for his plate. "Now, are you going to finish eating this? Or can we go finish the window? Because the day's not getting any shorter, and by my count, there are still three more windows to go. And I, for one, would like to see moonlight outside the window when I go to bed tonight. Wouldn't you?"

What he wanted to see when he went to bed that night was her.

And that was something that was just not going to happen.

Because his last name wasn't Smith.

Fiction or not, it was Fortune.

*Chapter Eight*

"Mom. I'm fine here. Last time I called, you promised you were going to stop worrying about me."

"How can I stop worrying about you?" Karen's voice sounded loud through the receiver against Ariana's ear. "Your father wants to drive out to this Paseo place and bring you home. You've been there nearly two weeks, honey! There's no reason why you need to keep imposing on those people while you wait for your car to be fixed. How are you going to pay your bills when you're not even working? How are—"

Ariana barely had a chance to register that Jayden had walked into the kitchen, where she was using the wall phone, before he reached past her and plucked the receiver from her hand.

He raised his eyebrows at her. "Y'mind?"

She couldn't have responded if her life depended on it. Primarily because she was too busy staring at his bare chest above the faded blue jeans hanging low around his lean hips.

Since the "day of the windows," as she'd come to think of it, they'd both been careful to keep to their respective, circumspect corners. She knew the only reason *she'd* been successful at it was because he hadn't so much as brushed against her, even inadvertently.

Not once. In ten whole days.

Even now, while taking the phone right out of her hand, he managed to do so without touching her.

He put the receiver to his ear and walked far enough away that the coiled phone cord stretched out to its full length.

But that just left Ariana's eyes free to explore the sculpted lines of his back. To study the stark line of demarcation just visible above the waistband of his jeans. To admire the tanned skin above and the paler skin below.

And to pick out the few droplets of water that were still clinging to his shoulder blades from the shower he'd obviously taken.

The shower was part of his routine. Get up before the sun, work until the afternoon heat got really serious, then come in and shower away the sweat and grime that went hand in hand with repairing barns and fixing fence and working cattle. Over the last few days she'd learned that meant anything from giving inoculations to tagging ears to weighing to castrating. This time of year, though, he'd said they were mostly working with the calves that'd been born in the spring.

She'd also learned that if she timed it right, she could often catch a glimpse of him on the back of one of his horses as he came back in for the day.

She'd even managed to snap a few photos of him with her cell phone without him noticing.

But even though she'd learned his routine well over the past two weeks, this was the first time he'd strolled into the kitchen looking half-naked.

She quickly swiped her hand over her forehead and hoped her cheeks didn't look as hot as they felt while she listened to him speak into the phone.

"Mrs. Lamonte, this is Jayden Fortune. Sorry to hijack your phone call, ma'am, but let me assure you that Ariana's not imposing. Fact is, she's been real helpful lately."

She glanced his way and his carefully neutral gaze roved over her face.

"That's right, Mom." Despite her better intention, she stepped over to him, speaking loud enough for her mother to hear. She held up her palms as if Karen could see the bandage strips there. "Jayden put up a new barn wall this week and I helped." Helped as much as she could, at any rate, once he'd shown her how to hammer a nail without hitting her own fingers. She'd hammered so many nails she'd earned blisters even through the work gloves he'd given her to wear.

"I appreciate your hospitality on my daughter's behalf," she heard her mom say, "but would you put her back on the line, please?"

"Yes, ma'am." He set the receiver on the countertop and stepped around her.

Ariana picked up the receiver and told herself that it was her imagination that the hard plastic felt warm from his brief grip on it. "I'm here, Mom."

"Seriously, Ariana. About your work? You haven't been online anywhere. You didn't put up a fresh magazine blog this week or last. Mrs. Wysocki was in for her teeth cleaning this morning and she just couldn't wait to pump me for the reason why."

"Mrs. Wysocki needs to worry less about what I'm

doing than what the Empress of—than what her own daughter Juliette is doing. She has to testify soon in Judge Rivera's sexual-misconduct trial, if I remember." From the corner of her eye, she watched Jayden flipping through the pile of mail on the kitchen table.

As if he were aware of her attention, he angled his head and gave her a sideways look.

She tucked the phone in the crook of her neck and studiously picked the corner of one of the bandages on her palm. "And I haven't posted anything online because the library internet has been down. But don't worry. I still have a job. People are covering for me at the magazine and I got my latest story submitted on time just like usual." She'd had to dictate it over the phone, which had been a pain, but it still had worked. Which meant she didn't have another column to write until next month. At which time, she would certainly be back home again.

The thought of getting back home, of getting her life back on its usual track, ought to have been a relief.

"And what about that book of yours?"

Ariana stiffened, holding the phone more tightly against her ear. She hadn't told anyone at work about her book deal but she had told her parents. How could she not have shared that momentous news with them? The day she'd been offered the deal had been one of Ariana's proudest. But she didn't want Jayden overhearing something that would only end up upsetting him.

"It's coming along fine, Mom." If *fine* could be described as not having done one single thing.

Her mother's sigh was noisy. She clearly wasn't convinced. "Well, what about your car? How's that coming along? Daddy and I were concerned when you paid for it outright with your book advance. It would have been wiser to put some of that money in your savings. Or at least you could have bought some furniture to replace the hand-me-downs you've had since college."

Again with the book? "My furniture is fine, Mom. And so is the investment in my car. Charlie—the guy who's doing the work—was still waiting on one last part when I talked to him Wednesday." Jayden had given Ariana the keys to his truck to drive into town and use the library. She had stopped to see Charlie on her way back.

The boat had been gone from his garage, only to be replaced by a showy new pickup truck and a John Deere tractor. Charlie had shown her the progress he'd been making on her car, though. And he'd tried to explain about the mechanical damage he'd discovered once he'd started working on it. Everything he'd said had gone over her head. But he'd assured her that her insurance had approved the work and all he was waiting on was the part, which he didn't expect to get for another few days.

"So you'll be driving home soon." Ariana's mom was still talking in her ear. "Daddy will be awfully glad about that. He's not at all comfortable with you staying under a strange man's roof. Of course, he thinks all men are just after one thing where his baby girl is concerned. The only reason he can sleep at night is knowing you've got a built-in chaperone from that SEAL boy." As if Ariana were still seventeen instead of twenty-seven.

Ariana thought it best not to share the fact that Nathan hadn't been around for the last few days. And even when he *had* been around, he hadn't been the least bit chaperone-y.

"Just make sure you let us know this time before you get on the road," Karen continued pointedly.

"I will, Mom." Ariana let the cord re-coil itself as she walked back toward the phone's base on the wall. "I've got to go now. Love you." She quickly slid the receiver onto its cradle.

Jayden was tearing open one of the envelopes and he glanced up at her. "Everything good on the home front?"

If he'd been able to hear her mother's comments about the book, he didn't appear interested.

"Same as usual." She headed for the refrigerator and pulled it open. When she'd first blown in with the tornado, the refrigerator had been stocked to the gills. In the two weeks since, it had become nearly empty. Which meant that figuring out things to fix was becoming increasingly challenging.

She ought to have stopped at the gas station for some groceries when she'd gone into Paseo the day before yesterday. But she'd already been feeling foolish for reminding him that she'd lost her driver's license in the storm, so she really shouldn't be caught driving anywhere until she got it replaced. He'd just given her a look and dropped his truck keys on the table in front of her.

Having to ask him for money on top of everything would have been just too much. And he hadn't remembered to offer.

Which was why the refrigerator was now in its current state.

No milk. He was a grown man, but he still drank gallons of it.

No eggs. She'd learned straight off that he and Nathan could plow through a half dozen a day before taking off at the crack of dawn.

No bread. Deborah Fortune made it from scratch and even the frozen loaves were gone.

No fresh lettuce or tomatoes or fruit. Though Ariana had discovered a garden near the house, it had been leveled by the storm.

And she suspected that the half carton of cottage cheese

on the bottom refrigerator shelf was growing the world's next great antibiotic.

On the positive side, there was a slab of leftover rib eye, from when Jayden had grilled the night before, and an onion.

She pushed the refrigerator door closed and pulled open the metal bin partially filled with potatoes that she'd discovered the week before.

She could make a hash with the potatoes and steak, she supposed. Though it would be better with fried eggs on top—

"Forget the food."

She looked over her shoulder at Jayden. It was silly to feel light-headed just from the sight of his bare chest. She'd seen bare chests before. Had even been up close and personal with a few of them. What was the deal with Jayden's, then?

"So? Do you want to go or not?"

The owner of said chest was giving her an impatient look and she felt her face flush. She'd completely missed whatever it was he'd said and had no idea where he'd asked her to go. Still, she answered, "Uh, yeah. Sure." No matter what it was, she was determined to pick it up in context.

Only Jayden just continued standing there. Watching her. And after a moment, his eyebrows went up. "You going to change?"

She looked down at herself.

Despite her reluctance to invade his mother's clothes closet, necessity had simply won out. She could only wear the same combination of jeans, cami and two tie-dyed shirts for so long without losing her mind. Which was why she was currently wearing one of his mother's long-sleeved denim shirts. She had the sleeves rolled up. And even belted around her waist, the long shirttails made for an adequate dress. It covered her more than some of the sundresses hanging in her apartment closet. Plus, it was cooler than her jeans. "I know it's hardly high fashion, but—"

"But you'll be more comfortable on horseback wearing jeans," he said drily.

She hid her surprise behind an obliging smile. The only time he'd asked if she knew how to ride a horse had been on the day of the windows. "True. I was just waiting for you to, uh—" She gestured toward him with her hand. "You know, change also." She hoped her face hadn't turned as red hot on the outside as it felt on the inside. She turned on her too-loose, borrowed tennis shoe and inadvertently stepped right out of it.

She barely managed to keep from pitching forward onto the kitchen table and scooped up the offending shoe during the momentum. "Your mom has big shoes to fill," she said breathlessly.

"I'll tell her you said so."

It was too hard keeping a smile in place, and it died the second she ducked out of the kitchen.

Whether they'd reached a truce or not, she seriously doubted that Jayden intended to tell his mother one single thing about Ariana, once she was out of his hair. And she knew, without question, that he particularly wouldn't say anything about her so-called Fortune hunt.

She closed herself in Deborah's bedroom and quickly pulled on her jeans. She'd washed them that morning and had taken them from the dryer while they were still damp. They were dry now. But barely. Then she pulled on the closest thing she had to a real bra—the shelf-lined cami. She was just reaching for one of the hardware-store T-shirts to pull over the cami when Jayden knocked on the door.

She pulled it open.

His eyes skimmed over her from her face to her bare toes and back up again. His gaze left a trail of heat in its wake as surely as if he'd physically run his fingertips up and down her. "I just came to tell you to wear a pair of boots. Mom's boots," he added, as if she didn't have the sense to know he hadn't meant Ariana's high-heeled red ones.

"Fine."

His eyes roved over her again. "And put a shirt on over all that." His fingers waved. Evidently meant to encompass her "that" which she'd intended on covering anyway.

An unwise spurt of contrariness bubbled inside her. "You're going to stand there half-naked, but I have to wear a nun's habit?"

He snorted, and before she knew it, he'd slid a finger beneath one of her cami straps. "Habit?" With a quick tug, he pulled the scooped edge of her cami down just far enough to reveal the wings of her butterfly tattoo. "Not even close."

She yanked her strap back over her shoulder. If she could only hate the way her skin was tingling, things would be ever so much easier. But she didn't hate it.

She longed for it.

And whether she was awake or sleeping, she couldn't get away from the intensity of it.

"Don't make the mistake of thinking I'm easy on top of everything else," she warned.

"Believe me, sweetheart. Nothing's easy about you."

Her skin prickled even more. She abruptly turned away and snatched up the shirt she'd fully intended on wearing to begin with and yanked it over her head. She looked back at him as she worked her hair free. "Satisfied?"

His gaze roved over her and she actually felt dizzy.

Then he suddenly cleared his throat and turned on his heel. "Don't forget the boots," he said as he walked away.

Ariana's breath rushed out. She leaned against the tall chest of drawers for a moment. When she felt a little steadier, she pulled on her mismatched socks and opened Deborah's closet door again.

Jayden's mom had several pairs of cowboy boots. Ariana chose the most worn-looking pair and sat on the edge of the bed to pull them on.

They were just as loose on her feet as the tennis shoes, but at least they weren't so easy to step right out of. The fact that she had to tuck the legs of her narrow jeans inside them didn't hurt, either.

She rubbed the dwindling tube of lip balm over her lips and left the room.

The kitchen door was open when she got there and she went outside, spotting Jayden. He was pulling on a blue plaid shirt and it flapped loosely around his lean hips as he disappeared into the barn. Sugar was trotting along at his heel.

Her heart did a slow cartwheel inside her chest at the sight.

There just was no way to deny it.

She pulled the kitchen door closed behind her and followed after them.

Even though she'd spent hours this past week working on the barn wall repairs with him, her first step inside the barn had her nose wrinkling. Not because the smell was unpleasant. Far from it. There was the expected smell of horseflesh, yes. But even more, it smelled like fresh wood and hay and the cleanser Jayden used when he swept down the aisle at the end of nearly every day.

There were two fans at either end, suspended from the rafters. They helped keep the air flowing and the flies down, and as she walked down the center aisle, she could feel the air tugging at her hair.

At the moment, none of the horses were in their stalls. Nathan, she knew, had taken two of them with him when he'd gone out on the range earlier that week. Two others, she saw through the open door at the other end of the barn, were tied to the railed fence surrounding the pasture.

Since she'd been at the ranch, she'd gotten close to the horses only a few times, and that had been to feed them carrots over the top of the sturdy fence standing between them. And even though she'd sooner choke than admit it, the thought of getting up on the back of one now was more than a little daunting. But she wasn't going to give Jayden another opportunity to point out what a city girl she was.

Not if she could help it, anyway.

"You going to stand there chewing your lip all afternoon?"

She looked over to where he was pulling a saddle from the rack. "Maybe," she admitted.

His eyes crinkled slightly. "Ridin's easy."

"Says the man who grew up doing it." She rubbed her hands down the sides of her jeans. "What do I do?"

"Carry this on out to Daisy and Jobuck. You can hang it on the rail." He set the saddle on her outstretched hands.

"Holy mama." The weight was unexpected and she had to hurriedly adjust her grip or drop the unwieldy saddle right on her feet. "How much does this thing weigh?"

He'd grabbed two saddle pads in one hand and hung a second saddle from his shoulder. "That's Mom's saddle. It's a light one," he said, leading the way from the barn. "Less 'n thirty pounds."

"So much for thinking I work out at my gym often enough," she muttered. He'd buttoned up his shirt and shoved one tail of it haphazardly into his jeans, which left her plenty of rear-end beauty to ogle as she followed. It helped distract her from the fact that for every step she took, she had to sort of push the saddle along with her thigh. It made for a Quasimodo kind of pace.

At the fence surrounding the pasture, she managed to heave the saddle onto one of the rails like he did without sending it toppling onto the other side. Then she started gnawing the inside of her cheek as the horse closest to her turned its head toward her and gave a loud snuffy huff.

"Think she smells good, do you, Daisy?" Jayden rubbed his hand over the horse's back and looked at Ariana where she was hovering. "Come closer. She'll sniff you up real well but she's not going to bite." He matter-of-factly took Ariana's hand in his and set it on the horse's warm back. "See?"

"Sure." Between the supple feel of the short, coarse hair under her palm and the warmth of his calloused one holding it in place, she was awash in sensation. And the way Daisy swung her head around to eyeball Ariana made her wonder if the horse knew it, too.

He stroked their hands across the horse a few times. "All smooth. They're already groomed, but you still always want to check and make sure nothing's there to irritate her when she's saddled."

His hand left Ariana's and he stepped away for a moment, and she quickly swallowed, sharing another look with Daisy.

Then he came back with the saddle pad, and once he'd shown Ariana how to make sure it was placed correctly, he grabbed the saddle and gently situated it on top of the saddle pad.

Explaining all the while, he fastened the front cinch. Then the flank cinch. He glanced at her where she was standing next to Daisy's enormous head. "I'm not using a breast collar." As if Ariana even knew what that was. "And we don't really need the flank for where we're heading this afternoon, but it'll make things feel a little more secure for you."

"Ah. Thank you?"

His lips twitched and he looped the reins over the horse's neck with one hand and hung his other fingers on the stirrup. "Come on. Left foot up in the stirrup if you can reach it. I'll tighten things up a little more once you're up."

Nervousness fluttered up her chest. She stroked Daisy's cheek. "What if I fall off?"

His lips tilted. "Then you'll get back on." He moved, gesturing for her to take his place standing next to the saddle. "But you won't fall off. Daisy's the steadiest ride we've got. She's been around a long time." He scratched the horse beneath her neck as they switched spots. "Haven't you, girl? Not that it's polite to talk about a lady's age, but she's twice as old as Jobuck."

Ariana blew out a puff of air. She stretched her foot up and was grateful not to hear one of her seams rip as she fit the toe of her boot through the stirrup.

"Okay. I s'pose you could find a hundred people to tell you a hundred ways to mount a horse, but here's how I learned." He moved her left hand from where she'd grabbed the saddle horn and placed it instead near the horse's mane not far from the edge of the saddle pad. "Usually you'd have the reins in your hand like I do." His left hand nudged hers. Then he guided her right hand to the back of the saddle. "Some people grab the far pommel. Some the cantle. This is the cantle. You're only looking for balance when you push yourself up. Not pulling. Pushing. Keeping your weight toward the horse while you're doing it. Got it?"

She let out half a laugh. She felt like she was being stretched on a rack. "Sure. Right."

When he'd been saddling the horse, she'd noticed that one of his hands had maintained contact with Daisy the whole while. And when his hand left Ariana's to find her waist, she realized he did the same thing with her.

She couldn't decide if it was unsettling or comforting.

"I'll give you help if you need it," he said. "Once you're off the ground and feeling balanced standing there in the stirrup, swing your right leg over. Try not to kick Daisy in the process. She doesn't like that much."

"Who does?"

He laughed softly and the sound of it was almost music to her ears. He hadn't laughed like that since…well, *since*.

"Get some good spring going here." His hand touched her thigh. "It'll help a lot. And *push*."

She pushed, barely feeling his hand fall away from her waist as, by some miracle, she swung right up into the saddle, completely bypassing the whole stand and balance part, but nevertheless ending up with her butt where it belonged.

She laughed, surprised by the exhilaration she felt. Not to mention being able to look down on him for once.

It was a novel experience.

"I feel very high up here," she admitted.

"You're a natural." His hand left her boot and he ducked under Daisy's head and checked her right foot in the stirrup after she'd stood up in them when he requested. "You're shorter than my mother." He ducked back under again and adjusted the front cinch some more. The process had him standing distractingly close to Ariana's thigh. "I figured I'd need to shorten the stirrups, but I don't."

His brown hair was slightly lighter on top. Sun kissed. She caught herself just in time from reaching out to ruffle her fingers through the short, thick strands. His hair wasn't much lighter than Daisy's but she knew very well that it was so, so much softer.

"Long legs, I guess." She absently pressed down one of the bandages striping her palm.

His gaze lifted, catching hers for a moment that seemed to stretch. "Yeah."

Then he took a step back, breaking the moment.

He scooped up the cowboy hat he'd left hanging over a fence post and put it on his head. "Just get used to the feel of Daisy under you for a few minutes."

"Mmm-hmm."

She watched him stride back into the barn and leaned forward over Daisy's neck. "Be gentle with me, okay, girl?" Daisy shook her head and shifted, and Ariana quickly straightened, grabbing the saddle horn as she rocked. "I hope that's your way of saying yes."

The horse standing next to them—Jobuck—also shifted, tossing his head and pulling against the rope tethering him loosely to the fence rail, and Ariana gave him a wary look. "Behave over there, would you, please? I'm still new in town, remember?"

Then Jayden returned carrying a coiled rope, a canteen and a longish pouch from which he pulled a pair of leather gloves. He handed them to her. "They're the softest ones I could find," he said a little gruffly. "But they'll give your hands a little more protection."

Stupidly touched, she pulled them on.

In a matter of minutes, he had Jobuck saddled. The younger horse didn't stand quite so placidly in place as Jayden worked. "Cut it out," he said easily as the horse seemed to deliberately bump against him. Jayden just pushed back with his shoulder against the horse and he settled.

It was a reminder that Ariana didn't really need that

the horses could run the show if they so chose. "Have you ever been hurt by a horse?"

"Not intentionally." He looked up at Ariana as he fastened the bag to the back of his saddle. Next came the canteen and the rope. "Don't worry about Jobuck. He's just feeling frisky."

"What's the rope for?"

"In case."

"In case of what?"

His lips twitched. "In case you don't behave yourself."

She made a face and his smile widened. "In case," he said again.

She supposed when it came to a rancher, "in case" probably covered a lot of possibilities.

He replaced the horse's halter with the bridle and reins. But instead of mounting Jobuck, he led both horses around to the front of the barn, not stopping until he'd practically reached the storm-cellar door.

Ariana pointed toward it. "Did it get all dried out down there?"

He glanced at the cellar door. "Probably by now. Haven't worried about anything down there enough to look."

He checked the cinch on Ariana's saddle one more time before handing her the reins. "Hold 'em in your left hand." He showed her. "You want 'em easy and loose for Daisy, but not so loose she worries you're not in charge. Yep. There you go. Keep 'em up like they're a cup of coffee you don't want to spill."

"Coffee!"

His eyes glinted. "Figure that might resonate more than the usual ice-cream-cone comparison. Drape the rest over on your right. You're green, so you can hold the horn if you need to. Otherwise just let your free hand relax."

"Relax. Because that's so easy to do."

He was smiling as she watched him swing up onto Jobuck's back and she nearly swallowed her tongue.

How on earth had she gone her whole life without realizing just how sexy the sight would be of a man climbing on a horse? Even though she knew Jayden had worn an army uniform for most of his adult life, at that moment it was hard to picture it. Not when he looked so completely and utterly where he belonged on the back of a horse.

His smile widened and his eyes glinted. "Ready?"

Her stomach danced around. And she knew at that particular moment that it had absolutely nothing to do with a horseback ride and everything to do with him.

"Yes." The word slid from her lips. "I think I am."

## Chapter Nine

They rode through grass. And more grass.

And Ariana realized that she'd been wrong when she'd first thought that it all looked the same. In the thick of it, there seemed to be an endless variety of colors and textures and smells.

And the sounds. She wasn't sure why she'd ever thought of the country as being so quiet.

There was buzzing. There was chirping. There was the quick rush and flap of wings as birds scattered almost from beneath their hooves when Jayden decided it was time for her to trot. At which point she was pretty sure that the loudest sound in the entire county was her teeth clanking together as she bounced ungracefully in the saddle. She didn't know what to grab. The saddle horn to help the jouncing or her chest to stop the bouncing.

"Relax your knees," Jayden called. "Squeezing with your legs isn't going to help. Lighten up your spine and let your hips rock more. Sorta like you're bouncing on a yoga ball."

She couldn't help it. She laughed. "Yoga ball?"

"You've been on one, haven't you? You look like the yoga sort with the way you go around exercising every morning."

She hadn't thought he'd noticed anything she did in the mornings. Aside from keeping food on the table and the coffeepot brewing. "Yeah, I do yoga." She nodded, only to bite her tongue. Which, strangely enough, just made her laugh that much harder. "This is awful!"

He was grinning. "How do you think it feels from Daisy's perspective?"

"Oh, great. Now I feel guilty for hurting her, too."

He pulled up Jobuck and Daisy slowed as well, taking a couple of steps, then just stopping altogether.

"She's patient," he assured her. "She knows you're learning." He brought Jobuck closer until there was only a few feet between them. He pulled off his hat and reached over to plop it on her head. "Your nose is getting sunburned."

She pushed up the brim so she could see from beneath it and warned the pitter-pat going on inside her chest not to get too excited.

"When we start trotting again, imagine keeping your seat bones in contact with the horse. Then once we do a slow lope, you'll feel more of a wave motion and it'll get easier. Graciela once told me she thought sitting the trot was sort of like learning to follow your partner during sex. Close your eyes if you have to."

He was waiting for a response. She merely nodded. It was all she could manage because she suddenly couldn't seem to think a single, coherent thought.

His eyes crinkled and they set off again.

When she felt Daisy picking up speed beneath her, transitioning from that easy, swaying sort of walk into another trot, she had to clap one hand on his hat to keep it from blowing off her head.

She closed her eyes.

She didn't know if she bounced any less, really.

But she certainly enjoyed the image of him behind her closed lids.

She wasn't sure how long they rode, but she was pathetically grateful when they finally stopped in the shade of the trees surrounding a large, meandering pond where an old-fashioned-looking windmill slowly turned.

The hot sunshine had sent sweat dripping down her spine. Even inside the gloves, her hands were so wet that when she peeled them off, the bandages on her palms dropped off, too.

"Here." Jayden leaned toward her from Jobuck's back, offering the canteen.

"Thanks." She was breathless. She'd lost count of how many times Jayden had her move in and out of a trot. In and out of a lope. Enough times, though, that she'd actually felt like she was getting the hang of it. "I didn't know riding a horse was such a workout." She twisted off the cap and drank thirstily. The water was cool. Vaguely metallic. And entirely refreshing.

"That's how Nathan and I keep our girlish figures."

She coughed a little as she swallowed. The day Jayden Fortune and his brother were in any way girlish would be the day the earth started spinning in the opposite direction. Even though she hadn't met Grayson, she figured he had to have been cut from the same cloth, too.

She swiped her arm over her mouth and took another drink, then screwed the cap back on.

Jayden had already dismounted and led Jobuck near the edge of the water, leaving the reins loose.

"You're not afraid he'll run off?"

"I'll keep an eye." He walked back toward her and took the canteen. "But he's usually pretty good being ground tied. Particularly when Daisy's around." He pulled off the cap and tilted his head back as he drank.

His throat was tanned and sheened with sweat.

And she felt desperately in need of something to fan herself with, just from watching him.

Then he looped the strap of the canteen over a tree branch and took the reins that she'd draped around her saddle horn and walked Daisy nearer to Jobuck. "Need help getting down?"

She shook her head. "I don't think so."

"Just go in reverse pretty much. Get your right foot out of the stirrup. This time grab the horn with your right hand. It'll keep you from getting anything hung up on it as you come down."

"What would get hung up?"

He waved vaguely. "Your, uh, shirt."

She frowned.

"Just trust me," he said. Then he sighed a little impatiently. "Graciela once got hung up on her bra," he said abruptly.

She raised her eyebrows. It was difficult being blithe when she felt more like baring her teeth. "Just what exactly went on between you and Graciela? I thought she was supposed to be the older woman who got away?"

"Nothing to write home about." He gestured to the horse. "Swing your leg over." He waited while she did it. "And now lower it on down." His hands surrounded her hips when her foot hit the clover-covered ground and she slid her left toe out of the stirrup. "Good job."

Daisy's warm body was in front of her. Jayden's warm body was behind her.

It was safer to focus on the horse. She patted the side of Daisy's neck and pulled off Jayden's cowboy hat. Even though it was straw, her head immediately felt cooler from the fresh air and she shoved her hand through her hair, flipping it away from her neck. "Is the pond deep enough to swim in?"

"Thought you didn't swim."

"I don't."

"Well, as it happens, it's only a few feet deep, anyway. Good for wading in, but that's about it." His hands fell away from her as he gave her space. "Though if you want to strip off and give it a shot, don't let me stop you."

She gave him a look.

He spread his hands. "I'm just a guy, sweetheart."

"You're not *just* anything."

His smile was faint and entirely wicked. "It's fresh water, though. That old windmill's been pumping up water since the fifties."

She looked up at the metal-framed structure situated on a slight rise above the trees. The fan part of it was turning slowly with a distinctly rhythmic squeak.

In conjunction with the buzz of bugs and the chirping of birds, it was almost musical.

"Fifties, huh?" She tucked the gloves in her back pocket and yanked her T-shirt off as she walked toward the water's edge. "That was before your mother came to Paseo." She crouched down and swished her shirt through the clear water, glancing back at him.

He'd hooked his thumbs in his front pockets. His shoulders seemed particularly massive and his expression had closed. "So?"

She swallowed a sigh and straightened. Every muscle in her legs protested.

"I'm not digging for details," she assured him evenly. "Paloma told me about your mother and the Thompsons. Irv— No. Earl. Earl and Cynthia Thompson. They're the ones who took in your mom before you and your brothers were born."

"Yeah. So?"

She wrung the water out of the T-shirt and pulled it back on over her camisole.

The cooling relief it brought was immediate.

She swished her legs through the short, thick grass growing at the water's edge as she walked along it. There were a few boulders along the pond bank that would have made a decent enough spot to sit, except her butt didn't feel ready for contact with anything just yet. Especially a hard piece of rock. "So, nothing. I was just wondering if the Thompsons were the ones who put in the windmill, that's all."

"Yeah. They were." His thumbs came out of his pockets and he pulled down the canteen from the tree branch. "They were like grandparents to us. They both died when we were in high school. Within a year of each other." He waved in the direction of the windmill. "There's a small cemetery over there. That's where they're all buried."

"Do you know what happened to their daughter?"

He took a swig of water. "Car accident is what most people say. Suicide by car was more accurate, though. Earl told me about it one night."

"How terrible."

"She was pregnant, too. Like Mom."

Ariana winced. "So, not just one life lost, but two."

"Yeah." He tossed the canteen strap over the branch again and moved around the horses where they were chowing down on the bright, green grass to sit on one of the boulders. Apparently a couple of hours in a saddle were nothing to him. "I used to wonder if Mom would have stayed here like she did if things had been different. If Earl and Cynthia hadn't needed us all so badly to fill the void after their daughter died."

She imagined him as the boy he'd described. The one who'd wanted to be anywhere other than tiny little Paseo, and her heart squeezed. She perched gingerly beside him on a slanted rock. "Did you ever ask your mom?"

"She said the only family who mattered was the one we'd made here."

So many questions. Questions she couldn't ask because she didn't know what might or might not lead to the matter of Jerome Fortune. And more than anything, she didn't want that ruining their time together.

"I never knew my grandparents," she told him. "It was always just my folks and me."

"No wonder you're spoiled."

She gaped. "I'm not spoiled!"

His coffee-colored eyes were lighter than usual because of the bright sun. And when they looked right into her, the world stopped.

*I love this man.*

The realization flowed through her.

But then he was speaking again, his smile widening. "Okay. You're not spoiled."

The world started up again. She managed to lightly roll her eyes, even though inside she felt like she was reeling. "Darn tootin' I'm not. I've been living with one pair of underwear here. No makeup. No cell phone. No internet. Have you heard me complain?"

He scooped up water in his hand and splashed it around his neck. "No underwear. Hadn't thought about that."

She cursed her thoughtless tongue. At least her red face could be attributed to the hot day. And just because she couldn't get the notion of loving him out of her head didn't mean he had to know it.

She grasped for a change of subject. "How, uh, how long do you think it will be before the Ybarras can start rebuilding their house?"

"They've already started."

"What?" She wobbled a little on her perch and instinctively grabbed his arm to steady herself. She felt his muscle flex, and then he stood, whether needing or wanting to put some space between them, she didn't know.

Then she told herself she was being overly sensitive, because all he did was head over to retrieve the canteen.

"Nathan was over there before he headed out to check the north section," he said before taking a drink. Once he capped it again, he held it out toward her. "He told me they'd already poured a new foundation and started the framing."

Her fingers brushed his as she took the container. "Amazing."

"Even in tiny Paseo, things *can* get done quickly."

"Clearly." Just not when it came to getting parts for her car. She had no complaints on that score, though, as it gave her a reason to still be there. She had her back to the water and she stretched out her stiff legs as she sipped the water. "So, seriously. About Graciela…" A bee buzzed by her face and she jerked back, swatting at it.

Unfortunately, she didn't factor in the angle of the rock on which she sat and she felt her butt sliding back. Her arms sawed and her legs went up.

She had only enough time to see Jayden's startled expression before she hit the water. It sloshed up over the rocks, splashing her in the face, and she had a moment's panic before she realized just how shallow the pond really was. Her rear end was on the bottom, her face well above the surface.

She sat in deeper water when she was in her bathtub at home.

She swiped the water from her face and looked up at him.

At the edge of the pond, he stood there with his hands on his hips and a broad grin on his face.

Dry.

"You all right?"

She finished capping the canteen that she'd somehow managed to keep aloft the pond water and tossed it onto the grass. "Aside from busting my dignity?" She put her hands down in the water, prepared to push herself upright, but they slipped against the slick bottom and water splashed up and over her shoulders. "I don't know what's growing on the bottom here, but may I just say *ick*?"

He laughed outright. "It's just grass, sweetheart."

"Easy for you to say." Stupidly, something sweet was jiggling around inside her chest from the sound of his laughter. She tried finding some purchase with her boots, but the heels just seemed to sink farther into the bottom of the pond. "Sure there isn't quicksand under here?"

Still chuckling, he leaned forward, stretching out his hand. "No quicksand," he promised. "Maybe some frogs and water bugs. A snake or two."

She grimaced, tried scrambling out of the water, only to land yet again with a splash. Not even a beautiful, graceful splash. Just an unbecoming flop. Because, naturally, that's what would happen when you realize you love a guy.

"I was kidding about the snakes." He was still grinning. "Come on, city girl. Give me your hand."

"I guess I should be glad you're not going for your 'in

case' rope to haul me out." She held out her hand and he caught it, circling his long fingers around her wrist.

She yanked.

He snorted, easily planting one foot in the water to keep himself from being pulled down into the water beside her. "Nice try. You think it'd be that simple? Other hand now."

She made a face but gave him her other hand and he hauled her clean out of the water. She bumped flat against him and his hands went to her waist.

Before her nerve endings had a chance to fire too brilliantly, he pivoted to set her on the dry grass.

"There you go. No harm done. Except for a little pond scum." He pulled a long, slick piece of grass away from her neck and tossed it back into the water.

She smiled. And gave him a healthy shove.

Healthy enough to unbalance him and watch him land on his butt with a big splash.

She laughed as she propped her hands on her soaking hips. "Watch out for us city girls."

He angled his head, giving her a considering look. "I suppose you think we're even now."

She nodded. "I suppose I do." She scooped up the canteen and took another drink. Then she capped it once more and eyed him. "You just going to sit there among the water bugs and frogs?"

"Maybe I'm enjoying the view."

There was no question he meant *her.*

She resisted the urge to look down at herself, because she knew what she'd see. The human equivalent of a drowning rat. "Sure you are. Because this is a really attractive look." She squished her way to the flattest boulder and sat on it to pull off the boots. She upended them and water poured out. "I hope I haven't ruined your mom's boots, too."

She heard him splashing and looked over to see him standing in the pond and sloshing his way to the edge.

"Y'ought to worry more about ruining mine." Unlike the rest of him, his voice was dry. And somewhat muffled by the shirt he was taking off. He didn't even bother with the buttons. He just pulled it straight over his head. Then he tossed it at her and it landed with a wet slap against her chest.

It was almost impossible not to ogle him when his body was just so impossibly perfect. "Your boots got soaked the day we met," she reminded him. "They survived that, didn't they?" She threw the shirt back at him.

He caught it in midair long before it could hit him. "You do realize that we still have to ride *back* to the ranch, right? If you were feeling saddle sore before, it's nothing compared to how you'll feel after riding in wet jeans."

"I would've been riding in wet jeans whether you took a little bath in there or not."

"Except I could have given you my dry shirt to wear."

"With wet jeans."

"Not if you took them off."

She raised her eyebrows. It was all she could do to keep it light. "Riding in just my dainties? You must be joking."

His eyes were amused. "We are gonna have to get our jeans dried out, though. Unless you'd rather walk, we'll both be in for a pretty uncomfortable ride."

Being soaked from the pond had momentarily taken her mind off her stiff legs. "So walking, we'd probably get back around midnight?"

He chuckled. "It wouldn't take that long." He spread out his shirt over a tree branch, then sat on a rock and worked off his boots. Then he pulled off his socks that she could tell were nowhere near as wet as hers. Then he stood and started unfastening his jeans.

She couldn't help the strangled sound that emerged from her throat and flushed when he looked at her. His eyebrows rose a little. "Something wrong?"

"Aside from you having way too much fun at my expense?" She pointed an accusing finger at him. "That's what you're doing."

He spread his hands. "Considering history, you've shown an aptitude for taking off *your* clothes." Then his grin broke loose and his hands fell away from his pants. "Truth is, I don't know if our jeans'll dry faster with us wearing them or not." He walked barefoot through the soft grass over to where the two horses were still grazing and unfastened the bag from his saddle.

He came back and handed it to her.

"It's like a fanny pack," she said, unzipping the nylon bag to find a collection of granola bars and a small first-aid kit inside.

"Cantle bag," he corrected her, looking like he wanted to laugh.

"Well, you attached it to the fanny part of your saddle." She pulled out one of the bars and tossed the bag back to him. "Thank you. Aside from the failure to pack a spare change of clothing, you're very prepared."

"Thank the army." He sat down on the grass, then took a bar for himself before lying back. He had one leg hitched over his other upraised knee. "Wet jeans or not, this is the life," he murmured. He tore open the wrapper and bit off half the granola bar.

He'd made himself similarly comfortable that first day in the storm cellar and she couldn't help smiling a little at the sight. She tore open her own bar and took a bite. "Did Graciela really get her bra hung up on a saddle horn?"

"She really did."

"And she really said…what you said she said about the trotting thing."

He'd finished his granola bar and he rolled onto his side, propping his head on his hand. The muscles in his arm bulged. "She really said what I said she said."

He was laughing at her. No question. And she was still left wondering what had really gone on between him and the beautiful older woman.

"Did you ever sleep with her?"

His eyebrows shot up. "You don't hesitate to ask questions, do you?"

"Not usually," she admitted.

He rolled onto his stomach, propping himself on his arms.

There was no real reason for her mouth to run dry, but it suddenly did. "Well?"

"Yes, I slept with her."

Her jaw went tight.

"I was all of six years old and she was babysitting me and my brothers," he added. "Why's it bother you so much?"

"Who says it bothers me?"

He just looked at her.

She focused on the faint scar above his eyebrow. "She's very beautiful now. I can only imagine what she was like when she was younger."

"She didn't hold a candle to you."

There were probably a hundred books written about the wisdom of trusting a handsome cuss's flattery. She'd written a blog or two about it herself.

But he wasn't just any handsome cuss. Not anymore.

"I'm not fishing for compliments."

"Generally speaking, truth is rarely complimentary. It's just truth."

Something inside her chest squeezed.

"Come here."

She hesitated. But it was a lost cause. It had been from the first time he'd smiled at her. She moved off the rock to sit on the grass growing around the base of it.

"Closer." He extended one arm toward her, his palm up, fingers curled slightly.

She focused on his palm, on the ridge of calluses that were plainly visible.

He had a working man's hands.

Without thinking about it, she found herself moving closer to him. "When's the last time you slept under the stars?"

Instead of looking surprised by the odd question, he just slowly slid his palm over her forearm, setting off a rush of heat through her veins. "About a week before I met you."

"Out camping or something?"

He shook his head and drew his hand down to hers. He slowly pressed his larger palm against hers and her head swam.

"Out, uh, checking your cattle like Nathan's been doing?"

He shook his head again and steadily separated her fingers with his.

She swallowed and moistened her lips. "Then why?"

His eyes lifted to hers. They were clear brown and so much more addictive than any amount of coffee could ever be. "Because there's no place better than being beneath the Paseo sky."

"To sleep?"

He reached out his free hand and slid it along her jaw. His thumb slowly brushed against her cheek.

She felt herself being drawn down toward him.

"Just to be," he murmured.

Then his mouth slowly brushed against hers.

Tasting.

Tempting.

And no matter how smart she wanted to be where he was concerned, she couldn't stop herself from leaning into him. From tasting him in return. From parting her lips when his kiss deepened. From winding her arms around his back when he drew her down onto the soft, fragrant grass with him.

She couldn't stop herself from sucking in a quick breath when his hand slid over her belly, pulling up both her soaking T-shirt and the cami beneath. Or from threading her fingers through his hair when his lips followed his hand.

"If you're going to stop me, say so now," he murmured as he worked his way upward, pulling the elastic-edged shelf bra above her breasts.

She couldn't find words if her life depended on it. She lifted up enough to finish pulling everything off over her head. And then it wasn't his hands running over her but his gaze, and she felt weak from it.

He leaned over and kissed her butterfly tattoo. Slowly he worked his way to one nipple, then over to the pulse pounding madly at the base of her throat.

The grass beneath her tickled her back and the heat from the afternoon sun beat down from above, glowing even when she closed her eyes.

She wrapped her hands around his head and pulled him up to her, pressing her lips to his. "Jayden—"

He went still. Then he levered his chest up from hers. "You want to stop."

She shook her head as she opened her eyes and looked up into his face. The sun was behind his head and the aura surrounding him was nearly blinding. "I want you to never stop," she whispered.

He was silent, while all around them, the sound of nature seemed to get louder. The buzz of grasshoppers. The warbling and chirping of birds. The squeak of the windmill.

Then his lips brushed against her cheek. "I'll do my best," he murmured against her ear, before his lips burned their way once more down her neck. Past the pulse. Beyond the butterfly. He slowly kissed his way along her breasts, down the center of her belly to her navel, not stopping until he reached the button of her jeans. He freed it with a soft pop. "Lift."

She raised her hips and he peeled the soaking jeans and her frivolous white panties away.

"Don't leave me here like this alone." She managed to slide her fingers beneath the waistband of his jeans and he caught her fingers, dragging them away. He kissed the tips of them before letting her go long enough to work out of his own wet things.

And then he was settling against her, and she exhaled shakily, because she had never felt anything quite so momentous in her life as the weight of him. The heat of him. The need for him. As if her entire life had simply been marking time until this very moment.

She slid her hands over his wide shoulders, down his back, all the while hovering on the agonizing precipice of waiting as his strong fingers gripped her hips, staying her motions.

"You're sure?"

She twined her legs around his and nodded, pressing her mouth against his because she wasn't sure that she could hold back words that she didn't dare admit. Fortunately, it was answer enough and she shuddered when he slowly pressed into her, filling her so perfectly she wondered how she would ever be the same again.

Then his hands slid up to find hers again, their fingers meshing. "I knew it." His voice had gone rough. Husky.

She could already feel herself tightening around him. She could hardly manage to form words as he rocked against her, making the pleasure inside her build and build.

"Knew...what?"

"How you'd feel." Then his breath hissed between his teeth as she arched sharply, winding her legs even more tightly around his hips. "Perfect."

But she was already beyond hearing as he emptied himself inside her and she cried out, startling a nearby bevy of quail into scattering.

All she knew was that he was right.

There was no more perfect place than being beneath the Paseo sky.

With him.

## Chapter Ten

Jayden's cotton shirt dried long before hers did and he pulled it over her head. "More than your nose is getting sunburned."

"And you're not getting sunburned?"

"I'm already mostly leather," he murmured, kissing her shoulder through the shirt.

She smiled, because she knew better. His upper torso was deeply tanned and felt like satin covered muscle. "Not your under-the-swimsuit bits," she said.

He gave a choked laugh. "Bits?"

She lifted her shoulder and twisted her fingers through his.

They were picking their way barefoot through the clover around the pond. And even if it ought to seem odd that he was wearing only his still-damp jeans and she was wearing only his wrinkled plaid shirt over her panties that had quickly dried in the sun, she didn't care.

"I suppose you'd prefer something a little grander sounding."

"I'd prefer words other than *little* and *bits*," he allowed wryly.

She laughed and he suddenly pulled her around to face him, twisting his hands in her long hair as he kissed her.

Despite the lethargy still clinging to her, she felt heat streak through her and she swayed unsteadily when he finally lifted his head and started walking again.

They passed the windmill and she stopped to look up at the tall structure. She reached up and wrapped her hands around one of the horizontal bars running between the corner pieces. The pipe running straight down from the top slowly moved up and down and connected to another series of pipes near the ground, one which clearly ran toward the pond. "Considering the noise this thing makes, I thought it would be rustier."

"It's not rust that's squeaking. It's the sails and the sucker rod." He stopped close against her and set his hands on either side of hers. "We've gotta keep it running. Can't depend only on rain that's either too little or too often." He tapped the metal bar. "This baby keeps the place irrigated and the cattle from drying up. We have three more mills farther out, too. Nathan'll be checking on 'em while he's out. Make sure they weren't damaged during the storm that delivered you."

She leaned her head back against his chest as she squinted up at the slowly revolving fan blades. Sails, he'd called them. Such an evocative term. "It's kind of beautiful, isn't it?" The afternoon. The windmill. *Him.*

"Mmm-hmm." He lifted the plaid shirt and slid his arm around her bare waist. "Only times it's not real beautiful is when we have to climb up and repair something." His fingers grazed her breasts, circled her eager nipples.

"View's great, but it's still a pain in the butt and seems to only happen when it's either hotter 'n hell outside like today or cold as a witch's heart."

She was having a hard time breathing. Particularly when his leg slid between hers and she felt him, hard and insistent against her backside. And even though she felt a rush of dizzying want all over again, she closed her hand over his, stilling his motions. "I want to." How badly she wanted to.

"But?"

She rubbed her temple against his chin. Despite her cautioning hand, his thumb still managed to taunt her sensitized nipple and heat collected low inside her. "But I'm too sore," she admitted in a raw breath.

"You'll get used to saddles and horseback riding." He slid his hand from beneath hers.

Regret was like a physical noise, joining the cacophony of sound around them. "I'm not talking about being sore from the horse."

He dipped his head and kissed the side of her neck. "Guess that makes up for the *bits* bit," he said in a low voice. His hand didn't leave her, though. It slid leisurely over her rib cage.

She exhaled shakily and rested against him, feeling more than a little mesmerized by the motion of the windmill. The turn of the sails. The up-and-down glide of the rod. The no-longer-random trajectory of his fingers. "Jayden—"

"Sshh." His hand covered hers where she was still holding on to the metal bar. His other hand—the provocatively tempting one—moved inexorably southward. "Just let me do this."

She inhaled sharply as his fingers breached the edge of her panties. She wrapped her fingers around his strong wrist. Whether to stop him or urge him on, she wasn't sure. "But what about you?"

His fingers delved between her legs, gliding slickly. He made a low sound of pure appreciation that rumbled from his chest, through her spine and straight to her heart. He pressed his mouth against her shoulder and his voice dropped even deeper. "This is for me." His clever, marauding fingers swirled against her and she couldn't hold back a sigh of pleasure. "You know what a fantasy this is?"

She rolled her head back and forth against his chest. "No."

"After this, I'll never hate repairing windmills again," he murmured. His thumb roved over the knot of nerve endings and she gasped.

"Trust me, sweetheart." His fingers dipped. "Let yourself go. For me."

And she did.

Eventually, they made it to the small cemetery he'd mentioned earlier, where the Thompsons were buried. The grassy patch was surrounded by a white picket fence that looked in pristine condition. It made a few of the headstones that it surrounded look even more ancient by comparison.

For the first time in a long while, she wished she had her cell phone with her so she could take pictures. She didn't need to ask who was responsible for maintaining the fence around the family plot. Because she understood that the ones buried there were considered Jayden's family.

She put her hand on the gate. "May I?"

"Sure."

She undid the latch and stepped through. The oldest of the headstones were the farthest away from the gate, situated among the roots of the enormous tree standing guard over the cemetery. She knelt down, barely noticing the way her calves and thighs protested, and read the inscriptions on the simple stone markers. "Eighteen ninety-five. Nineteen-oh-two."

"Earl's grandparents." Jayden flicked a leaf away from the deeply weathered granite. "They were some of Paseo's first settlers. Came from Boston originally." He gestured toward the three markers next to them. "They had four children. Earl's dad was the only one who lived past fifteen." He moved around to the next row where the headstones were noticeably brighter, the edges less worn. "Kees Thompson. Earl's father."

She read the marker. Jayden had pronounced the name like *Case*. "I like that name. Very different."

"His wife, Mary." He pointed at the accompanying headstone. "Nothing unusual about her name. Not until you get to Mary Junior." He stopped in front of a third headstone. "Earl's sister. Only woman I've ever known that actually used Junior in her name."

She brushed her fingertips over the engraved surname. "Thompson. Mary Junior never married?"

He shook his head. "Died when we were little."

She moved around to look at the last and most recent row of headstones. Earl. Cynthia. Caroline and child. "So sad. Every generation lost a child before they should have."

He leaned over to brush away the leaves accumulated at the base of Caroline's square headstone. When he straightened, he was holding a large silver ring. "That's a new kind of leaf," he drawled.

She smiled and reached out to take it. Only to frown as she studied it more closely. "It's part of a loose-leaf binder." A big one. She worked the ring apart. "See?"

He was still brushing away debris and held up a piece of bright pink plastic. "Belonged to this, I expect."

Her stomach tightened as she took the jagged remnant. "You had a notebook like this in your car, didn't you?"

Her mouth suddenly ran dry. She nodded.

"Wonder if anything else from your car landed around here. We should take a look. In case."

She wasn't sure how she'd managed to forget the inconvenience facing her when it came to replacing her driver's license and everything else that had been in her wallet. "It doesn't matter." She couldn't seem to tear her attention away from the piece of plastic binder.

Jayden noticed. "You okay?"

There was a knot inside her chest. "I kept all my research and notes in this."

"For the magazine."

She started to nod. But then she looked at him and couldn't make herself do it. She couldn't tell him an outright lie. Not anymore. Not when she'd already crossed every single line she'd sworn she'd never cross.

The self-imposed oath had been simple.

Until now. Now that she knew she was in love with him.

"For my book," she said huskily.

His eyebrows rose. "A book? That's great. You never said you were working on—" He broke off. His eyes narrowed. "What kind of book?"

"A biography." She had to forcibly swallow down the knot when it moved from her chest into her throat. "An unauthorized biography."

His lips tightened. He folded his arms across his wide chest. Arms that only minutes earlier had surrounded her with such thrilling tenderness. "Let me guess. About Gerald Robinson?"

"Jerome Fortune."

His lips twisted. "They're one and the same."

How could she make him understand? "And everyone

knows everything about Gerald! At least everything he's let everyone know. But nobody seems to know anything about Jerome. Not once he supposedly died thirty-some years ago."

"What were you hoping, Ariana?"

Her nerves tightened. Because he never addressed her directly by name. And it felt so, so much worse than it should have.

"Were you hoping you'd be here long enough to grill my mother when she returns?"

"No!"

"To dig into her past just because you think writing some damn *unauthorized* book gives you the right?"

"I would never do that." Her eyes stung. "Not now."

"Why should I believe you?" He advanced on her, looking furious. He plucked the pink plastic out of her numb fingers and held it up between them. "Because you've been so honest and up-front about everything so far?"

"Because I fell in love with you!"

A muscle worked in his tight jaw as his gaze drilled into hers.

She pulled in a breath that seemed to burn. "I fell in love with you," she repeated huskily. "Whatever ends up in the book, it won't involve you."

It seemed impossible for his expression to sharpen even more, but it did. "Because you believe he's not our father."

She chewed the inside of her lip. But she'd already determined she couldn't lie. And what did it matter now, when he was looking at her with such anger? Such distrust?

"No. I do believe he is your father."

A barrier seemed to slam down behind his eyes.

"But no matter what I believe, I'm not going to write about it," she insisted even though her head told her it was useless. "Not about you. Not about your brothers or your mother."

"Then what *are* you going to fill the pages with? Details about some other slob you pick up off the street and sleep with for a story?"

She felt the blood drain from her face. Even though it took every speck of strength inside her, she managed to lift her chin. She wasn't a tramp and she wasn't going to apologize. "I never came here trying to prove you were Jerome Fortune's son. You know that. You *have* to know that by now."

"The only thing I know is that you could've mentioned the book from the get-go. And you didn't. That's as good as a lie to me."

"If I'd been trying to prove that you weren't his son, would you still feel the same?"

His expression remained cold.

But no colder than the yawning hole that had opened up inside her.

She set the metal ring on the edge of poor Caroline's headstone, then turned and walked away.

She knew he followed after her. Not because she could hear his footsteps in the clover and grass. They were just as silent as hers. But because she could feel the drilling of his eyes through the space between her shoulder blades.

She was out of breath by the time she made it all the way around the pond again, and she pulled off his shirt, turning to hand it to him.

His gaze dropped for the briefest millisecond, but she was damned if she'd cover her bare breasts now. Instead, she snatched up her cami from the rock where she'd spread it to dry and tugged it over her head. Then the rough cotton T-shirt and her jeans that were still more wet than not.

She ignored the clamminess and pulled on her socks and his mother's too-large boots.

"Ariana."

It was practically a command and she hesitated.

"Don't rush around the horses. I don't want you spooking them."

Not that he didn't want her getting kicked. Just that he didn't want her scaring his horses.

He'd pulled the plaid shirt on, but the buttons weren't fastened and it flapped around his lean hips after he'd pulled on his own boots and headed toward the horses. They'd never strayed far from where they'd left them, and even though it felt like they'd whiled away an entire day beside the pond, it could only have been a couple of hours.

A couple of hours for her to taste heaven.

A couple of hours for her to lose it just as surely.

She looked away from him, blinking hard at the stinging in her eyes.

Then she lifted her head and threw her hair behind her back. She walked over to where he stood with Daisy and put one hand on the horse's withers, the other on the cantle, and mounted.

Focusing on the top of Jayden's tousled head, she pulled on the leather gloves then held out her hands for the reins.

He silently handed them to her, then mounted Jobuck and led the way back to the ranch.

No swaying, gentle walk this time. No exercise in trying to sit the trot. He didn't even make a soft clucking sound. Jobuck just moved smoothly into a steady lope and Daisy kept pace.

He couldn't have made it any clearer that he wanted to get away from her.

All too quickly, they were back at the ranch and Daisy aimed straight for the wash rack at the back of the barn.

Ariana wasn't showing off any particular skill she'd learned that afternoon. That was all Daisy.

"I'll put her up," Jayden said when Ariana dismounted. His expression was still closed. She knew there was no point in arguing. Not about helping to unsaddle the horse and groom her like she knew he always did after bringing one of his horses in. Nor about convincing him that the book she was writing didn't matter.

Because if it truly hadn't mattered, why had she really kept from mentioning it?

She silently handed him the reins and walked through the barn. She didn't even notice the little red vehicle sitting near the house until she practically walked right into it.

"Hey there, Miss Lamonte." Charlie came down from where he'd been sitting on one of the porch chairs. "Was just beginning to think I wasn't goin' t' find you." His skinny face had a happy smile. "Got that part today after all." He waved at her car. "She's spit-shined and ready t' go."

Her eyes burned. "I see that, Charlie." Because she was badly afraid she was going to lose it and cry, she walked around the vehicle, working hard to study it. She couldn't see a single scratch. No dents. No damage.

It was as if the tornado had never crossed the car's path at all.

She bent over and looked blindly through the window. "It looks perfect, Charlie." She surreptitiously swiped her eyes and straightened.

"Runs perfect, too," he assured her. He pulled a sheaf of folded papers from the back pocket of his overalls. "Just gotta get your signature." He spread the papers out on the hood of the car and fumbled in his pocket again to produce a pen. "Insurance companies always want things good 'n' official."

She took the pen and signed her name.

"Gotcha a full tank of gas as well."

"If you tell me how much I owe you, I'll have to send you the money." Her insurance wasn't going to cover gas.

"Nah. Jayden took care of it a few days ago when he told me to make sure your tank was full."

Naturally. Even before he ever knew there was a book at all, he'd wanted to make sure she had no reason to hang around. Not even at the gas station in Paseo.

"Thank you," she said huskily. "I never expected you to deliver the car to me like this."

"No trouble. Wanted to give it a good test-drive anyway." He refolded the papers and pocketed them again. "Figure Jayden won't mind giving me a hitch back to my place." He handed her the key fob.

"No doubt." She gestured toward the barn. Her eyes were still burning, and if she didn't get away soon, she was going to make a fool of herself in front of the mechanic. "He's taking care of the horses if you want to go talk to him. I'm going to have to excuse myself." She plucked at her jeans. "Managed to get myself all wet—"

"Sure. Sure." He tipped his grease-stained ball cap and took a step toward the barn. "See y' later, now."

She couldn't even manage a garbled response. Her throat was too raw with unshed tears and she just went straight into the house.

Sugar hopped up from her bed in the kitchen and followed close on Ariana's heels as she walked to the borrowed bedroom where she changed out of her wet things and back into Deborah Fortune's denim dress. Then, moving fast and trying not to trip over the poor dog, Ariana stripped the bed and remade it with the fresh sheets kept in the hallway linen closet. She silently apologized for breaking her mother's rules when it came to comingling laundry and shoved the sheets and the towels she'd used into the same washing-machine load and started it running.

She fed Sugar a treat and gave her a kiss on her silky head.

Then she went back into the bedroom and grabbed up the rest of her belongings and went outside to the car.

She did not look at the barn.

Did not look at the storm-cellar door.

She just tossed everything in the passenger seat.

And she drove away.

"Jayden, what's this?"

Jayden looked up from the ledger he was supposed to be updating to see his mom standing in the kitchen doorway. She'd been back a week now. It meant an improvement in the coffee situation again, though it also meant having to endure her speculative looks when she thought he wasn't aware. "What's what?"

She set a small shipping box on top of his ledger book. She'd already opened it. "Came in the mail today."

Disinterested, he glanced inside the box, then felt his nerves pinch at the sight of the glossy magazine sitting inside.

"Ariana sent it. Obviously." His mother knew they'd had a "guest" while she'd been gone. He pushed the box aside and picked up his pencil again. But the row of numbers he was staring at were gibberish.

"Not the magazine." Deborah lifted out the latest copy of *Weird Life* and set it on the table. "This." She plucked out a bank check and waved it in front of his face.

He sat back, hiding his annoyance. It wasn't his mother's fault that he'd felt more like an angry bull than a human being since she'd been back.

Actually, he'd been that way since Ariana had driven away without so much as a "thanks for nothing."

He took the check and tossed it on top of the magazine. "She's just paying me back for expenses." She'd been keeping a list, she'd said. He remembered how she'd smiled at him that day she'd picked out those ugly tie-dyed shirts. That day, he'd thought her smile could light the county.

He stared harder at the gibberish.

"A thousand dollars in expenses?"

His mother's voice penetrated. "What?" He looked at the bank check. Ariana's scrawl was distinctively messy but the amount was plain. His fingers curled, crumpling the check like the garbage that it was.

"She included a note." Deborah pulled the next item out.

Despite the fact that his mother had left the contents inside the box for him to see, she'd clearly been through it at least once.

He pushed his chair back on two legs and folded his arms. "Why don't you just tell me what you want to say? You've obviously read it already and drawn your own conclusions." She'd been trying to pump him all week about Ariana. About his mood. About every damn little thing on the entire damn little planet.

His mother's lips thinned. "Watch your tone with me, Jayden Fortune. You're not too old for me to box your ears."

God help him. "And I'm too damn old for this bull—"

She raised her eyebrows.

"—hockey," he amended through his teeth. Which was ironic as all hell, because his mother could swear a trucker into blushing if she so chose. He thumped his chair back onto its four legs and he took the small, folded sheet of paper from her and flipped it open between his fingers.

"'For lodging and incidentals,'" he read. He shook his

head, actually seeing through a haze of red. "Incidentals!" He shoved away from the table, ripping the note into shreds. "Incidentals?" He tossed the paper up like confetti.

His mother had leaned casually back against the table. Her long hair was still more brown than gray and hung in a long thick braid over her shoulder, and she toyed with the ends of it, like it was the most fascinating thing on the planet. "Quite a reaction for a girl you say was *just* an unintended houseguest."

His jaw was clenched. He was not going to discuss Ariana with his mother. Because if he did, he'd end up telling her what his beef was.

And that was *not* going to happen. He was not going to question the decisions Deborah not-really-Fortune had made a long time ago.

No way.

No how.

Deborah let go of her braid and sighed. "Honey, *please*." She gestured. "If I weren't already suspicious about what went on between you and this Ariana Lamonte—" she picked up the magazine and flipped it open to a page with a small photo of Ariana in the corner "—I would be now, just because of your behavior. I wouldn't even have needed Nathan to tell me there was something personal going on between you. Clearly, she left an impression. You've been like a dog with a sore paw since I got back." She set the opened magazine down, and the small photo of Ariana—looking unfamiliarly sleek and sophisticated with a brilliant smile—stared up at him.

"She was only here for a couple weeks," he gritted out. "Nothing important happened."

"And I am the Queen of England." She straightened and brushed her hands together as if she were dusting away the entire matter. "Fine. I know you too well. If you don't want to talk, you won't talk. Who am I but just an old woman who wants to see her sons in happy relationships?"

He snorted. "Right."

She raised her eyebrows again. "You think that's so strange, Jayden? That I'd like nothing better than to see you and your brothers settled down with nice girls? Maybe give me a grandbaby or two I can bounce on my knee before I'm too old to bounce anything?"

"Don't act like you've got one foot in the grave. There's plenty of time for…for stuff like that." He'd never seen a more active woman than his mother. She had to be to keep up with Grayson's tours. And when she wasn't doing that, she was keeping up with the ranch. Considering neither Jayden nor Nathan had been around a lot once they'd joined the military, that was saying something. "And since when have you ever wanted babies around, anyway?"

The very subject of babies was like an annoying itch between his shoulder blades. Because he knew damn well that he and Ariana hadn't used any sort of protection when they'd made love. And what kind of man was he to not even think to ask if she'd been on the pill? Damn. He used to lecture the kids coming up in the army about safe sex, and he turns out to be no better?

"Why wouldn't I want a grandbaby around? It's a normal enough desire. Traditional—"

He snorted again. "Traditional? You, traditional?"

Her lips tightened. "And what is that supposed to mean?"

"Come on, Mom. You chose to have Nate and Grayson and me when you weren't even married. I know it's common enough now, but back then? You were totally on your own. If it weren't for Earl and Cynthia—" He broke off and shook his head. He couldn't let his thinking go down that road, because it kept leading to the very thing he refused to question.

What if Ariana had been right?

He braked hard on the untenable thought.

"Oh, Jayden." Deborah pulled out a chair and sat in it. Her brows pulled together as she smoothed her tanned, lined hand over Ariana's article about the Ybarras. "Of course I chose to have you. I loved all three of you before I even *knew* there were three of you. But I never wanted to do it on my own. Circumstances just turned out that way."

"It's none of my business what the circumstances were."

Her steady gaze softened. "When you were little, you used to badger me all the time for details about your father."

His jaw tightened even more. He'd badgered. Until he'd made her cry.

"And then one day you stopped." She tilted her head slightly. "I always figured that eventually you and your brothers would be old enough for the truth. But none of you ever brought it up again." And this time when she focused on the end of her braid, there was sadness in her face. "And so neither did I." Her slender shoulders rose and fell. Then she let go of the braid again and lifted her chin slightly.

It reminded him way too eerily of the way Ariana had tended to do the same thing.

Like she was facing something she couldn't change.

Deborah looked at the magazine again. "She's a beautiful girl," she murmured. "I don't know if she's a nice girl as well or not. But she certainly wrote a wonderful article about Hector and Paloma. And she has certainly left an impression on you, good or bad." She nudged the magazine closer to the edge of the table and stood. She touched his shoulder. "It doesn't matter if it was only two weeks, son. I fell in love with your father after just two days. We met in New Orleans during what ought to have been the worst times of our lives. We'd both left behind unhappy family situations but once we met—" She broke off and lifted her hands. "Everything bad that had gone before just didn't seem so important anymore. If Ariana matters to you, then do something about it." She smiled slightly and started to leave the kitchen.

Sugar got up from her bed, sending Jayden a reproachful look before following.

He pinched the bridge of his nose, trying to quell the ache there.

"Mom."

She hesitated in the doorway.

He lowered his hand, meeting her eyes and wondering what the hell he was doing. "Where did the name Fortune really come from?"

She didn't look away. "From your father. It was the only thing of his I could give you. That I could keep."

The knot that had been in his stomach for too long now tightened even more. "So, you were married to him."

She shook her head. "In my heart? Yes. But not legally. I could have been. But I wasn't."

"Why not?"

"I was afraid."

"Of what?"

"It doesn't even matter anymore. It all happened so fast. He proposed. When I hesitated, he believed it was because I didn't love him enough." She lifted her shoulder. "By the time I realized I was pregnant with you, it was too late. He was already gone. And even though I tried to find him—" She shook her head. "It was too late."

"Why?" The question came from somewhere deep and sore inside him.

"Because he died." She looked sad. "He was the only man I ever really loved and I realized it too late. Don't be like me, Jayden. Whatever your issue is with that young writer, don't let pride—or fear—keep you from having more than just this ranch in your life."

"His name was Jerome." It wasn't a question.

Something flickered in her gaze. And even though he hadn't asked for confirmation, she still nodded. "Yes. It was. Jerome Fortune."

## Chapter Eleven

He should have called her first.

Why hadn't he called her first?

Jayden stared at the apartment building across the street and tried to shut off the thoughts inside his head.

The only reason he had the address of Ariana's apartment at all was because of that damn check she'd sent him.

Incidentals.

Even though he knew now just how right she'd been about Jerome Fortune, that comment of hers still pissed him off.

He'd thought maybe he'd have cooled down a little about that fact during the long drive from Paseo to Austin.

But he hadn't.

And now he was looking at the apartment building where she lived and second-guessing himself even more.

Which also pissed him off.

He didn't like second-guessing himself. And it was her fault that he was doing so.

He looked at the passenger seat next to him. He'd have brought Sugar with him, but he hadn't wanted to subject her to a trip somewhere unfamiliar. Instead, the seat held only a yellowed, faded newspaper.

The newspaper that had been in the storm cellar all along, if Jayden had ever bothered to actually look at it. The newspaper that his mother had collected herself, after he and his brothers had been born. The newspaper confirming, once and for all, that Jerome Fortune—heir apparent to some financial empire in New York who'd disappeared years earlier as a young man after a questionable suicide—had been declared officially dead.

He was a lot less interested in the story of Jerome Fortune or Gerald Robinson or whatever the hell the man wanted to call himself. Despite finally knowing the truth, Jayden still thought of him as nothing more than a sperm donor. Everything Jayden was—everything his brothers were—they owed to one person.

Their mother.

He blew out a breath and studied the high-rise apartment building. Landscape lights were starting to come on in the lush, well-maintained grounds that surrounded it.

*You could've just called her.*

Except he'd never particularly thought of himself as a coward. If anything, he tended to rise to challenges too quickly, rush to judgment too quickly.

He gritted his teeth and let out an impatient sound. Then he pushed open the door and got out. He waited for traffic to clear and jogged across the street. Even though it was closer to evening than afternoon, it was still hotter 'n hell, and he was sweating when he strode through the sleek, modern entrance to the building.

Which only reminded him of their last afternoon together out by the pond, at the windmill.

Before she'd run off.

What kind of woman ran off during a fight? Particularly after just claiming that she supposedly loved you?

He jabbed the elevator button and rode up to the sixth floor. When he found apartment number 629, he jabbed the doorbell even harder than he'd hit the elevator button.

First thing he was going to do was tell her that the next time they argued about something, she needed to damn well stick around and keep up her side of the argument.

None of this cut-and-run crap.

Only she didn't answer the door.

Not when he jabbed the doorbell the first time. Nor the second. Nor when he kept his finger pressed on it for an entire minute the third time.

He knew it was working. He could hear the strident buzz through the door.

So could the dog living in the apartment next door. The thing had started barking at the second buzz and was still barking when Jayden finally turned and stomped back to the elevator.

He should have called her first.

He rode the elevator back down to the ground floor again and returned to his truck. It was Friday. Three weeks ago, he'd been convincing Ariana to come in out of the storm with him.

How could so much have happened in such a short time?

His mind was buzzing in so many directions he wanted to kick something. But of course he couldn't. He was supposed to be a reasonable man. Maybe not the most patient, but still reasonable.

The street was congested with rush-hour traffic and he stood at the crosswalk. She'd told him when they first met that she loved the city. Considering the location of her apartment in what he was assuming was the downtown area, she obviously got plenty of *city*.

Frankly, after two years of peace and quiet back in Paseo following his stint with army life, the busyness was enough to make him break out in a rash.

He added that to his saddlebag of complaints.

How could any sane woman ever prefer this to Paseo?

He looked up at the sky. He'd bet once it was dark, there'd still be too much city light to see the stars.

"Jayden?"

He turned around and there she was.

Walking toward him wearing one of the shortest skirts he'd ever seen with one of the ugliest shirts he'd ever seen.

He dragged his attention up from those beautiful long legs, skimmed over the *Paseo Is Paradise* T-shirt and met her eyes as she stopped a couple of yards away.

She'd pulled her hair back in a sleek ponytail. Her face was made up and her dark eyes looked even darker and more mysterious.

And wary. Definitely wary.

Once he got over the physical shock of seeing her, he realized everything about her—from the way she clutched her soft, oversized purse to the way she seemed poised on the balls of her flat-heeled sandals—looked like she was ready to run.

"What are you doing here?" she asked him.

"Looking for you." Obvious, yeah. "What other reason would bring me to Austin? *Incidentals*, Ariana? That's how you categorized what went on between us?"

Her lashes—they were twice as long as he'd remembered—swept down. But not before he'd seen a spark of temper.

At least that was something familiar.

As was the tie-dyed T-shirt. Strangely enough, it looked

pretty good with the short black skirt that showed off her legs.

And it made him hope that maybe he hadn't entirely blown things with her.

"I guess I don't have to ask if you received the package I mailed." She hitched the strap of her purse higher on her shoulder.

"It came today."

That surprised her. Her gaze flicked up to his, then away. "I see."

She couldn't possibly. "Can we go up to your apartment and talk?"

Her chin lifted slightly. "I don't think so."

His jaw tightened. "So we're going to do this right here on the sidewalk with people walking by us every ten seconds?" He smiled tightly at the bicyclist who wove around them.

"Do what, Jayden?"

"Are you going to cut and run every time we have a disagreement?"

Her lips rounded. "I— What? Cut and run?" She glared. "Should I have stayed and let you accuse me of being a...a slut for the third time?"

"I didn't accuse you of being a slut."

"What would you call it, then? As if I'd sleep with—"

"I'm sorry."

Her lips slowly closed.

"If you wanted to turn the knife, the note with the check did the job. Four words is all it took. 'For lodging and incidentals.'"

"I told you I was better on paper," she muttered.

She was good on paper. Really good with words. She knew just how to use them to make her point. "The article about the Ybarras was amazing. Before I left Paseo, I stopped by their place to drop off the magazine for them."

She opened her mouth again. "I mailed—"

"I know. They already had the copies you mailed to them. Paloma said to tell you *gracias*. She was already planning to frame one copy and figuring out where to hang it in the new house."

The corners of her lips curved faintly. "How is their house coming?"

"Framing is already done."

"Even in Paseo, things can get done quickly." She side-stepped so another bicyclist could pass and looked toward her building. "I'm glad for them."

The sun behind him shone over her profile.

"You were right," he said abruptly.

Her lashes lowered again. He could see the slow breath she took. Then she looked at him. There was no need to elaborate. She knew that he was talking about Jerome Fortune. "I'm sorry."

"It means you've got at least *one* meaty chapter for your book."

She chewed off some of the pink lip gloss on her soft lips. "No."

"You can't write a book about the man's secrets and not include my mother."

"I'm not writing a book about Jerome Fortune. Not any-more." She shifted. Her hands were wrapped so tightly around her purse strap, her knuckles were white. "I returned the advance yesterday. I, uh, also resigned from the magazine."

If she'd announced she had married the Pope, he couldn't have been more confused. "Why?"

"Because I can't write any more stories about the Fortunes. I'm too involved—" She chewed off a little more pink shine. "I'm not objective enough. I'm too biased now. So you'd better cash the check fast if you don't want it to bounce."

He ignored that. "You love writing."

"Yeah, well." She shrugged one shoulder. "Maybe I'll try fiction this time." She gestured toward the apartment building. "I need to turn in my notice on my place before the manager's office closes or I'm going to be on the hook for another month of rent that I can't really afford anymore. So—"

"Did you mean what you said?"

"Uh. Yeah. As it is, I'm probably going to have to sleep in my car if I don't tuck my tail and go home to Mommy and Daddy. Mom changed my childhood bedroom into a gift-wrapping room—" she air-quoted it "—but she'll be okay. She'll content herself by telling me 'I told you so' about the way I handle money."

He shook his head, as if to clear away her answer. "No, I was asking if you meant what you said about *me*." From the look in her eyes, she knew good and well what he'd meant.

"Jayden—"

"Do you love me or not?"

Her lips firmed. "God knows why, considering you're such a patient soul, but yes."

It all oozed out. The anger he'd harbored since she'd bolted from the ranch.

The worry that he'd damaged things beyond repair.

"I love you, too."

She huffed. "No, you don't."

He took a step toward her. The fact that she didn't take one away from him he took as a good sign. "I do. You make great coffee."

Her lips compressed.

"What you do for an ugly tie-dyed shirt is amazing."

She rolled her eyes, flushed a little and crossed her arms.

"The things that you make me feel are nothing short of a miracle."

Her eyes flickered. She looked away.

"I don't know what else to do here, Ariana." He took another step closer. "This isn't exactly familiar territory."

"You haven't been to Austin before?"

"I haven't been in love like this before."

Her jaw shifted. "Tess—"

"Was a pale comparison. If I had a ring, I'd pull it out right now and go on bended knee." He hadn't even considered where they'd go if he could get her to forgive him. But the second his words were out, he knew they were right.

Her eyes widened and focused on him. "So what's stopping you?"

"I drove straight here from Paseo. Do not pass go. Do not stop at jewelry stores."

She lifted her chin. "You still have a knee, don't you?"

"Okay. Fine. You want me to grovel a bit. I can live with that." He grabbed her arm before she could avoid him and pulled her off the sidewalk. At least the main part of it where bicyclists and pedestrians were constantly passing them. Then he dropped to one knee.

"Jayden, I wasn't serious—"

"But I am." He closed his hands over hers. "Ariana, I don't know what to offer you that you can't already do for yourself. You're nearly ten years younger than me. When I'm sixty, you'll—"

"—still be in love with you," she said huskily. She pulled on his hands. "Get up, former Sergeant Fortune. I can't handle you being all sweet and tender like this. It makes me nervous."

"I'm trying to propose here, sweetheart. Don't ruin the moment."

"Yeah, honey," said a heavyset woman with gray hair who passed them on her way into the building. "Don't ruin his moment."

Ariana flushed. She pulled harder on his hands, but he still resisted and she huffed. "Fine. But you don't have to propose just because you think—" She broke off.

"Because I think what?"

"I don't know! I don't know what you think. I don't know what *to* think. You come here after everything and—" She shook her head. "Dammit!"

He stood up and stepped closer until his chest touched the words on her T-shirt. "Do you want me to get you some paper so you can write it down?"

Her eyes flashed at him. But the glint of tears in them nearly undid him.

He slid his hands along her jaw and tipped her face up to his. "I love you," he murmured. "That's what I think. That's what I feel. I'm going to keep loving you no matter what you say here on this sidewalk. I'm gonna love you when I'm sixty and you're a hottie fifty-year-old grandma."

"Grandma!" The word escaped on a gurgle of choked laughter and tears. "I'm twenty-seven. If I'm going to be a grandma at fifty, you're planning on some fast work. Not to mention putting some big expectations on that grandchild's parent."

"That grandchild's parent would be *our* child."

"I know that."

"Okay, so maybe you'll be a hottie grandma at sixty. And I'll be a doddering old rancher at seventy."

"You'll never be doddering." She swiped her cheek, then made a face when her fingers came away black. "And you're making my mascara run."

"Sweetheart, I've seen you in pond scum. You're always beautiful to me."

She laughed and sniffed. "What am I going to do with you?"

"Take me upstairs? It might've escaped your notice, but it's hot as hell out here."

She took his hand and led the way into the apartment building.

It hadn't escaped his attention that she hadn't yet said yes.

But he'd take what he could get.

For now.

The elevator they rode up in was crowded. Too crowded to do anything other than stand close behind her as they rode up to the sixth floor.

When they walked down the hallway to her door, he could still hear that same dog yapping. "He ever quiet down?"

"Rufio?" She tapped her keys on the neighbor's door as they passed it and the dog yelped and went silent. "He just wants to know someone's out here." She unlocked her own door and gave him a diffident look before going inside. "Don't expect much," she warned.

He hadn't expected anything. All he'd thought about was her.

But the apartment was nearly bare. She had a patterned sofa that looked straight out of the eighties and a folding card table that was piled high with books and papers. A single floor lamp stood next to the table.

"Minimalist decorating style, I see."

She dropped her purse on the granite kitchen bar as she crossed the open room to the wall of windows on the other side. "Furniture detracts from the view," she said blithely.

The view of her in front of the Austin skyline was pretty perfect.

She spread her arms. "So this is the living area and the kitchen."

"Good. A tour. I was hoping."

She toed off her sandals and walked through the open doorway to the right. He followed. "Here we have the master suite. Another balcony, of course, because that's really what the ridiculous rent is for. The view—"

He pulled her to him and kissed her.

Her hands closed over his shoulders. Slid beneath the collar of his shirt. She pulled back an inch. "Don't you want to see the view?"

He rubbed his thumb along her cheek. "I'm looking at the best view there is right now."

Her eyes went dewy. "Jayden."

"Ariana," he returned softly.

She smiled a little and stepped back. Just enough to pull her *Paseo Is Paradise* shirt off. Then she took his hand and pulled him over to the bed.

And showed him real paradise.

When Ariana woke several hours later, Austin's city lights were shining through the bedroom windows.

And the mattress beside her was empty.

She had a moment's misgiving, before she realized that the light from the living room had been turned on. Which meant that Jayden hadn't left her.

She still couldn't believe he'd come to Austin.

Not even now, when her entire body still seemed to hum from their lovemaking.

She climbed out of bed, nearly tripping when her foot got caught in his shirt. She picked it up and pulled it over her head and went out to the living room.

He was sitting at her card table, reading an old issue of *Weird Life Magazine*.

Despite all the interviews she'd done with various members of Gerald Robinson's family, she couldn't imagine how Jayden felt now, knowing the truth. "Keaton Fortune Whitfield," she said. "British. Thirty-three. The newest great thing in architecture to hit Austin." She stopped behind Jayden and put her hands on his shoulders. They were tense. "He's quite a charmer. Recently engaged, I hear, to a waitress named Francesca."

"How'd he like finding out? You know. About—"

"Gerald?" She kneaded his shoulders and wondered if she'd ever get tired of the feel of his flesh beneath her hands. Probably not. "It threw him for a loop. You've all got that in common, Jayden."

He flipped the magazine closed and sighed.

She pressed her lips to the top of his head. "If you want to meet any of them, I'm sure I could arrange it."

"And say what? 'Hey, guys and gals. Meet your big brother Jayden'?" He looked up at her. His eyes were dark, pained. "These people—" He gestured at the stack of magazines. "They're all doing so much with their lives. And who is this Kate lady?" He picked up another issue of the magazine. "She looks a little older than Gerald's usual conquest."

"She's not one of his conquests." Ariana opened the magazine to the full spread on the petite business magnate. "Kate Fortune. She founded Fortune Cosmetics. Big, big company. Lots of money. Recently moved her headquarters from Minnesota to Austin and appointed Graham—one of Gerald's sons with his wife—as the new CEO. Big believer in all things family, even the ones she didn't know existed until recently." She looked at Jayden. "And who says you haven't done a lot with your life?"

"An army grunt?"

"Sergeant First Class Fortune," she corrected him. "I did some research. The rank isn't exactly a grunt. And your ranch isn't exactly a two-cow holding pen." She slid around him and sat on his lap, looping her arms over his shoulders. "Keaton was raised by a single mom. And Chloe Fortune Elliott was, too. You and your brothers have more in common with them than you think. You all have similar experiences."

"Yeah. Moms who've been dumped by Jerome Fortune."

"Actually, they all knew him as Gerald by then. Your mother is the only one who seemed to know the real Jerome." She chewed the inside of her lip. "I think he really loved her." She expected him to dismiss the notion. But he didn't. "What did your mother say about their relationship?"

"It was brief. Intense. He proposed but she didn't immediately accept, so he booked." He grimaced. "Then she tried to find him to tell him she was pregnant with us, but he was dead." His long fingers spread over her back. "I don't want to talk about him anymore."

She brushed her lips over his and felt such a thrill inside that she hoped it never ended. "Just one more thing."

He gave a noisy sigh.

"Okay, maybe two. But then no more talk of Gerald or Jerome. I promise."

He gave her a wry look. "All right. But make it snappy." His fingers drifted beneath the shirt. "I've got a powerful distraction here."

She wriggled, not even remotely able to keep from smiling. "This is serious." She tugged at his hand. "I can't think when you do that."

"Good." He nipped at her shoulder and returned his hand right where he wanted it. "Oh, yeah. Definitely makes two of us."

"Gerald is a very, *very* wealthy man."

He swore succinctly. "That's what I think about his money. Seems to me misery follows in his wake. Which—" he picked up the article about Keaton then tossed it down again "—evidently circles the globe. The guy has gotten around. No question."

"Okay. But here's the second thing." She caught her breath when his hand reached her breast. "I'm not so sure Gerald is totally the bad guy."

He snorted. "Right."

"Seriously." She turned to look at her work spread across the table. But of course the real guts of her research had been lost in the tornado. "Darn it, I wish I had—" She shook her head. "It doesn't matter. What matters is that I think Charlotte—she's Gerald's wife—knows more about things than she lets on. Well, maybe not about everyone. But she certainly knew about Paseo. Which tells me that she knew about your mom at least. Maybe even about you and your brothers."

"And you say you're not going to write any more articles? Not a book?"

"I'm not." She looked him in the eye. "I'm not, Jayden. I can't. Not anymore. I haven't written a single decent word since I left Paseo."

"I'm not so sure about that," he muttered. "But go on."

"You've heard your mother's side of things now. If you ever want to know the rest, you're going to have to get that from Gerald." Her thoughts were running a mile a minute through her head. "Or Charlotte, but trust me. *That* is not likely to happen. The only time I've ever seen her lose a speck of composure was when she let slip the name Paseo. You'd have better luck with Gerald. From all accounts, he's a hard-ass, too."

He slid his hand over her mouth. But his eyes weren't

angry. Just vaguely amused. And maybe, maybe a little accepting. "Enough," he said. He shoved the card table away with his foot and resettled her meaningfully on his lap. "Aside from the whole windmill thing," he murmured as he started to unbutton the shirt, "I've got a real appreciation for the way you wear my shirts."

So did she. Her skin felt like a million butterflies were dancing on her. "Take me to bed?"

"Every night from here on out, sweetheart. Every single night."

She tightened her arms around his neck and had a hard time not just purring when he lifted her right off the chair. She reached out and turned off the light.

And he carried her to bed.


"You're still sure about this?" Ariana pocketed her sunglasses as they stepped up to the massive front door of the Robinson mansion two days later. "Maybe meeting all of them this soon is too much."

"You're the one who suggested it."

"I know, but—"

He hit the door a few times with the heavy knocker, ending the discussion. "Sooner we do this, the sooner we can get back to Paseo. I do have a ranch to run, remember?"

She nodded. Even though she'd been at the Robinson estate several times, she still felt a knot of nervousness inside her stomach. Thank God she'd returned her book advance. She couldn't even imagine being able to write the biography anymore. She turned to him suddenly. "Just because I'm not going to tell Jerome's story doesn't mean someone else won't try."

His brows pulled together. "What?"

"The publisher," she muttered. "They'll find another

person to write it. I'm completely replaceable on that score."

The door opened and Ben Fortune Robinson stood there, looking as composed and polished as he always did. He was a handsome man, no doubt about it. Gerald made good-looking children.

She tucked her hand through Jayden's arm and was glad it wasn't as tense as she'd feared. "Hi, Ben. I appreciate you doing this."

"Ariana." The other man tilted his dark head. His intense gaze was focused on Jayden, though, as he stuck out his hand. "Ben Robinson."

"Not Fortune?" Jayden's words were a little terse, but he shook Ben's hand politely enough.

"Fortune Robinson. Sometimes." Ben's lips twisted in an eerily similar manner to Jayden's. "Depends on how pissed off with the old man I'm feeling," he admitted honestly. He backed away. "Come in. Everyone's waiting in the library. Don't worry, though. My mother and our…father are both gone for the day. We won't be interrupted." He pushed the heavy door closed after they entered and led the way through the lavishly elegant house.

"How's your wife, Ben?" Ariana asked him.

The man's expression lightened measurably. "Ella's beautiful."

"And the baby? Lacey, right?"

He nodded. "Almost six months old and just as beautiful as her mama." They'd reached a closed door and he pushed it open. "Here we are."

Even though she would have preferred to hang back, the hand Jayden held against the small of her back prevented it and she walked into the library ahead of him. When she'd called Ben to ask for the meeting, she'd told him everything she'd learned. Only because Jayden had wanted it that way. And as she studied the faces of Ben's seven brothers and sisters, she could tell that he'd also prepped them as well.

"Good Lord." Sophie, the youngest of Ben's siblings, was the first one to speak. "He looks like you, Kieran."

"No. The eyes are different." Zoe, the second youngest, stood up and came over to the doorway. "I think he looks more like Graham." She extended her slender hand toward Jayden. "I'm Zoe."

Even though he was looking increasingly uncomfortable, Jayden shook her hand. "Nice to meet you."

Thankfully, Ben took charge again as he drew them farther into the library. "Let me introduce you to everyone."

Ariana hovered in the rear of the somewhat crowded room where Olivia, the third youngest of the eight siblings, was leaning against one of the tall bookcases that surrounded the room. "He does look familiar," she murmured, more to herself, it seemed, than Ariana. "But not like Graham." Her brow knit together while across the room, Ben was inviting Jayden to sit at one of the chairs near the couch.

He sent Ariana a look and she gave him an encouraging nod. "They know about your mother, Jayden. Just ask whatever you want."

"Right," Ben said calmly. He'd been the first one to decide on tracking down however many half brothers and half sisters they had. It had been a unilateral decision that hadn't always been welcomed among the lot.

"I don't know what to ask," Jayden admitted, a stiff, crooked smile on his lips.

"Well, tell us about yourself, then," Ben amended easily. "Ariana said you were in the army for quite a while?"

"Yeah." Jayden's gaze traveled around the room. He took in the collection of priceless books. The original artwork. The statues. "My, uh, my brother Nate—Nathan— was a navy SEAL. Grayson rides rodeo."

"Three boys. That was a lot for your mother to handle on her own." Rachel—the eldest of the girls—gave him a sympathetic smile. Ariana was glad that she'd made the trip to Austin from Horseback Hollow, where she lived with her husband, Matteo. Of all the children Gerald had had with Charlotte, Rachel was one of Ariana's favorites. She was just so normal.

"At once, yeah." Jayden was nodding. He glanced at Ben and Wes. "You guys are twins. You know what it's like. Only there're three of us."

"Triplets." Olivia suddenly pushed away from the wall and crossed the room to grab the rolling ladder. She was muttering to herself as she climbed up to one of the top shelves and quickly started pawing through the books there.

"Olivia." Zoe was looking up at her sister. "What on earth—"

"It's here," she said. "It's got to still be here." She reached out and shoved the ladder over another foot without even bothering to climb off it first. "Ah." She snatched an album off the shelf. "I *knew* it." She tossed the book down to Zoe and quickly came down the tall ladder.

"Knew what?"

"Look." Olivia took the book—Ariana realized it was a small photo album—and flipped it open. She stabbed at the very first picture with a shaking finger as she practically shoved it in Jayden's face. "Is that you? You and your brothers?"

His brows pulled together. Ariana could see his temper building and she quickly went over, putting her hand on his shoulder as she looked at the old photograph. It was taken from a distance but the boys were clearly Jayden and his brothers.

"How'd you get this?" A muscle was working in his jaw, but his tone was at least shy of accusation.

Olivia sank down on the couch between Rachel and Kieran as if her legs wouldn't hold her up anymore. Her eyes were glazed with tears. "I found the book in Mother's study. I was—" She pressed her lips together for a moment, clearly struggling for composure. "I don't know. Maybe six years old? Mother was furious. She said the pictures were foster kids she and Dad were paying to support. She snatched it away and put it up there." She pointed to the shelf.

Even Ben looked shocked. "What? Why haven't you mentioned this before?"

"I didn't even remember it until now," Olivia said. She dropped her hand and stared at Jayden.

Kieran sat forward. "Mother *knew*?" He grabbed the photo album and flipped another page. To another photo. And another. "They're all here," he muttered, flipping faster. "Keaton. Chloe. And—" He squinted at their mother's hand-writing beneath a grainy photo. "Who the hell is Amersen?"

"The au pair's son. He lives in France. Amersen Beaudin," Graham provided, looking weary. "Remember Suzette?"

Wes took the album from his brother and paged through it. "That guy, Nash Tremont, that you have a lead on." He shook his head when he turned a few more pages. "These ones don't even have names. What the hell was she doing keeping this all a secret?"

The question seemed to spur comments from every single one of his siblings.

Jayden swore under his breath and grabbed Ariana's hand. "Let's go."

Ben tried to stop him. "Jayden. You don't have to go."

"I do." He gestured. "I'm sorry. I'll get used to all of you. In time. But whatever deal you've got going right now is about your mother. Not mine." He suddenly clasped Ben's shoulder. "I don't belong here right now. You understand?"

Ben nodded after a moment. "Yeah. Maybe I do."

Jayden nodded. He tightened his grip on Ariana's hand and he pulled her out of the room.

He didn't stop until they'd left the house entirely.

Only when they were out in the fresh air did he seem to draw in a deep, cleansing breath. "Wacko."

Ariana opened her mouth to protest.

"Not *them*. Charlotte."

"Oh. Well, yes. Maybe so." The woman clearly had more secrets than even Ariana had imagined.

He wrapped his arms around her and pulled her close. "What a freaking crazy family. No wonder you won't say you'll marry me."

"I never said I wouldn't marry you."

"You haven't said you will."

She pressed her mouth against the distinct cleft in his chin. Her heart was pounding so hard she could hear it inside her head. "If we end up having a son one day, you suppose he'll inherit your chin?"

His head reared back. His eyes searched hers. "I don't know. I sure like the idea of finding out."

Her eyes filled. "So do I."

"You're going to marry me, then?"

"I'm a little traditional about that sort of thing," she whispered.

"Dammit, Ariana. Is that a yes or no? Do I have to get a piece of paper for you to write it down on or what?"

She smiled. "Yes."

He looked positively frazzled. "Yes, *what*?"

She stretched up and brushed her lips over his. "Yes, I'll marry you. If you think that family is crazy, though, wait until you meet mine. My mother'll be sizing you up for a tuxedo before we get through the front door. And don't be alarmed when she calls you a handsome cuss. That's just a thing of hers. And Dad will want to show you his old Mustang. So if you can't describe what's under the hood of a car, we'd better get a book so you can brush up on it first."

He gave a bark of laughter. "I can handle a car. A tux, though? I'm not so sure about that." He closed his arm around her shoulders and directed her toward his pickup truck parked in the long, curving driveway.

"I don't care what you wear when we get married," she assured him. "Except for one thing."

He lifted an eyebrow. "What's that?"

"A ring," she said adamantly. "No way am I not going to advertise to the entire world that *you* are off the market."

"Sounding a little possessive there, sweetheart."

She raised her own eyebrow. "Have a problem with that?"

His smile was slow. "No, ma'am," he assured her. "No problem at all."

"Good. Now let's go home."

"Yeah. You never got around to turning in your notice at the apartment."

She twined her fingers with his, looking up into the face that she knew with every fiber of her being she wanted to look into for at least another sixty years. "I meant Paseo. Let's go home to Paseo."

And they did.

# *Epilogue*

The party was in full swing when Gerald slipped in through a rear door.

He shouldn't be there.

But knowing what he shouldn't do and actually *not* doing what he shouldn't do were two very different things.

Story of his life.

"Welcome to the grand opening of Austin Commons!" A pretty young woman dressed in red stuck a brochure in his hand before he had a chance to wave her off. "Do you know Mr. Whitfield? He's the architect of all this." She waved her graceful arm, meant to encompass the state-of-the-art office complex around them.

A part of Gerald's mind stayed focused on the attractive female. He'd spent a lot of years burying himself in the distraction of women. Stopping cold now, just because his whole family seemed to think they knew everything about him, wasn't all that easily accomplished. The other part of his mind was impressed with the building.

He honestly wished he could say he'd had a hand in developing Keaton's skill. Gerald had a healthy ego but not even he could claim credit on that score.

He took the brochure from the woman and strode through the building. Robinson Tech needed some additional space. He wondered if Keaton would be interested—

"Jerome?"

He stopped in his tracks, looking at Kate Fortune. She was the self-proclaimed matriarch of all things Fortune. All things that Gerald Robinson had pushed away a lifetime ago. "I told you before, Kate. I prefer Gerald."

The silver-haired woman dipped her head. She was ninety-one but looked younger than his own wife. "I know you did." She tucked her hand through his arm as if they were old, dear friends.

Maybe she thought apologizing last year on behalf of the world of Fortunes made them friends. Who the hell knew? Not Gerald, that was for sure.

He realized she was drawing him into the spacious atrium where at least a hundred people were gathered. He recognized a good portion of them. Many worked for Robinson Tech. Just as many were related to him.

He swallowed an oath when Zoe spotted him. So much for keeping a low profile. His daughter looked shocked at first, then delighted as she separated herself from her husband, Joaquin Mendoza, and headed his way. Gerald didn't mind Joaquin too much. He was smart and he doted on Zoe. She'd always been his favorite, so he was inclined to like the man for that reason alone.

"Daddy." She reached up and kissed his cheek. "I didn't know you were coming." Her lashes hid her expression. "Is Mother with you?"

He almost laughed. He and Charlotte presented a united front only when they had to. And if she knew he was at one of his "other" son's events? That assuredly didn't qualify. "She's got one of her charity things," he answered vaguely. "Who are all the men over there with Joaquin and Alejandro?" Alejandro Mendoza had been more of an ac-quired taste. Gerald still was getting used to the fact that his daughter Olivia—sensible and pragmatic like him—was engaged to marry the entrepreneur. At least Alejandro hadn't stolen Olivia away to Miami, though. He wasn't sure how he would have stopped it, but he would have tried.

"Alejandro's cousins," Zoe was telling him. "They're the ones going into business with him. I told you about them last week at dinner. Mark, Rodrigo, Chaz, Carlo and Stefan. Don't tell me you weren't listening. They're from Miami, remember? They're going to be renting space in this very complex."

"Of course I remember." He squeezed her shoulder. He didn't. But she didn't need to know that.

A flash of long dark hair caught his eye.

Deborah had had hair like that. Even after all these years, he could remember the feel of it in his hands. The scent of it. Of her.

But the girl with the hair was young. As young as his own daughters. She was that reporter, he realized. The one who'd written all the articles that had so annoyed Char-lotte.

He'd gotten a kick out of them.

Which, naturally, had annoyed his wife even more.

But then, what was life without the small pleasures?

He looked down at Zoe. "Are you having fun tonight?"

"Of course." She smiled. Zoe always found something to smile about. It was one of the reasons why it was so easy to love her. She was the antithesis of her mother.

Zoe's hand on his arm tightened. "Be nice," she warned.

"What?" He followed her gaze.

The reporter and a tall, steely-eyed cowboy were headed his way.

Gerald actually felt a knot in his throat. "That's him?"

"Jayden," Zoe whispered. "Yes."

The couple stopped shy of them a few feet. Zoe stepped into the void, giving Ariana a hug and reaching up to kiss Jayden's cheek. Her brother's cheek.

"Congratulations," she was saying. "I just received your wedding announcement in the mail this afternoon." She laughed musically. "You sure didn't let any grass grow under your feet." She held out her hand to Gerald. "Daddy, I know you know her name, but I'm not sure you ever met Ariana. Ariana Lamonte— Oh, it's Fortune now, isn't it? This is my father, Gerald Robinson."

Jayden's arm slid around Ariana's shoulders. "Yes, it's Fortune," he said evenly. His eyes stayed on Gerald's face.

"It was a small wedding," Ariana said.

"From what I understand, everything in Paseo is on the small side." Zoe's smile showed in her voice. "Your parents were there?"

Ariana nodded. "Of course. And Jayden's brothers and his mother."

Gerald tuned in more closely. For more than half his life, he'd been trying to forget Deborah. And he'd failed in every respect.

"I've read your articles," he said abruptly.

Ariana looked discomfited. "As it happens, I've left the magazine."

"That's a shame. Your pieces were one of the few that weren't drivel."

She smiled faintly, as if she didn't quite believe him. "Thank you."

He couldn't stop looking at Jayden.

"You have your mother's eyes."

And those eyes narrowed as if he didn't exactly appreciate the observation.

Though why would he, when it came from Gerald?

He looked at Zoe. "Sweetheart, would you and Ariana excuse us for a minute?"

His daughter immediately nodded. "Of course."

But Jayden shook his head. His arm didn't budge from Ariana's shoulders. "There's nothing for you to say that my wife can't hear."

Gerald hesitated. Not really because he was waiting for Zoe to move out of earshot, but because it took him that long to get the words past the tightness in his chest.

Maybe he was having a heart attack. It wasn't a novel idea. He'd just always figured when he went, it'd be in the bed of yet another woman who wasn't his wife.

Because all of those women, including his wife, had never filled the spot left by Deborah.

"I never knew about you and your brothers, Jayden. If I had—" He broke off. If he had known, then what? He hadn't fought hard enough for Deborah when they'd had their chance. "If I had, maybe things would've been different. For a lot of us."

From the corner of his eye, he saw Zoe's bright red dress—a flash of vibrancy among the traditional sea of little black dresses—as she returned to Joaquin's side. If things had been *too* different, he wouldn't have ever had Zoe. Or Ben and Wes. Not Sophie or Olivia. Kieran. Rachel. Graham. Because if things had been too different, he never would have married Charlotte. He was a miserable husband. And he'd never win awards for father of the year. But he did love his children.

Making them believe it had never been his strong suit, though.

Jayden was still watching him with that unsettling dark gaze.

"How is your mother?" He finally let the question loose. "Is she well?" *Did she ever marry someone else? Did she forget me as easily as I wanted to be able to forget her?*

"She's well." Jayden's voice was clipped. "A little surprised that you're not dead and buried somewhere."

The message came through loud and clear. One of his three eldest sons wished he was dead and buried. Chances were the other two felt the same.

Some things went beyond forgiveness. Gerald read that sentiment in Jayden's eyes.

"Don't tell her," Gerald told him, "but I've thought of her often." Every day.

Jayden's lips twisted. "I don't think so. Keeping secrets might be a biological trait you inherited from your father, but it's not a trait I intend to adopt."

"*My* father." Gerald grimaced. No matter what he did, how well or how fast he did it, nothing had ever been good enough for his old man. Which didn't alleviate the guilt he still felt about the way his father had died. "My father never kept any secrets from anyone. Particularly the fact that he hated the ground I walked on."

Jayden eyed the man. His father. It was still hard to accept. And right then, he wasn't sure that he didn't hate the ground Gerald walked on, too.

Ariana tugged on Jayden's fingertips. "It's late. Maybe we should be going."

Jayden curled his hand over hers, feeling something inside him calm again. "Soon, sweetheart." Gerald was his father by blood but not by anything else. But if he'd felt a smidgen for his mother what Jayden felt for Ariana, he'd had to have lived ever since knowing what he'd lost.

If for no other reason than that, he could almost feel a little sympathy for the man in front of him.

"I don't think this is the time," she murmured not entirely under her breath.

"Why not?" Jayden angled his head and focused on Gerald once more. "I didn't expect you to be here. But you are. And who knows when we'll see each other again." If Ariana reconsidered the book her publisher was still trying to get her to take on again, maybe. But in the past few weeks since they'd stood next to the windmill and said their vows, she'd been noodling with ideas for a thriller.

About an ax murderer.

He figured the ax murderer might win out. Mostly because his wife was incredibly imaginative and inventive.

And he planned to enjoy that facet of Ariana in every way possible for as long as the good Lord saw fit to keep him on earth with her.

And just that easily, he decided it didn't matter what he knew or didn't know about Gerald. Or Jerome. Or whatever name the man wanted to go by. It didn't matter that Jerome's father had been just as much a cheat as Jerome. With similar results. Jayden knew he wasn't going to be an apple off that tree, because he had Ariana by his side.

"You know what?" He looked into the older man's face. "It doesn't matter. I don't care if you know as little about your father's life as I knew about mine. I've got everything I want in this life standing by my side." He squeezed Ariana's shoulder and looked down at her face. "Are you ready to leave, Mrs. Fortune?"

She beamed at him and nodded.

And without another glance at anyone, they walked away, hand in hand.

\* \* \* \* \*

*Celebrate the holidays with your favorite family—don't miss the first FORTUNES OF TEXAS holiday special!*

*French entrepreneur Amersen Beaudin comes to Austin to investigate a business opportunity, kisses a cowgirl under the mistletoe—and just might be hooked on the holidays, American-style! But will his hidden connection to the famed Fortune family interfere with his chance at happiness?*

*Find out in*

*A FORTUNES OF TEXAS CHRISTMAS*
*by*
*Helen Lacey*

*Available December 2017, wherever
Mills & Boon books and ebooks are sold.*

*And catch up with*

*THE FORTUNES OF TEXAS:
THE SECRET FORTUNES*

# MILLS & BOON®

## *Cherish*™

**EXPERIENCE THE ULTIMATE RUSH OF FALLING IN LOVE**

# MILLS & BOON®

## EXCLUSIVE EXTRACT

When Charlotte Aldridge tells CEO Lucian Duval
she's pregnant, the handsome billionaire is adamant
his child will have the one thing he never did – the
love of two committed parents…

*Read on for a sneak preview of*
**THEIR BABY SURPRISE**

'I want to be a part of this baby's life on a daily basis.'

The knot of anxiety inside her twisted. 'That's not
possible, you know that, I'm moving away from London.'

'Don't move away.'

Charlotte gestured around her apartment. 'I need more
space. I need to be near my parents. To have family
close by.'

'I agree, that's why I believe you should move in
with me…and for that matter, why we should marry.'

She sank down onto the window seat below the open
window. 'Marry!'

'Yes.'

A known serial dater was proposing marriage. This
was crazy. Lucian had the reputation for being impulsive
and a maverick within the industry but his decisions
were always backed up with sound logic. And that quick-
fire decision making, some would even say recklessness,
often gave him the edge over his more ponderous rivals.
But he had called this one all wrong. She gave an incred-

ulous laugh. 'I bet you don't even believe in marriage?'

He rolled his shoulders and rubbed the back of his neck hard, his expression growing darker before he answered, 'It's the responsible thing to do when a child becomes part of the equation.'

This was crazy. She lifted her hands to her face in shock and exasperation, her hot cheeks burning against the skin of her palms. 'Have you really thought about what it takes to be a father? A child needs consistency, routine, to know that they are the centre of the parent's life. Have you considered the sacrifices needed? Your work life, the constant travel, all of the partying— everything about the way you live now will be affected. Are you prepared to give up all of that?'

Stood in the centre of the room, he folded his arms on his wide imposing chest, his eyes firing with impatient resolve. 'I don't have a choice. This child is my responsibility and duty, I will do whatever it takes to ensure that it has a safe and happy childhood.'

*Don't miss*
**THEIR BABY SURPRISE**
by Katrina Cudmore

Available July 2017
www.millsandboon.co.uk

# Join Britain's BIGGEST Romance Book Club

**50% OFF** your first parcel

- **EXCLUSIVE offers every month**
- **FREE delivery direct to your door**
- **NEVER MISS a title**
- **EARN Bonus Book points**

Call Customer Services
## 0844 844 1358*

or visit
## millsandboon.co.uk/subscriptions